Carry the World

a novel

by

Susan Fanetti

To Janine
So happy to see
you at RARE Paris!

Susan ♡
2022

THE FREAK CIRCLE PRESS

D1523256

Carry the World © 2018 Susan Fanetti
All rights reserved

Cover Design © 2018 Susan Fanetti
with images from DepositPhotos

ALSO BY SUSAN FANETTI

Light, Book 7.5
Lead, Book 8

THE NIGHT HORDE MC SAGA
The Signal Bend Series:
(The First Complete Series)
Move the Sun, Book 1
Behold the Stars, Book 2
Into the Storm, Book 3
Alone on Earth, Book 4
In Dark Woods, Book 4.5
All the Sky, Book 5
Show the Fire, Book 6
Leave a Trail, Book 7

The Night Horde SoCal:
(The Second Complete Series)
Strength & Courage, Book 1
Shadow & Soul, Book 2
Today & Tomorrow, Book 2.5
Fire & Dark, Book 3
Dream & Dare, Book 3.5
Knife & Flesh, Book 4
Rest & Trust, Book 5
Calm & Storm, Book 6

Final Books in the Night Horde MC Saga:
Nolan: Return to Signal Bend
Love & Friendship

As S.E. Fanetti:
Aurora Terminus

DEDICATION:
To all the women who carry the world, in all the ways they do it.

ACKNOWLEDGEMENTS:
Special thanks to my precious friends and priceless beta readers, TeriLyn Smitsky and Jess Brooks, for their keen insights and patient support.

And to the Pack Horse Librarians of the Works Progress Administration, who inspired this story, and who carried light and hope to remote places in dark times.

Prologue

Present Day

It was so hot in this attic, not even the dust motes moved. They hung perfectly still in air as thick as soup, in the stripes of desultory sun that pushed through the tatters in the decaying calico curtains over windows opaque with decades of grime.

A hank of hair had escaped Lizzie's ponytail and hung before her eyes. A drop of sweat ran down the path of its strands and plopped onto the rough plank floor. She pushed it behind her ear with the back of her wrist and then swiped her forearm across her face.

"Damn, it's hot. We should've got an earlier start today, Momma."

Her mother set a dusty box on the stack near the stairs and cast a glance around the attic. "Well, we couldn't hardly send Miss Grady on without settin' with her awhile. It'll be fine. The hard part's done. Got all the furniture down. All's we need now is goin' through these boxes. So let's get crackin'."

Lizzie turned away so her mother wouldn't see her smile. They lived in Chicago, Lizzie had always lived in Chicago, not counting college, but her mother, Lindy Ann Calhoun-Harris, had grown up right here, in Callwood, Kentucky, smack in the heart of Appalachia. Back home, her mother had no accent at all. She'd worked hard to lose it, insisting that nobody in Chicago would trust a cardiothoracic surgeon who sounded like a backwoods bumpkin.

But every time they came to Kentucky for a visit, Momma's voice picked up a strong hillbilly flavor, as if the taste of it sank into her the minute her feet touched Kentucky dirt. Or maybe it was that Kentucky stripped off the varnish of the big city and let the real Lindy show through again.

Lizzie liked it. When she was younger, she'd tried to emulate it, but Momma had thought she was poking fun, and she'd gotten mad enough not to talk to her for days. But she hadn't been poking fun at all. She simply wanted to have an interesting voice like that, not the Midwest, Gold Coast, prep school blandness she'd grown up with.

When she thought of Nannie, her grandmother, that was the first thing she thought of—her homey, homespun drawl that made every word more interesting, like each one was part of a story that deserved to be told.

A sad sigh escaped her chest as she thought of Nannie, up here in her attic. Nannie's funeral had been the week before. Now, Lizzie and her mom were packing up a long, fascinating life and selling it off or giving it away.

She closed the flaps on a box of old fabric, the third box full of striped and floral cottons which she'd learned were flour sacks, saved by her ever-frugal grandmother in case they might be made into quilts and dresses. When she set that box aside, she caught a glimpse of something shiny in the shadows under the eave. Rolling onto her knees, Lizzie crawled forward and pushed another couple of boxes—one an old hatbox she made a mental note to be interested in later—out of the way. Tucked right up against the low side of the peaked attic was an old wooden chest with thick leather straps, obviously handmade. The faint gleam she'd caught was one of the thick brass buckle latches.

Lizzie tried to unfasten a buckle, but the leather had hardened too much, after years of neglect. She found a leather handle at the side and tugged the chest to draw it closer—oh, it was heavy. The brittle leather of the handle broke after the chest had scraped closer by only a couple inches.

"Dammit," she muttered and crawled closer to get ahold of the chest itself.

"What you find?" her mother drawled like a girl from up the mountain.

"I don't know. An old chest. It's heavy as hell." With a determined pull, she drew the chest away from the eave, into a dusty stripe of sunlight. A thick layer of cobwebby dust covered its top. She managed to work the rock-hard leather and release the first buckle, and then with the same effort, the second came open.

"Huh. I never seen that chest, I don't think. Be careful openin' it. Who knows what kinda critters crawled up in there."

Lizzie tensed, ready to jump back if some kind of 'critter' crawled over her hand — or if the smell of its death wafted up. She pushed the lid up, and it creaked open.

The smell was of decay, but not unpleasant. Musty and rich, like paper, and a faint woodsy scent as well. At the top of the chest was some kind of leather bag, the leather cracked and stained dark in places, the pouch deep and wide. She picked it up — no, it was two bags, connected with a wide strap of stained leather. Lizzie thought she should know what this was, but she couldn't quite get there. She held the contraption up, so the two big bags dangled over her arms, and got there at the same time her mother said:

"Mercy, I know what that is."

"Saddlebags?" Lizzie guessed.

"Yeah." Her mother lowered the lid and brushed the thick layer of dust off the top, showing three letters carved into the top: ALW. Then she pushed the lid back open. "That's Mamaw's chest. Oh, Lizzie!"

Mamaw was Lizzie's great-grandmother. She'd died at age ninety-nine, when Lizzie was in middle school. Living so far away, seeing her only a couple times a year for a few days at a time, Lizzie hadn't ever built much of a relationship with her great-grandmother. Mamaw's mind hadn't been so sharp anymore, so mainly she'd just been the sweet old lady who sat in a rocker and watched her stories on the TV.

Lizzie hadn't even been particularly close to Nannie until high school, when her parents' marriage had imploded at the precise time her adolescence was exploding, and she'd spent a couple summers hiding in Kentucky so she and Momma wouldn't kill each other in Chicago. Then, she'd gotten to know her grandmother very well and love her as hard as she'd ever loved anyone. She was the reason Lizzie and her mother found their way back to each other.

Here in this hot attic, on this sad day, Lizzie's mother got down on her knees beside her and peered into the chest. She lifted out a roughly woven blanket with a strong musky smell and set it aside. Beneath it were books and papers.

Her mother lifted out a book like a homemade binder, covered in faded burlap and laced at the side with

11

a leather thong. "Did Nannie ever tell you about Mamaw—I mean, the way she was when she was young?"

Lizzie nodded. Mamaw had been a true hill woman, living up the mountain in a place called Cable's Holler, and nurturing a huge, boisterous family. Nannie had been the sixth of eight children growing up on a small subsistence farm, what Nannie always called a 'dirt farm,' in a cabin without real plumbing or electricity. It could not have been an easy life, but all her stories of her childhood were joyful ones. She looked on her mother like an angel.

"Mamaw was a book woman," Lizzie's mother said softly. "That's how she an' Papaw met. Oh, they had a love for the ages, they did."

Her mother opened the old binder to a yellowed page where a piece of aged paper was glued. The paper was full of typeface, as from an old manual typewriter, with a line in all caps across the top, like a title: STORIES, HOMEMAKING IDEAS, AND RECIPES, it read. In parentheses beneath the title, a line read: *Compiled by Mrs. Ada Lee Donovan, Callwood Pack Horse Library, Callwood, Kentucky, January 1937*. The rest of the page was filled with a description of how the contents of the book were compiled: from magazines and old books, and from ideas and recipes Mrs. Ada Lee Donovan—Mamaw, though she'd been Mrs. Ada Lee Walker most of her life—had gathered from friends and family, and from the people she served on the mountain.

Book woman. That was how Nannie had described it, too. As a young woman—a widow—during the Great Depression, Mamaw had been a Pack Horse Librarian. As part of a WPA program of the New Deal, she'd ridden way up in the Kentucky hills, bringing books and magazines to people too far removed from civilization to reach libraries, or sometimes even schools, on their own. They lived so far from the world that only pack horses and mules could reach them, so the librarians had ridden routes up and down and all around the Appalachian mountains, in any kind of weather, lugging books and supplies, bringing entertainment and news and company.

In college, Lizzie had taken some weird English course as an elective: The Literacy Narrative. She'd had no idea what that was, but she'd needed three more units to fulfill her Humanities requirements, and that one had fit her schedule, so whatever. She'd ended up kind of liking the class. For the final project, they'd had to write their own literacy narrative, tracing the history of and influences on their relationship with reading and writing, and Lizzie had done some research on 'book women' and on her own personal connection to them. She'd talked with Nannie on the phone several times and had gotten her to spin stories about her mother.

Lizzie had traced her history from Mamaw forward and made some lame conclusion suggesting that her own 'journey' to reading and writing had been guided by her ancestor, and she'd gotten an A on the assignment and in the course. She'd figured it was all teacher-pleasing bullshit, at which she'd always excelled, but the research actually had been pretty cool, and since she'd written that paper, she'd maybe thought of her family's 'legacy of literacy' differently. Her hillbilly great-grandma had loved books so much she'd risked her life to pass them around. Maybe coming up in the family that woman had made had shaped Lizzie truly. But she'd still never felt a personal connection to Mamaw, who remained, in her mind, the dotty old lady she barely remembered. The book woman Nannie had told her about was more like learning about an ancestor in a museum.

"It's like she made a book all herself," her mother said, flipping carefully through pages of handwritten and typed recipes, and pages from books, clippings from magazines and newspapers, hand-drawn pictures and clipped photographs. A few recipe pages had little crusty dots, as if a spoon had dripped sauce onto the paper.

Sitting cross-legged beside her, Lizzie studied the pages of the homemade book. "She did. It's a scrapbook — like, literally, made from scraps of things, like books that had worn out. When I wrote that paper, I read about these. Their books got read so much they wore out. They didn't have money to replace them, so they salvaged the pages they could and made them into new books. There's not many of these around anymore, I don't think. It's pretty amazing to find this. You didn't know about this chest?"

Her mother shook her head. "I heard stories all my life, but they was always just stories. I'd no idea all this was right here to see."

They'd come to a page with a handwritten recipe for sugar-crusted cornbread. Though there were several different kinds of handwriting on the pages, this one, a nearly picture-perfect facsimile of the Palmer method, seemed most prevalent. Lizzie brushed light fingertips over the page. "Do you think this is her cursive?"

"Oh yeah. I'd know that hand anywhere. That's Mamaw. Y'know, she was a schoolteacher for a spell, before she married Mr. Donovan. That'was her first husband."

Her mother's accent had suddenly grown so deep that she'd nearly said *'twas*. She nearly sounded like Nannie herself.

"Back in them days, schoolteachers couldn't work once they got married. But she was widowed after jus' a few years. Mr. Donovan died by a fever, and then she lost the farm and hadta move on home with her kin, but they wasn't doin' much better. That's why she signed on with the library."

As Momma rolled into her story, Lizzie sat back and closed her eyes, forgot all about the heat and dust, and the sorrow of loss, and listened to her mother spin a story in the voice of eastern Kentucky.

Part One

Chapter One

1937

Ada crouched down and squinted under the truck as Chancey checked the axle.

"I ain't know what to say, Mizz Ada. It can't take no more fixin'. It's jus' busted."

"How much for a whole new axle? Just replace it outright?" The question was entirely rhetorical; unless she could get a new axle in a trade for a bushel of corn, there was no price she could afford.

Chancey scooted through the dusty dirt until he was clear of the disabled truck and stood up. His head swung to and fro as he swiped the dust from his backside and then brushed his hands clean. "There's rust near straight through under there. Puttin' a new axle on this old heap'd be burnin' good money, ma'am. I'm sorry to say it, but I think your daddy's truck done rolled its last mile."

Turning a scowl that she'd once used on obstreperous pupils on the ancient Ford pickup, Ada sighed. "I don't know what to do, Chancey, if I can't get to town."

"I could fix up that old cart rig in the barn for you, get that in some shape. Then Henrietta could pull you into town. She's trained to harness, ain't she? Wouldn't need no payment—I owe you for helpin' me with them gov'ment papers."

Like many people in her community, Chancey was illiterate. Since her George's death and the hard times brought on by this terrible national economy, Ada had tried to earn some money, or at least barter for some food and services, by reading and writing for her neighbors. It wasn't nearly enough, but it was something. She and her father were trying to keep this old farm going, too, but it was just the two of them working, and four hands, with the occasional extra set from a vagrant come their way, weren't nearly enough to seed a good field or pull in a good harvest.

First she'd lost her husband, then she'd lost his family farm. Now she was living with her parents again, and they were about to lose everything, too. And they weren't unique. Every family all around them had the same story, or near enough like it. This world was nothing but loss, black and wide and deep.

Rich men had played gamblers' games with the stock market and sent the whole country reeling. It seemed to Ada like the people hurt the worst had hardly even *heard* of the stock market, much less invested in it, but they were the ones starving nonetheless.

Now she wouldn't be able to drive into Callwood with what little harvest they could reap. Getting to town would be a dawn-to-dusk endeavor, what with harnessing Henrietta and loading the cart, and then undoing it all when she got home. Her father wouldn't be able to do it; his back had been bad since last fall, when he wrenched it pulling stumps. He couldn't possibly sit a cart seat for the long ride to Callwood. Even the truck pained him. Ada would have to drive the team herself.

Accepting that truth, she sighed and answered Chancey's question. "Yes, Henrietta can pull the cart. I'd appreciate it, Chancey. That would be a big help. Truly."

Chancey flushed a shy grin and showed his gappy set of teeth. "Happy to help, ma'am. I'll jus' get started now, if it's the same to you."

She smiled. "Of course. Thank you. Don't work too late, though. I'll call you in for supper, if you'd like to stay." They could at least offer a neighbor a seat at their table. That was something.

"I'd take that kindly, thank you."

That evening, after Chancey had walked off toward home, promising to return in the morning to work on the cart some more, Ada cleared up the supper dishes and covered up the pot with the potato water. In the morning, she'd use it to mix up some bread dough. From the sitting room, where her parents sat, she heard the scratchy sound of the radio. The best reception came from Knoxville. Pausing at the table with the ceramic salt and pepper shakers in one hand and a wet rag in the other, Ada perked up her ears and tried to tell what show she was hearing. Ah, *The Green Hornet*. Her parents would listen to anything on the radio, but Daddy had been captivated by that new show.

She and George had saved up for months to buy that radio for her parents' fortieth wedding anniversary, two years back. By then her mother's eyesight had gone totally dark, and with them living higher up the mountain, Ada hadn't been able to keep reading to her every day like she'd done since her eyes began to fail. She'd seen the radio in a Callwood shop and put it on layaway without even talking to George first. Struggling under the weight of the mortgage his father had put on the farm, he didn't like credit or anything that even smelled of credit, but she'd known he'd understand. He'd always understood.

Now George was gone and she was back home and reading to her mother every night again, but that radio was still their most treasured possession.

She wiped up the table and spread out a fresh square of cheesecloth. Satisfied that the kitchen was tidy, she untied her apron, hung it on its hook, and went to join her parents in the sitting room.

The lights were off. Her mother didn't need them, and her father liked to listen in the dark, without distraction. Ada felt her way to the far side of the room and slipped her shoes off. She settled on the floor, framed by her parents' feet, and listened to the story. Her father's hand drifted down to settle on her shoulder, and she tipped her head to rest on it.

Times were hard. Life was loss. Ada hadn't known a day without strife and sorrow since George had come in early from the field with a face clammy and waxy pale but for bright red blooms of heat on his cheeks. Twenty-three months ago. She doubted she'd ever have another happy day in her life.

But sometimes, for just moments, everything felt a little bit fine.

Ada scooted the straight-back chair close to the bed and sat down on the frayed straw seat. They were alone in the bedroom; her father always left this moment to mother and daughter, and came to bed afterward. Ada knew he often stood in the hallway and listened as she read, but he didn't want to intrude on what he called 'his girls' time.'

"What story would you like next, Momma?"

She'd finished *Paradise Lost* the night before. Her mother was a fan of the classics. Though she had hardly any formal education at all herself, she was a smart woman and had been an avid reader and keenly interested in the world. She'd never been prouder than when Ada had gotten her post as a schoolteacher. In fact, Ada was fairly sure—though her mother had never said so—that she'd been a little disappointed when Ada had married and had had to give it up.

"Talk to me a little first, Ada Lee. There's somethin' eatin' you. Has been all night."

Ada was close to both her parents and always had been. She was the baby, come late in life, and their only girl. The whole family had treated her like the miracle they thought she was, and she'd been spoiled silly. Then, when she was still a silly, spoiled girl in pigtails, both her older brothers were killed in the same battle in the Great War. After that, in a house shrouded by grief, she'd no longer been spoiled or silly, but she'd been loved all the more deeply as the one bright spot in her parents' life.

She'd always been able to talk to them about anything, but her mother was especially astute, hardly even needing Ada to say the words to know what was troubling her. Since the hard shells of cataracts had blocked her pale blue eyes, she seemed even more perceptive.

"Just regular troubles, Momma. The truck broke down, and Chancey doesn't think it can be fixed."

Her mother clucked her tongue and shook her head. "You remember when your daddy bought that old truck?"

"I do. Off the lot in Callwood." Summer of 1929. They'd had a good few years, and 1929 had promised to bring in another good crop, so her father had decided he could afford to modernize a little. The truck had been eight years old then, and hard used, but well cared for. A few months later, the stock market had crashed, but that hadn't meant much right away, here in the shadow of the mountains.

Soon enough, though, it had meant everything.

"I told him then we ain't had no need of a motor car, but you know your daddy when he gets his mind on a thing."

"It gave us another seven years, Momma. More than that. And they've been hard years. I don't think it was a bad purchase."

"Maybe not, but we're back to the cart if the truck don't run, right?"

"Right."

"Your daddy's back is bad, Ada Lee. He tries not to let me know it, but I hear him. He can't drive a cart no more. Don't you let him try."

"I won't. You're right. Chancey's working on getting the cart and harness back in shape, and then I'll take the load in myself." She patted her mother's hand. "It'll be alright, Momma. Everything's gonna be alright."

Though the cluck of her tongue against her strong teeth and the cynical twist of her mouth showed her disbelief in that empty assurance, her mother reached out to the nightstand and felt the spines of the books stacked there. She tapped one. "Is that *Don Quixote*?"

"Indeed it is. You'd like that one again?"

"Yes, I would." She smiled and settled into the pillows, closing her foggy eyes. Though she was old enough that her hair, once the rosy gold Ada had inherited, had gone white, and her skin was loose and velvety, she was still a beautiful woman, small and slight but not frail. Not even the loss of her sight could make her vague or weak. "I always like to hear about that silly old fool."

Ada slid the volume from the middle of the stack and leaned close to the bedside lamp as she opened it. "'Chapter One,'" she read, "'Which Treats of the Character and Pursuits of the Famous Gentleman Don Quixote of La Mancha. In a certain corner of La Mancha, the name of which I do not choose to remember, there lately lived one of those country gentlemen, who adorn their halls with a rusty lance and worm-eaten target, and ride forth on the skeleton of a horse, to course with a sort of starved greyhound.'"

As she read, she caught the familiar flutter of her father's shadow in the corner of her eye, standing just outside the bedroom door, listening to the story.

When Ada read five chapters, her mother said she was ready to sleep, so she slid a tattered envelope into the book to hold their place and kissed her good night. It had escaped neither of them that this nightly ritual was the mirror image of one from Ada's childhood. She left the light on for her father and slipped out of the bedroom.

Her father was sitting in the kitchen with a glass of warm milk. He had a bad stomach, too, and on the single time she'd convinced him to see Doc Dollens about it, he'd been diagnosed with ulcer and told to keep away from spicy foods and to drink warm milk to coat his stomach. Ada wasn't sure it was doing any good, but her father wasn't one to complain.

"There's a bit left in the pot, if'n you want to set with me a spell," he said as she came in and set her hand on his shoulder.

Ada didn't have ulcer, but a bit of warm milk was soothing before bed. She took a heavy mug down from the shelf and poured the rest of the pot in.

"Now your momma's snug asleep, why don't you say all Chancey told you today."

"There's not much more to tell, Daddy. He says the axle can't be fixed."

His face drew into a severe scowl. He'd lived a long, hard outdoor life, and it showed on flesh as creased and cracked and burnt red as the bed of a creek gone dry, but his green eyes flashed keenly. "Damn if I ain't seven kinds a fool. I shoulda seen that hole was deeper than a puddle."

That was the source of this trouble: her father had driven over what he'd thought was a puddle and had turned out to be a tiny sinkhole, only a foot wide but at least three feet deep and filled with water. Here in mining country, sinkholes were common, and they could show up out of nowhere. The hit had snapped the axle nearly in two. But in health of both the human and machine varieties, often one problem turned out to be the thing that made a bigger problem known.

"The axle can't be fixed, but it's not the axle that's the end of the truck. The whole bottom's near rusted through. Chancey said it was a matter of days, maybe, before the motor just fell out." She reached over and set her hand over her father's. "It's alright, Daddy. He's going to get the rig fixed up to pay me back for helping him with his momma's papers, and I'll take the harvest in as soon as I can hitch Henrietta up."

"Corn's already sittin', Ada. Too much longer, we'll get rot. 'Twas a bad yield this year to start. Too damn much rain." A curse word never passed his lips when Ada's mother could hear, but he got them all out of his system when she couldn't. He finished off his mug of milk and wiped the back of his hand across his mouth. "We ain't gonna keep goin' much longer like this, baby girl. That note I took out a couple years back, it's gonna haunt us this year. Payments is already two behind, and I's hopin' to get even with this yield, but I don't know. I hate to burden you with such trouble, but I got nobody else to say it to. I don't know how'm gonna take care of your momma if I can't get food in this larder."

"Daddy. As long as we make enough to pay the bank, as long as we can keep this place, we'll always be able to eat. We've got the garden, and we've got the chickens for eggs, and Polly and Emsie for milk and butter. I can earn enough helping with paperwork to keep the animals fed, and the animals will feed us. We won't starve. The rest of it—well, someday things have got to get better. They just have to. We only need to hold on until they do."

He smiled and patted her hand. "Y'always been our ray of sunny light. Ain't never dark so long's you're here."

That night, after she kissed her father good night and tidied up the few dishes from their shared warm milk, Ada closed herself in the small room that, but for a far too brief spell when she'd been a happily married woman with a home of her own, had been her bedroom all her life. There wasn't much special about this room that showed the life it had held—no pictures or clipped photos of movie stars on the walls, no fancy, fanciful mementos of her childhood or adolescence, no keepsakes from friends. Since the death of her brothers, she hadn't had many fancies, or many friends. Only one good friend, who'd died of influenza when they were sixteen.

The only adornment of the plain-papered wall was her framed teaching certificate. Atop her bureau, leaning against the mirror, was a single memento from a long-ago carefree childhood: a faded, frayed, oft-patched ragdoll her Granny Dee had made for her, its red yarn pigtails gone dusky pink with age.

The furniture was functional—a narrow bed in an iron frame, a bureau topped with a swivel mirror, a tall pine chifforobe for hanging clothes, and, beside the bed, a simple two-shelf bookcase, stuffed with all the books she owned. Sitting on its top was a small milk-glass lamp and a short stack of the books she was currently reading. Always, she was in the middle of reading a few different books, choosing one according to her mood at any given time when she had a moment to read. Books weren't so easy to come by, and were luxuries besides, so she'd read those she'd acquired again and again—some, those she loved best, she'd read so often she had them memorized.

She shed her simple cotton dress, her plain slip and underclothes, her old, lace-up work shoes and darned stockings, and draped them all over the plain wood chair beside the door. Then she pulled her flannel nightgown from under her pillow and tugged it over her head. A sliver of wind came through the window she'd opened a crack and made the gown billow over her like a sheet on the line as it fell to her ankles. The gown was old and worn, and the flannel was soft as a lover's kiss on her skin. For a moment, she wrapped her arms around her waist, feeling the hard curve of her ribs, the sharp inward sweep of her waist, and imagined—remembered—what it was to be held by a lover. By George, her husband, her only lover.

This aching loneliness had become a part of her body, the weight as real and familiar as another limb. Tim

31

Conner down the road had come back from the Great War without his legs, and he spoke of terrible pains in the air where his knees should have been. Since she'd lost George, Ada thought she understood something of what Tim meant.

Allowing herself that small luxury of grief, Ada unfurled her arms and went to her bureau. She eased the pins from her hair and dropped them into a little glass dish. When her hair was loose, she ran her fingers through the mass and scratched lightly at her scalp, where the pins had poked for all the long hours of the day. Then she picked up her hairbrush and engaged in one of her few vanities: a hundred strokes, every night, to keep her long hair light and gleaming.

Her mother's hair and her father's eyes. All her life, people had said that to her — that she'd gotten the best features of both her parents. She'd heard it so many times the words had lost their meaning. But those features had captured George's attention, too. *Hair like fire, eyes like water*, he'd said, so many times, from the first day he'd spoken to her to the last day he'd lived. Through his eyes, through his love, Ada had first seen that she was pretty. Before he'd looked at her, the concept had meant nothing. Now that his eyes were forever closed, the concept meant nothing again.

But she kept her hair the way he'd liked it, and when she looked into the mirror, and saw her pale green eyes and red-gold hair, she imagined George looking on the woman he loved and whispering *hair like fire, eyes like water* at her ear.

Chapter Two

It took Chancey and Ada's father two days to get the rig ready, and then it was Sunday, so the corn sat another day until Ada could drive it into town. They lost a few bushels to rot in that time, but there was nothing for it. She'd go through those bushels and save what kernels she could, and grind them down for cornmeal.

Like all their neighbors in these Appalachian foothills, the McDaniel farm had never been much of a place. Just a single field of a few acres, rotating a few crops to keep the soil healthy. Some called them dirt farmers, but Ada's parents had always taken umbrage at that phrase. Still, there was no doubt that life in these parts meant scratching out each day straight from the ground.

On average, the yield was enough to keep the family sheltered and well and not much more. On good years, they had a little extra, to put in hot and cold running water, or buy a used truck. One year, after the wires came up this far, they were able to put electricity in. On bad years, years of drought or flood or infestation, it was all they could do to keep going.

Since this depression had started, there hadn't been any good years.

After they got the wagon loaded, Ada led Henrietta out from the pasture and got her into the harness. The big bay mare hadn't been harnessed for a few years, and she balked at the sight of it, tossing her head and digging her hooves into the dirt.

"Come now, girl," Ada crooned, stroking the mare's nose. She'd raised her from a filly and knew just the right tone so she'd calm. "We're going to have an adventure today, you and I."

Henrietta huffed noisily, unconvinced. But she lowered her head and pushed affectionately against Ada's chest.

"I won't make you work too hard, Hen. And when we get to town, I'll share my lunch. How's that sound?"

Her father chuckled. "You'd think that horse could understand what you're sayin', the way you make deals with her."

"Who's to say she can't?" Ada smiled over her shoulder at her father and then turned back to her horse. "You know what I said, don't you, Hen?"

Henrietta bobbed her head, like a nod, and Chancey, Ada, and her father all laughed.

When Ada tried again, Henrietta allowed herself to be harnessed.

"That's my good girl." Ada patted her neck and kissed her face. When she looked to her father and Chancey, they both stared at the harnessed horse, bemused.

"Women understand each other," she teased. "Well, I guess we're ready, as soon as I get changed." She might be driving the crop into town, but she had no intention of looking like a field hand when she did it.

"Mizz Ada," Chancey said, pulling his cap from his head. "I ain't sure a lady like you oughta go in town on your own. There's strangers on the road these days. Them hobo men. I could make some time and go 'long with you, if you like."

Her father nodded. "It pains me I can't make the ride myself. I'd feel better knowing Chancey was with you."

Chancey was a very nice young man, earnest and kind, but the mere thought of his endless prattle all the way to Callwood made her eyelids droop. One of the few benefits this hard trip offered was a peaceful time alone with her thoughts. And the men who walked the roads were looking for help, not trouble. They weren't monsters, but men only a single rung down the ladder from themselves. She had no fear of them.

"I don't need a chaperone. I know the folks at every homestead from here to town. I have trouble, I'll be close to help all the way. And if the worst comes, I've got the shotgun here behind the seat. I'll be fine." When Chancey opened his mouth to protest, Ada raised her hand and gave him her schoolteacher look. "I'll be fine, Chancey. Thank you for your help with the cart. You've done more than enough to pay me back for helping with your momma's papers."

The trip down to Callwood was twelve miles on dirt roads. In the old Ford, that was an hour or so. In the wagon, with a full load, it was more than five. Though she'd been up as usual with the dawn and on the road while the dew was yet heavy on leaves beginning to put on their fall colors, by the time Ada and Henrietta passed the town sign, the sun was at the peak of its arc. She had two hours to get her errands complete and be back on the road. Any later, and they'd be rolling the last miles in the dark.

Callwood was, by most measures, a very small town, a grid of a few streets, with only about three blocks of retail businesses, but to the people who lived in the hills, it was the biggest city most of them would ever see. Ada had gone to school in Lexington for her teaching certificate, and the first week in that city, she'd cried every day at least once, from sheer sensory overload.

Life in the hills was quiet. Few people had telephone or electricity, only about half had a motor car or truck. People moved at the pace their own bodies could go, and they followed the rhythms of the earth, busy in the light and quiet in the night. The farther up the mountain you went, the quieter — and harder — life got.

As Ada eased Henrietta and the wagon down Main Street, she felt as if she'd crossed a time shift of some sort. In the past few years, with the truck working, she hadn't much noticed it, but today, clip-clopping over the same street cars and trucks rolled over, she saw how much faster the world down here was moving — hurtling toward a different world entirely, one loud and harsh and far too fast.

Hers wasn't the only wagon on the road, but the drivers of motored vehicles were impatient with them all, honking loud horns and shouting from their windows. Henrietta's blinders kept her from spooking, but her ears swiveled constantly, and the skin over her withers shuddered at every horn and shout.

Their first stop was the mill — on the far side of the town from the mountain. Ada breathed out a heavy gust of relief as she finally guided Henrietta off the road and onto the mill lot.

There was a short line of other farmers bringing in their harvest. While Ada waited her turn, she noticed the grim expressions of the men walking back to their newly empty trucks, and a low burble of worry stirred on the floor of her belly.

Then she moved up close enough to see the sign advertising the rate, and the burble became a boil. That was a good twenty-five percent less than last year. She looked at the load in the wagon. It hadn't been a good year. They'd lost part of the field to cutworms, and heavy rains had ruined about a third of the rest. At the advertised rate, Ada guessed she'd barely have enough money in her purse to pay the bank note and the electric and buy the absolutely essential supplies on her list. She would have to be very careful and get very inventive this afternoon, because there would not be a cent left. What she came home with would have to do them through the whole winter, at least. Maybe a whole year.

That was just impossible. What she'd told her father the other night, that they would be able to make it with just what they already had, seemed like a fairy tale right now.

What would her parents do if they lost their home?

When it was her turn, she smiled, and felt it turn into the ridiculous grin that happened to her face whenever she was unduly anxious—like her first day at teachers' school, or her first date with George. Or their wedding night. She'd gotten a terrible fit of giggles that night, but he'd been charmed by them and patient with her as he showed her what it meant to love fully.

"Well, Mizz Ada! How do?"

"Hi, Pete," she said with far too much cheer in her voice. She took Pete's offered hand and let him help her down from the seat. "How are you?"

"I'm well, thank you. Surprised to see you, and in the wagon, too."

"The truck broke down. You know my daddy's back is bad, so I rode the load in myself." She cleared her throat and nodded at the sign. "That's not much, Pete. So much less than last year." She couldn't even say the number out loud. "You can't do better?"

At least Pete looked honestly unhappy about it. "I'm sorry, Mizz Ada. We had to drop our prices for grains and flours. Times is hard for everybody."

"I know. I just … well, I wasn't expecting it to be so low."

He dropped his voice. "Some folks're tryin' they luck in Holden. I hear tell they payin' a few cents more on the bushel. I won't take it wrong if'n you want to move on."

Holden was fifteen miles farther away. In the truck, she could have tried it. In the wagon, she had no chance. She wouldn't even make it before the Holden mill closed.

"I appreciate it, Pete, but we'll stick with you, take what you can give us."

While the mill workers emptied the wagon, Ada took her lunch pail off the seat and stood with Henrietta, feeding her apple slices. She'd eaten her lunch on the road but saved the apple for Henrietta, because she'd promised.

She watched the scale as her crop was weighed, and her heart sank. When Pete brought over a slim stack of bills and a handful of coins, she put the money in her purse and signed the slip.

Her mother was blind. Her father was injured far more than he'd admit. He didn't have more than a year or two left to work, even with her help, and they certainly couldn't afford to pay for help. Not even room and board, at this rate.

Ada didn't know how she was going to keep her parents going. Or herself.

She gave part of her money right back to the mill, in the front store, when she bought sacks of flour, choosing sacks with the prettiest patterns, to use them later for fabric. Then she guided Henrietta and the nearly empty wagon away from the mill and back to town, to bring the bank note current and then go to the store to buy what supplies she could still afford.

As she walked into Callwood Dry Goods, a bill in the window drew her attention. Arcing across the top, the letters carefully handwritten, were the words CALLWOOD PACK HORSE LIBRARY. Callwood had never had a library before, and the thought that she might have access to new books lightened Ada's heavy heart. Below those large, beautiful words were even prettier ones: SEEKS LIBRARIANS.

"'Scuse me, miss," a man said behind her.

Seeing that she was blocking the door, Ada ducked her head in apology and stepped out of the way. She stood before the window and read the whole bill.

The Works Progress Administration
of the United States Federal Government
seeks literate, healthy people with excellent horseback skills
for a new program to bring the joy of reading
to citizens throughout Eastern Kentucky.
Wages paid monthly.
Must provide own horse and tack.
Inquire at the Callwood Pack Horse Library,
24 Second Street, Callwood, KY.
Mrs. Edna Pitts, Head Librarian.

Wages paid monthly.

Wages paid monthly.

Wages.

Paid monthly.

By the federal government.

It didn't take much to understand what the job would be—riding up into the mountains, to the one-room schoolhouses and homesteads up in the hollers, where people lived who couldn't get down to towns like Callwood. She had taught up in a holler, so she knew. Most of those people were illiterate and didn't care about any book but the Bible, but they had children, and those children deserved to know the magic of books.

Ada was literate—more than that, she was educated. She was healthy. She had excellent horseback skills. In fact, her best friend was a horse. She and Henrietta could be librarians.

Leaving Henrietta to doze in her harness in front of the dry goods store, she turned and headed toward Second Street. If she got this job—and why wouldn't she?—she could shop after, maybe with a bit looser hold on her purse.

A simple hand-painted wood sign over a shop door on Second Street identified the new Callwood Pack Horse Library. That location had once been a music shop, but few people had money for luxuries like pianos and fiddles these days. It had closed up about a year back, and the windows had been covered over with newspaper and soapy swirls since.

Now, the windows were sparkling clean and covered with gathers of cotton calico. Ada dipped into her handbag and pulled out one of her few treasured possessions: a pretty scrolled compact with a curlicue letter *A* at the center. George had brought it home for her one day, out of the blue. It wasn't anything wildly expensive or luxurious, just a tin disc burnished with a bit of gilt, but it was the fanciest thing Ada had ever owned. She opened it now and lifted the little mirror to her face. She'd never worn makeup, but she wanted to be sure she wasn't wearing any smudges from the long ride down the mountain, or the dusty spell spent at the mill. Once she was satisfied that her face was clean, she tucked some errant strands of hair back in their pins, and made sure her hat was sitting right atop her head. She snapped the compact closed and slipped a pair of white cotton gloves from her handbag.

When she opened the door to the Callwood Pack Horse Library, she stepped in as Mrs. Ada Donovan, certified teacher, not Mizz Ada, desperate farmer's daughter.

The space was dim, and so quiet that Ada caught the door and closed it softly rather than letting it swing closed on its own. As libraries went, it wasn't much—about a dozen bookcases, each one no more than half full—but she was excited nonetheless. The desk in the center of the room was empty and there was no bell to ring, so Ada cleared her throat politely and called out, not too loudly, "Hello?"

"One moment," came a voice from out of sight. The voice was female but not feminine. Brusque and deep, but cultured, too. Mrs. Edna Pitts, she suspected.

A short, sturdy woman with a violently tight grey topknot and small round spectacles bustled up from behind a screen Ada hadn't noticed. She wore a dark grey dress and sensible black shoes.

"Yes. Welcome to the library. How may I help you?" She stepped behind the desk and took her seat, squinting—almost scowling—up at Ada.

"Mrs. Pitts? Mrs. Edna Pitts?"

"Yes. How may I help you?"

Ada offered her gloved hand. "My name is Ada Donovan. I'm here to inquire about the librarian position."

Now there was no doubt that Mrs. Pitts was scowling. She was hardly more than five feet tall, but Ada wasn't sure she'd met many people more terrifying than this dour woman. But when she spoke, her tone softened. "No, dear. I don't think you understand. The program is for traveling librarians."

"Up the mountain. Yes, I assumed. I live near Barker's Creek, about twelve miles into the foothills." Afraid to give Mrs. Pitts another chance to say no, Ada pushed on. "I got my teaching credential in Lexington a few years back, and I taught in Bull Holler for two years. I know these mountains. I've been riding all my life, and I've got a good strong horse."

"Why aren't you teaching now?"

"I got married four years ago."

Mrs. Pitts nodded with understanding, but then shook her head. "It's hard duty, dear. The route I've got left is a hundred-twenty miles a week, hard riding, high in the hills. You'd hardly be home to take care of your husband—or children, if you've got them."

"I don't. My husband passed. I'm a widow, and we never had a chance for children." They'd both wanted to start their family right away, but in the brief years they'd had together, no baby had come to them. Ada had desperately wanted children, but God seemed to have other plans for her.

"Already? How old are you?"

Though she thought both those questions were rude, Ada kept her composure and simply answered them. Now was not the time to stand on manners. "Twenty-six. My husband died twenty-three months ago." Twenty-three months, one week, and four days.

"Well, I'm very sorry for you," Mrs. Pitts said gently, and earned back a credit in Ada's estimation. She sat back and twiddled her fingers together, clearly weighing a decision.

"You have your own horse and tack?"

"Yes, ma'am. Henrietta's a big strong mare. Sixteen and a half hands. She's trained to harness, and she's surefooted in the hills. Twelve years old. I raised her from a filly."

"You have a teaching certificate you can produce? And a reference from Lexington?"

"Yes, ma'am. I can bring my certificate in tomorrow, and I've got the letter my advisor wrote when I got my first post, or I can write again for a new one, if you'd like."

"The letter you have will do." She leaned forward and peered hard at Ada. "Pardon my directness, young lady, but you don't seem very sturdy. You understand, this is a year-round position. All weather—rain, snow, storm, shine, you make your route no matter what, just like the postman. Starting in autumn like this—well, you're in for a hard go right from the first."

"I understand. I'm strong. I grew up on my parents' farm, working side by side with them in the fields. I know hard work. I can ride all day and jump down from the saddle at night. I can ride in cold or hot, dry or wet. I can do it."

That earned a small smile from her would-be boss. "We're more than the postman, in fact. We don't merely drop off a sack at a trading post. We go to every home, wherever it is. And it's more than dropping off books and collecting what they borrowed the last time. People want news, and companionship. Others, they don't trust us, and it's our responsibility to build that trust. Some people can't read and want to learn. Others just want to listen. We are bringing more than books to these people, Mrs. Donovan. We are carrying the world to them."

If Mrs. Pitts meant to warn Ada off, she was doing a terrible job. Ada was excited, not scared. This was the perfect job, even more than teaching. "I understand, Mrs. Pitts. It sounds like heaven to me."

"Hmpf," Mrs. Pitts grunted. "Well, I like your enthusiasm, and living up in the hills already, you'd have a head start on your route." She opened a drawer in the desk and pulled out a folded paper. When she spread it open on the desk, Ada saw it was a map of Callwood and the mountain to the northwest, showing some roads and dots for named places. Red lines wended up into the mountain, mostly away from any marked roads. "This is the route. All told, it's about two-hundred-twenty miles , over rough trail, sometimes hardly more than a tamped-down spot in the trees. You run the whole thing over two weeks, then run it again, so you're seeing all your folks every two weeks. You sleep at home as much as you can, but sometimes you won't be able to. It's up to you to know who'll offer you shelter if you can't get home. Do you understand?"

"I do." Ada's heart thumped a happy beat. This turn of talk meant she was getting hired.

"Once a month, you come in for a day of work here at the library—we'll all meet and discuss the weeks just past, and we'll take books with heavy wear out of circulation and put new ones in, if we've got them. That's the day you'll be paid. It's a government job, so the pay's not much. Twenty-eight dollars a month."

Ada's knees nearly buckled. Twenty-eight dollars a month would keep her family comfortable. It wouldn't make them rich, but it would keep the farm solid, and they'd be fed and warm and cozy through the winter. Twenty-eight dollars a month was a godsend.

"I understand," she said, because it would have been unseemly to squeal.

"You've got good sturdy clothes for this work?" She gestured at Ada's town dress and white gloves. "A dress won't do when you're riding twenty or thirty miles in a day. If you've got a feeling about women wearing trousers …"

"I don't. I wear denim trousers when I'm in the field. I've got boots with good soles, and a heavy coat. Mrs. Pitts, I've lived in the mountains all my life. I'm not a city girl, not even by Callwood's standards. I can do this work."

"Alright, then. Come back tomorrow with your papers, and we'll get you set up with the route."

Her new boss stood up and offered her hand. Full of hope, Ada clasped it. "Thank you, Mrs. Pitts. I'm ever so grateful."

As excited as she was, Ada had known too much loss in her life to be frivolous before she'd actually been paid for her new job. She was nearly as careful in her shopping as if she hadn't just been hired on for a twenty-eight-dollar-a-month job. Still, by the time the wagon was loaded with her meager purchases and she pointed Henrietta back toward home, the afternoon had gotten far too old. Even with the lighter load, and Henrietta's therefore quicker step, it would be dark or near to it before they reached home. Her parents would be worried.

But what she'd told Chancey and her father early that morning was true: She knew everybody from Callwood to home, and if she encountered a dangerous stranger on the road, she had the shotgun with which to defend herself.

As they passed the town sign, she snapped the reins and got Henrietta to pick up her pace a little.

She was about an hour or so from home when she came around a bend and saw a man walking up ahead, down the middle of the road. Before she was close enough to see much detail of him, she knew he was a hobo. There was just a look they all seemed to have—weary and weather-beaten. Instead of the bindle many seemed to carry, this one wore a brown canvas satchel hooked across his body. Ada had seen similar bags and was fairly sure it was military issue from the war.

It was a vulnerable place in her trip, about fifteen minutes past the last homestead and another fifteen before she'd be in sight of the next. The sun had nearly set, leaving only a dark pink ribbon around the edge of the world and the rest of the sky deep in its gloaming.

She glanced over her shoulder and saw the butt of the shotgun. It was loaded; all she'd have to do is reach back and grab it. Her father had taught her to shoot long ago. Unless the man was also armed with a gun—and she'd never met a wanderer who had been—Ada was in no danger from this tired, probably hungry man.

As she approached, he crossed to the side of the road, turned to face her, and stopped. He seemed older, she thought, in his forties or fifties, maybe. He might well have been in the Great War. He didn't try to wave her down, and she didn't stop. She couldn't. But as she pulled up alongside him, he fell into step with her, walking at the side of the wagon.

"Evenin'," he said.

"Evenin'." Feeling uncivil, she added, "I'm sorry, but I can't offer you I ride."

"I understand, ma'am. I don't mean you no harm, but you can't know that. If you was my woman, I wouldn't want you stoppin' for no stranger on the road."

She smiled and offered him a nod of shared understanding.

"Might I ask, though—you know where a tired man might find a place to put his head for a night? I don't need much, but I smell rain on the wind, so a roof'd be 'preciated."

"About a mile or so farther along, you'll see symbols on a post. They'll offer you the hayloft, and if you're polite, they might have some work for you in the morning. Work'll be hard to come by soon. Harvest's in."

"I know. I jus' got to get to Knoxville. Then I'll have a place for the winter."

Knoxville was more than a hundred miles away. He'd best not tarry if he wanted to get so far before the cold set in.

"If the Conners don't have work for you tomorrow, and you keep on this road in the morning, you'll come upon another set of good symbols about three miles farther on. That's my people's place. We don't have a good place for you to bed down on a rainy night, but we might have some work that'd earn you a meal."

"I'd take that kindly, ma'am." He doffed his cap and held it to his chest. "You're a beautiful angel, come upon me jus' as I was in despair."

Well, that was ridiculous, and this conversation had gone on too long and begun to get awkward, but she gave him a smile anyway. "You take care now."

He gave her a courtly bow. She snapped the reins, and Henrietta hopped into a trot.

Chapter Three

The hobo showed up the next morning, before the sun was full up.

Ada had just let the chickens into the yard and was tossing their feed when she saw him clear the dogwoods that framed the gate. He'd been right; it had rained most of the night, a soft, soaking rain that had left the world smelling fresh and new, and the first rays of sun on what promised to be a clear day turned the wet leaves and grass to diamonds.

He saw her and stopped, then pulled his hat off his head and waited for a sign from her.

She dumped out her apron and brushed the seed dust from her hand.

"Mornin', ma'am," he said as she took her first steps to him.

"Mornin'. Did you find a safe place to sleep?"

"Yes'm, I did. You was right. The Conners shared they supper and give a blanket for the night, and they loft was soft and dry. Thank you much."

The hobo symbols etched outside the Conners' gate would have told him as much as Ada had, but she accepted his thanks with a nod.

"Ye said there might be work here?"

She considered him now, in the clearer light of a new morning. He was polite, and spoke softly. He'd obviously been on the road a long time; his pants and canvas coat were heavily patched and needed more, and his boots were cracked and curled across the toe bend. His body was tall and skinny, his clothes hanging on his shoulders. His skin was the ruddy, roasted color that came with too much time spent in the elements. His hair was dark, short, and fairly well-kept. He was creased and leathered, ancient but somehow not old. His age might have been anywhere from thirty-five to seventy-five.

He was a hobo.

But was he a good man?

After Ada had breakfast made for her parents, she'd saddle Henrietta and head back to Callwood to finish the paperwork for her new job and get the information for her route. She'd be gone the better part of the day. Her father wasn't an invalid, but he wasn't strong anymore. He could use help finishing the work to end the season.

They'd helped men like this before; there were marks on their posts, too, made by men who'd passed through. Those marks said that a meal and work might be found here, and that the people who lived here were kind.

But since her father had hurt his back, Ada had never left her parents with a stranger on the property. She couldn't stay home today, and she wouldn't be home much in the future. Could she welcome a stranger and then go?

She and her parents had talked long into the night about their worries for her with this new job, and her worries for them. Both planks of worry leaned on the same thing: how much time Ada would be away. Her father thought her worry was silly, because he didn't yet see how much he could no longer do. He was much more concerned about her traveling into the mountains alone, up into the hollers where people were suspicious and aggressive in defense of what little they had.

But twenty-eight dollars a month was twenty-eight dollars a month, and no amount of worry could overbalance that need.

Deciding to let her father make the final call, Ada told the man, "I'm about to make breakfast. You can join us, and meet my father. If he's got work for you, he'll say. Not for pay, there's no money, but for food. Maybe another night's rest, but our loft's not as good as the Conners'."

The man smiled. "That's real kindly, thank you." He held out his hand. "Name's Joel Abernathy."

Ada shook with him; his hand was cold and hard, like quartz. "Pleasure. I'm Ada. My people are the McDaniels." She held back her own last name. She'd heard stories; a widow was more vulnerable to strange men with bad intent. They saw widows as easier targets—already experienced, no longer pure. Nothing to 'ruin,' so free for the taking.

This man hadn't yet given her cause for suspicion, and in fact had been downright gentlemanly, but Ada valued caution. Better he think her unmarried and untouched. And protected by her father.

As they walked toward the house, Mr. Abernathy said, "If you don't mind me sayin', Miss Ada, you've got a real pretty way of talkin'. You got schoolin'?"

"I'm a schoolteacher," she answered. "And a librarian."

"I'll be. Well, that's real impressive. I didn't much go to school, but I liked it when I did."

Mr. Abernathy was still there when Ada returned from Callwood that afternoon. The trip on horseback took not much more than half the time she'd spent driving the wagon the day before. She returned with her deep saddlebags full of books and magazines, and the ledger she'd use to log the borrows and returns, and the progress and key details of her route.

Not since George had been alive had Ada felt such a pure flush of hope for her life. This was good work. She would be able to use her skills and education. She'd be out in the world a bit, with long spells alone to think. And she'd be doing something helpful for her people in these hard times.

The afternoon was bright, though a brisk, winter-leaning wind had picked up and made the trees shake as if impatient to rid themselves of their still-soft cladding of leaves.

Mr. Abernathy was with Ada's father, patching the fence along the near side of the pasture. It looked like their helper had hewn new posts to replace those that had gone soft with age. This was the work she'd hoped he'd help with. They both turned and smiled as she clopped down the drive.

Sending them a wave, Ada rode to the barn to unsaddle Henrietta, brush her down, and give her the rest of the afternoon off. Starting tomorrow, Henrietta was going to be working hard almost every day.

She fixed supper for four that evening; her father had offered to let Mr. Abernathy sleep on the floor in their sitting room that night, since he'd helped all through the day. Ada felt a little uncomfortable about that. It was one thing to offer a meal or two for work, and if they'd had a decent place in the barn for a human being to sleep, she wouldn't have hesitated to offer that, but sleeping in their own house with a stranger under their roof, that didn't sit quite right with her.

But her father had offered without reservation, and Mr. Abernathy had shown them nothing but gratitude and respect. He said he wanted to be off with the first light because he had to get to Knoxville before the cold set in, and that was long miles of hard walking. That he'd be leaving at the same time she did in the morning settled her worries some.

After supper, he sat in the sitting room with her parents and listened to the radio. Ada cleaned up the kitchen and then sat at the table with the contents of her saddlebags, contemplating the map of her route and parsing out how long her trip would be each day. The route was laid out so that she'd travel fewer miles when she had more places to stop, and travel farther when the homesteads got more distant from each other. The last days of the first week, she'd go deep into the mountains, into the little nooks where the people hardly ever saw anybody but their own. Those days, the riding would be harder, and the chance she might get shot by a suspicious homesteader would be greater.

Her father had insisted she take a rifle with her, for bears and panthers and suspicious homesteaders.

The first day would take her up to Bull Holler, where she'd taught. She knew everyone in that area pretty well, and didn't expect trouble. One of her stops would be the schoolhouse that had once been hers.

"What's all that?"

Ada turned at Mr. Abernathy's voice. "Is the program over?"

"Yes ma'am. Your daddy's helpin' your momma to bed. She gets around pretty good for bein' blind."

"She's lived in this house a long time, and we make sure never to change anything. She knows where things are."

"You got a real nice family, Miss Ada."

"Thank you." She felt intruded upon. As cordial and helpful as this man had been, Ada couldn't seem to let go of her suspicion of him. It was unchristian of her, certainly. A man down on his luck was not a bad man, and he'd been nothing but kind. She and her parents were hardly a step above him in circumstances. And yet, she felt a dull beat of tension around him.

"What's all that you got there?" he asked again.

"I'm a librarian. A pack horse librarian. It's a program to bring reading materials to people up the mountain, who don't have access to books on their own. I'm just preparing for tomorrow."

"That's a real nice thing." Standing at her side, he picked up a book from a stack and opened it: *Treasure Island*. "This one's got pictures!"

It had woodcuts at the beginning of each chapter, showing a key moment from that chapter. "Yes." She felt uncomfortable with him so close, looming over her like he was, so she slid from the chair and stood as well. "I need to pack everything back up and turn in for the night. Do you need anything before I do?"

He gave her a long look, then closed the book and set it neatly back in place. "I'm sorry, Miss Ada. I don't mean to make you scared. I's jus' curious."

Hating herself a little for her prejudices, Ada gave him a smile. "You don't make me afraid, Mr. Abernathy. You've been very kind, and the work you did for my father helped him very much. I'm grateful."

"I had a job once. I had a woman, and a nice-enough little house, and a reg'lar life. Then the world went pell-mell, and I lost it all. Had a couple bad years after that where maybe I wasn't such a good man. But Jesus came lookin' for me and showed me what's what. Now I'm jus' tryin' to get by until the world rights itself again.

Y'understand? I don't mean nobody no harm. Jus' tryin' to make it through one day to the next."

"I understand. I hope you find what you need in Knoxville." She hadn't asked what Knoxville might offer, and she didn't mean to. Once he left the farm, his business was not hers.

His mouth stretched in a weary grin. "Thank you. It's prob'ly nothin', but a little hope never hurt nobody, y'know? At least it gives me a place to walk to."

When Ada woke the next morning, Mr. Abernathy was gone. The bedding they'd given him for the night was folded neatly and stacked on the seat of her father's chair. He hadn't even waited to get a good breakfast in him first. But two of the rolls left from last night's meal were gone from the covered basket on the table.

She stood before the window and looked out across the foggy morning. In her own discomfort, she'd made him feel unwelcome. He'd worked hard for her father all day, asking only for compassion and shelter in return, and she'd been suspicious. And with no cause—not only had he been respectful and cordial all day, but none of the men they'd offered assistance to over these past few years had treated them with anything but gratitude. She'd heard stories of bad men taking advantage, but they'd been only that: stories. She couldn't account for her discomfort. Maybe it was simply that she'd be away from home so much now, with her new job, and worried for her parents while she was away.

With a sigh, Ada sent out a little prayer that Mr. Joel Abernathy might find what he sought in Knoxville. Then she turned her mind to her own business.

Riding in the mountains had been one of Ada's favorite things to do from the moment her father had lifted her onto a saddle. Though she'd never been out of Kentucky, or any farther from home than Lexington, she'd seen pictures of places around the world—Asia, and Europe, and South America. Africa and India. Deserts and oceans. They all had their beauty, too, some of it mysterious and alien. But she'd never seen anything prettier than her very own Eastern Kentucky world.

Yes, life was hard here. Most people barely kept themselves sheltered and fed, and dying hungry was an ugly way to go. But, just as He'd done when He'd sent a rainbow to Noah, God had given the people of Appalachia all the natural beauty He could muster to remind them that He was good and full of love for them.

As she rode up on this first morning of her new job and all the hope it brought her and her parents, Ada pushed back her work hat and breathed deep of fresh mountain air, crisp with autumn chill. Sun had burned away the fog and left a sparkling bright promise of a day. The turning of the leaves had finally taken, and a new wash of warm colors surrounded her.

She'd dressed in a few layers—wide-leg denim pants, work boots, one of her father's heavy undershirts, a cotton blouse, and a canvas jacket—to account for the brisk morning and a day that looked to warm well, even as she climbed high. Her farthest reach today would be twelve miles up from home, with a return that would bring her and Henrietta back to the barn at dusk, maybe a bit later. There could be a swing in temperature of thirty degrees or more on her route, from dawn to dusk, from the foothills to the hollers.

Her saddlebags were full of her library supplies. She had a lunch pail and canteen tied to her saddle, and one of her father's hunting rifles, in the event of a bear or cat. She'd also tied up a bedroll, just in case trouble befell her and she couldn't get home or find better shelter before nightfall.

An hour after she left home, she made her first stop—a rambling, ramshackle cabin at the edge of Bull

Holler. A skinny dog stood on the warped porch and snarled and barked at her, his jowls flinging slobber, but he didn't come down. He was waiting for an attack order.

She knew the family who lived here, the Devlins — she'd taught their oldest children when she'd had her own school post. Remembering Mr. Devlin's hostility to strangers, as evidenced by his furious guard dog, Ada stayed mounted and called out "Mr. Devlin? Mrs. Devlin? Hello?"

A tattered curtain moved in a window. Ada smiled at it, hoping she'd be recognized and thought a friend. "Hello!"

The plank door creaked open, and she saw the muzzle of a rifle first. Ada held still and didn't react. She understood mountain people. They didn't want intruders, and some of them didn't even want company at all, but most wouldn't shoot unless truly provoked. They weren't animals. They were simply isolated people living hard lives.

Mr. Devlin followed that muzzle out and squinted at her. "State yer business."

"Mr. Devlin, hello! It's Ada … McDaniel." She used her maiden name, the one she'd had when she was a teacher, but it hurt to cleave George's name from her. "Remember me? I used to teach at the school."

"I remember you. What you want?"

"I'm working with a new program, bringing books and other reading materials up the mountain. I've got all kinds of things to read, I can leave a few and then I'll come 'round in two weeks and let you trade them out for something different."

"Like one o' them liberries?"

"That's right, sir. Just like. A library on horseback, and I'm a librarian, bringing it to you."

"You know ain't me or Jezzie c'n read. The little 'uns get they schoolin' at the school. What we need books for here?"

Mrs. Pitts had spoken about this at length, but Ada thought she would have done so even without the instruction; it seemed only right, and in keeping with the idea that they librarians brought the world up the mountain.

"Well, if you wouldn't mind me setting a spell with you, I can read to you. I've got newspapers, too."

Mrs. Devlin must have said something from behind her husband then; he twisted his head, looking over his shoulder, and his sharp Adam's apple bobbed brusquely as he spoke. Ada couldn't hear what he said, but she felt a quiver of anxiety nonetheless. She remembered the Devlins, and the bruises Mrs. Devlin often sported. This was a world in which women had a place, and it was more or less accepted that, if they stepped out of it, their men would put them back in it with as much force as necessary.

Even so, Mrs. Devlin had seemed to wear more bruises, more frequently, than most. Ada worried that she'd provoked marital strife simply by showing up.

"We don't need no books here, teacher. You go on and find somebody else."

"Alright. Thank you for your time, Mr. Devlin."

The man receded into his house and closed the door.

Ada turned and nudged Henrietta to walk on. The Devlins were part of her route, and she wouldn't give up, but she'd have to think about how to approach them in the future.

Though others had been more friendly than Mr. Devlin, only one house, where the Hoopers, an elderly couple on their own, lived, had welcomed her in. Mr. Hooper was bedridden, and Mrs. Hooper had all she could do to keep them alive. They subsisted on the help of their neighbors and what kindnesses came their way. Ada sat in their dim but tidy little room and read to them from the Bible. When she left, Mrs. Hooper took Ada's face in her bony hands and kissed her on the lips. "Yer a angel, Mizz

Ada. Sent straight from our good Lord to give us peace today. We thank you."

Ada rode away from that leaning cabin full of the pleasure of a good thing done—and also melancholy. Her parents were elderly, too. Not so old as Mr. and Mrs. Hooper, but her mother had been forty-five when Ada came to them, and her father three years older than that. Both past seventy now, they were too old to scratch out their own living.

She'd never considered her parents to be old until recently. They'd simply been her parents, older than she, and somehow eternal. Since she'd become a widow and returned home, and since her father had hurt his back, Ada had finally begun to see that her parents were in the last chapter of their lives.

But they lived well down the mountain and closer to the world than the Hoopers did. They had neighbors to look after them when Ada could not, and hope for help should trouble strike. They'd be safe and sheltered, and not alone, until the book of their lives closed.

Her old schoolhouse at the back of Bull Holler was easily the best stop of her first day. It came with a melancholy of its own—she'd loved those brief years of teaching—but the joyous clamor of children crowding around Henrietta before Ada could dismount was a wonderful, restoring experience. They'd known what she was as soon as they'd seen her, because their teacher had known. She emptied her packs of slim children's books—fairy tales and Bible stories, picture books and adventure yarns. One older boy, probably only a year or so from leaving school, took *Treasure Island*. She took their names and wrote them in her ledger, explaining when she'd be back to change those books for different ones.

When she and Henrietta walked away, headed this time down the mountain, the children waved and called out their goodbyes as if they were sending off a hero.

She'd lingered too long, and the sun had already dropped behind the mountain peaks. Her ride home would happen in gloom, and maybe finish in dark, but she didn't mind.

It had been a good day.

This was a good job.

Chapter Four

The first day became the first week, and then the second. By then, Ada and Henrietta had traveled her whole route and distributed a goodly portion of her books. There were some who wanted no part of her, neither her company nor her offerings, and she'd been run off a few places on the end of a cocked rifle, but most people were glad to see her, or at least willing to offer her and her horse a drink of water before they sent her on her way.

As she'd expected, the higher up the mountain she went, the less hospitable the people were. She was a stranger to them, and an agent of the government. Most wanted no part of her.

That didn't mean she wouldn't keep trying. It was those benighted souls, the ones so remote they didn't even have a schoolhouse for their children, who most needed the service she provided.

She'd made it home every night those first two weeks, but most nights she arrived at the barn in the dark, with her father and mother beset with worry. On three different occasions, her mother had wept with relief when Ada stepped into the house.

Mrs. Pitts had promised she could be home every night, weather or misadventure notwithstanding, and strictly speaking, it was true. But the days were too long. It was hard on her parents' nerves, and on Ada and Henrietta's bodies. She didn't know whether she was riding too slowly or spending too much time with the people she served, or getting too late a start—though she was on the road with first light.

Finally, on the Saturday afternoon following the completion of her first full circuit, with the most detailed information she could gather about her route, Ada sat down with her map and drew out a different scheme. No major adjustments, just a more sensible path, one forged by a hand that knew these mountains. Mrs. Pitt wasn't a mountain woman. She'd made the route without knowing the people up here and how they lived, simply by connecting dots on the map.

The mountains and their people were more than mere dots.

Ada had been an obedient child and was a compliant adult, with nary a rebellious bone in her body. She felt a touch discomforted, improving on a plan made by the woman who'd hand her her pay in a couple weeks, but something had to change. Riding down the mountain in the dark scared her a little. Bears and panthers prowled more freely under the moon, and were harder to see coming. Twice, she'd been confronted with eyes glowing in the moonlight and the low rumble of a warning growl. She and Hen had been still and quiet and eventually been left alone, but she wondered how long such fortune would hold out.

There was no one who'd check in on her and ensure she was following the route that had been set for her, and she hadn't been told in so many words that that route was sacrosanct. She wasn't exactly breaking any rules. So on the following Monday, Ada dressed in another set of layers — autumn in the mountains was nearly as crisp as winter down below — packed up her books and things, which now included a few of her own volumes and some recent papers she'd asked the people at church to donate, saddled up Henrietta, and headed up for her first day of second visits. Today, she meant to swap books with those who'd borrowed and try again with those who hadn't.

As she rode away from the barn, the kitchen window flashed a pale golden glow. Her father was awake. She'd made up what food she could the night before, but these days, making meals for him and her mother was her father's job.

"'I have set the LORD always before me,'" Ada read, "'because he is at my right hand, I shall not be moved. There for my heart is glad and my glory rejoiceth: my flesh also shall rest in hope. For thou wilt not leave my soul in hell; neither wilt thou suffer thing Holy One to see corruption. Thou wilt shew me the path of life: in thy presence is fulness of joy; at thy right hand there are pleasures for evermore.'"

She looked up from the Bible. Mr. Hooper had taken a turn since she'd first visited. He lay on his back, sucking rough breaths in erratic bursts, as if each one took more strength than he had. Ada wasn't sure he knew she was there.

Mrs. Hooper sat beside him, a straight-back chair pulled up close to the bedside so she could hold her husband's hand.

"I could send for a doctor," Ada offered, but Mrs. Hooper shook the offer away.

"Thank you, but no. Don't need no doctor. God takes us when He wants us, Mizz Ada. He give me and him a long time together, and I ain't nothin' but grateful for it."

"Is there anyone to help you?"

The old lady gave her a smile brittle with coming sorrow, but soft with peace. "Well, sure they is. We got neighbors, and Preacher Lawson comes 'round. We fine.

I'd like it much if you'd read from that pretty Bible s'more, though. Maybe Psalm 23?"

Ada didn't need to read to recite that psalm, but she flipped the onion-skin pages forward from Psalm 16 and held the book on her hands like an offering. "'The LORD is my shepherd; I shall not want.'" Mrs. Hooper picked up the verse with her, and they recited together the assurance that God was with them wherever they were, and always would be.

She stayed a while with the Hoopers, helping Mrs. Hooper prepare a small meal and sorting out some papers. Helping illiterate neighbors with their paperwork had been a way she'd earned money, or made trades, even while she was married, and she was happy to help people now as part of her job as well. As she saw it, and as Mrs. Pitts had explained to her, the books were simply the tokens she left behind. What she was really bringing the people on her route was companionship—in the form of stories and in her own presence.

On her revised route, she stopped at the Devlins' later in the day and approached warily, ready to face Mr. Devlin's rifle again. The dog wasn't on the porch, and Ada breathed easier. That probably meant Devlin was away, maybe hunting. She nudged Henrietta and came closer to the house. Two youngsters, one wearing a sagging diaper under a ragged sweater, and the other dressed in what had to be his father's undershirt, knotted up so it wouldn't drag, played in the dirt near the woods. The temperature was low for them to be so scantily dressed, but they didn't seem to mind the chill.

The Devlins had had five children when she'd taught four of them. These two were younger than the years since she'd taught, so they'd increased their brood by at least two.

Seven children. A family of nine living off nothing but this harsh land, with a man like Tobias Devlin at the head of their table. The thought made Ada's heart sore.

Mrs. Devlin came around the front, carrying a tattered reed basket mounded with wash just off the line. She stopped when she saw Ada and cast her eyes guiltily about.

"Hello, Mrs. Devlin! How are you?"

Jezebel Devlin had the looks of a once-pretty woman worn down by life and time. She was thin at the shoulder and thick at the hips. Her greying, mousy brown hair was captured in a few pins. Her flour-sack dress was so oft-washed the color and pattern had nearly worn away to a dull grey. She had a bruise on her cheek that looked to be a week or so old.

Maybe two weeks. Maybe the last time she was here, that sharp swivel of Mr. Devlin's head, that bouncing Adam's apple that Ada had thought meant harshly spoken words, had meant a blow as well. Maybe that bruise had been her fault.

"What you want?" Mrs. Devlin asked, her voice higher than her husband's but her tone the same.

"I've brought books and magazines again. I thought I'd see if you might have changed your mind."

"Like Tobias tol' you before, we ain't got no use for books here."

"How about for the children? I have books to help them with their studies, and others just for fun. Picture books for the little ones." She flipped a pack open and slid out a pretty picture book—a story told with only pictures, with no confusing words to make an illiterate adult feel stupid. Ada thought of it as an entry ticket: if they enjoyed the magic of a story like this, they might want more.

The exhausted mother looked across her yard to the little boys playing with rocks and dirt and sticks. She gnawed on her lip, and Ada understood: Mrs. Devlin didn't want to say no, but she would. Because Mr. Devlin had laid down the law. The way so many men did.

Ada had been blessed to have been raised by her father, who could be hard in his way, and stubborn, but was gentle in love. He treated his wife and daughter with devotion and care. Maybe if Ada had been a naturally rebellious child, or if she hadn't been her parents' only surviving child, come so late in their lives that her mother had thought the change had come on her and hadn't realized she was carrying until far into the pregnancy—maybe she would have known what it was like to have the law laid down, but that hadn't been the case in her home.

Nor had it been the case with George. He, too, had been gentle, and treated Ada as a partner in their marriage. She didn't think she could have fallen in love with any other kind of man.

She hadn't gotten to keep him long, but nevertheless, she'd been blessed.

"We can't have no books here. You gotta git," Mrs. Devlin finally said, casting another worried look around.

Just then, the older boy hit the younger with a stick, and the baby began to shriek. Ada and Mrs. Devlin turned in tandem. The baby was bleeding.

"Benny! What you do?!" Mrs. Devlin dropped the basket and ran to her boys. The basket fell to its side, spilling clean laundry onto the dirt.

Ada swung off Henrietta's back and hurried to pick up the laundry. As she set the basket right and pulled the top sheet, now dirty again, away from the still-clean wash, she heard the crack of Mrs. Devlin's hand on young flesh. She didn't look, but heard several sharp strikes. She draped the dirty sheet over one arm and picked up the basket.

"You git inside, boy!" Mrs. Devlin demanded, and the older boy — Benny — hurried red-faced into the house, holding both hands on his bottom.

Mrs. Devlin came back to the basket, the younger boy on her hip. Blood trickled down his face in a thin stream, cutting through a smear on his cheek where his mother must have wiped it.

She studied the wash in Ada's arms, fixing on the sheet that had fallen into the dirt, and her face collapsed into a mask of weary fear. "Oh no."

"What can I do to help?" Ada asked, not knowing what else to say or do.

But Mrs. Devlin shook her head. She set the baby on his bare feet and took the basket and sheet from Ada. "Please go 'way. Please. He'll be back soon. Yer gonna make it all worse."

It broke Ada's heart, but she knew it was true. "Alright, Mrs. Devlin. I'll go. I'll try again another time. You take care now."

Mrs. Devlin stood where she was and watched her go, her expression perfectly empty.

Good weather had held for most of Ada's first three weeks of riding. There had been a few sprinkles and some overnight showers, but for the most part, the days had been bright and the ripening autumn chill hadn't bothered her in her careful layers.

That changed at the end of her third week, on the day she rode farthest from home, high on the mountain, deep into the most isolated world of the hills. Cable's Holler.

Many hollers—most maps called them 'Hollows,' but in Ada's experience, no one who'd even *met* someone from this part of the world pronounced it that way—were almost like villages, tiny communities with a place for worship and schooling, maybe even a simple kind of store. If they didn't have a preacher or teacher living with them, they at least got a fairly regular visit from the itinerant variety. People lived in close enough proximity to each other to be neighborly and helpful—and to squabble, too, of course. To be a community.

But if you went up high enough, or dug in deep enough, that cohesion began to falter. The people who lived so far from the busy world wanted no part of community, either because they'd never known it and didn't understand it, or because they did know it and rejected it.

Nobody in the hills was what Ada would call *outgoing*—they were all suspicious of the world below and people who came from it. They kept themselves to themselves, as it was said. But the family that lived in Cable's Holler were hardly more than ghosts, as far as Ada had been able to tell thus far.

Cable's Holler was a dot on her map, and it was a discernable place on the mountain—a sudden valley, narrow and steep, carved into its craggy side—but it wasn't a community, not any longer. Not for a generation, at least.

It had no worship place or schoolhouse, nothing like a tiny store. Maybe once they had, but Ada saw no signs. There were four homesteads, but three had gone derelict; the families that had tenanted them had either finally died out or simply abandoned them. Only one home remained occupied, at the farthest reach of the holler, and showed signs that life was trying to live.

As cabins went, it was roomy, with a rare second story, and suggested that at some distant point in the past, the family had known comparative prosperity. It looked like it might even have been whitewashed once. But it had nearly gone back to nature now and looked only slightly more stable than its caving-in neighbors toward the head of the holler.

She didn't even know the family's name, or how many people lived there. On her first attempt to visit, no one had come out of the cabin, and she'd nearly decided that it, too, was abandoned, until she'd heard a child's voice inside, and then the soft rumble of a man's answer.

No amount of cajoling on her part had induced the occupants to come to the door, and Ada had eventually given up and gone on with her route.

Today, her second visit, she'd very nearly cut Cable's Holler from her path. Rain had fallen steadily on her head all day. The temperature seemed barely high enough to keep it from turning to ice. She was in her first foul temper of her librarian experience, and, seeing as she'd not yet received her wages, the allure of the work had washed away with the frosty rain dripping down her back. She wanted to go home, and Cable's Holler was a two-hour trek from her stop just before it. To what purpose? So she could pound on a door and peer through the tatters in decomposing curtains for fifteen minutes before giving up again and turning back?

Only one thing had her turning Henrietta toward Cable's Holler on this unpleasant, demoralizing day: it was her job. She simply didn't have it in her not to meet her obligations.

So she slogged over the muddy, rocky terrain, trusting Henrietta to know where to put her hooves down, and they made their way to the remotest part of her route.

The holler's valley was deep, and the sun was drowned in heavy rainclouds, so the dark was almost as thick as twilight when she pulled her horse up before the two-story cabin. Again, there were few obvious signs of life, but on a day like today, people were staying inside all they could. And she could smell that there was a fire going inside.

She swung down and landed in a muddy soup, but Ada's need to be presentable had died around the middle of the second week. She wasn't going calling. She was working, and the ride was hard.

Henrietta blew out an irritated huff and dropped her head. This day was no picnic for her, either. Ada patted her withers. "I'm sorry, Hen. We'll warm up at home tonight, I promise."

The horse snorted and pushed a sodden face against Ada's leg.

Ada untied her book packs, heaved them over her shoulder, and went up onto the bowed porch. She knocked on the door—not a plank door, but a solid piece of wood, sanded and turned, with a few remnant stripes of peeling red paint. Once it had been a very nice door. Once, someone had cared for this house like a home.

"Hello? It's Mrs. Donovan, from the Pack Horse Library!"

Nothing. She waited a bit, then knocked again; then, as last time, she heard the wordless roll of voices inside.

"I don't mean to be a bother, but it's mighty wet and chilly today. If you don't want a book, might I ask for a moment to sit by your fire before I go on my way?"

More rumbling. Childish voices, at least two, and a man's.

Then a deep voice, much louder, in two sharp syllables. "Bluebird!"

The latch shifted, and the door opened.

A tiny angel, with soft golden hair and enormous blue eyes, gazed up at her. She was five or six years old. Gleaming clean, though her little dress was ragged and her feet were bare. The room behind her was enticingly warm.

Ada smiled. "Well hello, miss. My name is Mrs. Donovan. People call me Mrs. Ada." She said it the way it usually sounded, the two syllables in Missus elided to *Mizz*. "What's your name?"

"I'm Bluebird," the pretty little girl answered, as Ada had expected she would. "You want to come in?"

"Bluebird," the man's voice said, now a tone of warning rather than halting.

Pretty little Bluebird dropped her head, but another voice, another child's, still young but older than Bluebird's, old enough to sound clearly like a boy's, said, "It ain't right, Pa. Please."

She didn't know this family at all, didn't know what kind of man these children's father was, or how he'd react to them or to her if she pushed her advantage here, but her instinct, without any evidence at all, insisted it was safe. Maybe it was Bluebird's sweet, clear face, or her gleaming smooth hair. She was well cared for. Maybe it was simply her name. Bluebird, a symbol of hope and happiness.

So Ada took the chance she had. "I would love to come in, Bluebird. Thank you so very much." She wiped her boots on the bare porch, the place before the door where most people kept a reed mat, and stepped into the shadowy old house.

Chapter Five

The room was large and warm. A fire crackled in a stone fireplace. But if not for little miss Bluebird standing right before her, smiling with shy sweetness, and a tall, gaunt boy, two or three years her senior, standing off a bit, in the middle of the room, Ada would have thought she'd stepped into a haunted old relic long past its use.

The plank floor was grey with age and wear. The walls were papered with newspaper, the pages obviously many years old, yellowed and cracking. The windows were covered with decaying curtains that hardly blocked light or sight.

A small, plain square table framed with four equally plain chairs, and two straight-back rockers, were the only furnishings in the room. No—there was a worktable in the shadows of a far corner, a wood cookstove and a pump sink, and what might once have been a pie safe, though it had lost its doors.

There had to be more, but the shadows were too deep. And the man whose voice she'd heard—where was he?

Something felt strange here. Unsettling. If she'd been a less practical woman, she might have honestly believed the place was haunted, and Bluebird and her brother were mere figments of a forgotten past.

Suddenly superstitious, Ada reached out and set her hand on Bluebird's shoulder. Bony and frail, but solid. Real. The girl's angelic smile brightened at her touch.

"You c'n sit by the fire, if you want," the boy said.

"Thank you." She let Bluebird take her hand and lead her to a rocking chair.

The fireplace was sturdy stone, with a heavy beam for a mantel. Now that she was closer, she saw a large cross-stitch sampler, framed carefully under glass, was centered on that beam, leaning against the stone chimney. It was a typical sampler, with the alphabet stitched in two neat rows across the bottom, and a stitched image of a cozy cabin, smoke wafting from its chimney, in the center. Stitched above the cabin were the words: *LORD BLESS AND KEEP US*, and the name *The Walkers* beneath them.

The dry warmth eased her fretfulness, and she sighed. She set her packs on the floor beside the chair and sat down. "Would you like to look at the books I've brought?"

The boy turned and looked into the shadows beyond the room. Ada looked the same way, expecting to see their father, but saw nothing except the edge of a newel post, where the stairs to the second floor must be.

Bluebird had settled on the floor beside Ada and was playing with the fastenings of her saddlebags. Ada leaned over and unwound the tie, then lifted the flap and opened the top. The saddlebags were weatherproof, but days like this, with steady, drenching rain, put that to the test. The edges of the topmost books had swelled a little. She drew a slim picture book from the pack and handed it to the girl at her side.

"Can you read, Miss Bluebird? That is *such* a pretty name."

The little girl flushed with pleasure. "My momma picked it. She named me Bluebird Hope Walker."

"Well, I think that might be the best little girl's name I've ever heard. Your momma must be wonderful."

"Our momma's dead," the boy said. His tone wasn't aggressive, or sorrowful. Simply flat.

Bluebird's big eyes went round. "Uh-huh. She died when I came."

"Oh, sweetheart," Ada said and brushed a finger under the girl's little chin. She turned to the boy, her hand over her heart. "I'm so sorry."

He held her gaze but didn't respond.

"May I ask your name?"

He glanced toward the shadows again before returning to meet her eyes. "Elijah."

"That's a very fine name, too. Would you like a book, Elijah?"

He shook his head. Like his sister, he was a beautiful child, with golden hair, not shaggy, but roughly cut, and soulful blue eyes. "We ain't got no school. Can't read."

Like every state in the Union, Kentucky had a compulsory education law, requiring students to attend at least grammar school. But when there was no school in reach, children like these were invisible to such laws and got an education only if there was someone in their family to teach them at home.

She glanced at that sampler. Someone had been able to read here. Their mother, most likely, who'd died when Bluebird was born—thus when Elijah was only two or three. Poor motherless children.

And a father afraid to make himself known. A widower. Ada turned again and studied the shadows beyond this room. She could almost feel eyes on her.

Turning back to Elijah, she smiled. "You know, I'm so grateful for the warmth you've offered me." She set her hand on Bluebird's silky head. "If you'd let me repay your kindness, I'd love to read you a story. Would you like that?"

"Please!" Bluebird cheered and held up the book she was flipping through. "This one!"

Yet again, Elijah turned to the shadows. "I guess it'd be alright."

He came closer and crouched beside his sister. "What is this story?"

"That," Ada said and held out her hand for the book, "is *The Three Musketeers*. There's a much bigger story about them that someday you can read if you want, but this is just one of their adventures." She pulled Bluebird onto her lap. Elijah stood at the side of her chair as she began to read.

After a few pages, she heard the sound of a door open and close heavily, but no one had come through this room. She looked out the window, through the tattered curtains, and saw a figure in the rain—a man, tall and broad-shouldered, hunched into his coat and hat. He went to Henrietta.

The horse didn't know him and shied a bit when he took her reins. But he must have spoken kindly to her, because she went easily with him, out of sight. Ada forgot the book as she watched, wondering if Henrietta was safe.

"That's Pa," Elijah said. "He'll be takin' your horse to shelter, outta the rain."

"That's very kind of him. I'd like to make your father's acquaintance."

"Pa don't like people," Bluebird said, brushing her little fingers over Ada's cheek. "You got spots."

Ada laughed. "Those are called freckles, and yes, I do."

"I want freckles, too."

"God decides about freckles, I think, Bluebird."

"Then I'll ask Him when I say my prayers."

"Can you read some more?" Elijah asked.

"Of course." Ada picked up the story again.

This strange house was turning out to be her best stop of the day.

She read *The Three Musketeers* and *Little Sallie Mandy and the Shiny Penny*. Though the children couldn't read them, she signed both books out to Elijah and Bluebird, and a primer called *The New Path to Reading*, helping Elijah with the first few pages and promising to help him more when she returned.

Nearly two hours had passed, and she needed to be on her way, but still she'd seen no more of Mr. Walker than his hunched form collecting her horse. The rain had stopped, except for the dripping from the trees that would continue for the remainder of the afternoon.

As she returned her ledger to the pack and closed her coat over her clothes, Ada asked, "Do you children have enough food?"

Elijah answered, his brow creasing with offense. "Pa takes good care of us, Mizz Ada. We got all we need."

"That's good, then. I'm glad. I meant no offense, Elijah. I only wanted to be sure."

As Ada went to the door, Bluebird ran up and threw her arms around her legs. "Don't go! I like stories!"

Ada crouched to the girl's level. "I left the stories for you, Bluebird. And I'll be back. Do you know how to count?"

"Yes'm. One-two-three-four-five-six-seven-eight-nine-ten!"

Ada grinned. "That's excellent! If you count ten mornings and then four more, I'll be back, with more stories, and I'll read to you again, if you'd like me to."

"One-two-three-four-five-six-seven-eight-nine-ten-one-two-three-four!"

"That's exactly right! Well done!"

Bluebird hugged her again. Elijah shook her hand like a young gentleman, and Ada went out the door, still without having met their father.

She followed the path she'd seen him take Henrietta and found, behind the house, a small barn that was more lean-to than full structure. Most of it was little more than windbreak, with only three full walls and a partial fourth. Henrietta was tied under shelter. A dairy cow, an aged Holstein, was penned under cover as well, tucked into the nook where there were three solid walls. She heard a sleepy bleat and peered through a rough doorway into the shadows of the small, fully enclosed area. A few goats seemed to be clustered inside at a far corner.

Beside the barn, behind the house, was a small patch, less than a quarter acre, that had mostly been harvested, though a few vines of small pumpkins remained. A small chicken coop made a far wall boundary for the garden; it was closed up against the poor weather.

Henrietta was still saddled, but she was dry and munching contently at a box of dried mountain grasses. Her bridle had been removed and was hanging on a post. She was tied with a rope halter. Mr. Walker had taken very good care of her.

Ada peered into the protected part of the rough little barn. Aside from the pen of goats, she saw only hand tools, and some bundles of mountain grasses hanging from the ceiling to dry.

Mr. Walker provided for his family with what he could grow in that little patch, what this old cow and few goats and chickens could give, and what he could hunt or forage in the wilds.

She turned toward the post where Henrietta's bridle hung, and nearly jumped clear through her skin. Mr. Walker stood there. His hat was tipped low over his face, and his head canted down, as if he studied his own boots. His trousers and coat were both a dark grey that had once been black, and his hands were shoved into his coat pockets. He was like a dark, hulking specter.

"Oh!" she gasped when she could breathe again. "You startled me."

He lifted his head, and Ada nearly gasped again. Over the course of the afternoon, she'd conjured an image of Mr. Walker in her mind, but the man before her was not remotely the same. This man was ... well, he was handsome, in a rough kind of way. Or maybe not handsome, but interesting-looking. Ada found herself fascinated, and her eyes focused on all of him in turn.

He was taller than she'd even realized, and broader as well. His face was made of harsh angles—square jaw and chin bristled with greying hairs, sharp cheekbones, heavy brow, blunt mouth. His hair was dark and shaggy under his hat. She couldn't really see his eyes, under the shadow of his hat and that serious brow, but she could almost feel them boring into her.

"Mr. Walker."

"You were good to my children," he said, and she recognized the voice as the one she'd heard earlier from the other side of the door. Pitched low, it rumbled is if it traveled over a rocky riverbed on the way to his mouth.

"They're wonderful children. I was happy to spend time with them. I left some books, and I'll be back in two weeks with more. If that's alright by you."

He stood still and didn't answer. Ada was sure he was staring and wasn't sure what to do. Then he touched a finger to the brim of his hat and walked away.

Ada watched him walk to his house, his broad back hunched again. She didn't know what to make of Mr. Walker.

Ada's father switched off the radio, and the new report went silent. The three souls of their little family sat in silence for a moment. The report had been full of turmoil in Europe and around the globe.

"I'm glad you're a woman, Ada Lee," her mother said to end the quiet. "It sure sounds like they want to make another war like before, and it'd kill me to send my last child to die like the first two."

"Don't you worry 'bout that, Bess," her father said. "What's goin' on over there's none o' our affair. President Roosevelt, he musta learnt from before. He won't send no more American boys to do Europe's dyin'."

"Well," her mother said and pushed herself up from her chair. "Leastwise, we don't gotta worry 'bout our girl." She turned a wry, sightless look on Ada, turned right to her as if she could see her. "All's we got to worry is if she falls off the mountain in the dark. Or gets et by a panther. Or gets shot by a somebody thinks she's up to no good in they business."

As her mother made her way to the kitchen, holding a hand out to be sure of her way, Ada rose from the floor and followed.

Her mother was at the plate of cookies on the table. In the month she'd been riding the mountain, Ada had taken to spending Sunday afternoons baking, making breads and biscuits, cookies and pies for the week. She liked something sweet in her lunch pail, and she liked to leave something sweet for her parents to enjoy as well.

A batch of pumpkin cookies had been her last of the day. She'd harvested the bulk of the pumpkins on Saturday afternoon, and had canned enough for them to eat through the winter and to use for trade, too. Her mother's pumpkin soup was famous among their neighbors.

"Momma, what I do, it's not dangerous."

Her mother sat at the table and nibbled at a cookie. "Sit down, Ada Lee."

Ada sat.

"You know I was raised up there in Red Fern Holler. Till I went off on my own, I hardly ever saw a stranger wasn't lookin' to collect a tax."

"I know, Momma." She'd visited her grandparents in the holler when she was a girl. She was no stranger to the mountain, not before she'd taken this job nor since.

"Ever' time I hear you ride off, I wonder if you ain't gonna get shot by somebody don't want a stranger snoopin' at his door. Or maybe Hen'll put a hoof down on a loose rock, and you'll fall off a crag. Or a bear'll stand up right in front of you. Ever' time you go, I worry I'll not see you again."

"Momma ..." she reached over and covered her mother's hand with her own.

"Don't tell me you're safe, Ada Lee. A woman alone ain't never safe. I know we need you to take this wage. You and your daddy, you try not to let me know the way things are, but it's my eyes that went, not my head. I know. I can taste when you're stretching ingredients to make 'em last. I can hear when Zeke don't turn the lights on. And I know good and well how much he hurts when he tries to work hisself. So I know we need what you can earn. I jus' want you to tell me you know how dangerous that mountain is, and that you're bein' smart as you can be."

"I am, Momma. I changed my route so I can be sure to be home before full dark. I keep a rifle with me, and I keep it loaded. I'm being as smart as I can be. And tomorrow, I'll go into Callwood and get my first wages. Then we won't need to stretch the flour and sugar or keep the lights out so much." With twenty-eight dollars in her purse, she meant to stock well up on supplies.

"That's well and good, but it's you I care most for. I need you to come home, Ada Lee. Ever' night. I need to know you're here with us."

Ada squeezed her mother's hand, hardened by work and bent by arthritis. "I will be, Momma. Always."

Chancey Maclaren ran around the front of his truck and opened the passenger-side door. He'd offered Ada a ride into town this morning, and she had happily accepted. After spending twenty-six days of the past month in the saddle, she was glad to give Henrietta this day off—and her own backside as well. Besides, riding in the truck with Chancey meant that she could dress up nicely for her librarian meeting.

"How long you need, Mizz Ada?" Chancey asked as he helped her to the sidewalk.

Ada thought about that and checked her wristwatch, another treasured gift from George. She wore it only for church and special days. It was ten minutes to ten in the morning. "Well, this meeting starts at ten and goes for four hours, and then I'll need to do some shopping."

He dug under his canvas jacket and pulled his heavy old pocket watch from his overalls. "I'll meet you at the front of the dry goods store at three o'clock, then. That alright, Mizz Ada? If'n you ain't done shopping, I'll help. I wouldn't want you carryin' nothing heavy or dusty in that pretty dress."

"That's perfect, Chancey. Thank you."

"Always happy to help you, Mizz Ada." He grinned and ducked his chin a bit. He stood at the side of his truck like a guard while she went into the library and didn't get in and pull away until she went to the window and waved him away.

Ada turned to face the library and grinned at what she saw.

Her first time here, Mrs. Pitts had been alone, and the space had been quiet and a bit gloomy. Ada had loved it, because of the books and the order and the peace, but it had felt lonely, too. Today, however, two large tables had been brought into the main part of the room and pushed together, and circled with plain chairs, and seven women besides Mrs. Pitts milled about that meeting space. They all faced her and offered her smiles of welcome.

"Mrs. Donovan, excellent." Mrs. Pitts bustled up. "You may put your coat and things over there"—she indicated the other side of the room, where coats and bags and lunch pails lay neatly scattered over another long table—"and I'll make introductions. Then we'll get to work. You're the last in, but that's understandable. You've the farthest to come."

She set her things in amongst the others, then stood for a moment with her back to the others, feeling a flash of awkwardness. She'd taken the last route and was the last to arrive today. How naïve was she compared to the others? How would she be judged?

After a moment, her practical soul took hold of such silly worries and shook her back to sense. With a quick smooth of her dress and a check to make sure her hair was in place, Ada put on her professional teacher's smile and went to the others.

Mrs. Pitts was still standing, but the others had taken seats. Only two remained empty — the one Mrs. Pitts stood behind, at the head of the table, and another at the end of one side. She went to that chair.

"Ladies," Mrs. Pitts said with an arm outstretched toward Ada. "Please welcome Mrs. Ada Donovan to our ranks."

The other women nodded, smiled, or said "Hi Ada." Ada returned their greeting with a nod and smile of her own.

"Ada comes to us from Barker's Creek and has taken our last route. We've got this corner of Eastern Kentucky covered now, ladies. So let's all introduce ourselves and get down to our business of the day."

As her fellow librarians introduced themselves, they said where they lived and what route they had. Ada focused on remembering names, but she was also struck with a powerful feeling of community. These were mountain women, too. Mrs. Pitts might have been sent in by the government from away—Ada wasn't sure about that, but suspected it was true—but her fellow librarians knew the mountains just like she did. They were women doing a service for their own people.

They were all literate, of course, but they weren't all teachers. Only one other librarian had been a teacher. Another had been a reporter for a newspaper that had gone bust. The rest were simply women who loved books and needed to earn. Every one of them was either married or widowed.

She sat and listened as they talked, describing their victories and challenges, complaining about the string of days of wet weather, fretting about the cold to come, exchanging hints for keeping their feet dry and warm inside their boots. They talked about books that had been lost or ruined while out on loan, and others that were getting, in the words of Mrs. Tolliver, "just loved to death, so much the strings are coming loose from the bindings, and they're all but loose pages."

After Mrs. Owens had mentioned a trouble she was having with one family, and her concern for the children there, Ada piped up. "Yes, I have a family or two I'm concerned about as well."

They all turned to her, and Ada felt a bit shy, like she'd interrupted where she ought not have. But Mrs. Owens said, "A family like my Cranes?"

"Something like, I think. The Devlins. Mr. Devlin has been very hostile to me, and I'm worried about his wife and children. He beats his wife, it's clear. And when last I visited, the youngest children were hardly dressed, though the temperature couldn't have been more than fifty degrees. They won't even let me dismount. I'm not sure what to do, but I'm worried."

"We can't meddle, Mrs. Donovan." That was one of the older women, a staunch lady of about forty, Mrs. Castle. "We can only cause more harm if we meddle. Unless Mrs. Devlin is asking for your help?"

"No. She's not. She wants me to stay away."

"I say," offered Mrs. Galway, "To you and Mrs. Owens—keep these families on your route. At least, you can see if things get worse, and if Mrs. Devlin wants help, you can help her. Leastwise, your visits let her know she's not forgotten."

"I agree," said Mrs. Pitts. "Don't give up, ladies. Keep yourself safe, of course. I trust your judgment to know when a home's not safe for a visit, and to make a note of it in your ledger. But remember our mission. It's more than books we bring."

"We carry the world," several of the women said, their wry grins and sidelong looks suggesting they heard that line frequently and had made it a joke among them.

Ada liked it. She didn't think it was funny at all. It was important.

Part Two

Chapter Six

Jonah checked the last knot, found it tight, and stood back. "You did good, boy."

"Thank you, Pa." Elijah frowned at the sled, studying his work in tying down the load. He was a serious boy, and took compliments and approval with no special pleasure Jonah could see. They two were cut from the same dark cloth. Bluebird favored her mother and brought them all the light they had.

"Now. What'll you do while I'm away?" Jonah asked his boy.

"Stay inside. Bar the door. Keep the rifle close, but out of Bluebird's reach. Keep her close and safe."

"If somebody comes, what'll you do?"

"Get the rifle and take Bluebird under the stairs. Stay quiet till they leave."

"If there's trouble for me, when will you know?"

"If morning comes and you ain't home."

"And what'll you do?"

"Pack Bluebird up nice and warm and walk down t'store in Red Fern Holler."

Where Jonah was headed today. It was a long trek, and slick today, but the path was fairly clear, so long as more hard weather didn't block it or bury it. If he wasn't home by dark, it would be trouble that kept him away, but better the children wait until dawn to find help.

Elijah was eight years old. Too young to be in charge, maybe, but he was born older than his years, and since his momma died, when he was two, he'd featured himself as Jonah's right hand.

If not for these children, Jonah would have walked himself off a cliff the day he'd put Grace in the ground. He lived for them, and only them, and he hated to leave them so long on their own. But he couldn't take them down the mountain with him today. The ice storm last night would make the way hard. They were safer home.

More importantly, he might have to humble himself before Hez Cummings at the general store to get the supplies he needed to keep the children through the winter. He didn't want them to see him beg.

"Alright then." He set his hand on his son's shoulder and drew him back toward the house.

Inside, Bluebird sat on the floor near the fire, flipping through the latest picture story the book woman had left with her. Every couple weeks, that skinny little redhead would tromp up to the cabin on her big bay mare and bring books for the children to choose from. Bluebird adored her, sure she was an angel. Elijah maybe thought so, too, though he was quieter about his affections.

Jonah didn't know what he thought about her, except she was a stranger, and he didn't like those. The more she showed up, the less a stranger she felt, and he liked that even less. He hoped the onset of a hard winter would keep her down the mountain before his children got too attached to her.

Elijah went to his sister and knelt before her. "Bluebird, Pa's goin'. Go say 'bye."

She looked up and smiled. Mercy, how much like her momma she looked. Grace knelt primly by her side, as beautiful as the day he'd met her, and gave him the exact same smile.

Jonah wasn't a superstitious man, and he didn't put much stock in God, not since Grace was taken so cruelly from him. He thought it more likely that his mind conjured the vision of his wife out of grief and wishing than that she was truly haunting him, but he didn't care one way or the other. She was with him and had never left, and that was all that mattered.

All his life, Jonah had lived high on the mountain in Cable's Holler. He'd been born in the same cabin his children were born in, the same cabin his father and grandmother had been born in. Once upon a time, when he was a child and then a young man, the holler had been a community and even managed to thrive a bit, with three other families calling that quiet nook high in the side of the mountain their home. They'd made regular treks down to Red Fern Holler in those days, traveling together every Sunday for services and to do trade with the bigger community there. That was how he'd had the good fortune to meet and court a pretty, yellow-haired preacher's daughter named Grace.

It had been a good life. Simple and quiet, and not easy, but full.

But then, a year or so after he'd made Grace his wife and brought her home, a sickness came and took most of the people of Cable's Holler, including his parents and younger sister. The ones who'd survived that hellish winnowing packed up and walked away. All but Jonah and Grace. He couldn't leave the house his great-granddad had built, and she couldn't leave him.

They'd lived together alone in the holler for near three years, and they'd been happy, with no need of more than the mountain offered up, except for a couple trips a year down for supplies.

She'd delivered both their children with no more help to her than what Jonah could give her. When the bleeding wouldn't stop after Bluebird came, and the fever struck her the next day, he couldn't go for help—he couldn't leave her or their children, and even if he could have left Grace on her own, he didn't know how he could carry a newborn and their boy still in diapers down to Red Fern Holler for the healing woman, or to send for a doctor.

It was the first time ever he'd felt real isolation. Not even when his parents and sister died had he felt trapped on the mountain. In those weeks of illness, they'd had a doctoring man up three times, but everybody still died anyway.

But sitting at the side of their bed, holding a squalling, hungry newborn, while Grace moaned and thrashed until she was quiet evermore, Jonah had hated the mountain with his whole heart.

He'd meant to pack up his children and walk away from Cable's Holler. But the morning after he'd buried Grace, he'd woken with both children sleeping in his arms, and he'd found his wife sitting on the bed beside him, propped against the iron headstead, dressed in her pretty, wedding-night dressing gown, looking as beautiful and happy as she'd been that night.

She'd followed him around most of the day, but never left the walls of the house. When he went to the barn, or out into the woods, she'd stayed behind.

She wasn't transparent, like he imagined a ghost would be. She wasn't solid, either. She was an image, a memory, a wish. That was all, and he was too sensible a man to think otherwise. But it didn't matter. She was here, and only here. So Jonah and their children stayed, and made the life they could, alone at the top of the mountain.

It wasn't long before he began to talk to her, and she to answer him. Not in words anyone could hear, not even him, not with his ears. But she spoke to him nevertheless.

He knew right well only he could see her. She'd never shown herself to their children, which was as good a sign as he could imagine that she was a figment of his loneliness and not an actual ghost. If Grace could give her children comfort, she would. Still, he never questioned her presence.

That he saw his dead wife every day was no sign of madness. It was the reason he was sane.

Today, when he went away to carry what wares he'd mustered for trade, Jonah would leave his children and his dead wife behind. He hated this day fiercely, every time it came around.

He hunkered low and opened his arms. When his little daughter ran up to hug him, her mother, who'd died of fever four days after bringing their girl into the world, set her hand on his shoulder. He could almost feel its weight.

Under the best conditions, when the path was clear and dry, and he wasn't pulling the cart or the sled, the walk down to Red Fern Holler was about two hours, and about half an hour more than that back up. Pulling the cart added about another hour each way. Today, with a few inches of snow on the ground from a fall several days earlier, and another half-inch of hard ice skimmed over the top from last night's storm, Jonah pulled the sled, and it was near noon before he made Red Fern Holler and Hezekiah Cummings' general store.

This holler was much bigger than his own, with enough people to constitute a village. Still too remote for cars or trucks to reach, they managed with horses and mules, and Hez kept his store pretty well stocked. He was also open to trade with men like Jonah, who'd forsaken the world below—or, as in his own case, had never known much of it in the first place.

He pulled the sled down from the woods and onto the holler's wider path, wide enough to be considered a road. There weren't many people out of doors—the day was cold and the ice still held—but those he saw gave him a distant, civil nod, which he returned. All the people of Red Fern Holler were known to him, and he to them, but they also knew he wasn't someone who'd flex his jaw with them.

At the head of the holler, he pulled his sled up before the general store and climbed the wooden stairs.

His feet had long ago given up their complaints about the cold and were little more than dead stone in his old boots, but he wiped those boots carefully on the reed mat before he opened the door and went in.

The store was warm and smelled of cinnamon. Hez's wife sold baked goods and sweets. Jonah's belly rumbled, but he ignored the pang and went to the counter, pulling his hat from his head and smoothing down his hair as best he could without a glass to see the success of his effort.

There were no other customers in the store, and no sign of Hez or his wife, either. Jonah waited, as patient as he could be.

"Jonah!" Hez called, coming up from the back. "Good to see you, friend."

"Hez." Jonah made himself extend his cold hand and let Hez Cummings grip it and shake. "Hope you been well."

The niceties of social activity were hard for him. Most of the year, he spoke only to his children.

Hez's expression of friendly welcome faded. "Well, it's hard for ever'body, you know. With all that's goin' on in the world, gets harder every year."

Jonah nodded vaguely. He didn't know what was going on in the world, but he agreed that every year was harder than the one before.

"I guess you come down with somethin' to trade?" Hez asked.

"Yessir, I do. Got the sled out front."

Hez patted him warmly on the back. "Lessee what you got, then."

Jonah was a simple man but not a stupid one. He understood that Hez Cummings considered himself his better, and believed he offered charity when he made a trade with him. Jonah understood it and hated it, but he had no other option. Maybe it was charity after all, then.

They went back out into the cold. Jonah unfastened the ties his son had so carefully tightened and turned back the waxed canvas tarp. On the sled were twenty neatly bundled packs of hewn logs for firewood, two dozen tanned deer hides, and two crates of Mason jars of canned pumpkin.

All the people in and around Red Fern Holler, all the people who shopped at Hez's store, could chop their own firewood, hunt their own game, and can their own pumpkin. But he had nothing else he could do to earn for his family. All he needed was to make a trade for supplies he couldn't make on his own. He counted on his work making convenience for those who had other work they could do. Like Hez himself. Likely, the storekeeper used all Jonah's firewood bundles for the store itself.

Jonah didn't care. He worked hard, and offered the fruits of his labor.

Hez eyed the sled critically. "Well, like I said, things get tougher ever' year. I don't know what-all I can do for you, but let's see. What're you lookin' for in trade?"

He didn't like to talk, but there was no time in his life more important to be friendly and conversational than now. With a stone of worry pulsing at the bottom of his gut, Jonah made his list. "Four sacks of wheat flour, three of sugar, a couple boxes of salt. A pack of that soap I get. A box of nails. Lamp oil. And a new whetstone." Hez's expression showed a readiness to dispense hard news, so Jonah pushed on quickly. "There's a panther skin under the deers. Maybe that'll get me some shoes for the children. They grow faster'n I can keep up." He'd meant to hold that back a bit and get deeper into the negotiations before he threw in the panther skin, but he wasn't good at haggling. Desperation was a poor bargaining position.

At the mention of a panther skin, Hez's eyes took on a greedy gleam. Panthers were tough game to bag, no matter how seasoned the hunter. "You got a panther?"

"Yessir, I did. Come across him on a hunt. We had our sights on the same buck. I got 'em both." He was a bow hunter, so he'd had the chance to take both the panther and the deer—a rifle shot at the panther would have sent the deer running.

Hez laughed and slapped him on the back. "Well damn, son! Lessee it."

Jonah folded back the pile of deerskins and exposed a beautiful tawny panther hide. Another benefit of bow hunting: no singe on the coat. With the right shot, and a good skinning, the hide showed no sign of violence at all.

"I gotta tell you, Jonah. I's all set to make this trade hard on you. I ain't lyin' when I say things is bad. But this—I can take this down below and fetch a fine price. I know just who to take it to. So let's get this load inside, and then you can get what you need. All what you said, and some warm clothes for you and the young'uns, too."

Jonah took a breath deeper than he had since he'd stepped onto the Red Fern Holler road. That panther skin had saved him from the need to beg, and the fear of need. "Thank you, Hez."

The storekeeper clapped him on the back again, and they undertook to offload Jonah's little sled.

An hour later, Jonah's sled was packed again, with all the supplies on his list, and coats, a few pieces of warm clothes and underclothes for the children, and new boots for them all. As he fastened the tarp down over his supplies, Esther Cummings bustled from the store and trundled her girth down the stairs.

"Wait, Jonah."

He stood straight and turned, waiting.

Esther held out a little tin bucket, with a piece of checkered cloth tucked over the top. "Some sweets for your babies. I missed 'em today."

Jonah took it and lifted the cloth. Inside were two sweet-smelling muffins in colorful paper, and a few bright red hard candies, wrapped in cellophane. He lifted his eyes and shaped his mouth into a smile for her. "Thank you, Esther. They'll be real pleased."

She patted his arm. "You take care, Jonah Walker. You hear?"

"Yes, ma'am. I will." He tucked the pail under the tarp, set a finger to his hat to bid Esther Cummings farewell, and put his shoulder to the hard work of pulling the sled up the mountain.

It was late afternoon when he reached home—still light, but the halfhearted sun pushed sidelong through the trees and made long shadows. The cabin was quiet, and he was glad to see a cozy swirl of smoke waft from the chimney. The children were indoors, and Elijah had kept the fire going all day. He was a capable boy.

Jonah pulled the sled behind the house, and stopped short when he saw the barn. The book woman's mare was tied in the sheltered, open-sided half. Her head drooped in a contented doze.

The book woman was regular in her visits, and Jonah kept count of the days. She wasn't due for two more days. He'd made sure not to leave on a day she'd show up.

Leaving the sled behind the house, he went in the side door, moving quietly. Always, he felt the need to be stealthy when she was around; he didn't like strangers, and she made him particularly wary.

"Find ... me ... Daddy," he heard Bluebird say, her little voice slow and stuttering. Was she calling him? Did she know he was home? Jonah stopped in the dark hallway and listened, trying to understand. All he could see was the glow of firelight in the doorway to the front room.

"That's perfect, Bluebird," the book woman said, earnestly.

"Find me, Daddy," Bluebird repeated happily. "Daddy! Find me. S—huh ... huh ..."

"Do you remember what the sound is when 's' and 'h' are together?"

Bluebird didn't answer, not so Jonah could hear, at least.

Elijah answered, though. "It's 'sh,' like 'shoe' or 'sheep.'"

"That's right, Elijah."

"Sh-sh-uh," Bluebird tried. "Sh-uh-tuh. Shu-tuh. Shut?"

"Very good! Shut."

"Shut yuh … yuh … It's too hard, Mizz Ada."

"Would you like Elijah to help?"

"Yes, please."

Elijah's voice picked up. "Shut your eyes. Shut your eyes, Daddy," he read.

The book woman had been teaching his children to read. When she visited, she spent an hour at least, often more, with them. At first, she'd simply read to them. Then, Elijah had wanted to read for himself, and she'd given him books to help him learn. Bluebird hated to be left out of anything, so now she was learning as well.

Jonah had never spent a day in a school and had never learned to read. He knew the alphabet, and he could write his own name. He could cipher numbers enough to make trade or build something. He knew the word 'flour' from 'sugar' and 'salt.' But little more than that.

He recognized his wife's name to see it, and his son's, but not his daughter's. Grace had lived long enough to give Bluebird her name but not to show him the shape of it.

There was a sampler above the fireplace that Grace had made; he could read that, because she'd told him what it said. There were two more samplers hanging on the walls of their bedroom, one commemorating their marriage and another Elijah's birth. He could look at those and know what they said. But that was the limit of his understanding of written words.

Grace had meant to teach their children, but she'd died before she could. Jonah stood alone in the dark hallway and listened to this woman he didn't know take that sacred task over for his wife, heard how she was succeeding, and his stomach soured.

He was glad his children were learning; there was no schoolhouse near enough for them to attend, and they had no other way to learn but from the books this woman brought, and the lessons she could teach. But it wasn't the book woman's job to teach them. Their mother should have had the chance.

And where was Grace? Normally, when he returned to the cabin, she waited for him at the door, at the limit of her reach. But he'd come into the hallway and been alone.

The irrational notion that the book woman had somehow chased the memory of his wife from the house caught Jonah by the throat, and he surged forward, coming into the front room as if he meant to fight her. He drew up short as soon as he crossed the threshold.

Seated at the fire was the book woman, with Bluebird settled snugly on her lap. Elijah had pulled a stool up and sat beside them. He held a little balsa airplane Jonah hadn't seen before. The woman held the book so all three could read.

The firelight framed the whole picture in rosy glow. The woman's red hair seemed blaze. She was pretty, and young. He'd heard her tell the children that she was a widow, but she seemed too young for that. Then again, he knew as well as anyone that no one was too young to die. Or to be left behind.

Now, they all looked up at him, surprised. They'd been so wrapped up with her they hadn't heard him return.

"Pa!" Bluebird squealed and squirmed free of the woman to run to him. "Pa!" Jonah dropped to the floor and caught her in his arms as if he hadn't seen her only hours earlier. "Look what Mizz Ada brung me!" Bluebird leaned back and showed what was in her hand—a little knitted toy. A bluebird, on a bit of rubber string. She let it drop, and it bobbed on the string, its blue wings flapping as if in flight. "Look! It's a bluebird, like me. Bluebird of Happiness!"

I want to name her Bluebird, so you'll never be without happiness. Bluebird Hope.

Though the memory of words her dying mother had once spoken pained him, he made himself grin. For his children, especially for his little girl, Jonah kept all his smiles. "Just like you."

"I hope it's alright," the book woman said. She'd stood and had come a few steps toward him. "I hope I didn't …"

Blushing so hard her freckles seemed to fade, she let her words die out, and Jonah wasn't sure what she was trying to apologize for.

"We didn't expect you today. I wouldn't've been away if—"

"Oh, no. I'm sorry." She jumped her words over his, and he stopped. "There's a big librarians' meeting in a few days, with people from the national office, so I had to change my route around a little. I'm sorry to come unexpectedly."

At the reminder that she was a government employee, Jonah's face cramped in distaste before he could stop it. The woman blushed harder and dropped her gaze to the floor. She wore mannish clothes, heavy trousers and boots, and a thick flannel shirt, but her hair was braided prettily, and her features were so delicate she still looked like a lady.

It made him uncomfortable to look at her. "It's gettin' late, and the cold is makin' the way slick again. If you mean to get down the mountain today, you should go." It crossed his mind that he should offer to let her stay the night, but he didn't want her here so long.

Her eyes—large and round, the soft green of a mountain stream—flared wide. "Of course. Yes. My parents'll be looking for me." She went to the door, where she'd hung her coat, scarf, and hat on a hook. Her big saddlebags rested on the floor beneath.

"Well, children." She turned back to Elijah and Bluebird as she slipped her coat on. "Keep reading, and I'll see you again in two weeks."

Bluebird pushed away from Jonah and ran to her. "Bye, Mizz Ada!" she cried as she wrapped her little arms around the woman's legs. "Thank you for my bluebird!"

The woman bent low and hugged his daughter back. "You're welcome. And thank you for reading to me today."

When Bluebird let her go, she turned to Elijah and held out a cordial hand. "And thank you, young man, for your fine hospitality today. You are a wonderful host."

His serious son blushed all the way to the roots of his blond hair, and smiled softly as he shook hands with her. "'Twas a pleasure, Mizz Ada. Thank you for my airplane."

"You're ever so welcome."

"I'll walk you to your horse," Jonah said. He was unsettled by all he'd just witnessed, disheartened and somehow ashamed, and strangely restless, too, and he wanted the woman gone. He picked up her saddlebags—they were heavy, full of books—and opened the door.

That night, Jonah put his children to bed. Though they were fortunate to live in this big old cabin his great-granddad had built, the winter nights were too cold to sleep at a distance from the fire. The children slept on pallets before the hearth, where they could keep warm. Soon, Jonah would join them, but for a few nights yet he would sleep in his own room.

Bluebird slept with her new little knitted toy cradled close to her heart. Elijah set his balsa airplane on top of the book the woman had left him, both on the floor beside his pillow.

They had toys, he'd carved boats and horses for Elijah and little dolls for Bluebird, but he'd never seen them treasure tokens like they treasured these the woman had brought them from the world below.

Jonah sat at the table and watched them settle into their night's rest. When he was sure they were asleep, he took the candle and went across the hall to his own bed.

For the whole afternoon and evening, since he'd returned from Red Fern Holler, Grace had kept away. He couldn't remember a day in six years he hadn't seen her, standing in a doorway, sitting with one of the children, standing at his side as he tried to make the food she'd made. Every time he thought of her in this house, he saw her, quiet and smiling and with him.

But tonight, he was alone as he shed his suspenders and used the last of the washing-up water to clean his face and neck. He rinsed the cloth and pushed it under his undershirt, washing under his arms the way she'd always insisted he do. The room was cold enough to show his breath, but he didn't mind the chill. There were quilts piled on the bed to keep him as warm as he could be.

After he toweled off, he turned the covers down, first on her side, and then on his. He sat on the chair by the bureau and pulled off his boots, then stood and unfastened his trousers, noting that the top button was loose and soon to pop, and slipped them off, draping them over the back of the chair so he could put them on again in the morning. He arranged his boots under the chair. Grace didn't like an untidy house, and she'd trained him to be tidy as well.

Still alone as he slid into bed, he brushed his hand over her pillow. He'd never washed that pillow since her passing, only fluffed it every now and then in the sun. For a long time, the feathers and cotton batting had held the smell of her. Though he was sure the scent had faded years ago, the memory of it remained keen whenever he put his face to that pillow. It held her scent the way the house held the sight of her. They kept his memory sharp. That was all it was, he knew. Only his memory, his mind conjuring visions to keep him company.

So why wasn't she here with him tonight?

"Grace. Darlin', where are you? I need you." He spoke the words in a reverent whisper, hardly more than a breath, the way Elijah and Bluebird said the prayer Jonah made them say every night because their mother would want them to.

Getting no answer, Jonah blew out the candle on a sorrowful sigh and settled his head on his pillow.

I'm here, my love. He heard her sweet voice in his mind, and he opened his eyes. In the blue light of the winter moon, he saw her. She lay on the bed, her head on her pillow, facing him.

"Don't go 'way like that."

I'm here. As long as you need me, I'll be here.

Jonah set his hand on her pillow, as if his palm cradled her cheek, and fell into sleep.

Chapter Seven

Jonah stood back and watched Elijah milk Petal, their aging cow. Bluebird leaned on his leg, her arm hooked tight around his knee, watching her big brother just as carefully.

"You're doin' good, boy." It had taken him a bit to get the rhythm right, long enough to try the sweet old girl's patience, but now he had a steady tempo, and milk hit the pail in a smooth stream with each careful squeeze of a teat.

The cold was brittle this morning, and Petal didn't give as much milk when the freeze was hard, but it was enough for them to get by for a little while.

"I wanna try, Pa."

"Not yet, baby girl. When you get big as Elijah, then you can try, too. You can feed the goats with me, soon's the milkin's done." Three of the four does were carrying kids for the spring, and that was great good fortune. Their young ram had done his work.

When Jonah and Grace had started their life together, this little homestead had done pretty well for itself. That was before the sickness which took most of their family and neighbors, and before the fever that took Grace and left him alone with two children. In those days before, in addition to a happy, vibrant life, they'd had another, younger dairy cow, and a good strong horse to pull wagon and plow, and a heartier plot for planting, one that yielded enough to sell.

But the sickness had come, and then Grace had died, and there just seemed to be a pall hovering over the holler after that. Junior, the horse, had fallen on a trip to Red Fern Holler and broken his leg, and Rosie, the other cow, had simply fallen over dead one night, for causes mysterious to Jonah. He'd butchered them both and fed his family from their meat, but when it was gone, he had no way to replace them. Such animals were valuable, too valuable for simple trade, and Jonah no longer had the means or the will to earn money, certainly not enough to buy livestock.

He had an arrangement with the Dickersons down in Red Fern Holler to breed Petal to one of their bulls often enough to keep her milking—they kept the calf, and he kept Petal's milk. But she was getting old, and the way to and from Red Fern Holler was getting too hard for her. One day soon enough, he wouldn't be able to get her there, or she wouldn't catch a calf if he did, and she'd go dry. Jonah wasn't sure what he would do then. Hope their ram kept his girls pregnant so they'd produce milk, he reckoned. His children were young; they needed milk to grow strong. He knew that.

The milk pail was a little more than half full when Petal stamped a hoof and lowed sharply. Elijah flinched back, releasing her teat, and glanced over his shoulder.

"Did I hurt her?"

Jonah shook his head. "S'alright. She's just tellin' you she's done. Take a look at her udder—see how soft it is?" Elijah looked, and touched, and nodded. "She give you all she got. Tell her she's a good girl an' go on an' take the pail inside. I'll lead her out. You did good, Elijah."

His son stood and nodded, and showed little sign of pride or pleasure in his accomplishment. He set the stool aside and hoisted up the pail, careful not to jostle it. Before he left the barn, he went to Petal's head and patted her softly.

"Good ol' girl," he crooned. "Thank you kindly for the milk today."

Jonah watched him walk slowly to the house, keeping the pail level, bearing too much weight on his immature shoulders. As long as Jonah could remember, his son had felt the need to be a help to him, a partner in running their family. He couldn't remember when he'd placed that burden on him, or ever meaning to, but of course he had. He did lean on the boy, in precisely the ways Elijah felt the pressure.

"Pa, I wanna feed the goats."

Bluebird, on the other hand, felt free to be a little girl, to be cared for and carefree, and Jonah and Elijah both bent backward to make sure she always was.

"Alright, girl. I'm gonna put Petal out in the sun first. Then we can open up the goats. Do you want to help with the chickens, too?"

"Can I put eggs in the basket?"

"If you're real careful not to drop 'em, you can."

She made a little cross over her heart. "Cross my heart and hope to die."

Never before had she made that old sign or said those words, and he didn't know where she could have picked them up. Jonah remembered them from when he was a boy, and around people more. In those days, they'd been nearly meaningless, just a thing children said and did to seal a promise. But now, they struck him painfully, and he dropped into a crouch and grasped her arms.

"Don't ever say that, Bluebird. Don't you ever say that again, you hear?!"

He'd scared her, and her big blue eyes—Grace's eyes, both the children had Grace's eyes—grew wide and round as supper plates. Her pretty little lip quivered and pushed out, and Jonah's heart cracked a little as she began to cry.

He pulled her into his arms, pressed her little head to his chest. "I'm sorry, baby girl. I'm sorry. I didn't mean to speak so harsh. But don't ever hope to die. That's a bad thing to say or think. Where'd we be without you?"

She didn't understand what he was saying, he knew she didn't, but she held onto him until her burst of tears spent itself. When she squirmed in his arms, he set her back and pulled his kerchief out to wipe her face dry.

"Do you forgive me?"

Sniffling, his little girl nodded. "I wanna feed the goats."

"Why don't we go 'head and do that now, and I'll put Petal out after." When she nodded, he kissed her forehead and stood. She took his hand, and they went to open the goat pen and feed the goats.

Since the book woman had first knocked on their door in the fall, no amount of weather seemed to deter her from her route. She'd shown up in torrential downpour, in snowfall so heavy the air had gone white, in whipping wind, in cold so bitter one's breath puffed out and froze in place. On those bad weather days, she stayed a bit longer, until she was warm or dry again, but she always left after an hour or two, mounted up on that big bay, whose coat had gone shaggy and thick, tromping off back down the mountain.

Over the months of her visits, every two weeks, on a schedule he could track, Jonah had come to respect her. She was skinny, seemed hardly more than a frail little city girl, and talked like one, too, but she was tough as old leather under that pale, delicate, freckled exterior.

He'd come to respect her, and his children had come to revere her, but Jonah had yet to say more than a handful of words to her or spend more than a few brief minutes in her company. He stayed close to home on the days he expected her — and except for that one day when she'd surprised him, she came every two weeks exactly — but he didn't get too close. She was there for the children, not for him. He didn't want her, but they did.

They counted the days, too, and waited at the windows to see that mare emerge from the front of the holler. Elijah fussed all morning, making sure there was enough firewood, and the front room was tidy, and there was food and drink to offer her. They both stacked the books they'd borrowed neatly on the table, ready to hand back to her before they selected something new. 'Mizz Ada Day' was their favorite day.

Mrs. Ada Donovan was her name. He'd only heard her say her name like that once, but he remembered it. She was a widow. He remembered that, too. But he thought of her as 'the book woman.' He felt a strange flare of emotion, something faint and far from his understanding, when he thought of her as anything else.

So he stayed close to home, but away from her. He tried to keep busy, but sometimes he simply stood in the shadows of the hallway and listened. She made the children happy, and he was glad of it. But it worried him, too. When she came to them, she brought with her a kind of loss.

Since that day Jonah had come back from Red Fern Holler and found the book woman in the front room with Elijah and Bluebird, Grace disappeared when the other woman was in their house. She stayed away most of the day after the book woman left, too, not returning until the children were asleep and Jonah was alone with his thoughts and his need.

On this day that the book woman was due, the weather was good. It had been nearly a week since there'd been more snow, and the temperature had risen high enough to loosen the ice from tree branches. The sun shone brightly, making a world of crystals, and melted ice and snow plashed lightly all around. Jonah had spent the past couple hours chopping trees down, and then turning them into logs to restock the woodshed, and he'd grown warm enough in his exertions to cast off his heavy lined coat.

He was behind the house, carrying a load of rough logs into the shed, when he heard his children cheer. The woman had arrived. Jonah stacked the logs and went out, grabbing his coat and pulling it on as he went around to the front. As had become her custom, she'd pulled her horse—Henrietta—up at the corner of the porch, on the side closest to the barn, and looped the reins around the porch rail.

As had become his custom, he loosed the reins and led the docile girl to the barn, where he relieved her of her bridle, fixed her with a halter and tied her to the wall. He filled a bin with some of Petal's favorite dried grasses and hung a bucket of water beside it. She nickered appreciatively and dug in.

She was a beautiful horse, nearly big enough, and powerful enough, to be a draft breed. Jonah suspected at least there was some draft horse in her bloodline somewhere. Honestly, it wouldn't have shocked him much if there were mule, or maybe mountain goat, too, considering how well, and how often, she got around this high up the mountain.

Her saddle and tack were well used but well cared for. When the weather was bad, Jonah would unsaddle her and get her some relief from the wet tack, but today, he left her saddled. After spending a moment offering her some affection and sweet talk, he went back to his work.

She'd stayed surprisingly long today, considering that the weather was good. Jonah finished chopping wood, checked on the animals, checked the fence line on the pen, and ran out of outdoor work for the day. He finally went in the side door and stood in the hallway, as he often did, listening.

She was reading them a Christmas story. Was it Christmastime?

The children didn't know about Christmas, or birthdays, or any holiday. Jonah hadn't celebrated a day since the last one he'd celebrated with Grace.

That strange flare of unknown emotion struck him, and he went to the doorway. As usual, they were seated together by the fire, the woman in the rocker, Bluebird on her lap, Elijah seated on a stool at her side.

Bluebird wore a bright red knitted cap with a big white puff atop it, like a snowball. Elijah had a red and green striped scarf wrapped several times around his neck. The woman had brought them gifts again.

"Is that Santa Cows?" Bluebird asked, pointing to the page.

"Santa *Claus*," the woman corrected. "Yes, that's him. In some places of the world, he's known as St. Nicholas or St. Nick."

"Saint? Like a Bible man?" Elijah asked.

"Exactly. He's a holy man, too. 'Santa' means 'saint' in some languages."

"Why doesn't he come to our house?" Bluebird asked.

Jonah's insides heated to a boil. He didn't know if he was angry or sad, if this was offense or regret he felt, but something was wrong. This was wrong.

"We live too far from people, Blue," Elijah explained to his sister, with the accidental wisdom of a child trying to understand for himself. "He can't find us."

"But you come, Mizz Ada. You find us. Can you bring St. Santa next time?"

Just then, the book woman saw Jonah in the doorway. She looked up, meeting his eyes, and he saw something go through hers—guilt, maybe? No, he didn't think so. The opposite of guilt. Condemnation. She was judging him.

He came all the way into the room, asserted his position as the master of this house. "It's late. You need to go."

"No, Pa!" Bluebird protested. "We need to finish the story!"

"It's time, girl. She needs to get home before it's dark."

"I can leave the story with you, Bluebird. Then you can practice re—"

"No. Take that book away. Children, you can pick different books."

Three sets of eyes—two blue, one green, all large with shock—stared at him. He held his ground. "We got no need of Christmas here. Santa can go where he's wanted."

"I want him!" He'd made his little girl cry again, twice now in one week, but he couldn't give her this. Not this.

He looked to the woman. "It's time for you to go."

She cleared her throat and nodded her concession. To Bluebird, she smiled. "Don't fret, sweetheart. I'll help you pick a better book. And Elijah, how about that book about airplanes?"

Jonah couldn't watch his children's disappointment any longer. He strode to the front door. He went out and around the house to get her horse ready.

She came around the house before he could lead her horse forward. Fully swaddled in her heavy coat and gloves, her neck wound with a scarf much like the one she'd brought for Elijah, except this one was pink and purple, she marched up to him like she had a motor. She was angry. Her eyes flashed with it, and her face was flush with—

She was bruised. Her cheek was discolored near her mouth, and her bottom lip was split. The bruising was fresh, a day old at the most.

He knew what he was seeing. Though his life was quiet isolation now, he'd grown up in a community and had been in, and seen, his share of fights and beatings. She'd been hit. Punched in the mouth. Who in tarnation had punched this small woman?

There were men who hit women, he'd known a few, but nobody was lower in his mind than that.

His hand came up without a thought, aiming to cup her cheek, and she flinched from his touch.

"Who did that to you?"

Ignoring his question, she heaved her packs over her horse's rear and then spun to face him and lashed out with the thing that had driven her so emphatically to him. "How can't you tell your children about *Christmas*?"

Her outrage had blunted the crisp edges of her refined way of speaking, and he heard the mountain in her words. She'd had schooling to polish up her shell, but she was like him down deep.

He could ignore her just as well as she could him. He reached for her face again, and this time she didn't duck away quickly enough. He cupped her cheek and brushed his thumb over her lip. She gasped and quivered under his touch, and her clear-water green eyes softened, losing some of the heat of their anger.

Jonah felt a long-dead urge cramp uncomfortably inside him, low in his gut. He turned his mind from it at once and dropped his hand.

"Who hit you?"

"It doesn't matter. It's none of your concern."

"And my children are none of yours. Bringin' 'em books don't make you they momma."

She blinked, and for a second Jonah thought he'd hurt her feelings. But then she said, "Of course not. But pretending the world doesn't exist doesn't mean you and they aren't in it. Christmas, Mr. Walker. *Christmas*. The birth of Jesus Christ. Your children deserve to know the love of the Lord."

His bitterness flared out in a harsh laugh. "Why? What love's he showed us?"

"You can't mean that."

"Why not?"

"You named your son Elijah Moses, Mr. Walker. Two of the Lord's greatest prophets. And your daughter is Bluebird Hope, a name that positively *sings* His love. If you have no care for the Lord, why name them with so much faith in Him?"

"They momma named 'em. Do you see her here with us?"

Again, her attitude cooled, and she dropped her head a bit. "No. They told me she passed on. I'm sorry."

Jonah grunted. He didn't think he'd said so many words in one exchange to anyone but his children in years, certainly not words so full of feeling, and he was running out of them.

"I lost my husband, too. It hurts every day. But the Lord doesn't forsake us in our grief. He sustains us. He gives us hope. You have your children. His love for you is in them."

Again, Jonah had nothing to say. All he could do was stare. And hurt.

When she realized he meant not to answer her, she sighed and relented. "I'm sorry, Mr. Walker. I didn't mean to overstep. I love Christmas, and I was excited to share it with the children, but of course it's your right to teach them about the world as you see fit. I hope it's alright that I made them each a gift."

Surprise loosened his tongue. "You made them?"

"Yes. Just the hat and scarf."

"That somethin' you do for all the young'uns you see?"

She blushed and didn't answer. No, then, she hadn't made gifts for all the children on her route. Only his.

The notion sent a painful spasm of guilty pleasure through him, and the befuddling pang made his words harsh. "You ain't they momma."

He'd hurt her again. "No, I know. I'm sorry to have offended you."

It bothered him to see her humbled like this. That fire she'd stormed up to him with was completely doused now. "I ain't offended. Jus' — they momma's special."

A tenuous smile perked up the corners of her pretty mouth. "Yes. I know she was, because you and she made such wonderful children together, and because … because you still miss her so."

Feeling as if he'd done, or was doing, something shameful, Jonah shot his gaze sidelong toward the house. There was no one watching from the windows. They were empty.

"You won't be safe if you don't leave now," he said when he looked again at the woman. "The way'll freeze again when the sun drops."

"You're right. May I come again as usual?"

He nodded. "The children count the days."

She smiled fully then, so wide she winced a bit when the stretch pulled at her wounded lip. An angry ember kindled in his chest for the man who'd done that to her. The worst kind of man, who'd strike a woman. Jonah's hand lifted again, seeking to touch her mouth, but he caught himself and forced it back down before he did.

She mounted her horse with grace and ease. "Until then, Mr. Walker."

Before she could turn, Jonah grabbed the bridle and held her horse in place. "When's Christmas?"

Her head tilted to the side. "You don't know?"

He stared up at her and didn't answer. If he knew, he wouldn't have asked.

"The day after tomorrow. Today is December twenty-third."

Two mornings later, his children woke to gifts under the little tree they'd brought in the day before. There wasn't much, Jonah hadn't had the time or the resources to do much, and he didn't tell them the lie that a fat man had snuck into their house in the night, but Elijah had a new slingshot, and Bluebird had a little birdhouse for her bluebird to live in. That day, they made a pie from pumpkin he'd canned in the fall, and that evening, Jonah pulled his children close by the fire and told them what he remembered of the story of baby Jesus and the three wise men.

That night, after the children were asleep, Grace finally came back to him. She'd been away for two days, since the book woman had told their children about Christmas. Never in all the years since her death had she left him alone so long.

"I thought you went away for good," he whispered when she sat on the floor beside him. He slept in the front room with the children now, on the floor near the fire, since the winter had set in hard.

I'm here, my love. As long as you need me, she said in his head.

"I'll always need you, darlin'."

She smiled, but no more words in her voice came to him.

Chapter Eight

"Papa, I wanna feed the goats. That's my chore."

Jonah tucked the quilts more tightly around his ailing little girl. He set his palm on her forehead and worked hard to keep the frown from his. Three days now, she'd been feverish.

His children didn't get sick. They'd been hurt once or twice, a bruise or a cut, but they'd not been truly ailing all their lives, and now his little girl lay listless on the floor before the hearth.

Three days.

Her mother had lived four days with fever before it had overcome her.

Jonah hadn't felt this twisting terror since, but it was keenly familiar, known to him as well as any sworn enemy would be.

For his girl, he shaped a smile on his face as he used his big kerchief to wipe her nose gently. "Today, you get to be a princess like in the stories the book woman tells you. Jus' lay by the fire whilst Elijah and me do your biddin'. Ain't that nice?"

It was the woman who'd made Bluebird sick, he was sure. She'd sneezed daintily a few times when last she was here, two weeks ago, and dabbed at her nose with an embroidered handkerchief. She'd brought sickness up the mountain with her.

Sickness had taken all his kin, all his folk, but these two children, while he'd been hale and hearty all the days of his life. His children had both been just as strong, until the book woman had come and carried up the poisonous world below with her.

If sickness took his children, too, he'd grab that woman and throw her off the mountain before he cast himself off as well.

He knew just where he'd do it. He often sat on that cliff edge when he was lonely and despairing, and needed some time to let himself feel it. He'd sat there near the whole day after he'd buried Grace, leaving their two little babies alone in the cabin for hours while he pondered jumping and following her to whatever waited beyond.

When some kind of instinct, strong as a shake, had stirred him to remember them, he'd returned to find them both squalling, soiled, and hungry. Their two-year-old boy and newborn girl. He'd nearly abandoned them to die in agony and terror.

Grace had first appeared to him the next morning.

Bluebird's little lip pushed out, and she shook her head. "It's lonesome. I don't like to be alone."

He brushed his hand from her forehead over her soft golden hair. "You ain't alone, baby girl. Brother and me, we'll keep close to the house, jus' do what we gotta, then we'll be right back to give you sugar milk and biscuits. Elijah can read to you from your book."

"Can you read it?"

"I don't read, honey." For the first time, that truth shamed him. The children had never asked him to read before, or made mention that he didn't, and he didn't consider it a fault that he'd never learned. Most people he'd known in his life couldn't read, and in his life he'd rarely felt the need for it. The few times he had, Grace had been there to read for him.

Grace had been sharp as a honed blade, and sometimes she'd read to him from her little collection of books, but she'd never made him feel he was less because he couldn't understand most of those symbols as words.

"I don't read," he said again, "but I can tell you a story. That be alright?"

Bluebird's puffy eyes drooped as she nodded. She tucked her little bluebird under her chin and curled up to sleep.

Jonah set his lips on her hot temple. "You be well, baby girl. You get well."

145

Jonah and Elijah stood and stared at the carnage inside the chicken coop, a mess of bloody feathers and bone. By the look of it, only two hens had survived, tucked deep in the rafters as if their fright had been so keen they'd remembered they had wings. He saw no sign of the rooster, either alive or dead. He dug around in his gut and tried to find any thread of hope. If the cock had survived, maybe the flock would, too.

A fox had obviously got in and had himself a real feast. By the look of it, more than one. Maybe a whole pack.

The attack would have made a huge commotion, and on a quiet night he'd likely have been able to save most of the flock, but they'd had a storm, the kind that happened when the tail end of winter lashed at the nose of oncoming spring, full of roar and flash. Jonah hadn't heard anything but the weather.

He had a good strong catch on the coop door, meant to be both storm and fox proof, but it hung loose at the edge of the door, as if it had never been engaged at all.

Jonah looked down at his boy, whose face was warped with worry. His attention drew Elijah's like a magnet, and the boy turned that fretful look up to him.

Not yet nine years old, he was. His birthday was coming near Easter. A month or so from now, he thought. Easter was a moveable feast, so he couldn't be sure.

Jonah had followed the sun and the seasons as his only calendar for more than six years, but since two days before Christmas, he'd been trying to keep track. He couldn't read, but he knew the calendar. He knew the days of the week and the months of the year, and he knew how many days in each month. He thought it was the beginning of March. The third of March, if his count was right. He'd considered asking the book woman to bring up a calendar sometime, but since Bluebird had taken ill, he now meant to drive her off for good the moment he saw her horse headed their way. He'd drive her away on the end of his rifle if he had to.

"I locked it, Pa," Elijah said, his voice aquiver. "I swear. I did it right."

Jonah believed him. Elijah was a dutiful, careful boy. And if he'd made a mistake, treating him harshly now wouldn't undo it. Whether a mistake had been made, or the storm had simply undone the lock somehow with a freak twist of the wind, Elijah would feel the consequences. They all would.

"Alright." He set his hand on his son's trembling shoulder. "S'alright, boy. But we gotta clean this up and see what's left, and we gotta do the rest of our chores, and get back to your sister and take care of her. I need you to be strong and careful and quick as you can be, you hear?"

"Yessir, Pa. I can do whatever you need me to do."

"We gotta get the mess cleaned up and cover the blood with sawdust and shavin's 'fore we let the goats out. Animals don't like bloodscent, 'less they's hunters like foxes. I don't want the ram going mad tryin' to protect his pregnant ladies. Get the wheelbarrow, and fill it full from the woodshed. I'll deal with the bodies."

"Can we ..." Elijah swallowed, then started again. "Can we eat 'em, at least? What's left, I mean?"

The question made a little flash of pride in Jonah's chest, and he smiled. "That's smart thinkin', makin' somethin' good outta bad, but no. They's too tore up, and we don't know what the foxes might had in 'em. Germs and such. That's why only some animals eat carrion. They got special stomachs can sort out the rot and sick from the good. Our stomachs ain't like that."

"How we gonna get by without eggs, Pa?"

"We got two hens, at least. They won't lay for a bit, till they forget they was so scared, but they'll lay again, give us a couple eggs a day, maybe. Until then, we'll get by like we always do. Jus' a little less variety in what we eat." He thought about the biscuits he'd made up yesterday for supper, fluffy and rich—a family favorite. Those might be the last for a while. "Then in a few weeks, when spring's full in, I'll find somebody in Red Fern Holler who'll trade for a few chicks, or a full-growed cock, if we need one, and we'll rebuild the flock. We'll make do, boy. We always do."

The book woman came, as usual, in the afternoon. All day long, Jonah had meant to tell the children that the woman couldn't come in today, that Bluebird was too sick for visitors, and he'd never found the strength to do it. These days were their favorite days, and his little girl had perked up a little as the day went on. She wanted 'Mizz Ada,' wanted new stories, wanted the company of this woman who was, it pained Jonah to realize, the closest thing to a mother she'd ever had.

She was not Bluebird's mother, however, and she had made his little girl sick.

Elijah sat at the window, on the lookout, since lunch. When he called out, "Here she comes!" Jonah still had not told them the book woman couldn't come in.

But he grabbed his jacket and did something he'd never done before. "Wait here," he ordered his son, and he went out to meet the woman himself.

She pulled up as he came toward her, and he saw wary surprise in furrows of her brow. "Mr. Walker, hello."

"You need to turn around, go back down, don't come back. We don't want you here no more." He'd reached her horse, and he took hold of the reins near the bit and tried to turn the horse himself. Henrietta liked him fine, but she didn't take orders from him, not when her rider was mounted on her. The mare dug her hooves in and tossed her head.

"Excuse me?" the woman asked. "What happened? Is something wrong? Are Elijah and Bluebird alright?"

"Bluebird's ailin'. She's real poorly with a fever, and you brought it to her."

Her hand went to her chest in that feminine show of shock that came to all women naturally. A leather riding glove, rough and sturdy as a man's work glove, covered her hand, but he knew the slim, elegant fingers inside it, the way light freckles sprinkled over ivory skin.

"Oh no. Oh, I'm so sorry. Yes, I did have a cold. I had to stay home a day with a fever. There's something going around, a lot of people have been feeling low, but I didn't know I was ill myself when I was last here. It's not deadly, except for the weakest people, the old and infirm. It makes you feel slow and sore for a few days, but most people have gotten well."

"She never was sick a day till you brought sickness up here."

"I'm sorry, Mr. Walker. I don't know what to say. There's a tonic people are taking, to ease the symptoms. It helps. I have some with me. May I give some to Bluebird?"

"Who give you the tonic?" In his mind, doctors and healers and witchy women were all alike, but he was curious nonetheless.

"Doc Dollens. He has a practice in Barker's Creek, where I live. He takes care of me and my parents, and all our neighbors."

Barker's Creek was farther up the foothills than he'd thought she lived—far enough up that he'd actually heard of it and knew where it was. He'd been that far down himself, when he was younger. She truly was a mountain girl, no matter how she talked.

"Doctors brought medicine when the sickness took the folk here in the holler. My ma and pa and sister, too. Didn't help 'em none. They all died anyway."

"You're talking about the influenza outbreak, about ten years ago."

Jonah didn't answer; he couldn't remember if that was what it had been. His life had shrunk to a tiny point since then, and old memories languished in the shadows, but the word 'influenza' seemed familiar, and the time was right.

She didn't need him to speak to know his answer. "I'm sorry. That was very bad, all through the county. My best girlfriend died then, too. There was no cure for it.

What's going around now isn't nearly so bad." She leaned back and dug in a leather pouch hanging from her saddlebag. When she sat straight again, she had a small, dark bottle in her hand. "This isn't a cure, either, but it will help her sleep and make her feel more comfortable, so she can rest and let the cold run its course and leave her. Then she'll be well."

Jonah stared. From the moment Bluebird had first shown illness, he'd decided to get rid of the book woman once and for all. Even as he'd been unable to tell his children in advance, he'd meant to send her away and figure out the explanation later. Now he had hold of her reins and had told her to go, but he couldn't follow through.

That bottle might make Bluebird feel better. The woman had brought the sickness, but she might also have brought wellness. And the children wanted her.

"I can't lose Bluebird." He hadn't meant to speak. He certainly hadn't meant to say those words to this woman, in that tone, so full of fear and weakness.

A spasm of emotion turned the compassion and concern she'd shown since he'd told her his little girl was sick into something like sorrow. She dismounted and landed on the ground right in front of him. Turning her head up to meet his gaze, she set her gloved hand on his chest. "You won't, Mr. Walker. She will be well again. May I see her?"

He'd meant to send her away. Instead, he nodded and walked with her toward the cabin, still leading her horse.

Bluebird had been happier and more energetic from the moment the woman had walked into the front room. She'd sat right on the floor, keeping his daughter tucked snugly in her covers while she drew her close, and they'd read together for most of a book. Bluebird tried to read for a bit herself, but after a few pages, she lost the energy for it, and the woman held the book while Elijah read to his sister. Then she'd given Bluebird the tonic. His little girl had twisted her little face into a knot of disgust at the taste, but she'd taken it all at the woman's sweet urging.

Now she slept deeply, in calm repose, her breaths deep and slow, without the awful rasp she'd taken on in the past two days.

The woman and Elijah sat side by side near her and talked about the book Elijah had chosen. They weren't really reading, as far as Jonah could tell. Their talk was different, more like a conversation about what the book said. It was something about steam trains—how they worked, and how the rails were built. Didn't seem like a storybook at all.

In all the months of the book woman's visits, Jonah had never spent so much time in the same room when she was with his children. She'd always made him uncomfortable, though the reasons had changed in some way he didn't care to understand, so he'd always found work to do that kept him at a distance. Today, his worry for Bluebird had held him close. But he was still uncomfortable. Even more, in fact. He felt like an interloper in his own house.

When he ran out of things to do in the front room, he sat at the table and simply watched the woman with his children. Bluebird slept comfortably for the first time in days, curled at the woman's side. Elijah leaned against her as they studied that book. They spoke quietly together, making a cozy closed circle.

She'd emptied her saddlebags when she'd come in, and made neat stacks of the books so Elijah could choose his next one and she could record as returned those the children had borrowed before. Jonah contemplated those stacks. Some of the books were small, hand-sized, and shaped like bricks. Others were more flat, though the covers were bigger. He knew that the brick-shaped ones were for grownups, without many pictures, and the bigger, flatter volumes were picture books for children.

Every book looked like it had been read hundreds of times and didn't have many more times left in it.

There were also a few tattered magazines and some folded newspapers. And her ledger book, where she wrote in pretty, curlicue writing with an ink pen. Jonah guessed his children's names were in that book, but he didn't know the letters of that kind of writing, so he couldn't recognize Elijah's name, and he'd never seen Bluebird's name in any kind of writing at all.

But there were two other books that caught Jonah's attention. They were bigger, with covers done in fabric. One had a binding of leather lacing, and a simple burlap cover, and the other had metal rings through it, with a flowered cover. Those, he couldn't make sense of.

He picked up the topmost one, with the leather lacing, and flipped open the burlap cover. A piece of white paper was pasted to the first page, with a lot of words, like the printing in books. He flipped to another page and found two pages of a book pasted there. For the next several pages of this strange book, another book's pages were pasted there. And then a picture from a magazine, showing a smiling woman holding a tray of cookies. Under that picture were more words, and numbers, too. He thought it might be a recipe. Probably for the cookies.

Every page had something pasted to it, either a page from something else, or an artfully cut picture, or something printed on white paper like the first page had been, or something written in the woman's pretty writing. There was a smear of red on one page that Jonah first thought was blood, but it was another pasted-on picture of food with writing underneath. He didn't know what kind of food it was, but there was red glop on the top of it, so he decided it was a recipe, too. He put his nose close and sniffed the smear. A faint hint of tomato.

"It's a scrapbook," the book woman said, and Jonah sat back so hard the chair rocked. He looked around, and gathered his bearings, wondering how long he'd been studying the book. Bluebird slept quietly. Elijah sat near the fire, close to his sister, reading. The book woman stood so close to Jonah he could smell her. Under the scent of the fire she'd been sitting near, and the horse she'd been riding all day, there was something with flowers.

"Huh?"

She smiled. "That's a scrapbook. All we librarians have been making them. Our books are being read so much they're falling apart, and there's no money to buy more, so we're trying to make books of our own. We take pieces of books that have fallen apart, or old magazines we can't circulate any longer, and save what we can by pasting them in books like this. Some of us write our own stories, or retell fairy tales and folk tales, and type them up, too. One of my colleagues is a lovely artist, and she illustrates her books. I'm not very good at drawing, but I try to find pretty pictures. We also add helpful things, like important news stories, or sewing patterns, and household hints, and recipes. That there," she tapped the page with the red smear. "I cut that out of a magazine. It's a recipe for spaghetti sauce."

"Spaghetti?" He'd never heard such a word. It felt alien in his mouth.

She nodded. "Noodles. They come from Italy. The sauce is good, and not hard to make, and you don't need spaghetti noodles to do it. If you've got canned tomatoes, it's easy. I've made it and put it on chicken. It's delicious."

Jonah thought of the dead chickens he'd spent his morning cleaning up and disposing of. He'd found most of the rooster some distance from the coop. The old boy had put up a fight.

They didn't eat chicken here, unless a hen stopped laying. He couldn't afford to keep a meat flock. He hunted for their meat. "How 'bout grouse? Would it work on grouse?"

"I'm sure it would. Would you like to borrow this book?"

He stared at the page, the tiny black symbols that meant so much to others and nothing at all to him. He closed the book. "Nah."

The woman surprised him by pulling out a chair and sitting at the table with him. "I can teach you to read, too, Mr. Walker."

A refusal leapt immediately to his tongue, but it got stuck there. Jonah sat in place, his jaw locked on the word *no*, and considered the woman before him. With her hat, scarf, gloves, and coat off, and the cardigan sweater she wore beneath it as well, she looked like the small, pretty young woman she was. Not even her mannish clothes, the plaid shirt and the heavy trousers, could camouflage her femininity.

Slim shoulders and a long neck. Pale skin, dusted everywhere with faint freckles. Soft, small mouth, the bottom lip fuller than the top, like a pout. Big green eyes, warm with kindness and compassion. Her red hair was in its usual braid, loosened by the hat and the wind and a long day so that its natural wave puffed lightly around her head. The firelight behind her made it glint and shimmer like a halo.

Bluebird thought she was an angel. Right now she looked like one. So beautiful and sweet.

As Jonah comprehended where his thoughts had taken him, and what feelings those thoughts had enlivened, shame crashed down on him with the buffeting force of a thunderclap.

The word he'd needed to say finally came free. "No." He shoved the book away and stood. "Time for you to pack up."

He'd hurt her again with his brusqueness. Her warmth cooled, and she began to gather her things without another word to him. When she had her books and papers packed up in her bags again, and she'd said goodbye to Elijah, she came back and set the medicine bottle on the table. "Give Bluebird a spoonful when her cough or her fever is bad. It'll ease her pains and help her rest. But no more than one spoonful, nor more than twice a day. Too much could make her sleep so deeply she forgets to wake up."

"Don't you need it?"

"I'm well again. But should I need more, I can get more from the doctor."

Jonah couldn't bring himself to thank her, but he wrapped his hand around the bottle and managed a nod.

He let her go to her horse on her own, her heavy saddlebags slung over her shoulder. When she stepped through the front door, bundled up again against the last of the winter cold, she turned back. "Am I still welcome here?"

A beat or two passed before he could make himself answer. "For the children."

His children needed her. But there was nothing in himself that needed her. Not her.

Chapter Nine

"Easy now, baby girl. Don't squeeze."

When he was sure Bluebird's hold on the chick would keep it but not hurt it, Jonah dropped his hands from hers. The small yellow puff looked right at her and peeped. His little girl giggled happily.

She was well. Whether it was the medicine, or the sickness had simply run its course, or some blend between them, two days after the book woman had left, the fever broke. Two days after that, his precious girl was herself again. He'd fussed after her for another week more, fearful she'd weaken again, but by the end of that next week, she was whiny and combative from being cooped up. For the past two weeks, she'd been at her normal activities and back to her natural happiness. She was well.

Neither he nor Elijah had fallen ill at all.

Spring had come fully in. The days were lengthening, and the sun was warming. All but the most stubborn bits of snow, those tracks that lived in the shadows of ancient trees, had melted from their tier of the mountain. New leaves were budding on the trees and the ground cover, and the wildlife had stirred and filled the forest and sky with bustle.

Elijah's birthday had gone by a few days earlier. He knew the day exactly because the book woman had brought up a calendar on a recent visit. He'd intended to ask her to do exactly that, but then Bluebird had taken sick, and he'd decided he didn't want that woman bringing anything else to them ever again. And then she'd shown up with medicine, and he'd changed his mind again. In all the confusion she'd got boiling in him, he'd never asked. But she'd known anyway. They now had a paper calendar from the Callwood Mill hanging on the wall by the front door. And now both children knew their birthdays for the first time in their lives.

He'd felt awkward about marking Elijah's birthday, after letting so many go by unnoticed. Grace had been alive for only the first two, and they'd done what they could to make those days celebrations, but Jonah couldn't replicate that. They'd lost too much since then.

There was no cake or special meal, but he dug into the back of his bureau and found a token to give as a gift: Grace's father's pocket watch, a keepsake she'd held dear. It was a heavy piece, not real gold but fine enough nevertheless, with a steam train etched into the case. Jonah didn't know the time, but he wound the watch to make sure it still worked, and it began a steady, soft ticking at once.

Elijah had been awestruck, and now carried it with him everywhere, checking it frequently, studying its face as if it held more answers than the likely incorrect time.

Bluebird had been envious, but then Jonah had come home from Red Fern Holler, after trading an afternoon's labor for five new chicks, and she'd been mollified by the babies. And her birthday was coming up soon, in May. He knew that date as well. He'd find something to make for her or give to her to make her day special as well.

There was only one other date in the past seven years he remembered, four days after her birthday. He'd stopped tracking the days then. This year would be the first since that he'd know when that date came around.

He tried not to dwell on that.

Since Christmas, Grace had been with him less and less. He hadn't lost her yet, but he could feel her drifting away, taking the last wisps of herself from him, and no amount of pleading in the dark night alone in the room they'd shared could tie her to him. He'd seen her only once in more than a week, and a few weeks had gone by since he'd heard her voice in his head.

Losing that last tiny bit of her he'd been able to keep had opened a new sore inside his chest that throbbed with every thought of her. A throb so keen it threatened to bring him to his knees. So he tried not to dwell, and focused instead on his children and their good hearts and wellbeing.

He picked up another chick from the little box and turned it over. Gently, he squeezed its tail end, and he smiled at what he saw. "Look here, Bluebird."

With the chick she was holding, a little pullet, tucked under her chin, still held in both hands, she looked. And made a face. "What's that?"

"That's what shows he's a boy. This is a cockerel. He'll grow up to be a rooster."

"Like Mister was?"

"Like Mister was. And he'll help the hens have more chicks. And soon enough we'll have a bigger flock and more eggs."

"But we won't let the foxes get 'em, right Pa?"

"That's right, baby girl." He'd figured a new way to lock the coop door, and had taken to walking the yard after the children were asleep, to make sure everything was closed up tight before he bedded down himself.

He turned the cockerel right side up and brushed his thumb over its soft yellow head. This boy was a good sign. Maybe this spring would be good for them.

It had been a long time since he'd had a thought like that.

As always, Jonah double-checked his pack, made sure his field-dressing kit was where it belonged, counted out the cartridges for his rifle.

Ammunition was a great expense, well more than he could bear comfortably, and he used it like the precious resource it was — almost never, in fact. He had a substantial array of firearms, handed down to him from generations past. There was even an old musket from a forebear who'd fought the redcoats long ago, and a Kerr's Patent revolver, carried by his great-granddad during the Civil War. But those guns were relics, and he'd let all but two rifles fall into poor repair.

Circumstances had not yet forced him to trade away these pieces of family history, and he wasn't sure he'd ever want to. Most weren't good for hunting, and he didn't like the idea of scattering out so many ways for people to kill each other. People who had guns tended to find them necessary. Jonah himself found them to make more trouble than they fixed, even in hunting. So he'd left his guns to rot in a locked chest, though trading them or selling them might have brought comfort to his family.

Guns had hurt his family, too. Not only in war. Also simply in anger and despair.

Few folks lived this high up the mountain, and most of those few were of families that had staked their claim generations ago. Jonah's family were practically newcomers, from that perspective. He was the fourth generation to live in this house, and his children were the fifth.

There were two ways to prosper way up in this thin air, and they both had to do with the land: coal or timber. You could scrape by with a plot for growing, have a little surplus to sell, as Jonah usually did, but the soil was too rocky to grow a real cash crop. But if there was coal under your feet — and there was often coal — or if the forest was strong, you could make a real nice life for yourself.

Jonah's great-grandfather, Jackson Cable, had been a younger son from a wealthy family, down in Kentucky horse country. He'd been an officer in the war that had torn apart the country, and ravaged the South, and after it, he'd fled into the mountains to turn his sight away from the ruination of all he'd known. All his family was dead. All his history was gone. He'd dug up what he'd buried before he'd left to fight, staked himself some land up high, and made himself this home in what quickly became known as Cable's Holler.

He'd built this house, far grander than most other dwellings in the hills, but far humbler than the mansion he'd grown up in. And then he'd stripped the land of its timber and sold it for profit to the rebuilding world below.

Jonah had been told the story of his great-grandfather and Cable's Holler from the time he was old enough to sit still and listen. His father's mother was Jackson Cable's only child, born right here in this house and never lived a day anywhere else. She was the first to love the mountain. Her father despised it—though he was wildly prosperous by the measure of the mountain folk, he'd never again been truly wealthy, never approached the luxury he'd known as a child. He held hate in his heart for the war that had ended his way of life, and he was a bitter, brutal man.

When Jackson shot and killed his wife and then himself, their daughter, Isabelle, Jonah's grandmother, stayed on with her new husband and baby boy, but she closed the timber operation and let the forest reclaim itself. In that way, she made the life she wanted, humble though it was.

By the time Jonah came into the world, the Cable family had been the Walker family for two generations already, and its circumstances were much reduced. But they were still the leaders of their little community, the people who'd built up around them while the timber was falling and stayed when it stopped, and Jonah had grown up well and happy, unaware of his isolation.

Over the years, the family had sold or traded away most of the baubles and trappings of prosperity. Now this old house was mostly empty of anything beyond the essentials—and some might say not enough of those. But Jonah still held on to a few old things, more out of a sense of futility than nostalgia. Most of those useless things, he let time to do them what it would.

This rifle, a 30.06 bought by his father, he kept well and kept with him. Another one, a smaller .22-caliber, he kept up, too, and had taught Elijah to use. For protection.

He could count on his hands the number of times in his whole life he'd shot his rifle except in practice, and every one had been when he'd had no other choice. Thankfully, Elijah had never yet had to shoot at anything but a bottle on a post.

Jonah brought the 30.06 with him whenever he left the homestead, but it was a bow he hunted with. Quiet and clean. He could make his own arrows, and they didn't spoil the meat of the kill, or its hide.

"When can I hunt with you?" Elijah asked, watching Jonah pack up for a hunt.

Bow hunting required more strength and skill than the gun. Elijah couldn't yet pull a strung bow—not Jonah's, at least. He'd considered making him something smaller, but hadn't decided whether that was a good idea.

"Not till your sister can stay on her own. You know that, boy."

Relenting quickly, Elijah couldn't stifle a short-tempered huff.

"It's important work, tendin' Bluebird and keepin' the homestead safe. I count on you, Elijah. What you do helps me do what I gotta do. You get that?"

"Yessir. I jus' … I don't like it when you're away."

Jonah put his hand on his son's shoulder and squeezed. "I don't like it, either. But we need meat. I'll be back quick as I can, soon's I bag a kill. Then I'll need you to help me butcher and smoke it."

His serious son nodded. Jonah gathered Bluebird up for a hug and left his children alone while he went to find them food.

Jonah went out the front door. A powerful spring storm had lashed the mountain all day, driving the rain sidelong and whipping the trees wildly. Lightning and thunder had blown bad temper unabated since morning.

Elijah stood on the porch, his arm looped around the post. He was dripping wet, and the spring was not yet truly warm. Certainly not today, when storm clouds had shrouded the sun all day.

"Come on, boy. Come sit for your supper." He took hold of his son's arm and tugged gently, but with determination. "She's not comin'. The storm's too bad."

"She always comes." He turned and looked up at him. "Always. Rain, snow, wind, it don't matter. Mizz Ada always comes."

168

"It's near dark, Elijah. If she comes now, she'd have to go down in pitch black. She wouldn't be safe."

"She always comes."

Jonah let Elijah's arm go and stood beside him, squinting into the grey gloom, the rain so hard and fine it closed off the view. He was right. The book woman had come in all manner of weather before, including storms like this. She'd never missed a day. Every two weeks, once or twice a day or two early, but never late. Now that they had the calendar, she'd taken up a habit of showing them the day she'd be back, marking it down right before she said goodbye.

But she wasn't coming today, and it was too late to keep expecting her. The sky had never gotten much light all through the day, but night would fall soon.

"Elijah, come inside. Supper's ready."

"What if somethin' happened to her?"

The thought had crossed his mind as well, but she was a good horsewoman and knew the mountain near as well as he did.

"It's been stormin' this bad all day long. If she even tried to get up the mountain today, the weather drove her back soon enough. She's home and warm by her fire, I reckon." He set his hand on Elijah's shoulder. "She knows this mountain, and she and Henrietta make a fine team. She's fine, but she's not comin' today. She'll come soon's she can, you know that. Come on, boy. We got a warm fire and good food inside."

His son nodded and complied, but he looked out to the woods until Jonah got him inside and closed the door.

He'd kept the fire stoked all day, and the front room was cozy and warm, crackling with good heat and aromatic with venison stew with dumplings bubbling in the pot. He got his children to the table. Bluebird was sad and cross as well, missing the book woman just as keenly as her brother, and the two of them sagged at the table, resting their heads on their hands.

Jonah tried to be patient with them. They were good children, obedient and good-natured, and he asked much of them both. They should be allowed to feel and show their disappointment, he thought. Grace would have thought so, too. But he felt odd as well, jumpy and frustrated, and it took a force of his will not to snap at his children. He ladled stew into their bowls and served them up glasses of milk. Then he served himself and sat at what passed for the head of their little table.

He stretched his arms across the corners of the table, offering his hands. The children set theirs in his and reached across to touch their fingers together, which was as far as they could reach.

If their mother had been there, she would have sat at the other end of the table and joined them all more tightly. Jonah had that thought every meal.

"Bluebird, it's your turn."

Usually, she enjoyed saying grace, and recited the little prayer with gusto. Today she sighed heavily and mumbled, "Dear Father, kind and good, we thank Thee for our daily food. We thank Thee for Thy love and care. Be with us Lord, and hear our prayer. Amen."

"Amen," Jonah and Elijah said together.

He'd let God fall away from their lives, except for these little ritual moments of prayer, at bedtime and mealtime, that he'd known Grace, the preacher's daughter, would want her children to know. These moments caused him pain like any other that should have included her but didn't, but in their simple ritual, their rote recitation, he'd been able to preserve them. They required little of him but to hold his children's hands and say 'Amen.' He considered them honors to Grace, not to the God she loved and he'd discarded.

"Wait, Pa," Bluebird said as Jonah picked up his spoon.

"Yeah, baby girl?"

"Can I add a prayer?"

"You want to say more?"

She nodded.

"Alright, go 'head."

This time, Bluebird squeezed her hands together and clamped her eyes shut, as she did at bedtime. "Dear Father, please keep Mizz Ada safe. She was s'poseda come today and didn't and I'm scared she's sick or hurt. Please let her be alright."

"Yes, Father," Elijah whispered, and Jonah saw that he had his hands folded and his eyes closed, too. "Please watch over her."

"We love her," Bluebird said. "She brings us books and tells us stories and makes us things and takes care of us and" — her little voice had taken on a moan of worry — "and we love her."

"Please don't let her be hurt," Elijah said.

"Amen." Bluebird said it first.

"Amen," her brother echoed.

The children picked up their spoons and began to eat. Bluebird sniffed softly and wiped the back of her hand across her eyes.

Jonah sat, stunned, and stared at the center of the table. His heart thudded heavily in his ears.

After that prayer, Jonah found himself peering out the window himself several times during the few remaining hours before he put his children to bed. Bluebird wanted them all to sleep in the front room, the thunder frightened her and made her worry more for the

172

book woman, so they pulled their winter pallets out and made their beds near the hearth again.

Once they were down for the night, Jonah went to sit at the table as he often did, to think in the quiet dark. He no longer waited for Grace. It hurt too much to wait and not see her, and he so rarely saw her these days.

For all these years, she'd promised to stay with him. *I'm here as long as you need me*, she'd said, time and time again. That she was disappearing suggested she didn't think he needed her anymore. But he did. He always would.

But she wasn't real. He knew that, or knew it as well as anything else. She was in his head, only his head. If she was disappearing, then, something in his head had stopped conjuring her. Something inside him, the thing that knew when she was needed, no longer had the need.

But he needed her. He did. He always would. He would.

He looked out the window into the stormy dark. There was nothing to see; the cloud cover was too thick for moonlight or starlight to push through, and all that was left was an impenetrable black, broken occasionally by jagged blasts of lightning.

One hit just then, lighting the yard with a white light as bright as midday, then a quick flicker before it went dark. Jonah leapt to his feet and ran to the door.

173

Flinging it open, nearly losing it in the wind, he jumped out into the night.

He'd seen something in the yard. The blackness was back, and the howl of the wind clawed at his ears, but he ran surefooted off the porch toward what he'd seen. If he was wrong, and it was something else, he could be running into deadly trouble. But he didn't think he was wrong. The image was burned into his eyes like a photograph.

Henrietta.

"Mizz Ada?" The name felt odd to say, and he realized he'd never said it before. "Mizz Ada?" Under the snarling storm, he heard the horse whine, but no human voice accompanied it.

Another, softer flash of lightning flickered and showed him the horse—saddled, exhausted. Riderless.

"Hey girl." He tried to keep his voice calm. When he reached for the drooping reins, she whined again, an agonized sound more like a screech, but she didn't shy. "Hey, girl. It's alright. I got you. I reckon you wanna get warm and dry, yeah?"

He began to lead the horse toward the barn. The very first step she took, she faltered badly and cried out. She was hurt.

"Alright, girl. We'll take it nice and slow. You're alright." He set his hand on her neck and walked right alongside her. Something was wrong with her left front leg, but he needed real light to know what. She limped, whining, but came with him.

"Pa?" Elijah was on the porch, his thin arms crossed over his bedclothes. Each lightning flash, faint or bright, gave him bare hints of information of the world around him.

He wanted to reassure his son and send him back to bed, but he needed the help. "It's Henrietta. Mizz Ada's not with her."

"Oh no!"

"Easy, boy. I need you calm. I'm gonna get this girl safe, and then I'm gonna go out an' look for her."

"I knowed somethin' was wrong!"

"Elijah! Get dressed. Try not to wake your sister. Get the lantern and come out to the barn."

His son snapped into action. He turned and hurried back into the house. Jonah eased the horse back, moving across the yard by feel.

He got her into the barn, out of the rain, and tied her in the little space beside Petal's stall. He felt around on the wall for the lantern and pulled a match from the box. Just as he got it lit, Elijah was out, running through the rain, holding his hand over that lantern as if to shield it from the storm.

When both lanterns were hung and throwing light around the barn, Jonah examined Henrietta's leg. It didn't take long. There was a long gash through her left shoulder.

The rain had washed it out enough that he could see it was deep. He put his fingers to the edges of it, crooning softly when she shuddered and huffed at the pain he'd sharpened. The blood was sticky. The wound was fairly fresh, but not brand new. A few hours, he thought. There were two other gashes, one on either side, not nearly as deep or long, but oriented in the same way. There was at least an inch between each gash.

Elijah leaned down and peered at the gash. "That's bad, ain't it?"

"It ain't good. But it's clean, and that means she can heal. You know that salve we use on Petal when her teats get sore?"

"Yessir."

"Get me that, and the mendin' box from the cabinet inside."

"What about Mizz Ada?"

He wanted to go immediately, but the night was pitch black and he didn't know where to start. At least he knew he could help the horse. "How you think she'll be about us lettin' Henrietta be hurt longer than she need to be?"

That got Elijah moving, and he ran toward the rain.

There was something else, too, something Jonah didn't want to say to his son. Something that terrified him for going out into the woods—not for what might happen to him, but for what he might find had already happened.

He was fairly sure Henrietta had been swiped by a bear.

Chapter Ten

Jonah set out to search for Ada at the first sign of morning light. By then the terrible storm that had sat on the mountain all the day and night before had finally gasped its last and left a sodden, foggy mess behind. But there was enough light and quiet for Jonah to search.

He'd hunted these woods all his life and was a good tracker, but there were no tracks to follow. Not even Henrietta's hoofprints remained in the yard; the driving rains had erased them completely in a yard so muddy it seemed to wave like water, and the winds had torn limbs from the trees. He spent a moment wondering if the horse could help him, might know the way she'd come and lead him back along it, but that wound on her shoulder was bad, and she'd come up lame if she didn't rest it. Horses were valuable; Jonah had felt the death of his horse four years ago every day since.

More than that, though, Ada loved this mare and would be heartbroken to lose her.

Ada.

Near three full seasons, the better part of a year, she'd been visiting the cabin every two weeks, and only in the past few hours had he let himself say or think her name. He couldn't remember why he'd shied from it at the first, but he understood that, at the last, the thought of her had become stronger in his head than he could bear, and her name seemed like it would conjure her even more powerfully.

The way Grace's name had always, until recently, conjured her.

He left his frightened, fretful children alone, with the usual strict instructions to keep together and stay in the house. Bluebird asked him to promise to bring Ada home—*home*, she'd said *bring her home*—but Jonah couldn't promise. He didn't know what he'd find, if he found her at all. Worry of his own sat like a hot stone on the floor of his belly.

In the morning light, he was more sure than ever Henrietta had been attacked by a bear, but he didn't know if she'd encountered the beast after she'd lost Ada, or if they'd been attacked together. He didn't know why the bear had taken only one swipe, if the horse had fled and the bear had turned its full attention on an abandoned Ada, or if the storm had simply dissuaded him from the chase.

Where was Ada? How had she and her horse been separated? Something bad had happened, clearly, but what? And how bad?

Without tracks to follow, Jonah followed his instincts.

He cast his mind back to things she'd said over the months, talking to the children about her travels. She went to Red Fern Holler on the same day she visited them. So he started off on the regular trail, keeping his eyes and ears sharp as far as he could see and hear in every direction.

At its best, the last few miles of the trail were narrow, steep, and difficult, barely passable by anything but the most surefooted person or beast; Jonah's holler was its end, and for years, only he, and now she, had traveled it. There might be a few souls who made their home even higher than he did, but not on this side of the mountain. Storms had washed out the better paths over the years of his isolation, and Jonah had found no cause to undo Nature's will. Anything that made visitors feel unwelcome had been a boon in his mind.

And yet, Ada had wended her way to them, as undeterred by the remoteness of his home as by his aloofness when she reached it.

Moving slowly, stopping every ten feet or so to peer into the woods and listen sharp, Jonah made it down about a mile and a half before he hit a sudden new cliff, and a fresh gully about fifteen feet below. A great hunk of the mountain had shorn off and slid down. Even this unfriendly path was impassable now.

His instinct flared bright. Was this what had happened? Had Ada gotten caught in the slide? If so, Henrietta had found her way above it, to the only place she knew on this part of the mountain.

He stared down the sheer muddy slice in the side of the mountain at the water rushing through the newly formed stream at its bottom. That water rushed with force; he knew it must connect to an established water source. Probably one above it. There were only two possible sources: Cable's Creek, or the small lake it fed from, Willow Lake. Jonah's own well shared an underground source with Willow Lake. Even in the height of summer, the water from the pump was so cold it made one's teeth ache and tongue numb.

If she'd fallen in the slide and was still in that water, there was no way she was alive. A bear attack, if that had happened to her as well, might be some kind of brutal mercy, compared to freezing to death in mountain ice water.

Following an instinct that had cemented to a bitter certainty, Jonah eased sidelong across the top of the slide until he found a place where he could work his way down. He landed feet-first in the new stream and gasped at the cold — so cold the water was slushy, and nearly up to his knees.

He stepped out and followed the flow of the water.

She was about a hundred feet away, at the end of the slide area, where a massive chestnut oak, centuries old, had defied the will of the mountain and stopped the slide. The new stream rushed against the trunk and tried to divert downward, but scattered over the ground instead. There was danger of that rushing water causing another slide, but Jonah barely entertained the thought. Ada lay near the base of the tree, out of the stream but still soaked by it, sunk into mud and washed in the icy spray.

He dropped to his knees beside her and instantly sank several inches in mud. She was unconscious, and even the flow of water hadn't washed all the blood away. Her ginger hair was stained with it above her ear, and her waxed canvas jacket bore a large red stain at her waist. There was a jagged tear through the stain.

His head began to shake to and fro, but he didn't know if it was denial or despair. She was pale, so pale, inhumanly pale. Her lips were greyish blue, as was the tender skin around her eyes. As he pulled a glove off, he knew the truth before he set his fingers beneath her nose. She was gone. There was no way she could possibly still be alive.

But a faint warmth tickled at his fingertips. Breath? Or wishful thinking? He gathered her into his arms, and even so cold as she was, her body was soft, pliable. Laying her flat across his thighs, he opened her jacket and her shirt, apologizing to her modesty with a thought, and lay his head on her chest, above her cotton underthings.

It was faint, and far too slow, but her heart was beating. She was still alive. As he sat there, he saw the source of the bleeding near her waist—a tear in her side that matched the one through her coat. The bear, he reckoned. A swipe so powerful had to be a bear.

"Ada?" He slapped lightly at her cheeks, but got no response. "Ada. Come on, darlin'. Come back."

Still nothing. There was a gash in her head, too, topping a swollen mound in the space between her temple and her ear. He'd brought what medical supplies he could, but in these conditions, there was little he could do for her. So, with a desperate hope that the cold would work to keep her wounds from bleeding too much more, and that he wouldn't do her more harm getting her to safety, Jonah gathered Ada up and surged back to his feet.

She moaned then, and Jonah felt a gust of relief. "That's it, darlin', that's it. Stay with me."

His cabin was still closer than anywhere else, and he didn't know the condition of the way below. That rushing water could have made more mudslides, or might yet. Home was the safest route. He had to find a way back up this slide and back to the path to his house.

It took him hours, and his shoulders and arms burned like fire, but he got her back to the cabin. She'd moaned a few times in his arms, and each one was like a promise—she was still alive.

Elijah and Bluebird ran out onto the porch as he approached. Bluebird wailed in fear, seeing her angel draped over her father's arms. "Oh no, Pa! Mizz Ada's hurt!"

Elijah's face cramped with fright, too. But the boy asked, "What can I do?"

"Stoke up the fire, and get the pot boiling. I need hot water and that ointment." His medical skills were rudimentary at best, but he had no other option but to do what he could.

He carried her into the house, went through the front room, across the hall, and into his room. He'd laid Ada gently on the bed and stood straight before he understood what he'd done.

It took his breath away.

He'd laid her down on Grace's side, set her head on Grace's pillow. Her wet, bloody, muddy head on the pillow that had held his wife's scent, and then the memory of her scent, for seven years.

Feeling a crushing weight of loss and guilt in the midst of this crisis, Jonah darted a glance around the room. Grace wasn't here.

Ada moaned again, and Jonah focused his attention where it belonged, on the living woman, badly injured but alive, before him.

Working carefully, he eased her boots off, and the sodden socks inside them. He gently worked her arms from the sleeves of her jacket. The guilt coming at him from every direction made his fingers tremble, but he opened her shirt. Under it, she wore a light cotton thing, like the top half of a slip. Grace had called them camisoles, and he'd found them powerfully alluring.

He cast every piece of that thought out of his head.

But he had no choice with the next thing: she was bleeding, wounded. A gash in her side. He had to get to her skin. And he had to be sure he found every place she was hurt.

"Pa?"

Elijah was at the door.

"Yeah, boy."

"Here's the ointment, and the water's on the fire. What next?"

"I'm gonna need all our winter blankets, and the mendin' box."

"You gonna sew Mizz Ada up like you did Henrietta?"

185

"I reckon I gotta. She's got a couple deep cuts. Once she warms up, they'll bleed."

"Is she gonna be alright?"

He paused and gave his son his full attention. "I don't know, Elijah. She's hurt bad, but I'm gonna do what I can, and you're gonna help me."

"Yessir, I will. Bluebird wants to help, too. I told her to pray."

"That was good thinkin'. Go on now, do what I said. Close the door." He didn't want his son to see Ada when he opened the rest of her clothes.

When the door was closed, he pulled the folding knife from his trousers and sliced through the camisole. The wound at her side was angry, the edges waterlogged, but fairly straight. Again, he thought of the gashes on Henrietta's side. It looked as if Ada and her horse had encountered a bear together.

Trying not to focus on her body—her shoulders were freckled, too; he saw that and wouldn't let himself look farther—Jonah eased the sodden, filthy clothes from her top. Then, with another wave of guilt slamming over him, he opened her trousers and eased them off. Now, all she wore was a filmy pair of undershorts. Muddy water had soaked through her pants to stain those shorts, but Jonah left them on. He couldn't steal all her modesty away, and the only sign of blood on them was at the waist, near the gash in her side.

Now that he'd exposed her legs, however, he saw that her left knee was easily twice the size of its right mate and bright red with swelling. She'd wrenched it. He grabbed a little stitchwork pillow and pushed it beneath her sore knee, then got down to the work of examining her for more injuries.

He found no others of note. Besides the gash in her side, the blow to her head, which had begun to bleed again, and the swollen knee, she had an array of bruises and scratches that showed what a hard night she'd had, but nothing that would require special care. Her skin was deadly pale and cold, though, her lips and fingernails that terrible shade of dusky blue, and it bothered him that she wasn't shivering, and hadn't moaned again since he'd put her to bed. Again and again, he laid his head on her chest to hear her heartbeat—still weak, but there.

When Elijah knocked, Jonah drew the top quilt over Ada's body. The boy brought in a pail of hot water and the mending kit, and Jonah began the work. He had no whiskey or any other way of easing her pain as he cleaned and stitched her wounds, but she never reacted. He made a dozen stitches, as even as he could, in her side, and another half dozen in her head, working slowly around her hair, and she never even flinched.

He was worried. No—he was frightened. She was holding onto life by a thread as frail as spidersilk. What would his children do without their Mizz Ada?

What would he do? He shoved that thought aside with the others.

After he cleaned and closed her wounds, he washed her with more hot water, wiping the mud and blood from her frigid skin. Then he took a flannel nightgown from one of Grace's bureau drawers and eased the clean, soft fabric over her, and bundled her under as many covers as he had to spare.

By then, the day had gone to afternoon, and he'd hardly thought of daily chores, or feeding his children. So he forced himself to leave her resting and try to be a father for a while.

The chores had been done, and Elijah was making butter and sugar sandwiches with applesauce for dinner. Not much of a meal, but Jonah was impressed nevertheless.

Bluebird was on her knees by the fire, her little hands clasped together, her mouth moving silently. Had she been praying the whole day?

"Hey, baby girl." He sat next to her and brushed his hand over her back.

She opened her eyes and peered at him over her praying hands. "Is Mizz Ada better? Did God listen?"

"We found her, and that's a prayer answered, right?"

"But is she better?"

He didn't know how to explain this to his little girl, who was so innocent of anything beyond their holler. "She's real sick, Bluebird. I don't know if she'll get better. But she's here, with us, and that makes her better than when she was lost."

"I want her to be all the way better."

"Me too, baby girl. Me too."

Ada began to shake in the middle of the night. Jonah had stretched out on the worn rag rug beside the bed, where he could rest and keep watch, and he was brought to full wakefulness by the sound of the headstead drumming against the wall. He rolled at once to his feet and lit the candle on the bedside table. Ada lay on her back as he'd arranged her, still unconscious, but shaking so hard her teeth knocked loudly together. A loud sound came from her, not a moan or a whimper, but her breaths coming through her violently shaking chest.

Since he'd gotten her home, she'd never yet woken or made a sound or move until this wild quaking.

His mind full of the crimson light of agonized memories, he laid his hand on her forehead and found what he feared: she was burning with fever. Her skin was as hot and dry as a banked coal.

Had he sewn infection into her wounds? He'd tried so hard to clean them, but all he had was the bag balm for medicine. He'd never been a drinking man, never kept liquor in the house, not even moonshine, and had no other thing that might kill infection.

He'd thought of that tonic she'd brought up several weeks back. There was half a bottle left. It had helped Bluebird so much, taken away her discomfort and let her rest. But it had always put her into deep sleep, and Ada had been senseless for hours. He was afraid what that tonic might do to her. He didn't understand about medicines, when and why and how they worked. But he knew medicines could hurt as well as heal.

She was shivering cold but burning hot. He understood the way fever tore a body apart; he'd seen it time and time again. He'd watched it happen to his parents, his sister, his wife. He'd seen the pain in his daughter, but she'd survived.

Because of the tonic?

He didn't know. But he had to do something.

He was halfway to the door, on his way for the bottle, when he remembered.

This isn't a cure, but it will help her sleep, Ada had told him when she'd brought the tonic. *Let the cold run its course,* she'd said.

Ada didn't need help to sleep. She needed to wake. The tonic wouldn't help her do that, or cure the illness inside her.

This was illness was brought on by injury; maybe it didn't need to run its course. Maybe it could be helped. He could find his way down to Red Fern Holler in the morning, leave Elijah to watch over Ada and Bluebird, and ask Hez Cummings to send for the doctor. And get word to Ada's kin as well. He couldn't do this alone. He needed help.

In the meantime, he had to do what he could to ease her suffering.

There was one other thing. He'd done it for Grace, when the fever had racked her like this. His impulse then had been purely love, nothing but desperate, terrified love, and burgeoning, devastating grief, but it had eased her in her pain.

Jonah sat on the chair beside the door and pulled his boots off. He shed his suspenders and undid his trousers, leaving him in nothing but his union suit and socks. Then he climbed into bed, under the heavy mound of quilts and blankets. He eased himself to Ada's trembling body and turned her gently, bringing her against his chest, and wrapping her in his arms.

She shook so hard he had to clamp his jaw so he wouldn't bite his tongue as his body picked up her quakes.

Oh, she was so horribly hot. Like he held a live flame in his arms.

"Shhh," he breathed. "Shhh. It's alright, darlin'. I got you. Stay with me. Don't you go."

It might have been a few minutes that passed, or an hour, but finally she began to settle, and when she did, he could feel her breaths become a bit deeper. And then he felt her hand move. It was caught between them, pressed to his chest, and he felt it turn, and the fingers curl. Her nails scraped lightly on his skin. She'd hooked her fingers into the placket of his underclothes, where the buttons were open at his throat. In the first movement she'd made since he'd found her that might have been intentional, she'd taken hold of him.

"I got you." he whispered again.

Ada seemed to sleep calmly the rest of the night, but she never cooled, and shortly after Jonah left the bed in the morning, she began to thrash. It was different from the shivers but still ghastly familiar to him. He thought it was pain, now, that unsettled her so. Maybe it meant she was closer to wakefulness, but it hurt to see her hurt.

Leaving Elijah in charge, he went down to Red Fern Holler at the first light of dawn, and moved as quickly as he could. The washed-out trail was bad, with another, smaller slide farther down, but he was able to get around it and make his way to the store.

Ada was known in Red Fern Holler, and well liked. Hez sent down for the doctor, and with word for Ada's kin, at once, and sent Jonah back up with bandages and a salve from Esther, as well as a few sweets for the children and a pot of chicken broth for Ada, once she was strong enough to take it.

The doctor came that afternoon—Doc Dollens, the one who'd given Ada the tonic. He was weary and filthy, but he washed up and had Jonah take him straight to her. She was still insensible and hot. Her skin that had been so awfully pale was now red and shiny, which was even more awful to see.

The doctor had a black bag with him. While Jonah leaned against the wall by the window, watching carefully, within one step of Ada should she need him, the old man spread a cloth across the bedside table and laid out an array of strange instruments.

"How long's she been like this?" the doctor asked. He spoke a bit like Ada did, with some schooling in his accent, but he'd kept more mountain in his words than she had.

"I found her yes'day mornin'," Jonah answered, "'bout two miles down the way. She'd took a bad fall and got washed out in the storm, looked like. Maybe somethin' worse'n that. Her horse took a hit from a bear, I reckon—I got her in the barn. I think Ada mighta done, too. She ain't woke since I found her. She got the shivers bad last night, and been thrashin' and moanin' like this today."

The doctor nodded and focused on his patient.

He tapped a little red hammer on her good knee, on her wrists and elbows. He put a contraption in his ears and set a metal disc attached to it on her chest, pulling the nightgown away to lay it right on her skin. He put a glass tube in her mouth and frowned when he took it out and studied it. He had a strange little device with a tiny bright light, and he opened her eyes and shone it into each one.

"Has she voided since you found her?"

Jonah didn't understand the word. "Voided?"

"Has her body done any business?"

Oh. Jonah shook his head. The only soiling of the sheets so far had been blood and mud. "Not yet. But I ain't shy 'bout all that. I tended sick before. Don't bother me none." It might bother Ada, who was a lady, and not kin to him. He'd have to take care of her in intimate ways he'd normally have no business in, but it couldn't be helped. He'd tend to her the way she needed, whatever that was.

"Every day, startin' now, I need you to try to get water in her. 'Least a cup, more if you can. Her body needs to do its work. That'll help her get this fever out. Even if you gotta squeeze water between her lips with a cloth, do that. It might make her sick. If it does, clean her up and keep tryin'."

"Yessir."

With another acknowledging nod, the doctor checked her wounds. "Did you close these up?"

"Yessir. Yes'day. I tried to clean 'em up good, and I used the medicine we got after I sewed 'em up."

"What medicine is that?"

Jonah answered with incipient shame. "Bag balm."

The doctor chuckled quietly.

"Did I do wrong? Did I hurt her?"

"I don't think you hurt her, no. Bag balm's a fine salve. Probably better than that goop Esther gave you. If you keep the pot clean, then I reckon you did her some good. And these stitches aren't bad. Did you use a straight needle?"

Jonah nodded. "One I use for mendin' coats. And the balm pot's clean. Doc, is she alright?"

"No, Mr. Walker. She's real ill. Her fever's far too high, and that knock on her head is a bad one, in a dangerous place. It worries me she's not been conscious in more than a day. But you didn't make her this way. If she lives she'll have you to thank for it, by the sound of it."

"If?"

"She's real ill, like I said. She needs to be in the hospital, but we can't take her down the mountain, not till she's much stronger. You've done a good job carin' for her so far. If I give you some instructions and make a regular visit, you reckon you can nurse her?"

Jonah didn't hesitate. The thought of her going away from here in this state was far worse than the idea of tending to her. "Yessir. Jus' tell me what to do."

Before Doc Dollens left, he wrote down instructions, and explained them in detail. It was a lot. Jonah had Elijah read them and make sure they both understood. Then the doctor checked the children over as well—the first time one had ever looked on them—and pronounced them in excellent health, though both a bit too thin.

They all were always skinniest at this time of year. The garden hadn't had a chance to yield yet, and winter stores had reached their end. This last storm had torn the patch up pretty bad, too, which boded poorly for the coming year. But Jonah couldn't spare a thought for that problem yet.

Before the doctor left, Jonah took down the dark bottle of tonic. "I got this here medicine. I had a thought to give it to Ada last night, but I didn't know what it'd do. It helped Bluebird when she ailed a while back."

The doctor took the bottle and peered at it through his spectacles. "This is one of mine."

"Yessir. Ada brung it up when sickness was goin' 'round. It gave my girl some ease. Should I give it to Ada?"

"No! No, don't do that. This slows down the body. It takes pain away and lets patients sleep, but right now, Ada's body is workin' too slow, and she's sleepin' too much. If you'd given this to her last night, she'd be dead right now."

Jonah's breath stopped and swelled in his throat. He'd very nearly killed her.

The doctor handed the bottle back, but Jonah stepped back, holding his hands up. "I don't want that here."

"It's got its uses, Mr. Walker. Just not this. No medicine's a cure-all."

Jonah shook his head. "I don't want it."

"Alright then." He put the bottle in his black bag. "I'll be up again day after tomorrow, early as I can. If there's trouble before that, get down to the Cummings' place, and they'll get word to me."

"You got word to her kin?"

"I did. They know she's alive and recoverin' someplace safe. I won't tell 'em much more than that for now, till she takes a turn one way or the other. Her folks are gettin' up in years, she was a late-in-life child, and this worry's takin' a toll. But there's lots of folks prayin' for that sweet lady, all up and down this mountain."

Jonah could believe it. Ada Donovan made an impression.

Ada didn't wake all through the day, and she seemed in much more pain, but Doc Dollens had confirmed that her moaning and writhing was preferable to senseless stillness. If she could feel discomfort, she was close to consciousness, and there was hope.

He squeezed cool water between her hot, slack lips. At first, it seemed like she'd take it fine. Then she sicked it up, all without waking, and started to choke. He turned her to her side until the spasms passed. Then cleaned her up and tried again, hoping at least some of the water was staying down.

She had the shakes again that night. This time, Jonah didn't hesitate. Already stripped to his union suit, lying on the floor beside the bed, he rose and went to the other side to climb in with her. He didn't bother to light a candle.

This time, he had to mince his steps so that he didn't stomp on his children. They could hardly bear to be away from Ada and both had begged desperately to be allowed to sleep in this room. He'd been unable to think of a reason they shouldn't, and it gave him comfort to have them here as well. Maybe it helped Ada, too. Maybe she could sense she wasn't alone.

He got into bed and eased her into his arms. As the night before, she shook hard for a while and then finally found some quiet.

"George," she murmured, and Jonah almost missed it.

Or had she said Jonah?

"Ada?" He leaned his head back and tried to see in the dark. "Ada, you with me?"

She didn't answer. Jonah held her close and gave her all the warmth and strength he could.

Part Three

Chapter Eleven

Oh, she hurt. Fire and ice gushed through her in alternating waves, carrying sharp blades of pain.

Sometimes those blades would close around her arms or legs, would grasp her and move her, shift the flow of fire and ice.

But always there was pain, flashing light and dark, hot and cold. Always pain.

Hurt thumped through her from her head to her legs. Every beat of her heart was an explosion. Ada tried to move, but she couldn't. Not even her eyelids would obey her commands. She tried to speak, to call out for help, but the sound that left her slack mouth was little more than a mewl.

Shh, shh, darlin'. I got you.

A man's voice. George's? Was she with George?

George was dead. Was she dead, too? Was she lost? Had he found her?

Mustering every ounce of energy she could find in this terrible dark, she managed to form his name but barely had the breath to utter it. "George?"

The dark swallowed her up before she could listen for his answer.

Ada realized that her eyes were open. She didn't know how long they had been. The world was dark, except for the red pain pulsing in her head. She was weak and hurt everywhere, and the world was pitch black, but she was in it. She was hot, too hot, but not on fire. She felt a strange kind of agonized calm.

She tried to move and found that her body was in her control again—but the pain was too much to bear. Even the blink of her eyes was like claws digging in. And she was constrained in some way—not paralyzed but bound. Was she a prisoner? Was the pain from someone hurting her? A shock of fear grabbed her, but ebbed away almost as quickly.

Not bound. Held. Strong arms around her. Breath riffling her hair. A heartbeat, steady and sure.

Had George found her? Was this Heaven?

She found her hand and managed to move it despite the keen ache of the attempt. She brought it up to her chest, pushed it into the narrow space, where she was pressed against that strong heartbeat. A chest. A man's chest. George? Spreading her hand on the warm body against hers, she tried to speak his name, but no sound came. Her mouth was dry and cracked as a baked brick.

Suddenly, she knew it wasn't George who held her. This chest was different. Hair tickled her fingertips. George had no hair on his chest. This chest was harder than her George's, and she had a sense that it loomed over her. This man was bigger. The scent was different, too. Not George's. But familiar, somehow. Safe, somehow.

Finding the energy to move again, she tipped her head back—oh, it hurt so much—but the world was black as pitch, and she couldn't see.

She didn't know who this was, or where they were, but there was no danger here. The man who held her was a tether, she was sure of it. He held her to this world.

Did she want to stay? What if George was looking for her on the other side? She'd felt him close by, only moments ago, it seemed. What if all she had to do was let go, and she'd be with her husband again? Her sweet, kind man, who'd been with her for too short a time.

Did she want this world?

Or the next?

Ada came back to daylight. This world, not the next. She opened her eyes and sealed them shut again at once. Sunlight streamed over her and stung. Fire still burned all through her, but it was deep, like the core of the earth. She didn't feel the flames licking her skin anymore.

In fact, she felt a brush of cool over her leg.

Prepared now for the bright, she opened her eyes again. Her sight was foggy with lack of use, but she blinked, and blinked again — her eyelids felt singed by the heat of her eyeballs — and details came into focus. She was in a room. Faded flowers danced across the walls, disappearing now and then under white curls. Wallpaper. Old and peeling.

She was in a bed. A bedroom.

Another brush over her leg, warm and soft, then cool, like a breeze. "What?" Her voice croaked.

The brushing stopped. "Hey there." A man's voice. "Hey."

Ada closed her eyes, summoned her focus, and opened them again. Mr. Walker crouched beside the bed. He held a twist of wet cloth in one hand. With the other, he pulled covers over her bare legs.

"You in there?" he asked.

"Mr. W—Walker?"

He smiled. The expression was surprising, as if she'd never seen this man smile before. Had she?

"Jonah. That's my name."

"I don't ... what?"

Jonah Walker set the cloth aside. Ada heard a soft splash when he did. Then his hands—big and coarse, sweetly cool and a bit damp—scooped her hand up, and he leaned close and spoke softly. "You got real hurt in the storm some days past. You recall?"

Her mind was a muddle. She knew him, and herself, but could not possibly conceive why she was where she was, or even begin to find a memory of something that might have happened.

She tried to shake her head, but the movement blasted white-hot agony through her neck and around the side of her head. A moan crawled up from her chest as she squeezed her eyes shut.

"Easy now," he murmured. His voice was so gentle, so deep and slow. "Don't push."

"Hurts."

"I know, darlin'. I'm sorry." One of his hands left her. "You think you can try to take a drink? Got some good fresh water right here."

"I don't ... know."

Her throat felt like it was full of steel wool. Oh, she wanted water. But the thought of lifting her pounding head horrified her. She eased her eyes open and found him right there, his eyes full of kind concern. He'd always looked on her with such cold wariness before, when he met her eyes at all. But she'd seen this look in his eyes for his children.

Bluebird and Elijah. Where were they?

"Let's try," he said and set a cup on the table beside the bed. Moving gently, he slid an arm under her shoulders. It hurt, and she cried out, but he could not have been more gentle, and he didn't pull back. He eased onto the bed, using his body to support hers, and brought her up enough that she could take the cup he offered. She rested on his chest. Broad and firm.

The first trickle of cool was like fire rolling down her throat. But the second was bliss, and she fixed her mouth to the metal side of the cup and swallowed as much as she could. She tried to lift her hand to hold the cup, but something vicious bit her side, and she winced, but still tried to drink. Water spilled at the corners of her mouth.

"Hey, hey," he said and firmly, yet gently, forced the cup from her lips. "You been havin' trouble keepin' it down. Best take it slow." He slipped from the bed and eased her back to the pillow. Somehow, he'd managed to slide another in, and she was propped a bit higher.

"How's that settin'?"

He meant the water. Actually, it was sloshing around in her belly like it couldn't find a place to be. "Not sure."

"Try to keep it if you can. If you can't"—he bent and lifted a tin pot from the floor—"that's what this here's for."

Ada had spent all the energy she had orienting herself in this room, forming a conversation with Jonah Walker, and having a drink. She drifted back into darkness before she could say or hear another word.

Sound was the first sense that woke. Ada heard a soft, young voice, each word canted up sweetly at its end, very close by. She opened her eyes to a room lit with candles but not wholly without natural light. Dusk.

Bluebird sat on the bed, cross-legged, with a picture book across her lap. She was reading aloud. She wore a faded and patched pink pinafore dress, and her hair was in two little braids, tied with the pale blue ribbons Ada had brought up for her on one of her visits.

She wasn't supposed to bring gifts to her patrons, and she certainly wasn't supposed to favor some over others, but Ada hadn't been able to help herself. The

Walker children were special, and so much in need. She'd been driven almost at once to give them anything she could. Mrs. Pitts said the librarians were carrying the world up the mountain. Ada wanted to give Bluebird and Elijah the world.

There were others on her route just as hungry, just as lacking in their clothing and shelter. In fact, there were children on her route whose homes were half as stable and strong as this one, or even less. The Devlins, for instance, living under the tyrannical fist of Tobias Devlin. He'd tried to bring Ada into his tyranny once, and had hit her in the face. Now she saw the Devlin children only at their schoolhouse, and stayed clear of their father.

Jonah Walker was no tyrant. She'd seen no hint of violence in the man. He took good care of his children, and showed them deep love. He was patient with them, and they were happy. His own aloof suspicion of her and the world she came from hadn't tainted their good natures. His love for them was so deep and pure that it shielded them from his own unhappiness.

But they were isolated from the whole world. No friends but each other. No schooling, no knowledge of anything in the world beyond their own holler. And in that, they were in desperate need. The books she brought them, and the little tokens, had literally carried the world into their lives.

They'd cleaved to her quickly and fervently. She wasn't simply a book woman to them, and they weren't simply patrons to her. This house was her favorite on her route. These children were by now as dear to her as if she'd been lucky enough to have carried them in her own body.

To have this little girl reading so sweetly at her side eased Ada in body and soul.

Before she let herself be known to have woken, Ada took a few moments and arranged her thinking. Though her main memories and the ideas that formed what she knew of herself and the world, and of the Walkers, were clear and right at hand, recent memories, including the understanding of why she was here, were like loose twists of remnant string. Each thought wanted to twine with all the others, and each time of waking required this act of untangling.

She was at the Walkers' house, in Cable's Holler. She'd been hurt in a storm, had serious injuries to her head and side, and a significant but less severe injury to her knee as well. She had no memory whatsoever of being hurt, or of the storm itself. Her memories were still in a jumble, but she thought her most recent one before this horrible pain was making breakfast for her parents. She'd lost whole days of time, starting from even before she was hurt.

How long had she been here? How long since the storm?

Five days, she thought, though her concept of time had been reduced to daylight and moonlight, and she couldn't keep track from one to the next. But Doc Dollens had been here twice that she could recall, three times in all, and Jonah told her he came every other day. He'd been here today, she thought. That made five days, unless she'd lost another large chunk of time. She'd been here five days, so the storm had been six days ago. If she was counting correctly.

Jonah Walker had taken care of her all that time. He'd found her, rescued her, saved her, and was nursing her back to health.

Jonah Walker.

Jonah.

She reached a hand out and clasped Bluebird's little bare foot. It was cool.

"Mizz Ada! You waked up!"

It took hard effort to sort words into sentences and find the breath to speak them, but she smiled and tried. "What are you reading?"

"*Snippy and Snappy*. Pa said it could make you feel better. Do it?"

"It does, yes. That's a good story. You're doing a very good job reading it." She truly was. She read nearly as well as her older brother, who had moved on to chapter books and adventure stories some time ago.

"Readin' is my favorite thing 'cuz the pictures go in my head and get big."

"That happens in my head when I read, too."

"You look kinda funny, Mizz Ada. Pa says your head hurts bad."

"It does. But it helps when you read."

"Alright. I'll do it more." Bluebird shifted on the bed, turning to sit against the headboard and canting the book so Ada could see the pictures.

Within a page or two, a shadow filled the open doorway, and Ada slid her eyes from the book. Jonah stood there, his arms crossed.

"Supper's on the table, Bluebird. Whyn't you set the book aside for now and go get washed to eat."

"I ain't done, Pa. There's"—she turned the pages to the end—"three pages left."

"If Mizz Ada wants, you can finish after."

Ada turned back to Bluebird. "Let's do that. I need a rest."

"Alright then." Bluebird closed the book and leaned over to put a very careful kiss on Ada's cheek. Then she scooted off the bed. Jonah stepped into the room to clear the doorway. When his daughter was gone, he came to the bed and crouched at Ada's side.

"You kept water down all day today. How 'bout some broth? Doc says you need to get some food in."

Every slightest move made her wildly dizzy and slammed a hammer in the side of her head. She was constantly thirsty, but her stomach rolled with every drink, and she'd been sick many times in the days she'd been aware enough to know it. Her middle ached horribly, and her side throbbed. She had a long stitched wound there; she'd seen it when Jonah had last washed her.

He washed her. He'd changed her nightclothes a few times. He'd tended to her in other ways, embarrassing ways, as well. Her thinking was hazy on the matter, but she thought he was dressing her in his wife's things. He was taking care of her.

The thought of it confounded her, made confusing feelings spin around her disordered memories and notions and turn it all into knots.

"What d'ya think?" he asked, and Ada remembered he'd urged her to eat.

Keeping water down today had been a blessing, and she thought risking something richer, even broth, would be counting her blessings a bit too early. She couldn't face being sick again.

"Not yet."

"You need food to get strong, Ada."

He said her name now, freely. Kindly. She'd known him since early last autumn, and it was now well

214

into spring. Months and months of regular visits, when she'd grown close to his children, come to love them dearly, while he'd barely looked at her, and never uttered any iteration of her name. Now he said the most familiar version as if he'd known her and cared for her all his life.

Each time he did, Ada felt pleasure flutter in her chest. It frightened her.

"I'll try tomorrow, Jonah." His name felt dangerous on her lips, but he wouldn't hear of her calling him anything else now.

"Alright." He smiled and sat at the edge of the bed, near her hip, easing his weight carefully, so as not to hurt her. "How's this doin'?" He put his hand on her head, cupping his palm at her jaw, and leaned in, using the candlelight to check her head wound.

"It's sore, but not like it was." She ached everywhere, was weak and dizzy, and the smallest act required heroic effort, but the steady pulse of nearly unbearable pain had abated. Now pain so intense only flared occasionally, when she tried for more than she could accomplish.

"Looks better," he declared. "Swellin's down. The cut's healing under the stitches." He came off the bed and turned, crouching again at the side. "Can I see?"

Ada nodded, and he pushed the covers away and lifted the nightgown. "This one looks pretty good, too.

And you ain't quite so hot. You're doin' better. But you gotta eat soon."

His hand rested on her side, over her ribs, just above the wound, and just below her breast, near enough that she thought she could feel the heat of his finger, almost touching the underside of that unimpressive mound.

The touch lingered. Ada brought her gaze to his face and found him looking, as if he were waiting for her. Their eyes locked. His thumb moved slightly, brushing an inch of her skin.

There was a pull between them, so powerful she nearly heard the hum of it. But she ached, and her mind was full of cracks. She was too weak even to sit up without his body to support her.

"I'm not ready," she whispered. She didn't know if she was talking about food, or something else.

"Alright. You let me know when you are."

She didn't know what he was talking about, either.

Ada felt much worse in the night. For each of the few nights she'd been conscious enough to notice, that had been true. As if the sun itself were her medicine, when it

216

fell fully away and the dark wrapped around the cabin, her fever rose, her aches redoubled, and her thoughts softened and became harder to hold.

Jonah and the children slept in the room with her, arrayed on the floor around the bed. They knelt at her side each night and said their prayers, and kissed her cheek before they settled onto their pallets to sleep. She was glad; she felt better when she wasn't alone.

And each night, at sometime during the deepest dark, when her health reached its nadir, and she despaired of ever feeling well or strong or warm again, Jonah had come into bed with her, to hold her and warm her as the fever trampled her.

She had a filmy memory, like a faded picture postcard, of him holding her in the same way while she was at her sickest. The memory was woven tightly with her memories of George, and her mind wanted to tell her it had been George who'd held her, but her husband was more than two years dead. If it had been him holding her, if he'd been waiting for her on the other side, she had chosen not to go with him.

She had chosen to stay here, in this world, and live without him.

On this night, the end of the first day when she'd been strong enough to feel she might become herself again, as Jonah settled the children and came to lie on the floor by her side, Ada reached out and brushed her fingers over his hand, as much as she could reach.

He stopped in the midst of fluffing out his quilt. "Ada? Alright?"

Ada had a question on her tongue, but now that the time had come to ask it, her tongue rolled up. All she could do was stare at him.

He wore only a union suit that might once have been white but had gone dun with wear. It was clean, though; he kept his home, his children, and himself neat as a pin. Even those things that were little more than rags were clean.

The cotton of his union suit had worn thin and showed his whole body, or enough of it that even her compromised, feverish brain could conjure the rest. He was tall and broad-shouldered; she'd always known that. And he was lean, too lean; those broad shoulders framed his body with sharp right angles, his collarbones lifted the top of his union suit up so that place where the buttons weren't fastened fell wide open and showed his throat and the top of his chest, and the curves of his hip bones pushed out the cotton knit farther down his body, where she tried not to let her eyes linger.

But he was strong, too. He had no extra meat on him, but the meat he had was muscle. His arms swelled with it, above his sharp elbows and below as well. His thighs were thick and ropy; the cotton stretched tight around them. And his chest and abdomen, which she might have expected to be hollow, were solid slabs of muscle.

She'd felt that chest, that abdomen, those arms. Each night when he held her and offered her comfort so she could manage her pain.

Ada didn't remember the storm, or how she'd been hurt. She didn't remember that day or night, or the next few days and nights. She knew her injuries. She knew Jonah had saved her. She knew Henrietta had come to him for help.

And she knew somehow that lost time, the mysterious event that had hurt her, had changed her life significantly.

Something stupendous had changed in Jonah, and in her.

She understood what it was, or what it might be, and it terrified her. And made her sad. She wasn't sure she was ready, or he was.

Or maybe it was all in her mind, and nothing she saw or felt or thought she knew was real.

But right now, she wanted to believe it was real, and not worry what it might mean.

"Ada?" he asked again and dropped the quilt. Stepping over it, he crouched beside the bed, close to her head. "What d'ya need, darlin'?"

Darling, he called her. She didn't think it was all in her mind.

Her tongue relaxed and remembered its work. "Will you … will you sleep in bed with me? From the start?"

He frowned and set his hand on her forehead. His palm was cool. "You feelin' the shakes comin' on?"

"No. Not right now."

His eyes were a deep brown, so dark they seemed depthless. They stared hard at her now, and she tried to find their bottom. As he understood why she was asking, he took a long, slow breath and didn't let it out.

Ada felt terrible. Her eyes burned and her head throbbed. Her joints ached, which made her sore knee feel like a hornets' nest, and her side itched. Every second that he stared and didn't answer drew energy from her, and she wanted to take it back. It had been a stupid, stupid, stupid thing to say, to ask, and she'd imagined everything. She wasn't clearheaded. The fever was making her delusional.

But she didn't take it back.

"Ada," he whispered, and his held breath rushed out. She waited for him to set her overheated imaginings to rights. "You want that?"

"I want you to hold me. Not because I'm shaking. I just want you to hold me. If you want it, too."

Another long, deep breath, held too long. Then he blew out the last candle. In the dark, without his answer, she didn't know what to think. She heard him rustling about, but couldn't place where the sounds came from in the small, crowded room.

Then the covers fluttered, and the mattress sagged and the bedsprings creaked.

"C'mere, darlin'," he said, lying at her side.

Ada moved her sore body to him and settled in his arms.

Chapter Twelve

Ada watched as Doc Dollens snipped the last bit of hardened thread and drew it carefully from her side. He set aside his snips and tweezers and leaned in to peer at the dark red scar. With his fingers, he pressed gently at its edges.

"How's it feel?"

"It itches a bit still, but otherwise it doesn't bother me. The sensation's a little like pins and needles."

He nodded. "The nerves there'll take awhile to knit back together. But it looks good. Jonah did a real fine job stitchin' it up. He's a good nurse."

"Yes, he is. Do you think a bear did that?" She still didn't remember how she'd been hurt, but Jonah thought a bear had attacked her and Henrietta. He'd nursed her horse, too, and just as well. Ada had seen Henrietta outside, enjoying the spring warmth. She was healed but had a nasty scar, too.

Jonah took excellent care of them both. He was so tender and solicitous that Ada's feelings were just as snarled as her thoughts and memories had been when she'd first woken.

"I can't say for sure, but could be. If so, you've got an angel on your shoulder, keepin' watch over you." Doc Dollens stood and put his hands on her head. "I'm gonna pull these stitches, too. The wound is closed." He picked up his snips. The pressure of his hand and the metal snips working a knot free hurt her, and she couldn't control a gasp and wince.

He stopped and leaned sidewise, peering over his spectacles at her. "Still sore?"

"A bit. Everything else feels much better, but my head still hurts."

"And the vertigo?"

She'd been wildly dizzy for days. "It's better. I can move about, if I go slowly and don't try to turn only my head. But if I do, or I move too quickly, it's bad as ever." She had trouble eating, too, because the dizziness brought nausea with it.

"I don't like that, Ada. It's been two weeks. The swellin's down, and the laceration is closed. If you're still hurtin' and dizzy, that says there's somethin' goin' inside. I didn't feel a fracture when I first examined you, and I don't feel one now, but I think there might be one. That's a fragile part of your head."

"What does that mean?"

"It means you need to take it real easy awhile longer, and protect your head like it's broken, because it might well be."

"How much longer?" She'd been away from her parents for two weeks. And from her job as well. They needed her wages.

"A couple weeks, at least. You won't get down this mountain until you're full steady on your feet. And you damn sure won't sit the saddle while you're dizzy."

"But my parents—"

He patted her hand and cut her off. "Your folks know you're safe and healin'. They got neighbors lookin' in on 'em, and they're fine. They miss you, but you know they don't want you to try to get home before you're strong enough. Think if you pushed yourself and somethin' happened, how they'd take that. And don't you worry about work none, either. Miss Avery at the Bull Holler schoolhouse and Esther Cummings at the Red Fern store, they both set up book exchanges for anybody on your route can get to one or the other. The people you see, they're swappin' library books you brought 'em, and havin' a potluck while they're at it. I went to the library in Callwood and talked to the librarian there, and you still got your job, and your pay. People love you, Ada. You brought somethin' good to their lives, and they're doin' what they can for you now."

Tears rushed forth and spilled from Ada's eyes. It hurt to try to stop them, so she let them fall. She was crying for so many reasons—because she was moved by the help and concern of people all around her, because she missed her parents desperately, because she was tired of being weak and hurt, and for reasons she feared to examine. Her heart hurt almost as keenly as her head.

"There, there." The doctor patted her hand again. "You're healin', Ada. You'll get home soon enough. Let's get these last stitches out. I'll be gentle as I can."

He was gentle, and the hurt he made was bearable. When he was done, he packed up his medical bag. "I want you to keep on tryin' to eat and drink. You're too thin. I want you to move around a little every day, get outside on fine days and sit on the porch like you've been, or in the yard a spell—but don't move about alone, and go slow. If there is a fine fracture in your skull, you don't want to jar your head at all. Try to do a little, but not too much. You hear?"

"Yes. I'll be careful."

He rewarded her with a smile. "Good girl. Now, with the wounds closed up and the stitches out, you can have a bath, so long's you get help gettin' in and out of it."

That was the first good news Ada had heard in a while, and it broke apart the shell of her self-pity. "That would be wonderful. May I wash my hair, too?" She hadn't washed her hair since she was last home to do it.

Jonah had tried to wipe it clean, but the mass still bore traces of blood and mud, and it hung heavy from her scalp.

It had only been the past few days that she'd taken on the task of cleaning her body with a bowl and a cloth. Jonah had washed her before that, until she was strong enough to sit up unsupported.

Doc Dollens took off his glasses and slipped them into the pocket of his shirt. "I don't know about that. Too much moving your head around. But if you can figure out a way, and *be careful*, the wound's not a reason to stop you."

"Alright. Thank you."

"I'll be up again next week, and we'll see how you're doin'." Once he felt confident that she would recover, the doctor had stopped coming up every other day. That was a long, hard journey to make so often. He gave her shoulder an affectionate squeeze, went to the door, and opened it.

Jonah stood right outside. His arms were crossed, but when the light from the bedroom slanted into the dim hallway, he relaxed and let them fall.

"She doin' alright, Doc?"

"She is," Ada heard the doctor answer. "She needs to take it easy awhile longer, and be careful about her head. I told her to get out and move around, but not go anywhere without help. If the vertigo makes her dizzy and she falls, she might go poorly again."

While the men taking care of her talked about her health, Ada rested back on the pillows and closed her eyes.

"Hey." Jonah's voice was at her ear, and his hand covered hers.

Ada opened her eyes. She must have dozed off. "Is the doctor gone?"

"Yep."

"Where are the children?"

"They's playin' outside. You want to go sit on the porch for a spell? I'll bring Henrietta up."

Each day seemed to bring a little more blue to Ada's mood. She was grateful for all the help and care, and she enjoyed being here with Jonah and his children, but she was ever so tired of feeling badly, and ever so confused about Jonah.

He cared for her as if he loved her, but he held himself off as well. Even those nights that he'd slept with his arms around her, he'd held something of himself away.

Ada felt it, too—the powerful draw to him, and the potent fear of that pull. Like they stood together at the edge of a cliff, holding hands, their toes hanging out over nothing but air. They were on the precipice of something, but neither of them would step their foot out and go over.

Of course they hadn't spoken of it. Ada could only interpret Jonah's actions, and make conjectures about what feelings might propel them. For her part, every flutter of feeling for Jonah came with a pang of shame. George had been dead for only about two and a half years. Not so long ago, she would have been able to name the exact count of year, month, week, and day since he'd passed, but now she knew it only as 'about two and a half years.' Somewhere along the line she'd stopped keeping such close count, and she didn't even know when. Was he fading from her? Was she erasing him? To make room for Jonah?

That thought had jagged edges. She felt unfaithful, and she recoiled from the precipice. But every time she thought of Jonah, every moment she was near him, the pull forward, to him, grew.

Lost in confusion, frustrated in her heart and with her body, impatient to get back to her life and reluctant to leave this cabin and its family, Ada felt heavy shadows creeping over her mood.

Jonah brushed a fingertip over her cheek. Tiny sparks of guilty pleasure lit up beneath her skin. "Ada?"

She realized he'd asked a question and reached back in her memory to find it. "Sitting on the porch would be nice, thank you."

He smiled—oh, how handsome he was when he smiled. "I'll help you get dressed."

She had no clothing of her own here, except what she'd been wearing that day she'd been hurt, and she didn't know where those were. Jonah had offered her his dead wife's wardrobe.

"I can manage on my own."

His beautiful smile faded, and Ada felt the pang of its loss. "The doc said …"

"I'll be very careful, I promise. You can bring the clothes to the bed, and I'll dress from here. I'd just like … I'd like some privacy, if I can." Some privacy, and some relief from the fretful fantasies that filled her mind when his hands touched her bare skin.

"'Course. 'Course you do. I'm sorry. I'll get you a dress."

A week later, the vertigo had receded considerably. Quick turns of her head or body still made it flare and sent the world tilting like a carnival ride, but the constant, low roll of nausea had passed. Ada was able to walk on her own for short distances and keep a straight line. Jonah fussed as if she'd been unconscious only days earlier and not three weeks, but she was firm, and he gave her a bit of room to improve her strength.

The end to the nausea allowed her to eat better as well, and she was doing what she could in that way to regain her strength. Jonah was a good cook, and they'd had more than his cooking besides.

In the three weeks of her recuperation, they'd had two visits from Red Fern Holler, bringing up prepared foods from the people there and small handmade tokens from the children as well. The men had used the opportunity to cut in a fresh trail. On the second visit, Mr. Cummings had handed Ada the McDaniel family Bible — sent up by her parents. That Bible had done more to lift Ada's spirits than nearly any other thing. She'd been so worried for her parents and so lonely for them. They were old, too old to be left on their own, too old to be burdened with worry for her. That Bible, the most special book from her father who'd never learned to read and her mother who'd lost the ability, said that they were well and waiting for her.

She wanted to go home to them. The farm itself, she didn't care for one way or the other; home had never been a building or a piece of land to her. If it was a place, her home was bigger than the little plot her parents owned. If her home was a place at all, it was this whole mountain range, from its peaks to the long tendrils of its foothills.

But her home was not a place. Home was people. Her people.

Ada sat on a rough timber bench behind the Walkers' house. Jonah was chopping wood, off somewhere nearby but out of sight, and the rhythm of his work made her feel calm and a little sleepy. She watched Elijah and Bluebird playing with the baby goats in the small goat yard. The little kids bounced and bleated, and Bluebird's joyful giggles joined them in a chorus. Elijah played, too, running so the kids would chase him, falling down so they'd climb him and nibble his hair. She was glad to see him so light and happy.

He was usually a somber boy — loving and friendly, but serious and keenly aware of his responsibilities and of their weight. He was very like his father in that way. But unlike his father, he burned with the desire for more in his life than this mountain. He'd never said it out loud in such clear words, but every book he chose was about the world beyond, and the ways to get there. He wanted to know about trains and airplanes. He wanted to know about the ocean, and cities, and other countries. He wanted to read stories from faraway places — adventure stories and mysteries, and things even stranger. Ada had once brought up a pulpy magazine called *Amazing Stories*, full of bizarre tales about Martians and other alien creatures, and Elijah had nearly wept when it was time to return it.

She'd intended to bring him up more like it, but Mrs. Pitts took that one out of circulation and forbade any others. She thought they were perverse.

Elijah wanted away from this mountain. Ada wondered if he would ever make the effort, or find the courage to tell his father of his dreams—or recognize them himself.

Bluebird, on the other hand, at least at this sunny age, was happy just as she was. She loved happy stories and silly stories and stories about princesses. In the humble, tattered world of her home, she *was* a princess; her father and brother—and Ada, too—treated her like their most precious treasure. She did her chores happily because she didn't like being left out. But she didn't feel them as responsibilities. Ada envied her a little, to be so joyful and carefree, so indulged and yet unspoiled, to feel so pampered despite how little this family had.

Easing herself from the bench, Ada walked carefully to the goat yard fence. Henrietta, who spent her days wandering loose around the house but never going out of sight, shuffled lazily to her. She was fully recovered and had been heartily enjoying her respite from the hard and nearly constant work of carrying Ada all over the mountain.

"Hey, girl," Ada crooned, and her horse nickered and nudged her shoulder. Ada grabbed a fence post to be sure to keep her footing. She stroked Henrietta's soft nose, and they watched the children playing tirelessly while the adult goats clustered in a corner, munching weeds and staring at the little ones with weary tolerance.

After a time, Henrietta ducked her head and stuck it in a pail that one of the children had hung on the fence post. It was empty, but when Henrietta raised her head again, her nose was wet. She huffed and tried again, snuffling around the bottom of the pail.

"Thirsty, girl?" Ada still wasn't supposed to walk around without someone with her, especially not outside where the ground wasn't smooth, but she felt strong and stable enough to go—slowly—to the well and fill the pail. "C'mon. Let's get you some water."

She left the children to their shenanigans and strolled to the house. Trailing one hand along its weathered boards as an extra caution against dizziness, she followed the house to its corner, where the well and the pump were located.

Most of the Walkers' land had heavy tree cover, and the sun dappled over the house. But at this end, the clearing that served as the center of the holler left a wide slant of unobstructed sunlight. The garden patch had been placed to make the most of it, and of proximity to the well. The woodshed was on this side of the house, too.

Ada arrived at the corner of the house and squinted into the suddenly bright sun. She lifted her free hand, the one that had brushed along the house, and shielded her eyes. And then her breath and heart and mind stopped.

She hadn't noticed an end to the rhythm of his work, but Jonah was no longer chopping wood. He was at the well, shining in bright sun. His suspenders were loose at his hips, and his shirt—a worn cotton with long sleeves and a frayed hem; he'd cut the top off a union suit that had given out at the knees — was draped over the stone side of the well.

He was bare to his waist.

Many nights since she'd been hurt, he'd held her closely. Many times, he'd supported her body with his, when she needed to sit up and couldn't, or when she'd been able to get up but couldn't walk steadily. She'd felt his strong chest many times in these last weeks. His underclothes were worn and snug, too, and left, she thought, little to the imagination. She thought she'd known what his body would look like.

She had not.

Now she stood, stunned to a stupor, with Henrietta just behind her, and watched as Jonah dunked his head in a bucket. He pulled back, tossing his head so his wet hair flew back, arcing droplets over his body. He combed his fingers through the dark mass and then scooped his hands into the bucket, filling them with water to splash his face and scrub over his chest, his belly, his shoulders, under his arms.

She'd known he was strong — lean and sharp-jointed but well muscled. But she'd been too naïve to conjure the true image of it in her mind. His muscles rippled. Each movement he made shifted planes and ridges through his torso, his arms.

In these weeks, she'd been deeply confused by her feelings for this man. Desire and guilt braided together into a rope that might choke her to death. What she wanted, what he wanted, it was all too snarled to make sense of. But not right now.

Right now, Ada wasn't the least bit confused by her feelings. She knew exactly what she wanted, and when she wanted it. This feeling had been gone from her for about two and a half years, but it was as familiar as the beat of her own heart, and so powerful she quite honestly ached. From her hips to her knees, she ached, so hard she moaned and crossed her arms over her throbbing belly.

She'd forgotten she was carrying a bucket, and it crashed to the ground.

Jonah flinched and looked over. Seeing her, he froze.

They stood like that, locked in place, staring at each other. The water droplets over Jonah's beautiful body dazzled in the sunlight as if he were crusted in diamonds. They spiraled and sparkled.

Ada was dizzy, more each second. She couldn't fall, or she might hurt herself badly again. She threw out an arm and grabbed the corner of the house, but it offered a poor handhold, and the whole world was beginning to twist and tilt. She slumped toward the wall, hoping it would break her fall.

But then Jonah was there. He swept her into his arms. Bare arms, bare chest. Sun-warm and water-cool.

The world went end over end.

She was in bed again when she woke, lying on the coverlet. Still dressed in one of his wife's dresses — she'd been a bit bigger than Ada, taller and bustier. The room was bright with sunshine, and Jonah's hair was still thoroughly wet. She hadn't been out for long.

He was still shirtless, too, and water dripped from his hair to his shoulder and down his bare chest, snaking slowly through the dark hair there.

"Ada," he said when he saw her open eyes. He crouched beside her. "How you feelin'?"

"Silly. I'm sorry."

"Don't be sorry. But you're pushin' yourself too hard, darlin'. Don't be in such a rush."

Another drop of water left his hair and began a journey down his body. Without thinking, Ada reached out and drew a fingertip along its trail.

Jonah drew in a sharp, short breath. She met his eyes, and again found herself trapped in their dark depths.

"Jonah," she whispered. That intense need was still on her, smothering guilt with desire and bringing clarity to her thinking. She wanted to feel his body on hers. If there would be guilt, if there should be shame, she was willing to feel it all later, if she could feel his body on hers right now.

Still trapped in her eyes, he leaned closer. He licked his lips. Ada licked hers. Anxious hope fluttered through her head like vertigo, but she was lying down and wouldn't fall.

He got so close she felt his breath over her lips. His hand came to her hair, and his eyes slid that direction. "Your hair's so pretty," he murmured. "Like fire."

Hair like fire, eyes like water.

Ada gasped and shrank into the pillow as the sound of George's voice filled her head.

Jonah jerked back like he'd been grabbed from behind. For a moment he froze again, blinking. Then he stood. "I gotta check on the children."

And he left the room so quickly he might as well have run.

All the confusion, the shame and loss and guilt, that had been tamped down by her need rushed back. Ada closed her eyes and let it all besiege her.

That evening, after the routine that had developed of supper, and then reading time with Ada and the children, and then bedtime for the children with their father—they slept in their own beds now, on the second floor—Ada went to the bedroom she was still sharing with Jonah. He didn't always hold her at night now, but they always slept together. He wanted her on the bed, because she was still recovering, and she didn't want to displace him from his own bed. Sleeping with him was yet another muddle of feelings: the warm safety and comfort, the burgeoning desire, the guilt of moving on, and the uncertainty that they were moving on at all.

She washed up and finger-combed her hair—she'd washed it twice since Doc Dollens had said she could, but she hadn't done much of a job of it; washing one's hair was difficult when moving one's head made one dizzy—then slipped into the nightgown she'd worn the past few nights. Maybe because she'd started wearing his wife's clothes before she'd been conscious to know it, Ada hadn't felt any qualm about wearing them at all. They were not hers, but they were all she had, and Jonah had offered them readily.

No qualms, but that didn't mean she didn't feel Grace Walker's presence in every room of this house, particularly this bedroom. She set the hand mirror down—Grace's, no doubt—and looked up at the samplers hanging side by side on the wall. The faded wallpaper curled down so that its corner nearly touched one of the frames. Candlelight flickered and made strange shadows of the loose paper.

One was a wedding sampler, with the names Jonah and Grace stitched inside two linked rings with a cross above them, and a date eleven years ago stitched beneath it. The other marked Elijah's birth, in April nine years past. A little blue baby basket adorned the center of that one, with the name Elijah Moses stitched beneath it.

There was no sampler for Bluebird. Her mother had sickened and died before she could stitch one.

The floor creaked, and Jonah stepped into the room. He glanced at the samplers and turned his attention to Ada.

"I got some things to say, Ada." His tone was solemn.

"Alright." Anxiety hurried her heart, but she held back any dizziness.

"If you're up to it, let's go sit on the porch." He held out his hand, and she went to him and took it. Walking with characteristic concern for her balance, he led her through the house to the porch.

They sat on the old rockers and looked out at the spring night. Ada waited for him to say what he had to say.

He stared out toward the woods as he began. "I ain't good at this — talkin', I mean. 'Specially about this. So let me spin it out."

She nodded.

"I love my wife. Grace. I've loved her ever' day since I met her. When she passed …" He shook his head and went quiet. When he spoke again, he'd moved on. "But she stayed with me even after she died. I felt her ever' day, still with me. I even saw her. She stayed in the house, but she was always here."

He cast an abashed glance her way sidelong, but Ada didn't judge him. Her heart ached, for his loss, and hers, and for the thing that it seemed he meant to stop before it could start. But she didn't judge him for seeing his dead wife. She understood what it was to cling to what you needed, even after it was gone.

Fixing his attention again on the dark woods, he continued. "I know 'twas my head conjurin' her. I ain't crazy. But it kept me goin', feelin' like she was here with me, watchin' over the way I raised up the babies she give me. Havin' her with me kept me openin' my eyes ever' mornin'."

He turned, and his eyes met hers. "I ain't seen her in weeks. In the winter, she started comin' and goin', bein' away a few days at a time, even if I called out for her. But she always came back. Then she jus' stopped, a few weeks back."

Ada's heart split open. He was telling her not only that he didn't want her, but that her being here had taken something crucial from his life. For these weeks, she'd been sleeping in his wife's bed, wearing his wife's clothes. She'd taken up his wife's space. Pushed her out of her place.

She'd misread every moment of the tension between them these past few weeks.

"I'm sorry." What else could she say?

He shook his head. "No, darlin'. Don't be sorry. I'm sayin' I kept Grace with me long as I needed her. When I didn't need her no more, I let her go. That's what I figured out. I think that's you. You made me see I could go on without her."

He paused, and Ada opened her mouth to speak, though she wasn't sure what she'd say. His meaning, or her grasp of it, seemed to shift with every sentence. She didn't understand what he was saying about her, about them, and she was afraid to guess.

Before she could force a sound from her throat, he put up his hand. "I know you had a good love, too, and your grievin' is still with you. You called out for him a lot when you was sick. George, his name is, right?"

She bobbed her head slowly, wary of vertigo and full of its emotional equivalent.

"I understand, and I ain't sayin' I need you replacin' Grace. You're too good for this life I got, anyways. You got all those folks who need you and love you. You b'long down the mountain where the people is."

"Jonah, I don't understand."

He chuckled lightly. Ada tried to remember if she'd heard him laugh before—or ever, with real humor. "No, I reckon you don't. I don't ken much of my own mind on this myself. I jus'—I got feelins for you, and they's all twisted up and confusin'. If I act improper with you, like earlier, I don't mean to. I jus'—sometimes, I want …" He sighed and stopped. The songs of night creatures swallowed up the unfinished sentence, and he didn't add another.

Ada focused hard and tried to parse out all those befuddling words. Was he saying he wanted her? She thought so. But so much of what he'd said complicated that idea. Was he saying that he wanted her but didn't think he deserved her? That was ridiculous. Was he saying he wanted her but didn't think she was ready to set aside her widowhood? That was reasonable, but not at all his decision. Was he saying he wanted her but didn't think she'd give up her life below to live in this isolated corner of the mountain, with no friends but him and the children, and little contact with the rest of the world? That was both reasonable and likely true. She loved this cabin, and Bluebird and Elijah. She thought she could easily fall in love with Jonah and might already have. But she could not give up her life and hide away up here.

242

He hated strangers and any notion of a bigger world. She did not. She didn't want to hide from that world. She wanted to help heal it.

And her parents were down below.

"You didn't act improperly earlier, Jonah. I have feelings for you, too. You're important to me. And the children, too. So much more than I can say."

He faced her again. "Could you live here with us?" Hope lifted his words.

But Ada shook her head, slowly. "I don't think so. Not isolated like this." Never had so few words hurt so badly to say.

With a halfhearted nod, he looked back to the black. "I know. This ain't no place for somebody like you. You got too much t'offer. I'm real sorry I acted outta turn today. It won't happen again."

Starting that night, Jonah stopped sleeping in bed with her. He slept on the floor in the front room, and Ada didn't protest, though she lay sleepless and lonely until deep in the night, each night. He kept a gentlemanly distance from her all the time, but he continued on with his devoted care as she completed her recovery.

Just more than a week later, Doc Dollens finally cleared Ada for the ride down the mountain and offered to escort her and Henrietta home.

Jonah presented her with the clothes she'd been wearing the day she'd been hurt, all except her camisole. They were clean and mended, and showed hardly any sign at all of the trouble that had befallen her.

Bluebird wailed unconsolably when she said her goodbyes. Elijah blinked back stoic tears. Ada chewed on her lip and held her own tears off, too.

When Jonah offered to help her into the saddle, she took his offer gladly, and felt a melancholy pulse of thwarted hope when his hand lingered on her leg.

"May I still visit, on my rounds?"

He squeezed her leg, and looked up at her with his dark, sad eyes. "We'll be countin' the days.

Chapter Thirteen

The way was long, and the new trail was unfamiliar. It took nearly twice as long to come down the mountain as it had the last time she'd descended. By the time she and Doc Dollens reached her parents' gate, Ada had come to understand very clearly that she was not quite at full health yet. She was sore and exhausted. Her head pounded, and that cruel vertigo pulsed at the base of her skull, threatening to unleash its fury at the slightest wrong move.

They pulled up before the barn. Doc Dollens dismounted, but Ada wasn't sure she could manage it. The thought of swinging off the saddle and dropping down from Henrietta's tall back seemed some distance past what she was capable of.

The doctor was more than twice her age; he had delivered her and been the only doctor she'd ever known. But he seemed unaffected by the rigors of their journey. He came to Henrietta's side and lifted his arms. "Easy now, Ada. Let me help."

Grateful, she leaned carefully over, closing her eyes against the swing of the world, and let the doctor bring her to the ground.

"Ada Lee!" her father called as she steadied her feet beneath her. Holding the doctor's arm, she turned toward the house. Her father was hurrying, in his lurching, painful trot. Her mother stood in the doorway, her arms outstretched and her face wrenched with tears.

"Hey, Daddy," she said and let herself be wound up in her father's arms.

"Oh, Ada, oh baby. We was so worried!" There were tears in his tone, but she knew he wouldn't let them loose.

"I'm sorry. I'm alright."

He unclenched and leaned back to squint hard at her. "You look alright. But pale. Doc, she's pale."

"I'm tired, Daddy."

"It was a long ride, Zeke. Ada should rest now. But she's gettin' strong. She's alright."

Her father let her go and turned to the doctor. He held out his hand. "I can't thank you enough, Doc. I know we owe you — "

"We'll work somethin' out." Doc Dollens cut him off as he shook hands. "Don't worry 'bout that now. Get your girl inside and set her down." He smiled at Ada. "Y'alright?"

"Yes. Thank you, Doc." She followed a sudden impulse and kissed his cheek.

He seemed a bit flustered, but managed a smile. "You're a fine woman, Ada Donovan. Well, g'day."

The doctor mounted up and turned to the gate. Ada and her father stood for a moment and watched as he rode toward the road.

"Let's get you inside, Ada Lee."

"I need to tend to Hen."

"I'll get her in in a bit. F'now, she can rest a spell as she is. Come see your momma." He squeezed his arm around her, and Ada relented. They headed to the house, where her mother waited, her arms still stretched wide.

"Momma." Ada went into those arms.

"Oh, Ada Lee! Ada Lee! We missed you so!" Her mother had no qualms about crying, and tears streamed from her clouded eyes. She put her hands on Ada's face, tracing every inch with her fingertips, moving into her hairline. In that way, she found the scar, and gasped as her fingers traced its full length. It no longer hurt, but Ada winced anyway. She didn't want them to know how badly injured she'd really been.

"Oh, my baby. Oh, your poor head."

Tears welled in Ada's throat. She swallowed them down. "I'm all healed up, Momma. I'm alright."

"I knowed that job was dangerous. What'd I say?"

"Let's get her inside, Bess. She had a long ride." Her father offered his arm for her mother to take and led her into the house. He reached back for Ada's hand and drew her in as well.

Everything looked the same. How strange, for something so momentous to have happened, and everything else in the world had gone on just the same. She'd had a similar feeling when she was in teachers' school and away in Lexington for long stretches of time, but this, though it had been only a few weeks, was doubly intense. She almost felt as if she had died in that storm and been reborn at the top of the mountain, while the life of the woman she'd been had gone on down here without her.

Her father set her in his chair and led her mother to hers. He pulled up a smaller chair from the side of the room and sat between them, closer to her mother, so they could both look on Ada from the same vantage.

She could see an interrogation coming, and she would answer all their questions, but first she wanted answers to her own. "How've you been? Did I see the field planted?" It should have been — Chancey had been planning to help them do it as soon as he got his own crop in, just after she'd gone up the mountain on a rainy, grey, chilly spring day. But that had been weeks ago. They'd needed her to help them get it going and keep it tended. Normally, her few days off from her route had been spent

248

helping her parents here; they couldn't manage well without her.

She'd wanted them to let the field go fallow this year, let her wages support them wholly, but her father wasn't yet ready to admit he was too old to farm, and he didn't want to rely on the daughter he yet hoped would find another good man and make an attempt at a life on her own again.

"You did. Chancey's been helpin' out, and Mort Edwards and his boys, too. And we had a few men come by lookin' to trade some work for a place to put they head and some bread for they bellies. One man stayed around near a week, helped me out plenty."

Her parents had always been kind to wandering men, and had always been treated well by them in return. She was glad there had been help for them. "And Momma? How've you been?"

Her mother smiled and reached out her hands, though she was too far away to touch her. Ada would have left her seat and come closer, but she was afraid to tempt the vertigo.

"I'm good as ever I am," her mother said as she set her empty hands in her lap again. "We missed you so, Ada Lee. You sure you're feelin' good?"

"I am. I was hurt, but I was in good care, and I'm well again."

"The doc said you was with one of your liberry folks?" her father asked.

She chose her words carefully, unsure how her parents would react to know she'd been with a widower and his children. "Yes. A family up in a high holler. They found me and nursed me." The thought of Jonah's tender care came to life, and she closed her eyes so she could see him clearly.

"Well, we owe them ever'thing, then," her mother said.

Yes, she did.

Ada and her parents spent the day quietly. Her father wouldn't allow her to give him any help with his afternoon chores, but he and her mother were both thrilled to have her back in the kitchen. Her mother sat at the table with her, and together they made a nice supper of beef hash and cornbread.

Her mother stirred the cornbread batter, and Ada could tell that her thoughts were mixing up into words while she did.

"You don't have to take up that job again, Ada Lee. We'll find a way without it. We always find a way."

"I like my job, Momma. I'm helping people."

"You almost died doin' it."

Ada thought about how to rebut that statement without lying to her mother, but she was too slow.

"I *knew* it. You was gone too long for it to be anythin' but deadly. A whole month, Ada Lee. More'n that. It took you a whole month to get back home. Y'almost died."

"I didn't die, Momma. I'm well. Completely recovered."

"What happened? Tell me how I almost lost you."

"I don't remember that day, except I remember leaving home in the morning. I only know what people told me, and they only know what they put together from when I was found. The storm was bad. I got caught in a mudslide and hit my head on something. That's what you felt, the scar from that. I lost consciousness. Henrietta went for help, and I was rescued."

"Who rescued you?"

"One of my families on my route. Hen went to their house, and they went looking for me."

"That's what you said. What I'm askin' is who. Who do we owe for our little girl's life?"

Jonah lived closed enough to Red Fern Holler to use it as his trading place. Only a few hours' walk from his cabin. Ada's mother had grown up in Red Fern Holler. She'd come down the mountain long ago, and they'd gone back up for visits only once a year or so until Ada's Granny Dee had died, and then not again. Nearly two decades had passed since her mother had been to her birthplace.

What did she know of the Walker family? It couldn't be much, not as it was now. Jonah's whole family had been alive back then. He hadn't been married yet. Ada didn't know how old he was, but there was grey in his stubble between shaves, and strands of grey mixed in with his hair's dark blend of gold and brown. Faint lines on his face, at his eyes and between his eyebrows. In his thirties, she thought. He'd have been a young man somewhere in his teens when Granny Dee died eighteen years ago.

She wasn't entirely sure why such caution seemed necessary, but she wanted to keep Jonah and the children for herself.

"The Walkers."

Her mother frowned. Ada could see her stretching her mind back, trying to remember. "I don't think I know the Walkers … 'less it's Paul and Dolly Walker, way up above Red Fern Holler. That the family you mean?"

She didn't know Jonah's parents' names, but 'way up above Red Fern Holler' described Cable's Holler. "Yes."

Her mother nodded. "They come down to the church for near ever' service. Had a couple children, as I recollect. I remember a gangly boy was the oldest. And a little girl, I think." She shook her head and felt on the table for the baking tin. "That was before Momma Dee died, though. They must be all growed up now, with families of they own."

She poured the batter into the tin, and Ada used the opportunity to change the subject before the questions got more complicated. "I'll put this in the oven. Then I need to stir up the meat."

Ada wondered if she'd ever met Jonah or his family in those days. She imagined him as a gangly boy, tall and full of angles, and smiled. Had he been naturally quiet and shy? Or had life's sorrow pulled him so far into himself?

"You're goin' back to that job, ain't you?" her mother asked as Ada closed the oven door.

"I am. I'm going to ask Chancey to drive me in tomorrow or the next day. I need to collect my wages, and I want Mrs. Pitts to know I'm ready to pick up my route again before she gives it to someone else." She was immeasurably grateful that she hadn't been let go during this time, but eventually, Mrs. Pitts would have no choice. Ada couldn't tarry.

"I don't like it." Her mother sighed. "But if it makes you happy …"

"It does, Momma. It's good work, and I love doing it."

"The money helps, it's true."

The money more than helped. Ada knew better than either of her parents how necessary her wages were. "As long as I'm in town, I thought I'd pick up a few things. But I've been away awhile, and I don't want to miss anything. Will you help me make a list?"

That night, after she read to her mother from *The Mill on the Floss*, and shared a lingering goodnight with her relieved, grateful parents, Ada closed herself in her small bedroom. She stood in the middle of the threadbare rug and considered the space. The same room she'd had all her life. The same bed, the same bureau and mirror, the same chifforobe, the same bookcase, the same books. The lamps were the only fairly new additions; they'd had no electricity when she was growing up.

She opened the chifforobe and brushed her hand over her few dresses. Her fewer pairs of shoes were lined neatly on the bottom. Just as she'd left them. Everything was exactly as she'd left it a month earlier. There wasn't even any dust.

She was home, and she was glad. Being with her parents again, seeing with her own eyes that they were well, that their lives were as stable as when she'd left, experiencing that profound relief, Ada felt the full impact of the worry and homesickness she'd been afraid to focus on while she was in Jonah's care.

In Jonah's care. That was what she'd been — cared for. Tenderly. Lovingly.

Everything here was the same, except for Ada herself. She felt different. Inside.

She felt lonely. She'd missed her parents desperately while she was in Cable's Holler, but she was homesick here at home, now, too. For Cable's Holler. For Elijah and Bluebird. For Jonah.

She went to the window and pushed wide the faded calico curtains. A full moon shone over her parents' bit of land. It looked like a wholly different world from the one Jonah and his children lived in. That world was steep and full of shadows, and life had to be wrested from its trees and carved from its stony ground. Here, the hills sloped gently, and the soil was richer, without rocks and roots in the way. Even in this time of universal need, this world seemed a kinder place.

A breeze kicked up, pulling the curtains through the open window and making the old windmill weathervane spin and squeak. Whippoorwills and crickets sang in the rustling trees and grasses. Ada leaned out the window. As the wind riffled her hair and pulled strands loose from the braid, she took a deep breath. She knew these sounds, these scents, these sensations. She'd grown up in this world, in this place.

She was glad to be home.

But her home was now bigger than this. It wasn't only her and her parents anymore. Now it was Jonah and Elijah and Bluebird as well.

There was no way to bring the top of the mountain together with the bottom. Though she could ascend and descend between them in a day, they were worlds that could not be joined.

And this was the one that needed her most. It didn't matter what she needed.

So she would live as she'd been living. The Walkers had always been special to her, and they would continue to be. She could honestly say that she loved them. Dearly. But they were not her family, and could not be. She would visit, she would carry the world to them as she did for all the people on her route. And she would return here every night and take care of her own family.

Ada backed out of the window and closed the curtains. She worked the heavy denim trousers — which had once been George's — off, folded them neatly, and set them on the seat of the straight-back chair. She slipped her socks off and set them on the trousers. Standing before the foxed glass of her mirror, she studied her reflection. The poplin shirt she wore had been George's, too. She'd altered his work clothes as much as she could to fit her considerably smaller frame. George hadn't been fat, but he'd carried a bit of weight in his belly.

Ada had always run skinny. When she'd been a young girl burgeoning into womanhood, and her body hadn't grown like other girls' had, she'd been deeply disappointed.

She'd never developed the beautiful round hips and backside her best girlfriend Kitty had gotten, or a bosom like the one that made the boys chase Kitty around on Saturday night as if they'd die if she wouldn't grant them a smile, but she'd finally grown a little bit of a chest. Not much to crow about, but at least she wasn't flat.

George had found her lovely. He'd always said so. He'd been a romantic sort, good with pretty words she could believe.

Hair like fire, eyes like water.

Watching herself in the mirror, Ada unbuttoned each button, slowly. There was a mended slash in the fabric, near her waist; she lifted the shirt and studied it in the golden lamplight. Jonah had sewn the tear shut, with small, even stitches in a white thread. She opened the shirt. Her camisole hadn't come back to her, and she owned only one brassiere she kept for dressing up, so she had nothing on beneath the shirt. The long scar of her wound was red and raised. She traced its length with a fingertip and felt nothing but the tingly absence of feeling. Jonah had sewn this tear shut as well.

Standing alone in her tiny bedroom, she pushed George's shirt from her shoulders and let it drop to the floor. Wearing only her plain cotton panties, she considered her body in the mirror. That scar on her side was the only visible sign of the change she'd undergone. Otherwise, she was the same skinny redheaded girl with too many freckles—over her face, her shoulders, her chest, her arms, her lower legs, the backs of her hands, the tops of her feet.

Like you stood naked in a frecklestorm, George had said, laughing, on their wedding night, the first time he ever saw her body.

Not a girl. A woman. A widow. She knew what she'd had. What she'd lost. What was missing. What she wanted.

Ada closed her eyes and cupped her hands over her breasts. Only George had ever touched her in this way. Since his death, she'd touched herself a few times, imagining that her hands were his, but it wasn't the same, and it saddened her to pretend to have what she never could have again.

Now, as she drew her fingers closed over her nipples and felt them tighten, a shadow of that melancholy hovered over her. But her body thrilled to the touch nonetheless. Because it wasn't George she was imagining.

Jonah had never touched her like this. He'd seen all of her body, and he'd touched her intimately, because she'd needed his help, though she'd taken over the most intimate care at her earliest chance. He'd never touched her but to tend to her.

Except that day he'd leaned in and touched her hair, when she thought he'd kiss her. When she'd wanted him to and then shied away.

She didn't know his touch of desire. But she imagined it now. It was his hand she conjured, his body looming over her, his voice at her ear, calling her *darlin'* in his deep, slow voice, its natural cadence almost reluctant, as if words gripped his tongue, fighting to stay back.

Kneading her breasts, imaging them in his hands, his rough palms skimming her skin, Ada moaned softly and dropped a hand down, over her belly, into her panties. She slid her fingers over her mound, drew one through the wet between her folds.

His hand between her legs. His breath on her shoulder. His chest under her cheek. She moaned again.

"Ada Lee?" A sharp knock accompanied her father's voice. "Y'alright?"

Ada jumped and pulled her hand from her underwear. "I'm alright, Daddy!" She scooped up the discarded shirt and slid her arms back into the sleeves. "Just getting ready for bed."

"You sure? Thought I heard somethin' in there."

Embarrassment made her cheeks hot, and she trembled with the need she'd stoked to a blaze. Wrapping

259

the shirt closed around her, she opened her door a crack. "I'm fine. Truly. I'm a little chilly, though. I'm gonna close the window."

He nodded. "Good idea. Radio said there's rain comin'. Don't look like you'll get to town tomorrow."

She held back a sigh and made a smile instead. "Maybe the rain'll pass quickly. If not, I'll spend the day with you and go to town the next day."

"That's good. It'll be good to have you here with us." He pushed on the door a little, and Ada let it open another inch or two so he could lean in and give her another kiss good night. "You get some good rest, Ada Lee. Your momma and me're sure glad to have you back."

"I'm glad, too. 'Night, Daddy. Sleep well."

Ada closed her door and rested back on it, her blood burning with shame and need.

Chapter Fourteen

Chancey opened the passenger-side door of his truck and offered his hand to help Ada onto the sidewalk.

He was slow to let go of her hand, so she slid her fingers free with a firm but gentle determination. "Thank you, Chancey."

"My pleasure, Mizz Ada. How long you gonna be, you think?"

"Not too long, I don't expect. I just want to make sure Mrs. Pitts knows I'm ready to pick up my route again. Not longer than it'll take you to get to Holden and back, I'm sure."

Like last year, this spring had been too wet and stormy, and the crops were suffering for it—getting in late and getting torn up once they started sprouting. It looked to be another year of poor yields. Ada's family would get by because of her job. Chancey had taken on work as a hauler to help support him and his mother. He had a job today to haul a load from Callwood to Holden.

"I'm real sorry 'bout that. Hope I don't make you wait."

"Don't you worry, Chancey Maclaren. I'll occupy my time just fine. We'll meet outside the store?"

"Yes'm, just like always."

Before she turned toward the building, Ada checked her look in the truck window. She'd made a special effort today, wearing her best outfit—a navy blue dress with white polka dots and a white spread collar, and a narrow, shiny red belt at the waist. She wore navy Mary Jane pumps and carried a matching handbag. And a small white straw hat with a navy and red grosgrain band. The outfit was a few years old, and probably a bit out of fashion, but Ada always felt strong and beautiful when she wore it. George had bought her the whole ensemble a few weeks after their wedding and spent nearly *five dollars* on it.

She'd lost a bit of weight while she was ill, and the dress hung a bit loosely on her. Examining herself in the window glass, she shifted and smoothed the collar. She'd pinned it so it wouldn't gap at her chest and show her camisole and brassiere beneath it.

"You sure look pretty, Mizz Ada," Chancey murmured at her side.

Chancey was twenty years old. Since she'd come home after losing George, he'd been sweet and quick to blush around her, and she thought he might be a bit sweet on her, but always he'd been a gentleman. In the days she'd been home after her illness, he'd been doubly attentive, and Ada was beginning to wonder if he might be getting ideas.

She'd be twenty-seven in a few weeks. Far too old for him. Besides, her heart was split in two and not available. One half was in the ground with George, and the other half was up the mountain with Jonah. Both halves were lost in the impossible.

"Thank you, Chancey. I'll see you at the store this afternoon." She gave him her teacher's smile and turned toward the Pack Horse Library of Callwood, Kentucky.

Since she'd first gotten the job, back in autumn when last summer's leaves were just beginning to think about their more colorful wardrobe, Ada had come monthly to Callwood for the librarians' meeting. She hadn't seen the place this quiet since that first day. But today, there was only Mrs. Pitts, sitting at her desk, her typical grey topknot, round spectacles, and austere dress all neatly in place.

She looked up as Ada closed the door, and smiled when she saw it who was. "Ada! Welcome back!"

"Hello, Mrs. Pitts."

The woman came around the desk, and bustled her round body to her with her arms outstretched. Though the saddlebags she carried made it awkward, Ada took the hug, surprised and touched.

"It's so good to see you, dear. How are you?"

"I'm well. It's good to see you, too. I'm ever so grateful you kept my job for me."

"Come, sit." Mrs. Pitts took her hand and led her to a table near the stacks. Ada set the saddlebags on the table, and they sat down together.

"You were hurt on your route, Ada. Of course we kept your job for you. What's more, the people on your route sent word to me asking after you and wanting to know how to help you. You've made quite an impression. I would even go so far as to say you're beloved."

Emotion washed over Ada, and she dabbed her eyes with gloved fingers. "I love them, as well. I'm very much looking forward to returning to my route. I can start again tomorrow."

Mrs. Pitts patted her hand. "It's Wednesday, Ada. Why don't you take the rest of the week off and begin again on Monday? If you feel strong enough for the work. If you don't, take a bit more time. Your health is the most important thing."

Occasionally, if she turned too quickly, she felt a kick of vertigo, but it passed before it could do more than make the floor swing once or twice. Otherwise, she felt right again. She was eager to get back to work.

But she wouldn't mind a few more days with her parents, that was true.

"I'm healthy, Mrs. Pitts, and ready to work. I'll begin again on Monday." She set her hand on the saddlebags. "What I've got here is the last books I had with me, and the latest update of my ledger. I'm a bit behind, but I heard that some of my patrons organized book exchanges among themselves, so when I see them, I'll do what I can to reconcile my records."

"Excellent."

"Many of these books, I'm sorry to say, were waterlogged when Henrietta and I found our trouble. Some, I don't think can be salvaged."

"Well, let's see what we've got. Do you have any time today? If so, perhaps we could go through these and see what we can save for scrapbooks."

"I have a few hours, in fact. My neighbor drove me into town, and he's working most of the day."

"Excellent. In that case, how would you feel about helping me write some fund-raising letters as well?"

Mrs. Pitts worked tirelessly to find funds to buy more books or find people and organizations to donate books to the program.

Ada grinned. Since Doc Dollens had brought her down the mountain, she'd been trapped in a battle between pleasure to be home safely and misery to be away from Jonah and the children. Today, sitting with Mrs. Pitts, discussing their good work and how Ada contributed to it, she understood fully that she had, painful as it was, made the right choice. She couldn't give this up. She wanted both, but since she couldn't have both, she had chosen rightly.

"I'd be delighted."

When Ada said goodbye to Mrs. Pitts early that afternoon, she'd written a dozen letters asking for donations of funds, reading materials, or other items to support the program, and she and Mrs. Pitts had sat together and salvaged what they could from damaged books and organized them for rebirth in scrapbooks. They'd worked together, the two of them undisturbed by anyone off the street or even a ringing phone, and done several hours of good work.

Ada had admired Mrs. Pitts and respected her from their first meeting. Over the months, she'd gained a distant sort of affection for her, as a student for a teacher. When she left the library on this day, she'd realized that Mrs. Pitts was a friend.

She also had her wages from the previous month. Mrs. Pitts had offered to advance her the wages for this month as well, and excuse her from the next meeting, which was coming up in just more than a week. But Ada wanted to see her colleagues. She enjoyed meeting day. The other librarians were her friends, too—and she'd recognized that long ago.

Chancey wasn't yet waiting for her in front of Callwood Dry Goods, and she didn't see his truck parked anywhere nearby, so she went into the store with her purse and her heart full, ready to do some shopping. She and her mother had worked out a list. As her mother had become more accustomed to Ada's earning, she'd allowed herself a few small luxuries here and there, like a better quality of yarn for her knitting. Her blindness hadn't stopped her fingers; she'd simply invented a way to keep the colors straight, and kept count of her stitches as she always had.

Today, Ada indulged in a tin of cocoa powder. Her mother's birthday was coming up, shortly before her own, and she enjoyed Black Forest cake. They had plenty of cherries, from the little grove of cherry trees in the back yard, but chocolate was expensive. She smiled at the thought of her mother's glee when she got her favorite cake for her birthday.

For her own part, Ada didn't really enjoy cake. She preferred pie. For every birthday since she was tiny, her mother had made her favorite peach pie. She still did, though Ada had to help now.

As she carried her little basket of needs and desires, and let pleasant thoughts of her parents and childhood flow through her, Ada browsed the whole store. She considered pretty hats and dresses, fondled shoes and handbags. The store didn't have a great many things to choose from, but Ada enjoyed her browsing all the same. It was nice to indulge in fantasy from time to time.

When she came to the notions area, the yarns, threads, ribbons, and other supplies for sewing and crafting, Ada chose some soft skeins in pale blue and cream for her mother's newest project. There was a display close by of novelty ribbons, with little designs woven into the grain—tiny flowers, American flags, little ivy vines. And tiny bluebirds.

Tears filled her eyes as she lifted the satiny white ribbon with those little bluebirds flitting down the center. She'd brought the Walker children gifts a few times before. She'd always favored them, and their isolation from others allowed her to do so with little guilt. But what she felt for them now was more than simple favor.

Starting Monday, she'd pick up her route again and visit all her families. Including the Walkers. She would see them every two weeks, as she had for three-quarters of a year. She'd grown to love Bluebird and Elijah in those visits; she hadn't needed to see them more often than that to love them.

Maybe it would be enough?

Could it be enough for Jonah?

Ada plucked the card of ribbon from its post. She'd buy two feet, enough for two ribbons for Bluebird's lovely golden hair.

Now. What for Elijah? And something for Jonah as —

Oh, she had an idea. Was it good? Or was it terrible?

Ada stood before the embroidery and cross-stitch supplies, staring up at the displays of samplers and patterns, and wondered at herself. If it was a good idea, she could give Jonah something important, something to show him how deeply she felt about that family at the top of the mountain.

If it was a terrible idea, she could slice his heart in two.

Deciding she could think more about it while she worked, Ada put her hand in the bin of blue embroidery threads and picked a lovely, rich shade, and another just like it. Then she considered the shades of red.

Chancey was much later than Ada had anticipated, and the sun was low by the time he pulled up before the store. By then, she'd exhausted every browsing opportunity the store offered, had spent as much as she could afford to spend, had strolled the blocks in sight of the store on both sides of the street, and treated herself to an ice cream soda.

She didn't want to stand on the sidewalk waiting, and look like a woman on the prowl, so she sat at the soda shop and nursed her treat, watching out the window, beginning to worry.

Finally, she saw his truck. He pulled up outside the store, running a front tire onto the curb. He nearly fell out the door and stumbled onto the sidewalk.

He was drunk. Good heavens.

Ada gathered up her purchases and left the soda shop. She hurried across the street. Chancey had gone to peer into store windows, his face to the glass and his hands shielding his eyes, so she had time to get to him before he went into the store.

"Chancey Maclaren! You are late, and you are drunk!"

He whirled around and made a jigging step to keep his tenuous balance. "How do, Mizz Ada. Y'ready t'go home?"

She held out her hand. "The key, please."

"Wuh? No'm, I wouldn' let a lady drive."

"I am going nowhere with you behind the wheel in this condition, and you won't get home safely on your own, either. I'm driving, or we're both staying in Callwood this evening."

"Can't do that. Got my momma."

"Exactly. So I will drive." She shook her upturned palm at him. "The key."

He dug into his overalls and produced a key for the starter. Ada took it and went to the truck. She opened the passenger door and waited for Chancey to crawl in. Then she put her purchases in the back and climbed in behind the wheel.

She didn't drive often, and hadn't at all for nearly a year, but even her rusty skills were preferable to the drunken carnival ride Chancey would no doubt have taken them on.

"Yer so pretty, Mizz Ada," Chancey mumbled. He'd been slumped against the window the whole ride, in and out of a stupor. "Prettiest thing I ever knowed."

Ada ignored him and watched the road. It had taken her a mile or two to refresh her skills with a clutch, but she was smooth and confident now.

"Y'think you'd ever see me like a man? I'd be good to you. Treat you good. Take care so you'd not hafta do all that ridin'. Keep you safe."

Oh no. She'd sensed a change in his feelings for her; she'd been right. But he was drunk, and it would do no good to try to speak plainly with him now.

He reeled up and made himself sit straight in the seat. "I's a good man, Mizz Ada."

"You're drunk, Chancey. Just rest. We'll be home soon."

Suddenly, his hand came across the cab and landed on her thigh. His fingers began drawing the skirt of her dress up. "I'd treat you so good. Like you deserve. Not lonely no more."

She slammed her hand over his and filled her voice with teacherly censure. "Chancey, stop! At once!"

But he clamped down harder and leaned toward her, trying to get his hand under her dress and kiss her at the same time. She tried to fight him off and drive, but he was bigger and stronger, and soon enough the truck went off the road, into the ditch. The front end crashed into the side of the ditch, and the impact hurled them both forward. The steering wheel stopped Ada with a painful blow across her chest and chin, but Chancey went forward and slammed his head into the windshield.

Her lungs screamed for breath inside a chest made of broken glass. Her chin hurt, and her neck. The world spun and swirled in a way she'd grown hatefully familiar with.

But she was alright. Feeling all that, being able to breathe despite the pain, she was conscious and not horribly hurt. But Chancey had sagged back to the seat, unconscious. Blood pulsed down his face from a gash across his forehead.

"Chancey?" She shook his shoulder, and he moaned. "Chancey, wake up! Wake up!" She gave him a harder shake, and his eyes fluttered open.

"Huh? Ow. Huh?" He blinked and tried to sit up straight. "Ow, ow." His hand went to his forehead, then came back down, and he stared at the blood. "What hap—" He turned to Ada. "Oh, Mizz Ada. Oh, I'm sor—"

"Don't worry about that. We'll talk about that later, when you're sober and patched up. We need to get help. Can you walk?"

"I—I think so. How 'bout you? You hurt? Yer bleedin' too!" He reached out for her chin, but Ada jerked away. She hadn't known she was bleeding, but she knew for a fact Chancey Maclaren would not be touching her again.

"I'm so sorry, Mizz Ada. I dunno—"

"Not now, Chancey. Now, we need help."

She pushed open the truck door and got out, landing in the muddy water at the bottom of the ditch. Oh, her good shoes.

Fueled by outrage more than anything else, Ada climbed from the muddy ditch in her best clothes, went around the truck, back down into the ditch, and opened the passenger door. "If you can walk, Chancey, then walk. We need to get to help."

It was well past dark when Ada got home. There was a strange man with her parents, a wanderer who'd come by looking to trade work for a meal. It was a fairly common occurrence, especially during the warmer months, but the last thing Ada wanted to face at the moment was a strange man. She was ashamed of herself for it, but she couldn't even try to be cordial. She glared at him, and he receded to the barn, which she supposed he'd been offered for a bed on this clear, warm night.

Her parents had only begun to worry for her lateness, but when her father saw the wound on her chin and her generally disheeled condition, he exploded into a dervish of anxiety and carried her mother along with him. Ada was weary and sore, but she let them fuss over her for awhile, assured them she was scraped up a bit but otherwise fine, and then escaped to take a bath.

Her chin was swollen and ugly, and she was bruised from her shoulders to her waist, but they'd crashed only a mile or so from Doc Dollens' place, so in addition to helping get Chancey's truck back on the road, he'd patched them up. And taken Ada home, because she wanted no part of being alone with Chancey, not even after he'd sobered up.

She didn't tell her parents why they'd crashed. They assumed Chancey was driving, and that was good enough. They didn't need to know that the neighbor they relied most often on for help had tried to force himself on her.

As she lay in the tub in a bathroom she'd left dark, Ada closed her eyes. The fresh memory of Chancey's clumsy, drunken paws filled her mind, and she pushed it away with memories of Jonah. Holding her, comforting her, being gentle always, always a gentleman.

Right now, she wished she'd stayed on the mountain.

First thing Monday morning, before the sun had done more than promise to show up, Ada and Henrietta were back at work. Their packs were full of books, and they had a nice lunch to look forward to. Her chin still hurt a little, and her chest hurt a bit more, but nothing that would slow her down.

Turned out it was just as dangerous in the foothills as it was up high.

Her families were thrilled to see her, and by the time she and Henrietta took a break for lunch at one of their favorite spots, Ada knew she wouldn't be home before dusk. Everybody wanted to linger a bit longer than usual, hear her story, tell her how they missed her. By the end of the morning, Ada had turned the story of her trouble into an adventure tale, buffing up the scary parts to make them thrilling instead, and turning Henrietta into the hero she truly was.

In the afternoon, she reached Bull Holler. She passed the Devlins' place with a pang. It still abraded her conscience that she didn't stop there any longer, there were children there, and Mrs. Devlin, who might need her help, but Mr. Devlin had dragged her off Henrietta and punched her in the face once, and he wouldn't get a chance to hurt her again. She wanted to help, but not at the expense of being hurt like that. Falling down the mountain in a mudslide was one thing, even getting in the way of a bear, but she wouldn't put herself in the way of actual malice, of somebody who wanted to hurt her just to hurt her.

Especially not while she had stitches in her face already.

So she passed by the Devlins' place and rode deeper into Bull Holler. The rest of her families here met her at the schoolhouse, where she'd once taught, and as they saw her riding down the middle of the holler, people came out of their homes, or stopped in their work, and called out to her, waving and cheering.

Grinning so widely her chin stung, Ada waved back and called out greetings. By the time she pulled up at the schoolhouse, she was trailing a whole parade behind her. Children spilled from the schoolhouse doors into the yard calling out, "Mizz Ada! Mizz Ada!"

She was born to do this work.

"Bobbi Lynn Devlin," Ada said as she wrote the name in her ledger. "*The Wind in the Willows*. Oh, this is one of my very favorite books, Bobbi Lynn. I hope you like it."

Bobbi Lynn, the oldest of the Devlin children in school, dropped something like a curtsey. "Thank you, Mizz Ada."

277

Ada had taught her when she was just a little slip of a girl. Now, she was nearly at the limit of her schooling. Ada knew her father would pull her from school as soon as he was able. Bull Holler was too close to the world for her father to defy the law, but he wouldn't let her stay any longer than he had to.

Hugging the book to her chest, the girl walked off. That was the last of the line of people, young and old, who'd checked out books. She closed her ledger and began to pack up.

The schoolteacher, Miss June Avery, came up with a smile and began to help. "We're all so glad you're back, Mrs. Donovan. We've missed you so. The children were worried for you. We all were."

Mrs. Donovan. That was her name, and she loved it as much as she loved the man who'd given it to her. But a strange twitch ran through her at the sound of it. Somehow, it didn't sound right. She shook that off and gave the young woman a matching smile. "Thank you. It's so good to be back, and to be well. And thank you, Miss Avery, for helping out while I was indisposed. Without you, I don't know what would have happened to my route."

"It was all of us. Near everyone wanted to help, and that was what we could do. And please, call me June."

"And you should call me Ada." Ada finished packing her packs and folded the leather flaps over them.

"May I ask a question, Ada?"

"Of course."

"Do you think there's more work like you do? Other routes?"

Surprised by the question, Ada left her packs for later. She turned and leaned back on the teacher's desk. "Why do you ask? Are things not going well for you here?"

"No, no. They're wonderful. Perfect. I love this post. But ..." She glanced around the schoolroom. The children were buried in their new books, and the adults had left the schoolhouse and gone back to their work. "But I've got a beau. He's proposed."

"Oh, that's lovely. Best wishes."

"Thank you. I'm very happy, but ..."

But the school board didn't allow married women to be teachers. She would lose her post before she'd gotten all the wedding rice out of her hair. Just as Ada had.

"But you won't be able to keep your post."

"Right." She huffed with irritation. "It's such a shame. It's Jimmy Crowder, right here in Bull Holler. I'm going to live within sight of this very schoolhouse. But they won't let me keep teaching these children I care so much for." She looked to Ada. "You're married, though, and working. What you do, it's close enough to teaching. I know this is your route, and I wouldn't want to take it from you, but I'd be happy to take another. Jimmy's even said he might ride with me sometimes, if I got a job like yours."

"I'm a widow, June."

"Oh. Oh, I'm sorry."

"It's alright. And you're not wrong. Most of the librarians I work with are married. I don't know of an open route right now, though. When are you getting married?"

"I'm not sure. I haven't said yes yet, because I don't know if I can give up my work. Jimmy wants to save up a nest egg first, too. Maybe a year or so."

"Well, things might change by then. Here." She opened her pack again and pulled her ledger and pen out. Tearing a blank page free, she wrote down Mrs. Pitts' name and the address of the library. "This is the head librarian. She's a good woman. When you need a job, go on down to Callwood and see her."

June took the page, folded it carefully, and put it to her chest. "Thank you, Ada!"

"Does this mean you're going to tell Jimmy Crowder yes?"

"Yes, I think it does!"

Ada had taught Jimmy Crowder in his last year of schooling. He was about twenty-two years old now, she thought. June Avery was probably about the same age. Only five years younger than she, but she felt suddenly old.

When she approached the gate to her family's home early that evening, Chancey Maclaren was sitting on the big, sunk-in boulder that marked their drive. That boulder was etched with symbols: two crossed beams, like a letter T, meaning the family gave food in exchange for work; a squiggly line, meaning they'd offer help if a man were hurt or ill; and a symbol like a smile with two round eyes, meaning a man might be allowed to sleep in the barn. That one had a little teardrop as well—the barn's roof leaked. One of the wandering men had explained these symbols and others to Ada last summer. There were checkmarks around the symbols, which meant others had come and agreed with them.

Chancey stood and pulled his hat from his head as she and Henrietta walked up. His forehead was black and blue and tracked with stitches.

Ada reined Hen to a stop. "Chancey, what are you doing here?" She hadn't seen him since Doc Dollens had sent him off home that night last week.

"I wanted … I needed …" He ducked his head and stopped. After a few big breaths, as if he were about to lift that boulder out of the ground, he looked up said, "I'm real sorry, Mizz Ada. I did you wrong. I did you wrong, and got you hurt."

"You did, yes."

"I don't know what got inta me."

"Whiskey, by the smell of it."

Dejection rounded his shoulders as he nodded. "It was them fellas in Holden. After I dropped off the load, they wanted me to go with 'em for a beer. I didn't think there's no harm in it, but then they kep' goin' and goin'."

Ada didn't drink. But she'd seen enough drunks to know once it started, it wasn't easy to stop. "You're forgiven, Chancey. Go on home."

"I can't, Mizz Ada. I 'member ever'thin' about that night. What I did was wrong, but what I said … I meant that. If you'd have me—"

"Chancey, stop. Please stop."

He stopped, and turned up such a pathetic face Ada nearly laughed—not with humor, but with pity. She mastered the impulse, however, and took on a teacherly attitude.

"I don't feel like that for you, Chancey, and I won't. You've been a very good neighbor and great help to my parents. I appreciate everything you do for them. But you're not more than a neighbor to me." Last week, she would have said he was her friend, but she was still too angry for the way he'd behaved to give him even that.

"I ruined my chance, didn't I?" he asked.

He'd never had a chance. "Find yourself a girl better suited to you, Chancey. Someone young, who'll look up to you."

"You're young. You're beautiful and young and smart and sweet."

Ada didn't answer. She looked down from Henrietta's back and waited for him to get it through his thick head.

"Alright. Good night to you, Mizz Ada." He put his hat on and slumped off down the road.

Chapter Fifteen

At the end of her first week back on her route, Ada pulled Henrietta up before the Cummings General Store in Red Fern Holler. Though she'd visited this holler often enough as a young girl, when Granny Dee lived here, there hadn't been much she remembered about it before she'd begun her work as a librarian. In the nearly year that she'd been riding the mountain, she'd rekindled old acquaintances and even gotten to know more about her own people on her mother's side.

The highest real community on the mountain, Red Fern Holler was small — only about eight homes in the holler itself and another six that could get to it within an hour's walk — but most of those homes held eight or ten or even more people, in several generations, and more than a hundred people called Red Fern Holler home. The Dickerson family held *five* generations; Big Pap Dickerson was nearly a hundred years old. Their cabin was a funhouse of half-thought-out additions, and not even in a schoolyard had Ada known as much commotion as went on throughout every day in that house, but she enjoyed sitting beside Big Pap and reading the Bible to him, and listening to his stories so old they were history.

The Cummings' store was at the head of the holler, and no one had seen her arrive yet. Ada had dismounted, untied her packs and slung them over her shoulder — she'd developed a callus near her neck from their heavy weight — and was climbing the steps up to the door when she first heard her name called out.

"Mizz Ada!"

She turned and grinned at the young man who stood on the path below her, pulling off his cap. One of Big Pap's great-grandsons. "Hello, Orville!"

"How do, ma'am! It's real good to see you!"

"Thank you! I've missed seeing everyone here. I'm going in to see the Cummings for a moment, and then I'll be by."

"I'll get out the word!" Orville Dickerson set his cap on his head and trotted into the holler.

By most standards, the Cummings' store didn't amount to much. They'd given over the front room of their moderately spacious cabin to the enterprise, and the room showed signs of a family life being lived around the wares for sale — the chairs beside the fireplace, the basket of knitting on the floor beside one; the kitchen at the back, framed off with a wood counter where Esther displayed her pies and other sweets; the stiff family photos on the mantelpiece. On laundry days too cold or rainy for wash to hang out, the Cummings' family laundry was swagged across the store.

The stock was neatly kept and arranged, but it was sparse, compared to a business like Callwood Dry Goods. More than anything else, this little store was a trading post, where mountain people brought what they could make or hunt or grow and traded it for something else they needed. There wasn't much in the way of real 'store-bought' merchandise the store could offer up here. Hez relied on barter nearly as much as anyone else in these parts; his store was just the nexus point for the transactions. But he did have a few things for sale: mainly sturdy clothes, tools, ammunition, milled grains, some household supplies, and a few special items like spices and sweets.

Red Fern Holler was a good two miles or so from any path wide enough to accommodate a full-size wagon, and at least twice that far from anything a car or truck could navigate. When Hez Cummings needed stock from the world below, he and his sons brought it up on their mules. Like others who lived in such remote locations, for bigger hauls he had a small, narrow cart that could be fitted with runners in the winter or thick wheels in warmer seasons, to be pulled by animal or man over the steep, rocky terrain, but that was hard duty, and used sparingly.

For the most part, Hez met a hauler at the farthest reach a truck could make it and carried his stock up the rest of the way on his mule.

She went into the store. Hezekiah Cummings must have heard her talking with Orville; he was already making his way to the door.

"How do, Mizz Ada!" He held out his hand, and Ada handed over her pack for him to carry. He didn't like women to exert themselves if they didn't have to.

"Hello, Hez. Something smells delicious. Is Esther around?"

"Esther!" he yelled, and then gave Ada a sheepish smirk. "She back in the house, tidyin' up. She got huckleberry pies bakin' — that's what you smell. How you feelin'?"

"I'm well, thank you. And thank you so much for helping get books shared while I was ill."

"'Twas all Esther's doin'. When she gets it in her head somethin' needs doin', ain't no soul on this earth can stop her."

The woman in question hurried up from the back of the house, wiping her hands on her apron. "My laws, Mizz Ada! We heard tell you'd be with us again soon! How you doin'?" She put out her arms, and Ada took her embrace happily.

"I'm well, Esther. And so grateful."

"Pssh." She waved the thanks away. "'Tweren't nothin' 'tall. Jus' a 'scuse for folk to get together and have a good time." Esther set her hands on her ample hips and squinted up at Ada. "Fact, how'd you feel if we made a reg'lar thing of it?"

"What do you mean?"

"Well, you know, we got the meetin' house, but these days, we's only got a sometime preacher come up ever' now and again, and we ain't had a teacher goin' on ten years now. We do what we can for God on our own, and for the young'uns, too. Mostwise, the meetin' house stands empty, though. But while you was ailin', we all met up there with the books we borrowed, and it was a right nice time. How'd you feel if we kep' that on, even now you're back? We can all meet you there, and do it up like we been?"

"That would be lovely, yes. I'll still visit the families that can't get to the meeting house, but I think a book party would be wonderful."

As Mrs. Pitts so often said, the Pack Horse Librarian program was about much more than simply delivering books. They were not merely a different kind of postal service. Pack Horse Librarians made connections— between themselves and their patrons; between their patrons and the writers of the books, and the characters and stories in them; between the mountain and the world below; and even among the people here in this quiet world above, where life was hard and people hunkered down sometimes and forgot they had neighbors.

They carried the world.

"I'll send Eddie out, have 'im round people up," Hez said.

"Orville was outside. He said he'd spread the word I was here."

Hez nodded and went out the front door, still carrying Ada's saddlebags.

Esther hooked her arm around Ada's. "Would you like a cup? I got tea and coffee brewin'."

"Coffee would be wonderful, thank you."

Esther led her back to sit at the narrow wood counter where her sweets were displayed. As she made up cups of coffee for them both, she asked, "You been up Cable's Holler yet?"

There was a tone in her question Ada recognized—the friendly, and mainly sincere, interest of a neighbor, but a tinge of hunger for gossip, too. "Not yet. That'll be my next stop today." And her last.

"Jonah Walker was real worried 'bout you in that storm. He come flyin' down the mountain 'fore we even opened up for the day, yellin' for help. Hez hadta drag Eddie from a full sleep to send him down for your doc."

She handed Ada a cup of hot coffee and sat down beside her.

Ada sipped her coffee and let Esther's observation go without comment. Of course there would have been some talk in this holler, where Jonah was known, that Ada had spent a month alone with a widower and his two children. The talk was probably not so far off the truth that had flowered during that month, which only made this moment now all the more awkward.

"Jonah, he's a good man. Rough 'round the edges, but a good man. I watched him grow up, y'know? Saw what he was like as a boy. Wasn't like he is now. I guess you know his wife died right after havin' Bluebird."

"Yes, I know." Though gossip made Ada uncomfortable, she found herself riveted now. To hear news of Jonah from the view of someone who'd known him always? That was a gift she'd not expected.

"He never was a giddy sort, but he was happy enough before. But that—'twas a sad, sad, thing, and him up there with two little babes, all on his own. Now and again, when he had need, he'd come down with 'em both strapped to him, front and back, and it was like two sweet, fat cherubs ridin' a ghost. 'Twas years 'fore he was like a livin' man again, though he still hunkered 'long the edge, not wantin' nobody's notice." Esther studied Ada for a moment before she went on. "Most life I ever saw in 'im in years was that day he come down for help for you."

Ada cleared her throat and took another sip of coffee. This time, Esther waited, letting the silence grow.

Finally, Ada said, "He took good care of me." She couldn't think of anything else to say that wasn't dangerous or private or both.

After another few moments of silent study, Esther nodded. "The Lord works in mysterious ways." She took a big swig of her coffee. "Well, I reckon the Walkers'll be pleased to see you."

Elijah and Bluebird were thrilled to see her. They both raced from the house as she dismounted, and Bluebird flung her little arms around Ada's legs with a squeal. Ada crouched low and pulled her into a snug, happy hug and accepted her flurry of wet kisses all over her face.

"You have a boo!" Bluebird fussed when she saw Ada's chin. She'd taken the two stitches out last night, but the cut was still red and a little sore.

"Just a tiny one. For just a tiny little accident. Like when you tripped on the steps and scraped your knees."

"That hurt real bad." She patted Ada's chin lightly.

"Yes, but it healed up fast, and you can't even see now, can you?"

The sweet girl stepped back and lifted her little dress — faded and worn at the hem, but clean, as always — and examined her unblemished knees. "Nope, can't see nothin'!"

Ada stood and went to untie her pack. "And how are you, Elijah?"

"I'm good, Mizz Ada. I read the whole book all the way through twice. I got some questions for the author man, though." He'd become fascinated with motors and engines, and the last book he'd borrowed had been a history of the railroad in America.

She drew the pack from Henrietta's back. "Do you? Well, would you like to write a letter and ask him your questions?"

His blue eyes went wide. "That's somethin' I could do?"

"Of course! I can't guarantee you'll get an answer, but there's no harm in trying."

"I'd like that, yes ma'am." He took Henrietta's reins and began to lead her to the barn.

Jonah always did that. Always. "Where's your father, children?"

"Pa's huntin'," Bluebird said and then sighed. "He goes huntin' ever'day now."

"Not ever'day, Blue." Elijah looked at Ada. Though he was only nine and innocent of nearly all the world but what she brought him in books, she detected a shade of understanding in his eyes. "Jus' the past few days."

The past few days. When he might have expected her to arrive for her usual visit. He wouldn't have known exactly when she'd be back, because she hadn't known exactly when she'd start her route again. Ada knew without asking that Jonah had first gone out a few days after she'd said goodbye, and if she hadn't arrived back at Cable's Holler today, he would have gone out every day until she had.

He was avoiding her.

She stared out at the quiet forest for a moment, hoping against hope to see him coming through the trees. Then she filled up her lungs with fresh air, squared her shoulders, put on a smile, and took Bluebird's hand.

She'd missed these children desperately. She wouldn't let her disappointment ruin her reunion with them, even if that disappointment was sharp enough to break her heart.

She didn't see Jonah for another month.

Not until her third visit since she'd started her route again. Nearly six weeks since she'd said goodbye and he'd told her they'd all be counting the days until they saw her again.

Well, the children had counted the days. But if Jonah had, it was only to make sure he was gone when she'd be there. It was even worse than it had been at first. Then, he'd always been there, though he'd kept his distance. Now, he was away from the house completely.

'Hunting.' They must have had a packed smokehouse, then.

Every time she rode into Cable's Holler, the children were there, celebrating her return, but they were alone. She'd tried to wait him out on her last visit, but she'd lingered far too long and had felt her way down the last few miles in deep dark. If the moon hadn't been nearly full, she would have had to stop and make camp in the woods, and she thought her parents might not survive the strain if ever again she didn't come home when they expected her. Especially not on a fair summer night of good weather.

By her third visit, umbrage had swamped her disappointment and sense of loss. She'd spent the month between her first visit and this one reliving every moment she'd shared with him, from their first words to their last, second-guessing her interpretations of his words, gestures, and acts. She tried to deconstruct her feelings as well, to tell herself that she'd been no more than ill and weak and grateful, that she hadn't fallen in love with him, but she'd failed. She knew her mind and her heart.

Sadly, she hadn't known his.

So she focused on Elijah and Bluebird, reading to them, listening as they read to her, talking to them about her life down below. She gave Elijah the simple form letter from the author he'd written, and shared his innocent joy at those few impersonal lines. She went out with them to see the growing kids and chicks. She sat at the table with them and helped them learn more than only reading. She gave them lessons on penmanship and writing, and on history and arithmetic, and she had plans to teach them art and music as well. She saw them only every other week, only a few hours at a time, but she was set on feeding their bright, hungry little minds as much as they could hold.

They were sitting at the table together and she was showing them a children's book about the American Revolution when the floor creaked heavily and they all turned toward the sound.

Jonah stood in the doorway. The day had been hot, as hot as it got this high on the mountain, and he wore only a cotton knit shirt, like one of his union-suit tops, under a set of faded overalls. He stared right at her.

"Pa!" Bluebird cried and got up to run to him. "You came for Mizz Ada!" She clutched his legs, and he set a hand on her head and tousled her hair lightly. His eyes didn't leave Ada's.

"Elijah, take your sister out back and start your chores."

Elijah rarely questioned his father, and he didn't do so now. He got up from the table and went to his sister. "C'mon, Blue." He led her out the front door.

Ada stood and smoothed the front of her clothes, self-conscious to be standing before him in dungarees and one of George's refitted cotton shirts. Which was patently absurd—except for the time she'd worn his dead wife's clothes, he'd seen her in nothing but men's clothes. In fact, he never had seen her in clothes she'd bought or made only for herself.

She had a green cotton scarf tied around her neck, and her braid wrapped around her head, because the midday had been muggy and hot, and she didn't like the feel of sweat running down her back.

"Ada," he said, almost too low to carry across the room.

"Jonah." Ada's tone was crisp, the way she'd spoken to sassy schoolchildren. She was hurt and angry, and she didn't bother to hide it.

"How are you?"

"Perfectly well, thank you."

He took a few steps into the room. Caught between competing needs to go to him and to keep her distance, Ada stayed right where she was. Her hand came up and caught the knot of her scarf.

"You know why I been stayin' away?"

Ada didn't respond. She desperately wanted to know the answer to that question, but she'd lost the ability to speak.

"I can't say goodbye to you again."

She hadn't expected an answer like that.

She cleared her throat and made words come. "Then why are you here now?"

"'Cuz I couldn't stay away no more."

"Jonah …"

"I know, I know. Nothin's changed. I'll get my head straight 'bout it. I reckon that's what I'm tryin' to do now. See you, then say goodbye, and try to go on 'bout livin' till you come again."

A month ago, she'd thought she might ask him if they could try to be closer, even though they couldn't be together all the time, if they might love each other when they could and, as he'd just said, go on about living until they could be together again. But that month had passed, and she'd been hurt. Now she understood that he was hurting, too. They'd only hurt more if they got closer.

So she didn't ask. Instead, she smiled and said, "I'm glad, Jonah. I've missed you, these past few visits."

He nodded but didn't speak.

Ada went to her pack. "I … I have something for you."

She'd piqued his curiosity, at least, and he finally came all the way to her. "What is it?"

Reaching into her pack, Ada closed her eyes and sent up a prayer that he'd take the gift as it was intended. She pulled out a carefully folded bundle of white linen and held it out to him.

He examined his hands before he took the bundle from her. Ada was touched by that care. He didn't want to dirty up her gift.

As he opened the linen, he bobbled the other piece inside it, and moved quickly to the table and set it down to finish unfolding. He spread out the piece and frowned down at it, and Ada fretted. She'd known from the start that to do this might be an overstep she wouldn't be able to retract.

An embroidered sampler commemorating Bluebird's birth. He had one for his wedding to Grace, and one for Elijah's birth, but Grace hadn't lived to stitch one for her daughter.

Ada had wanted to give him that token for Bluebird, but she'd known from the moment the idea had occurred to her that Jonah might think she was doing something only Bluebird's mother had a right to do.

Of course, he couldn't read it. Ada stepped to his side and reached out a trembling hand. But before she could explain, Jonah traced a finger over the bluebird in the center.

Ada had little talent for drawing or painting, but she could turn a nice stitch. She'd designed it herself, to be as close to natural as she could make it — the bird blue and white, with a soft red throat, perched on a branch full of dogwood blooms. Just like Elijah's sampler, it had Bluebird's first and middle name, and her birth date — Elijah had explained why the day was marked on the calendar hanging by the door, and she'd worked backward to the year — and then at the bottom, in the traditional way of samplers, the alphabet in three rows of the same colors. A scrolled border finished the piece.

His finger moved from the bluebird to the name above it. "Is … is … is this her name?"

At his question, Ada's doubts broke apart and blew away. His voice was full of wonder. "Yes. Bluebird Hope."

Jonah ran his finger over the stitches in each letter and spoke them aloud. "B-L-U-E — "

"Blue," Ada interjected.

"Blue," he echoed. "B-I-R-D — Bird?"

"Yes." She set her hand on his back. He was trembling, too.

"Bluebird." He swept his finger under all the letters of her first name, then began to trace the next. "H-O-P-E. Hope. Bluebird Hope." He stood straight and turned to her. "I never seen my baby girl's name before."

There was so much emotion in his face, in his eyes. His features had drawn in and pulled tight, and Ada thought it was pain she saw. Pain she'd caused.

"I'm sorry if—"

She couldn't get the apology out because Jonah's mouth was on hers. He'd clamped her head between his big, hard-worked hands, and covered her mouth completely with his own. She couldn't even take in the gasp the act had provoked.

His hands gripped her head painfully tight. His mouth ground on hers, rasping the pinprick stubble of his beard against her lips and cheeks and chin. He was trembling; those strong hands shook against her head— and Ada's heart sang. She could hardly breathe, could hardly think, and she didn't care. This was what she'd wanted for weeks, for weeks and weeks. She hooked her hands around his wrists—

He reared back, snatching his hands from her grasp, and gaped at her, panting and flushed.

"I'm sorry. Ah, Ada, I'm—"

"NO!" Ada lunged forward and caught hold of the bib of his overalls before he could reel backward more, out of her reach. "Don't be sorry, Jonah. Please don't be sorry! I want it! I want you!"

If she'd had a moment to think, maybe she'd have tempered her words. Maybe doubt or self-consciousness— or her lingering fretfulness that to love Jonah was to be

300

unfaithful to George—would have stilled her tongue. But she was overcome and breathless, and all she could think was to keep him, not to let him out of her reach again.

"Ada?"

"Please, Jonah. Don't go away."

He laughed, just two short syllables, too blunt to be a chuckle but not much more than that. Ada thought it might have held the first glimpse of true humor she'd ever seen in him, though it was cloaked in melancholy. "You're the one goes away, darlin'."

They both went away from each other—Ada down the mountain, and Jonah into the shadows. But he was right: she would need to go very soon, in mere minutes, so she didn't travel home in the dark.

She didn't care, and she didn't want him to care. It would be enough. They could make it enough. She tugged on his overalls. "Please."

Instead of coming to her, Jonah put his hands on her arms and drew her to him. He brought her all the way, until she was pressed firmly to his chest, and she craned her neck to keep her eyes on his.

He licked his lips.

Ada licked hers.

He bent his head.

She rose up on her toes. She lifted her arms, and he let them go, sweeping his hands around her back, wrapping each arm fully around her.

His mouth reached hers. This time, the touch was gentle, even hesitant. He brushed his lips over hers, back and forth.

Ada set aside every single thought in her head and devoted her whole self, mind and body and soul, to physical sensation.

He was so big and hard, and yet so gentle, so soft. Ada felt the silky-spiky touch of his lips and stubbly mouth through every part of her body, the pleasure rushing with her blood through even the tiniest of veins. Her fingers tingled as they curled into his hair. Her toes curled in her boots. Her heart pounded, filling her ears with the rhythm of her very life. She ached and throbbed in her deepest places.

He groaned softly, and his lips parted. Ada felt the touch of his tongue, and opened her mouth. Her tongue touched his, and she felt it like a starburst. It set off something in him as well — his hold of her tightened, and he lifted her up so her toes lost contact with the floor.

Her body touched his from her mouth to her toes. She felt his desire for her, pressing firmly against her thigh. An impulse shot through her, to wrap herself around him, to coil her legs around his waist and capture that part of him at the point of her body where it belonged, but she shoved the urge away. That wasn't the kind of woman she was. Not even married had she behaved in such a way, and this was her first kiss with Jonah. Or her second, she supposed, though she hadn't had a chance to participate in that first one.

Remembering himself, Jonah set her back on the floor and ended the kiss. He stayed close, however, resting his forehead on hers, bringing a hand up to slide it along the side of her head. "You are an angel," he murmured.

The light in this room had dimmed noticeably; the sun had set below the walls of the holler. The valley that was Cable's Holler was narrow and steep, and they were high on the mountain, so dusk came earlier here than elsewhere, but still — Ada had to go soon, or she wouldn't get home while there was any light. The moon tonight would barely be a crescent; the night would be pitch dark and dangerous.

If only she could stay the night. But her parents would worry.

She closed her eyes and blocked out the waning light. She held on to this man, who held on to her.

He moved to kiss her again, but stopped just before their lips met. Frowning, he leaned back, setting his hand on her chin. With his thumb, he brushed the scar, which was still red, but fading. "What happened here?"

"A silly accident." He didn't need to know more than that.

With a glance at her eyes, he accepted her statement as truth and kissed the scar. His lips skimmed up from that point to her lips, and Ada opened her mouth at once. She could kiss him like this forever.

The children chose that moment to return to the house. Talking together, they clomped onto the porch. Elijah was explaining about how chickens made eggs, and not getting very close to right. Ada made a note to add animal husbandry to her lessons.

With a breathy chuckle—and yes, that little laugh truly was free of anything but soft, sweet feeling—Jonah set Ada from him and turned to the door.

Feeling nearly as dizzy as she had when her head had been wounded, Ada gripped the back of the nearest chair and tried to reclaim some sense of equanimity.

Barely fifteen minutes later, Jonah walked Henrietta to the front of the house while Ada said goodbye to the children. He fixed her saddlebags behind her saddle and stood at her horse's head to watch her walk toward him.

Elijah and Bluebird were on the porch, arm in arm, waving. With that youthful audience, Ada refrained from falling into Jonah's arms. She simply smiled up at him and didn't touch him.

"Well, take care. I'll be back in two weeks."

He gifted her with another chuckle. What a wonderful sound that was, the light waft of humor from his deep chest.

"Ada."

As her name came from his lips, he took her hand and pulled her close. Right before his children's eyes, he bent and kissed her. His mouth was closed, and it didn't last long, but she was woozy nonetheless when he lifted his head from hers.

He studied her eyes, moving back and forth as if he read her thoughts. She saw the same thoughts, the same feelings, reflected in his dark eyes.

"I'll be countin' the days," he murmured. He stepped back and offered his hand to help her into the saddle.

Chapter Sixteen

Carrie Mae Kinder took one of Ada's scrapbooks down from a shelf. "I made that recipe for whatucallit — them stuffed peppers. 'Cept I didn't have no green peppers, so I scooped out some green tomaters. Didn't hold up too good." She blushed as she handed the book over to Ada. "Got some grease on the page. I tried to clean it up, but the words got smeared. Sorry, ma'am."

Inwardly, Ada sighed. If the words were smeared, she'd have to replace the page, and she'd typed that recipe up at the library. Outwardly, though, she smiled. "Don't worry, Carrie Mae. Recipes are supposed to get stained. That's what happens when they're used and enjoyed. I'm sorry the green tomatoes didn't work."

"Oh, they worked fine. I just mushed ever'thin' up and served it up that way, and they all ate it good. Made the squirrel meat taste real nice. You know squirrel usually got that funny smell, but with the 'maters it smelled fine."

"Well, that's good, then." She tucked the scrapbook into her pack and pulled out her ledger. As she sat down to write in the newest entry for the Kinder family, she glanced out the side window and saw that, up the hill, the roof had caved in on the Hooper cabin. She sighed. Sweet old Mr. Hooper had caught the same cold Ada had gotten the previous winter. He'd been so weak already, he'd apparently died within an hour of the fever setting in. Mrs. Hooper's family, the children who'd grown and left the mountain, had come and collected her, taken her from the only home she'd ever known, and in the months since, their old cabin, which had nurtured generations of life, was abandoned and falling to the will of the mountain.

"I hope Mrs. Hooper's happy," she mused.

Carrie Mae went to the window and peered out. "I know she is. She got her grandbabies all around her. And they in Georgia, where it's warm all the time. Sometimes, where you always been just ain't home no more, and you gotta make yourself a new one."

Home wasn't a place. Home was people. Without Mr. Hooper, that house she'd shared with him, and the mountain it was built on, was nothing but a place.

Ada finished her entry and returned the ledger to her pack. "You're right, of course. Is there anything else you need before I go?"

Carrie Mae turned around. "Next time, you think you could bring up one of them Hollywood magazines?

Dottie and Homer went all the way down to Callwood for they anniversary, stayed in a hotel and ever'thing, and they went to a pitcher show. Dottie ain't stopped talkin' 'bout it since. *A Star Is Born*, they seen. You know it?"

"I've heard of it, but I haven't seen it." Ada had only seen two pictures in her life, both with George, while he was courting her: *The Public Enemy* and *Dracula*. "I'll see if I can get a recent copy of a celebrity magazine for next time." Mrs. Pitts would probably have something to say about that; she thought reading material should be 'significant' in some way—by which she meant enlightening, practical, or thought-provoking. Convincing her that a celebrity rag was any of those things would take all of Ada's rhetorical skill.

"Thank you, Mizz Ada! I'd sure love to see them stars."

Reading should also be enjoyable. Fantasy and daydreaming had their benefits as well.

Ada had spent no small portion of her hours alone on the mountain engaged wholeheartedly in daydreaming. In a few days, her route would finally take her back to Jonah. She'd been filling the days without him reliving their kisses in every detail.

The Kinders were her last family on this day's route. Though she had more stops on this day than any other, and the day was usually almost as long as when she saw Jonah and the children, today Elmer Kinder and their boys had been out fishing. Only Carrie Mae and their baby girl at home, and Carrie Mae was making the most of her nearly empty house. Ada's visit there was much shorter than usual, and when Henrietta put her hooves on the road that led home, the sun hadn't yet touched the horizon.

Ada felt good. She had a couple hours of daylight left—a rare treat on her riding days—and it was a good summer day, with a blue sky full of puffy white clouds, the fresh, rich smell of a green mountain in the air, and a breeze soft enough to blow the humidity away without tossing things about. She and Henrietta had been treated to a nice lunch with one family, and a cool rest with fresh strawberries and cream with another, and now she'd be home in time to make a good supper for her folks. Henrietta would even get a chance to play in the pasture for an hour or so before she got put up for the night.

As she rode toward the gate, she decided she was going to take a long bath after supper and put some drops of rose water in. She'd lie there in candlelight and think of Jonah.

The first glimmer of disquiet she felt came while she was unsaddling Henrietta and brushing her down. Normally, her father came out when she got home. Either he met her as she rode up, or, if he was feeling sore and moving slowly, he showed up while she was grooming Hen. The few times he hadn't come out at all, he'd had a very bad day and was having trouble getting around at all.

She revised her plan for a long, soaking bath. Instead, she'd draw a bath for her father and put some salts in.

After she turned Henrietta loose—the horse celebrated with three big kicks and then tore off toward the trees—and tidied up the grooming supplies and her tack, she went out the front of the barn. The sun had met the horizon, and its color had deepened to ruddy gold. The house was quiet. No lights were on, but her father was slow to use electricity and never turned lights on until they were fumbling around in the dark. These days since she'd had this good job, Ada was more liberal in her use; she didn't like to squint at her ingredients or her stitching, or her books, so as soon as the natural light dimmed enough to obscure her purpose at all, she turned on the electric variety.

There was nothing particularly unusual around her—not precisely normal, but not beyond the reach of her experience. The most likely situation was that her elderly father, who worked far too hard for a seventy-five-year-old man, had had a rough day and was resting.

And yet Ada approached the house with foreboding.

She went in the side door, as usual, into the kitchen. It was dark and quiet. Two mugs were upended on the drainboard beside the sink, but there were no other dishes out, either clean or dirty. The coffeepot sat on the cookstove, but the fire wasn't lit.

For both her parents to be resting—sleeping—at this time of day would be highly unusual. In fact, it had never happened, in Ada's knowing.

"Daddy? Momma?" she called out, but not loudly. Something, some sixth sense, tamped down her voice. She got no response.

Now, Ada was truly frightened. Something was wrong. Very wrong.

In an act of pure, unreasoned instinct, she eased open a drawer and pulled out carving knife. Easing her way, careful where she put her feet, brandishing the knife before her, she went to the front room.

The first thing she saw was the radio. That gift she and George had saved for was smashed on the rug in the middle of the room. A table was upended, and the lamp that sat on it was shattered.

Where were her parents?

"Daddy? Momma?" This time, she barely made a sound at all. Her throat had cramped with fear.

She fumbled on the wall and pushed the switch, and the single lamp left in the room flickered on. That one bulb threw long shadows from the far corner, but Ada saw enough. There was a dark stain on the old rug, and a dark smear trailing from it, toward the hall to the bedrooms and bath.

Still holding the knife so it pointed outward, Ada crouched and put her fingers in that smear. It was cold and tacky. She brought her fingers to her nose, but she knew what she'd smell: blood.

"Daddy? Momma?" Tears landed on her chest, inside her shirt.

Pointing the knife toward the back of the house, Ada followed that sweep of drying blood.

Her father lay prone in the hallway. She saw his feet and legs first, and the hall was dark. She was falling to her knees in the sliver of floor at his side before she saw his head and face. His head was bloody and oddly shaped, with a strange blunt edge near the back, and a depression where blood had made a pool.

His eyes were open.

Remembering what she'd been taught, she lifted his wrist and checked for a pulse she knew she wouldn't find.

"Daddy! Daddy! Oh no!"

From her bedroom, her mother moaned.

"Momma? Momma!" Ada jumped up and hurried to her parents' bedroom, trying to remember to be vigilant but desperate to get to her mother.

She found her on the floor, curled into the narrow space between her bureau and the wall. Her arms were wrapped over her head.

"Momma! Momma!' Ada dropped the knife and ran to her. When she tried to hold her, to check that she was alright, her mother flinched and cried out.

"It's me, Momma! It's Ada!"

"Ada Lee?" She flung her seeking hands out, and Ada let her feel her face. "Ada Lee!" Her hands clawed at Ada, dragging her close. "Ada Lee!"

"I'm here, Momma. I'm here. I'm here." She held her sobbing mother as hard as she could.

"Is it over? Is he gone? Where's your daddy? Where's Zeke?"

Ada had dropped the knife in her hurry to get to her mother. She didn't know if it was over, or if the man who'd done this was gone. But she did know where her daddy was.

Ada burst into tears.

"I smell it."

"What?"

"Your daddy's blood. I smell it. He's gone, ain't he?"

She didn't know how long they'd sat together, wound together. Their tears had stopped at some point. When Ada lifted her head and looked around, night had fallen.

"Yes." The word broke in two as Ada said it.

But her mother didn't cry again. "I think I felt him go, when it happened."

Ada tightened her hold around her mother's small body. Now that the initial burst of cruel shock had eased, Ada could think around her heartbreak, and her mind spun, sorting out all the things that had to happen now, all the things she had to do.

First, she had to know they were out of danger.

"Momma, I have to check the rest of the house. I have to make sure the one who did this is gone." She had no idea who he was. In her mind, he was a monster, worse than anything the nightmares of her childhood had designed.

"No! No, baby girl, don't!"

"Momma, I have to."

"Don't leave me!"

"Momma, please. You were safe in this hiding place before. Just stay right here, and you'll be safe still." She didn't know that to be true at all, but she couldn't lead her blind mother around the house while she made sure the man who'd murdered her father was gone.

"I don't care about me, Ada Lee. I don't care if I live or die. But I don't want you hurt!"

Ada's chest was full of clawing beasts, tearing her heart to shreds. "Momma. Please. I have to check." She wrenched herself free from her mother's desperate grasp, fumbled in the dark for the knife, and went out of the bedroom.

She closed the door quietly. There were only three other rooms to check—her bedroom, the bathroom, and the little added-on room where the gas heater was. She pushed on every switch she came to and brandished the knife through each doorway.

They were alone. Just her mother and her, and her father's dead body.

In her room, her bureau drawers were open, and her things tossed about. She had only a few belongings of any real sentimental value, and only one thing of actual value.

The little box that had held the slim gold band that was her wedding ring was open and resting atop one of her brassieres.

Though there was space in the velvet for two rings, only hers had rested inside the box. She'd buried George with his ring on his finger. She'd taken her ring off on the first anniversary of his death, put it back in its special box, and tucked it at the very back of this drawer, for safekeeping.

That box was empty. Her wristwatch and the little gilt compact were missing as well. All her treasured gifts from George.

Had this been a robbery? Had one of the wandering men her parents so often welcomed into their home turned on them?

But they had nearly nothing of value to anyone but themselves. Wedding rings. A radio. Nothing else. Nothing worth a life. Her father would have given up any meager possession to keep his family safe.

Anything of his own. But would he have fought to his death for her wedding ring? Her father, who'd held her close so many nights as she'd grieved? Had he done that?

Ada's stomach howled at the thought. She bent over and vomited on her bedroom rug.

When she was empty, she reeled to her bed and sat down. She couldn't tarry; her mother was terrified. Ada had to make things right.

How could she? Her father was dead. Daddy was *dead*.

Another wave of nausea crashed over her, but she forced it away. No. She had to think.

She needed help. She needed the sheriff. She needed somebody to find the man who'd done this and make him pay.

Finding she couldn't yet let go of the knife, Ada pushed it through her belt and went back to her mother.

She was curled in the corner, just as Ada had left her. She gasped and flinched as the door opened.

"It's me, Momma. It's safe. Whoever it was is gone."

"Dick."

Ada helped her mother to her feet. "Who?"

"He said his name was Dick. He come to the house this mornin', lookin' for some work and a meal. He worked out in the field with your daddy, and they came in 'round lunchtime. Weren't long after, they was yellin' and smashin', and I hear your daddy moanin'. Then he jus' stop. Ever'thing went quiet. I don't what happened, but he said his name was Dick."

Ada cupped her mother's face in her hands. "Momma, listen. We need help, and we can't wait for a neighbor to come along. We have to go get help. We need the law, and I don't know … help. We just need help. You have to come with me. We're going to go out to the barn, and I'm going to hitch Henrietta up to the cart, and we're going for help. Understand?"

"We can't leave your daddy!"

"Momma! Daddy doesn't need us anymore." Ada clenched her face to fight a new wash of tears. Her mother's understanding finally came fully together, and she burst out in keening wails of grief.

Ada picked up her mother's hand, set it at the crook of her own elbow, and led her from the bedroom.

When they went through the hall, and Ada helped her around her father's body, her mother stopped and went to her knees. Still sobbing, she felt around until she found her husband's head, and she bent and kissed his bloody face.

"Find our boys, Zeke," she whispered as tears coursed down her creased face. "Find our boys and wait for me."

When she stood again, her face was covered in her husband's blood. Her tears collected blood as they ran down her cheeks and dripped red stains onto her housedress.

The sight was so horrible, somehow worse than her father's broken head, that it stopped all of Ada's volcanic emotions cold. Suddenly, she was made of stone, as dead inside as a statue. She had nothing in her mind or heart except her list of things she needed to do.

She led her mother out of the house, set her on a haybale, and went to call Henrietta back to the barn.

318

"Here. Drink this." Doc Dollens pushed a mug across the table at her.

Ada peered into the amber brew. "What is it?"

He sat in the chair across from her. "Just tea. Chamomile and honey."

She put the cup to her mouth and took a sip. The warm liquid slid down her throat but didn't warm her dead insides.

After another sip, she set the mug on Doc Dollens' kitchen table and looked across the table at him.

"How's Momma?"

"She's not hurt, Ada. I gave her something to settle her nerves, and she's restin' in the back room, but it don't look like he touched her at all."

That was something, at least. She hadn't thought her mother had been hurt, except in her mind and heart, but it was good to know for sure.

But her father was still lying dead in the hallway.

"I need to be at the house." She moved to stand, but the doctor set his hand firmly on hers and held her in place.

"No. Sheriff Guthrie's there, and he wants you both away so he can see how things are. I told Chancey to follow after, so he can see, too, and let us know anythin' Joe keeps to himself."

A humorless, numb laugh fell from her lips. Chancey was at the house, looking on her father's body, in the middle of this most personal business. She couldn't seem to unwind that boy from her life.

"You think you can talk to me about what happened? Maybe I can help you put things straight in your head."

Ada shook her head. "It happened while I was on the mountain. Momma said a man came to the house looking to work for a meal. He said his name was Dick. She heard a fight, but she didn't know any more." She turned and looked out the window at the black night. "He killed my daddy. They needed me, and I was gone, and now Daddy's dead."

The doctor took both her hands and shook them firmly. "That'll be just about enough talk like that, young lady. If you'd been home, maybe you'd be dead now, too."

The sound of an approaching motor claimed their attention before Ada could respond or think how she might.

"That'll be Joe, I imagine."

"I don't want him disturbing Momma."

Doc Dollens stood. "Then come on. You'll have to talk for her as much as you can."

She would have to take care of her mother. It was just the two of them now, Ada and her elderly, blind mother, and Ada couldn't leave her on her own.

Not for anything.

Or anyone.

Part Four

Chapter Seventeen

The crash and grunt stopped Jonah in his tracks.

He was heading back to the house, a brace of grouse and a surprisingly plump turkey slung over his back. He'd sighted two deer, but they'd been does with fawns at the teat, and he shot only for buck unless he was desperate. He wasn't desperate. The heavy rains of both spring and summer hadn't done his patch any favors, but they'd made lush grazing in the woods, and hunting had been very good for months. He foraged for wild-growing greens and fruits, and the patch was yielding enough to keep him and the children fed. He might not have much to trade with to put variety in their winter eating, but they'd keep fed, at least.

Now, he crouched behind an old fallen tree and set his kills on the ground. That grunt had been a bear.

Bears weren't really predators. Come across a panther in these woods, and you had a fight on your hands, or better yet a flight, unless you were a quick, sure shot. Panthers were meat-eaters, and a man was as good eating as anything else with warm blood. They stalked their prey, creeping silently through the woods, and attacked with full force. Fortunately, panthers preferred night hunting. You might come across one in the day, but it didn't happen often.

Bears, on the other hand, ate just about anything, from berries to meat to garbage, and only attacked to defend themselves or their space. Primarily day creatures, though they got up to some mischief in the dark, too, they were much more likely to cross a hunter's path. But if you lay low and let them mosey on about their bear business, more times than not, they didn't much care about men.

If you shot at one, however, you'd damn well better strike true. You were unlikely to get a second chance. And a true shot wasn't so easy; a bear's fur was so dense it was armor.

From his blind behind this thick, decaying trunk, Jonah scanned the area, looking and listening for the bear. Another crash and grunt alerted him to the direction, and he narrowed his eyes and studied the sun-dappled rise to his left. The underbrush was moving rapidly. Reaching back, he grabbed his 30.06. He preferred the bow, but this wasn't hunting. Neither he nor the children liked bear meat, and he had no need of the fur. If he shot this bear, he'd be protecting himself. The rifle was the better choice.

He braced it on the trunk and sighted in the direction of the noise and the fluttering ferns.

The bear bumbled into view, about a hundred feet away. Well in range. Placing his finger along the trigger guard, Jonah got ready. He'd let it go unless it made a move right toward him.

It grunt-roared again and slammed its head into the trunk of tree, almost as if on purpose. Then did it again. As it reeled away, Jonah frowned. That bear was skinny. Far too skinny for August, when it should be well into its efforts to fatten up for a winter's sleep. Was it sick? He looked up from the rifle and narrowed his eyes, trying to get a clearer understanding of the beast's strange behavior.

Reeling like a drunk down the hill, coming closer, it stopped and plopped onto its rear. Both front paws came up and went to its head, in a bearish caricature of a man with a headache. Or not a caricature at all. There was something wrong with the bear's head.

It dropped its paws, and Jonah saw the problem. Its head was caved in on one side, so severely that the eye on that side was misshapen. The injury had happened some time ago; any open wound was healed over. But that side of the bear's fur was filthy and matted.

There was no further evidence, nothing to say with certainty what had happened to this beast, but Jonah was certain nevertheless. This was the bear that had attacked Ada and Henrietta in the storm. Whether they'd been attacked before the mudslide, or after it, he didn't know, but at some point, their troubles had included a bear, and he was sure the same one was before him now.

Henrietta had caved in its head in the fray. He was sure of that, too. That horse was braver than any he'd known before.

Weeks — months, in fact — had passed since that spring storm. The bear had survived but was badly compromised. It wasn't able to fend well for itself. Jonah wasn't sure if he was acting out of mercy or revenge, but he aimed his rifle at the seated, miserable bear and put a bullet through its broken skull.

It fell over at once. Jonah cocked again and waited, aimed, to see if another shot was necessary. Its bony side heaved once, twice, three times, and then the bear let out a loud, miserable sigh and was still.

Rifle in hand, he leapt over the trunk and went to the carcass. He stood over it and considered what to do. He'd gone out today intending to hunt fowl, which he had done. If he'd come across a hearty buck, he might have tried for it, but he could carry a field-dressed buck over his shoulders. Even this skinny, damaged bear would be too heavy to carry like that, and he hadn't brought the litter with him.

It seemed a crime to leave a kill like this behind, but they weren't in such straits they needed to eat meat they didn't like — besides which, this mess of a bear was so skinny its ribs and hipbones showed under its dense coat.

That meat would be doubly bad—and possibly suspect as well.

He considered the coat. It was filthy, but otherwise good, except for around the head. An idea struck him. This was the bear that had almost killed Ada. She was to be with them again in a few days. That was enough time to get it salted and dried and set up for tanning.

What would she think if he presented her with its skin? Would she understand the gift as he intended it?

He thought of the gift she'd given him, the sampler that showed him Bluebird's name for the first time, and that put her name on the wall beside her brother's, where she belonged. That empty space had been like a hole in his heart, an infected wound, always pulsing its ache, reminding him of what he'd lost, what Bluebird would never know.

Now that space wasn't empty any longer. Not on the wall, or in his heart, or in their lives.

Grace was gone now. He knew she would never be back. But he didn't feel abandoned—nor did he feel unfaithful. She'd stayed as long as he'd needed her. She'd eased his way into a life without her, and she'd left when she'd known he was healed enough to go forward on his own.

What he might have with Ada, what he might build with her, he didn't know. It didn't seem like it would ever be akin to what he'd had with Grace, if they saw each

329

other only a few hours every two weeks. But it was good, and it would be enough. He felt something like happiness pushing through the black soil in his heart, and that was something he'd never thought he'd feel again. He wanted to protect her and love her and honor her, and that urge fulfilled him.

Could a bearskin, this particular bearskin, possibly convey all that, the way her delicate stitchwork and its sweet sentiment had told him how she felt?

Ada was a lady, refined and delicate. But she was also a mountain woman, strong and steadfast.

He went back to his gear and got out his field kit.

The next Mizz Ada Day was a bright, clear summer day, so warm and still that even the high perch of Cable's Holler was a little uncomfortable. The heat didn't slow the children down at all. They buzzed all day with excited energy, and Elijah wrote down a list of all the things he wanted to make sure got done before Ada got there, and make sure he showed her and told her when she arrived.

Bluebird wanted to wear all the different ribbons Ada had brought her at once, and she arrayed all the little tokens—the toy bluebird, and the winter hat, and a little plastic flower ring, and a picture book of her very own—on the porch railing.

Normally they were excited on Mizz Ada Day, but today, their buzz seemed doubly happy. Or maybe Jonah was simply sharing in it for the first time.

Every other visit for all the months she'd been coming, Jonah had felt some kind of discomfort: a wariness of strangers, or suspicion that she was getting too close, grief for the way Grace disappeared, or jealousy that his children, who did not remember their mother at all, were falling in love with her, or angst over the way his own feelings were changing. Finally, since she'd been hurt and he'd taken care of her, since he'd fallen in love with her as well, these past few visits, he'd felt a deep, pulsing kind of needy regret.

Then she'd given him that wonderful gift and he'd done something he shouldn't have done. He'd been so overwhelmed with love and need that he'd kissed her without thinking, without asking, without knowing how she might react.

She'd wanted more.

What that meant for them, Jonah couldn't say. Everything he'd said to her that night on the porch remained true: her world was bigger than his, and she brought good wherever she went. He couldn't keep her hidden away in the back of his lonely holler.

But he couldn't leave it, either. Not simply because it was the only home he'd ever had, but because he couldn't live down there among all those people, in that place he didn't know and would never comprehend.

His world was too small for her, and hers was too big for him.

So they'd have these little slivers of time. For Jonah, feeling hope and anticipation for a future, even a future mere hours away, for the first time in long years, these little slivers were more than he'd dreamed to have. He could only hope they'd be enough for Ada as well.

"Hold up, baby girl." He lifted Bluebird's floury hands off the ball of dough. They were making a wild blueberry pie for Mizz Ada. "What you doin'?"

"I wanna roll the dough. I'm big now. I can do it."

That had been her refrain all summer long, since she'd outgrown her shoes. She was big now, and could do it. Whatever 'it' was. She'd gotten a few hard lessons about what she wasn't yet big enough to do, but soon enough, she'd be nearly as capable as her brother.

"Alright, but let me help." Jonah pulled her to stand between him and the table. He scattered flour and brought the dough over. "First we gotta flatten it out a little and get it soft enough to work." He put his hands over his daughter's and taught her to make pie crust.

A skill he'd learned when there hadn't been anyone else to do it.

The sun was setting, and she hadn't come.

This time, Jonah didn't try to tell the children not to worry. The last time he'd done that, Ada had been lying in freezing water, on her way out of this world. So no, he didn't try to tell them there was no cause to worry. He was disquieted himself.

He wasn't naturally inclined to overreaction, and he understood that Ada was probably safe. Most likely, there had been some kind of inconvenience, and she was merely delayed. She had no quick or easy way to contact him if something had come up in her world that held her back.

But he remembered every second of that morning, every detail of what he'd seen at the bottom of that mudslide. How badly she'd been hurt. How close she'd come to dying.

So he hoped with all his heart and soul that she was merely inconvenienced, but he acted as if her life were in danger.

Dusk was on the holler, and night came fast inside its deep walls. But the moon should be nearly full, and the day had been crystal clear. He could get down to Red Fern Holler at least, and see if anyone had word of her there.

In the spring, he'd left his children in the house and gone looking for her—but then, Henrietta had come. He'd known something was wrong, and that it had gone wrong close enough to his home for Henrietta, badly hurt, to get to them.

This time, he didn't know what, if anything at all, was wrong, or where it had gone wrong. He didn't know where Ada lived, except that it was in Barker's Creek, which was far down in the foothills. He might have to go all the way down to the world below. On foot. He didn't know anything about that world, except that it was dangerous and strange.

He might be gone for more than a day. He might not make it home.

He couldn't leave his children. So he'd take them with him, at least as far as Red Fern Holler. Maybe he could ask the Cummings to watch over them.

And what about the homestead? The animals? If anything happened to their meager livestock, his whole little family would die before the winter froze hard.

Maybe he could ask for help for them, too.

Jonah didn't like to ask for something unless he had something to offer in return. But this was Ada. He needed to know she wasn't hurt again. He couldn't wait for a sign that the most reasonable, most likely, most benign answer was true. He had to know she was alright.

The people of Red Fern Holler loved her, too. While she was healing, she'd told him her momma's people were from there. To help her, they'd help him. Even if he had nothing to offer.

They needed to get moving before the night creatures, like panthers, stirred.

His children looked up at him with eyes full of worry. Bluebird had tears on her cheeks.

"Alright, children. We're goin'. Elijah, get that pair of boots you growed out of last, see if they fit your sister. I need you both to keep quiet and close to me, and boy, I want you to carry the .22."

When they made it to Red Fern Holler, the moon was risen, and the sun had set well behind the mountain, but there was just barely enough of the last gleam of daylight in the sky to feed Jonah's eyes. They hadn't met any kind of trouble on the walk.

As they'd approached signs of other people, Bluebird's worry for Ada had, in the way of young children, been dampened by her excitement. He hadn't brought the children down for more than a year. Esther Cummings treated them like special guests when they came, and Bluebird remembered her sweets and her hugs.

The holler was quiet and mostly dark. The store had closed up, and people were in their homes for the night. Looking up through the center of the holler, Jonah could see the faint glint of candlelight and lamplight in a few windows. All he cared about was the Cummings, and there was a glow in the store windows as well.

Taking the .22 from Elijah so the boy didn't make a mistake and drop the barrel down while Jonah was asking for help, he led his children onto the porch.

The door opened before he could knock, and Hez Cummings stood there, a rifle in his hand as well.

With a quick sweep of his eyes, he nodded. "Jonah. Here 'bout Mizz Ada, I reckon."

If Hez knew that, Ada hadn't made it to Red Fern, either. Jonah didn't know whether to consider that good news or bad. "Yeah. She weren't here neither?"

"No. We was jus' talkin' 'bout it. C'mon in." As he stepped back and cleared the door, he grinned down at Elijah and Bluebird. "How do, children. You growed a heap since you was here last."

Elijah stepped over the threshold and held out his hand. "How do, Mr. Cummings."

Hez laughed and shook his hand. "You're a good boy, Mr. Walker." He crouched to Bluebird. "And lookit how pretty you is, Miss Bluebird!"

Bluebird blushed and twirled her hair.

Jonah took a breath. His children would be well cared for here.

Back at the kitchen, Esther was coming around their table, headed for the front of the store. Their two sons, Eddie and Bert, both nearly grown, stood beside chairs at that table and watched.

Hez leaned his gun on the wall beside the door. "Set your gear here."

Jonah did as he was bid.

Esther corralled his children into a hug together and looked up at him. "Come sit. We was talkin' 'bout whether to worry."

"I'm worried. I'm goin' to find her."

Shifting her glance to her husband, Esther stood, then turned her gaze back on Jonah. "I knowed there'd be somethin' between you."

Jonah didn't answer, because he was too stunned to make words. The notion of people thinking about him when he wasn't around defied comprehension.

Everyone stood in a silent, awkward circle for a moment, as if nothing more could happen until he spoke.

"I need help."

Hez nodded. Esther stepped to Jonah and set her hand on his arm. "We'll keep the children with us. They'll be safe." She turned and smiled at Elijah and Bluebird. "How's that sound? You can help us in the store tomorrow. We went strawberry pickin' yes'day, and I'm making strawberry tarts in the mornin'!"

"Pa!" Elijah turned stricken eyes to Jonah. "I wanna go with you!"

"No, boy. I'm goin' now, in the dark. It's too dangerous."

"I can shoot! I can help! Mr. and Mizz Cummings c'n see to Blue! She don't need me! I can go!"

He was not leading his nine-year-old son down the mountain at night. "Elijah, no. Enough."

In the first fit of temper Jonah had seen in his son since he was just a toddling boy, Elijah stomped his foot and made a sound like a growl. The burst of bad feeling frightened his already anxious sister, and she began to cry.

In the way women always seemed to know what was needed, Esther immediately gathered Bluebird up in her arms and carried her to the kitchen.

Jonah went to his son and lifted his chin so the boy couldn't help but meet his eyes. He didn't try to avoid it. Instead, he glared up, his blue eyes full of righteous fury.

"It's dangerous, boy. You don't have enough skill in the woods yet. I'll go faster on my own."

"But what if somethin' hurts you, too?" Elijah's anger had dissolved and shown the true feeling: fear.

Jonah crouched down. The boy had grown so that from this position, Jonah had to crane his neck a bit to keep fixed on his eyes. "I promise I'll be back. I'll find Mizz Ada and be back. And when we're home together where we belong, I'll take you huntin'. Build up your skills."

Elijah nodded, somewhat mollified. Jonah stood again and faced Hez.

"Don't know how long I'll be. I got the animals up at the house."

"I'll send my boys up to see to things, till you're back."

In more than seven years, he hadn't trusted a soul with his home or his family, but now he had no choice. He'd asked for help, and he'd gotten it. He didn't hesitate to take it. "Thank you, Hez. I don't know how I'll settle this up with you, but I'll do it."

"Ain't no debt here, Jonah. We all want to know she's alright."

Chapter Eighteen

Large spans of this mountain were dense forest from the hills to the peak. Despite the moonlight, the way was deep with dappling shadows. Though he'd reached the Cummings' place in the last moments of twilight and hadn't tarried more than half an hour, it took Jonah the whole of the night to make it to the place he thought was Barker's Creek, nested in the rolling hills that were the roots supporting his own home.

In those hours of dark, Jonah had heard all manner of creatures roaming with him, and seen a few sets of eyes catching the moon's glint, but he'd been careful and quiet, and they'd let him be.

He'd kept the best eye out he could for Ada as well, looking and listening for signs of trouble, but he'd found nothing. No disturbance of the path, no cry for help or whimper of pain nearby. No Henrietta without her rider. No dropped gear. So he kept walking, and his hope grew that it had truly been mere inconvenience that had kept her from her route.

He cleared the forest in new sunshine, while the air was yet thick with the night's dew, and approached a small farmhouse. As he scanned the property—the large planted field, the neatly tended yard, the house with its solid porch, a barn with a bright red roof—he heard the slam of a wooden door and squinted in that direction. A man, woman, and boy who looked to be a bit older than Elijah had come out a side door together. They were walking to that big barn.

A creek burbled on the other side of the path, and Jonah was fairly sure it was Barker's Creek. But the last time he was here—many years ago, granted—it was still thinning-out woods this close to the creek, with no one living in easy sight of it. From where he stood, he could see three other homesteads, spread out on the downward slope from where this path became a road.

Had he taken a wrong way somewhere in the dark? Was this a different creek? Was he lost?

All he could do was ask.

Following the split wood fence that framed the homestead from the widening path, he came to a cross-beam gate across a gravel lane about ten or fifteen feet wide. In one direction, it led into the property, between the house and the barn. A red truck was parked near the barn. In the other direction, the lane arced onto the path Jonah was on, and here that path became a road. Where Jonah stood, it was maybe three feet wide and nothing but trodden dirt. But straight ahead, it became a real road, the likes of which didn't exist in his world. Paved smoothly with gravel and wide enough for two trucks to pass each other by. It was framed on either side by a narrow, deep ditch. The one nearest Jonah was about half full of water.

Sunk into the ground beside the gate was a sign, but Jonah could make no sense of its words. On the wood post that held the sign up were rough symbols, carved into the wood. He didn't know what those meant, either.

He needed to know where Ada was, and all he could do was ask. He hooked his rifle on his back, so he wouldn't appear ready to use it, and jumped this homestead's fence.

The family had gone into the barn. He headed toward it.

He was still a good twenty feet from the door when the man came through it. He had a shotgun in his hands, double-barreled and aimed at Jonah's chest. Jonah threw up his hands, as if they might shield him.

"We don't want yer kind here. Git yer beggin' ass off my land 'fore I blow it off!"

"I ain't a beggar. I'm lookin' —"

The man cocked the shotgun noisily and stalked forward. "You ain't deaf, so you knows what I said. Git!"

Jonah back-stepped quickly, keeping his hands up and his eyes on that shotgun. But he couldn't leave without asking. "Donovan! I'm lookin' for the Donovan place!"

"Ain't no Donovans 'round here. Git movin'!"

Donovan was her husband's name. He didn't know her family name. Were those the Red Fern people? No—her mother's family was from up the mountain. He didn't know her father's name.

He was at the gate. "Ada! I'm lookin' for Ada!"

That got the man to fire a barrel—not at him, but not far off to his side. "Next one goes in yer face. You lowlife no 'counts leave that poor woman be! Scum like you done enough already! GIT!"

Jonah vaulted the gate and ran down the road.

Now he knew for a certainty that Ada was near. He also knew with the same certainty that she was in trouble, but he didn't know what, or how he'd find her, if every homesteader behaved like that one had.

He'd have to keep trying.

He stopped at every home he came across, though he was much more cautious now, ready for the worst. He started telling them right off that he lived up the mountain, that he wasn't one of the men they called hobos, that he was worried about his friend.

It didn't matter. He faced three more gun barrels, and even those who didn't threaten violence wanted no part of him. Whether they ran him off with a gun, or just yelled at him, or didn't answer the door at all, nobody told him where Ada lived.

Something very bad had happened to her, though. Something down here in her world. As he failed again and again to get anything other than malice and threats from her neighbors, he put the picture together in his own head. A hobo had done something to her. Hobos were wandering men. They didn't come up on his mountain, and he'd only heard a stray remark about them here and there in Red Fern Holler. All he knew was that they were strange men walking the roads, looking for work, or a place to sleep, or simply a handout. Beggars.

And they all thought he was one of them. He was a poor man, and he didn't have much of worth in his life but his life itself and the lives of his children, but never before had he felt of less account than on this day. He looked down at his raggedy overalls and his cracked, curled boots, and he saw what these farmers saw: a hobo. A man with nothing. A man who didn't belong.

A man like that had hurt Ada. The notions that thought conjured, the things a man could do to hurt a woman, had Jonah's belly juices boiling. He'd hoped a mere inconvenience had happened, something she couldn't avoid and couldn't get word to him about, but no kind of pain. He'd been wrong.

But she was alive, at least. The way these people expressed their anger and suspicion toward him, he understood she was alive. Badly hurt, but alive. Not gone from him.

The people here knew her. They were her neighbors. Eventually, one of these houses would be hers. So he kept trying.

He came to a part of this village that seemed more familiar to him. The houses had more age and wear on them. The next gate was closed, as most of them were. A big grey rock was sunk into the ground beside the gate, for purposes Jonah couldn't cipher. It had had symbols marked on it, like he'd seen elsewhere, but these had mostly been rubbed away or marked out, and a large, angry "X" scratched over the smeared patch. Letters were written beneath it as well, in equally angry strokes, but he didn't know what they meant.

It gave him pause, all that anger struck on the rock. He considered the little farm on the other side of that gate.

There was a rusting truck parked next to a weather-beaten grey barn, leaning in a way that Jonah, who knew nothing about trucks, could see it didn't run. There was a little white house with a tidy grey porch. The roof on the barn looked ready to give up, but the roof on the house looked new, or close to it. A raised round patch of flowers bloomed in the yard. Weeds were starting to clutter up the flowers. The planted patch—an acre or so in size—needed tending as well.

The only signs that anyone had been home in a week or more were the chickens ambling about in their yard.

No—over there.

Jonah crossed to the other side of the gate and squinted into a pasture. It seemed empty, but a copse of trees bounded it on the far side, and Jonah thought he saw ...

A big bay horse, grazing amongst the trees. Too far away to be sure, but he was sure anyway. A mare. Henrietta.

He'd found her.

The gate wasn't locked, so he pulled the hasp and went through.

In the rush of excitement that he'd found her, and his hurry to get to her, Jonah forgot his caution. He was ten feet from that grey porch when the screen door crashed open and a young man—not much more than a boy, though he had a man's size—stormed out. He, too, had a rifle, and he didn't bother to brandish it.

He shot it, running down the steps right at Jonah.

White-hot fire tore through Jonah's middle as the shot found its target. It took him off his feet and sent him flying back. He landed hard on the grass near that round bed of flowers, his own rifle pinned uselessly beneath him, and heard the rifle cock again.

Elijah. Bluebird. The faces of his children rose into his mind as he understood he would never see them again. At least he hadn't left them in the cabin alone. At least he'd known enough to leave them with people who'd care for them.

"CHANCEY, STOP! STOP!"

Ada's voice rose up in a shriek, and Jonah tried to sit up. But his belly was on fire.

"GET AWAY!" she shouted, and his heart broke. She was going to drive him away, too?

But then she was there, her beautiful face like an angel floating above him, the day's sun turning her red hair into a blazing halo. He tried to see an injury, but all he saw was that gorgeous hair, and her sweet face, haggard with crying.

"Ada," he gasped. "Who hurt you?"

"Jonah!" She set her hands on the fire in his belly, and he groaned as she pressed down on it.

"Got shot."

"I know. I'm so sorry. I didn't—how did you know?"

She wasn't asking how he knew he got shot. His mind was filling with thunder, and the noise made it hard to think, but he knew she was asking how he'd known where she was. "You didn't come. Had to find you. Who hurt you?"

Her angelic face turned from him, and she looked at someone or something out of his narrowing range of vision. Her voice sharpened into an angry order. "Help me get him inside, and then go for Doc!"

The boy-man who'd shot him lurched into his view, and Jonah tried to get ready to fight.

"It's alright, Jonah. It's alright."

With Ada at his side, he let the boy-man lift him to his feet and drag him into Ada's house.

They helped him through the small house, into a small room, and laid him on a small bed. Jonah's belly was full of fire, and his head spun.

"Ada Lee?" a woman called out, her voice wavering with age.

"It's alright, Momma! This is a friend." Ada glared at the boy-man she called Chancey. "Go get Doc Dollens. Now!"

Chancey left, and Ada sat on the narrow bed at Jonah's hip and began to unfasten his overalls. Jonah tried to help her, but couldn't make his hands do what he told them.

"Ada Lee!" her mother called again. By the sound of it, there were a few walls between her and them. "What's goin' on?"

"Momma, I'll come to you soon's I can!" Ada's tone was sharp, and when she sighed, the breath carried a load of weariness.

It took all his focus and made the fire inside him roar, but Jonah brought his hand up and covered hers with it. "I'm sorry, Ada. I was … scared for you."

She lifted her wonderful pale green eyes, soft and clear as the sweetest cool water, to his. "I'm sorry. I couldn't get word to you. I didn't know how to tell you." Tears filled those eyes and made them blur.

"Who hurt you?" He raised his hand to touch her face, but saw his fingers covered in blood. He let his arm fall back to the bed.

She shook her head. "Not me. My daddy. Somebody …" her voice caught, and her tears fell. "He killed my daddy!"

Then somebody *had* hurt her, had taken a loved one from her. Jonah was intimately acquainted with that brutal pain. "Ah, darlin', I'm—"

"ADA!" her mother screamed.

"I have to go to her. She's blind, and she's been fearful since it happened." She had a cloth in her hand, folded neatly. She put the cloth inside his half-open overalls, along the side where he'd been shot, then lifted his bloody hand and pushed it over that place to hold the cloth there.

Fresh pain flared at the pressure, and he grunted, but managed to hold the cloth like she wanted him to. He didn't think he was dying. He hurt, and he felt weak and faint, but somehow he knew the wound wasn't mortal. From a range of ten feet or so, Ada's young friend had almost missed him—unless he'd been trying to wing him. That was possible.

"I'm sorry. I'll be back quick as I can. I need to settle her."

Jonah nodded, and she eased up to her feet. Before she left him, she bent down and kissed him on the lips. Surprised, Jonah didn't have time to react before she'd stood again.

"Thank you for coming for me. I didn't know when I'd see you again, if I ever would."

Then she turned and left.

Jonah tried to breathe around the pain, and, in this moment of sudden solitude, tried to sort his thoughts. A man had killed her father. From the evidence of this morning's events, Jonah knew it was a hobo, a stranger, who'd done the deed.

Her father had been murdered, and Ada was now alone with her mother. Her blind mother.

In one of their talks while she'd been recovering up on his mountain, she'd told him some about her parents. They were quite old, and her mother had gone blind later in life. In her own house, she wasn't helpless, but she couldn't be left alone, or go far beyond its walls. The only place she'd gone since her sight had left her, Ada had told him, was church on Sundays.

She couldn't be left alone. There was only Ada for her now.

Her father's death was why Ada hadn't come to him. Her mother's need was why she never would again.

That pain, of knowing he wouldn't have Ada even for the little sliver of time he'd thought he might, dwarfed the thumping pain in his middle.

But his loss wasn't the chief concern. Ada's pain was what mattered. She was close to her parents, devoted to them. And now she was without her father.

She came back in, now carrying a basket, and set it on the table beside the bed. No, it wasn't a table — it was a bookcase. There was a milk-glass electric lamp and a small stack of books on top. She set the basket on the books.

As she sat beside him again on the bed, Jonah looked around the room. The walls, papered in a plain pale blue with a faint stripe, were unadorned, except for one frame that held a paper with writing on it. The other furniture was a dresser with a mirror, not unlike Grace's, and a chifforobe against the far wall. Nothing but the books showed much of the person this room belonged to, but they were enough. He knew.

"This is your room."

She nodded as she opened the rest of the buttons at the side of his overalls and pulled the bib down. He looked at his side and saw that his shirt was soaked in vivid red, and there was a hole about the width of his finger in the fabric. When she lifted the shirt to show his belly, blood pulsed thickly but lazily from a corresponding hole in his side. Ada took the bloody fold of cloth from him and pressed it to the hole.

"Can you turn to your other side at all?"

Jonah did, clenching his jaw against the spike of pain.

"It went through. It went through. And it's far enough to the side I don't think it got any of your organs. I only know a little about anatomy, but I think I'm right."

With immeasurable relief, he lay on his back again. "That's good."

"Yes. Yes, it is. Doc Dollens lives just a few miles toward town. Chancey'll run and get his truck, and they'll be here in an hour or so, if Doc's home. I'm just going to bind this up until he gets here, alright?"

He caught her busy hands in his. "Ada."

She stopped and fixed her eyes on his.

"I'm sorry about your pa."

A twist of grief crossed her face. "Thank you. I'm sorry Chancey shot you. He thought you were a stranger and …"

"I understand. I'm jus' glad he didn't kill me."

Ada burst into a storm of tears. Ignoring the pain in his side and the blood still running from the wound, he pulled her into his arms, set her head on his chest, and held her.

By the time Doc Dollens arrived, Jonah's pain had doubled, and he was having trouble keeping conscious — or even to know when he was awake and when he was dreaming. He knew Ada had stayed at his side, but otherwise, the world had spun and swirled and faded in ways beyond his ken.

He knew the doctor was there, and felt the new pain of his work, and he tasted water when Ada gave it to him, but he wasn't sure when all that had happened or how often.

He remembered trying to tell the doctor about his children, where they were and how he needed to send word, he remembered how crucially important that had been, but he wasn't sure he'd managed to make the words.

His next moment of clear sense came in the late afternoon. He could tell by the light. Ada was sitting in a chair beside the bed, reading.

"Ada." He reached for her. His hand was clean. She'd washed him. He wished he could remember that. Now that he was noticing, he saw that he was bare-chested, wearing nothing but a bright white bandage around his waist. By the feel of the cover on his legs, he wasn't wearing much down there, either.

He hoped she hadn't washed him all over. He definitely wanted to be awake for that.

He'd tended to her in those ways, seen her beautiful small body, seeming frail but truly strong. Sprinkled with light freckles like gold dust. He'd tried to be a gentleman and not look on her where she'd want to be modest, but it hadn't always been possible.

At the sound of his voice and the reach of his hand, she looked up from her book and smiled. "Jonah. How do you feel?"

"Sore. Ada, the children. They —"

She took his flailing hand and held it to her chest. "They're with the Cummings. You said. Doc Dollens sent Chancey up with word. He's going to bring them down to us."

"No. They don't know that boy. They'll not give my children to a stranger."

"He's carrying a letter from the doctor."

A letter would have held no sway for him, but the Cummings could read. It might be enough to persuade them. He didn't like the idea of a stranger—the man who'd shot him, the man who'd been with Ada, who'd been the only man in this house—taking charge of his children, but he didn't know how he'd stop it now. And he wanted them with him.

He tried to sit up, but the pain was like a belly full of hot rocks, shifting with every move.

She sat on the side of the bed and pressed his shoulders down. "You're going to have to let me nurse you for a while, Mr. Walker. Doc Dollens says the wound is clean and the bullet didn't get anything but muscle, but you need to stay off your feet for a few days, and it'll be a week at least before you can even try to get back home—and that's only if you get a ride."

"The animals …"

"You have friends, Jonah. They will help."

He hadn't thought of anyone as a friend for years. But Hez Cummings had said he'd send his boys to look after the homestead. Maybe they'd stay up there as long as he needed to stay down here. He was too weak and tired to imagine an option, so he'd believe she was right and it was so.

She held his hand and studied it like she'd find some kind of secret in the creases of his knuckles. With her eyes away from his, something fell from her features, like a curtain dropping away, and Jonah saw how exhausted she was, how wan and slack.

"You look so sad, darlin'."

A mournful attempt at a smile flitted over her mouth. "I am. I lost my daddy so horribly, and I thought I'd lost you, too."

"When'd it happen? Mind me askin'?"

"Four days ago."

The day he'd killed her bear.

Without further prompt, she added, "It was a wanderer. My folks have always been kind to men like that, offering them a meal in exchange for help around the farm, or shelter in bad weather. They've welcomed them with open hearts since men like that started walkin' the roads, and never had a problem. But this one, I don't know what happened. He stole a few things, and maybe Daddy caught him doin' it. Momma only heard the scuffle. But he left my daddy with his head crushed. The sheriff said he beat Daddy with the radio we bought him. I found Daddy lyin' in the hall. I think he died tryin' to get back to my momma."

As she'd spoken, the mountain had come into her voice. Whenever she spoke with deep feeling, her heritage overcame her education.

"Ah, Ada," he pulled her hand to his mouth and kissed her knuckles. "I'm sorry."

She began to cry again. "I miss my daddy so, but there's so much more this means than losin' him. I can't leave Momma alone. I can't keep my job, and I can't go up the mountain. I don't know how I'm gonna take care of her, and I don't know how I'm gonna get by without seein' you!"

"I'm right here, Ada. Don't you fret."

She sniffed her tears to a halt and frowned at him. "Will you stay? Could you stay?"

He was sore and tired, and thinking was hard. He wanted Ada in his life. But this world was nothing he knew, and he was too old to learn how to live in it. Nearly everyone he'd met down here had wanted him dead. He was a stranger, and he didn't belong.

But the thought that he'd lose even the tiny sliver of Ada he'd hoped to have made his heart sick.

Too slow in his thinking, he didn't find an answer before Ada had one herself. Hopeless sorrow filled her face, and she nodded. "No, I know. You can't. Your home is your home."

"I don't know how to make it right, darlin'."

"I don't, either." She sniffed sharply and wiped her face with the hand he didn't have hold of. Her back went straight, and she let out a brisk, cleansing breath. "Well. I've got you now, and you're a blessing in time of darkness, Jonah Walker. I'm sorry you had to get shot to stay a spell, but I'm not sorry to have you with me. I'm tempted to pray for your slow recovery."

He pulled her close and kissed her. "You go on 'head and pray for that."

Chapter Nineteen

Chancey brought the children down the next day, and Ada brought them into the bedroom, where she'd insisted on, and rigorously enforced, Jonah's bedrest, allowing him to rise only when he needed to attend to his body's business.

He didn't fight her; in fact, he enjoyed her fussing. And he needed it. This gunshot wound was his first serious injury or illness in his life, and he'd lost a significant quantity of blood. Doc Dollens had told him to expect to be weak and wan for several days, and he hadn't been telling a story. Jonah was tired all the time and sore, and when he stood, the world rocked beneath his feet. If this was akin to the vertigo Ada had experienced, he was doubly sorry for her in retrospect. Now, he was happy to let her take his arm and lead him when he needed to handle his business.

This house had a room with toilet, inside the house, with a sink and a tub in the same room. Jonah had heard of such a thing but had never seen one before. He found it unsettling and unsanitary—and when Ada had shown him the pull to make water rise up in a noisy rush and carry off what was in the bowl, he would have jumped back if his belly hadn't been so sore.

He wondered where the water took it off to — not back to the well, he surely hoped — but he didn't want to talk to Ada about such things, and there hadn't yet been anyone else he could ask.

That strange inside-outhouse wasn't the only unsettling thing around in this world. The buzzing electric lights in every room hurt his eyes and gave him a headache. And sometimes a car or truck rolled by, its wheels grinding up the gravel road and its motor growling, which startled him every time. These were things he'd heard of but had never, or at least rarely, experienced, and they all made him feel jumpy as a bug in a burning log.

Even the air felt wrong. It seemed to have weight and lie on the floor of his lungs.

When — what was it, a day and a half after he'd been shot? — Ada led Elijah and Bluebird into the bedroom where Jonah sat, propped in bed, their eyes were big round saucers of trepidation and befuddlement, and he knew what they were feeling. A strange man had brought them to a strange place, where their pa was hurt, and they'd already been worried for Ada. Their world had been turned all the way over in this short spell of time.

They'd never been any farther down the mountain than Red Fern Holler, nowhere near any kind of electricity or motor, or hot water coming straight out of a pipe with a turn-knob.

"Pa!" Bluebird squealed and rushed into the room, climbing on the bed to throw herself into his arms. It hurt, she might as well have kicked him in his side, but he didn't slow her down. He wound his arms around her and held on tight.

"My baby girl. Were you good for Mizz Esther?"

"Uh huh we made little pies and I got to feed the chickens and play with Mary Jo she has a doll with yellow hair like mine. And Mr. Chancey took us for a ride in a *truck*! It's bumpy and goes fast and loud."

Jonah smiled over Bluebird's head at his son, who stood quietly beside the bed. "What'd you think of that, boy?" He'd become fascinated with motors, reading about cars and trains and airplanes in his library books, and telling Jonah all about them.

Elijah tried for a noncommittal shrug, but Jonah saw the keen light in his eyes. He'd been astounded. "It was alright. You got hurt."

"Just a little. I'll be fine."

Bluebird shifted on his lap, putting her little knee into his gut as she turned around. "And you found Mizz Ada and now we together and don't hafta be apart no more!"

Ada was still standing in the doorway. Jonah looked up and met her eyes. Two worlds full of impossible need crashed in the look they shared.

Jonah must have dozed off; he woke alone in Ada's bedroom. But he was not alone in the house. He heard the rumble of voices, a sound he hadn't heard around him since he'd been here. With the children in the house, activity and conversation had increased.

He lay there for a while, listening. He couldn't make out more than the general sense that people were talking, and who they were. His children. Ada. Chancey, that man-boy who was around far too much. And, he thought, Ada's mother. All out there, talking together. And him alone in here.

Ada had brought her mother, Bess, in to meet him last evening. She was an old woman, small as a sparrow, with white hair, soft, creased skin, and clouded blue eyes. Jonah had been struck by how anxious she'd looked, how tentative, as Ada had led her forward. She'd reached out small, withered hands, and Jonah had, as Ada had explained beforehand, allowed her to feel his face and shoulders. Only then had she spoken to him.

Now, out there with his children, he thought he heard ease in her tone, though he couldn't make out anyone's words.

Willing the pain to step back for a minute, Jonah pushed himself carefully to a fully seated position and eased his legs off the side of the bed. All he had on were his summer drawers, which was a problem, but Ada had washed his overalls and left them, folded, on the top of her bureau. His shirt, she hadn't been able to get clear of the bloodstain. But at least he had his overalls. The bullet had just nicked the very edge on the front. It had gone through the back, but that didn't matter much.

Could he get into his overalls on his own, still woozy with blood loss, his side stitched up and aching, and all his muscles around his middle still feeling oven-hot?

In the short time Ada had been taking care of him, she'd been attentive enough that he'd had no need to call on her; when he'd needed her, she was there.

Just now, the only need he felt was for company. He was lonely, and the people he loved were just barely out of his reach. But he didn't know if he could get to them on his own.

He didn't want to call out for her, especially not with Chancey around. Jonah wasn't a jealous man, maybe because he'd never before had call to be, but he didn't like that boy. The way he hung around this house, like he was waiting for something. The way his eyes seemed to fix on Ada always. Not to mention the way he'd shot him.

Jonah would be dumbstruck if the boy was more than eighteen or so, half his own age. But something in that boy made his hackles raise up.

Using Ada's bookcase as a support, Jonah levered himself to stand. Then he put his hand on the wall and waited for the room to stop dancing around, and the fiery waves of fresh pain to ebb. Eventually, he found that his feet were fairly steady and his legs would hold him, as long as he took it slowly. He made his way to the bureau and picked up the folded overalls.

He'd never thought about how he put his clothes on before he'd gotten shot. Everything, every kind of movement, even breathing, hurt. He let the denim unfold and lay out down his legs, and thought about how to get this done without falling over or tearing up what was only just starting to heal.

He was going to have to sit down again, wasn't he? Which would mean getting back up again.

Jonah sighed and shuffled to the bed.

Though he'd been brought through the house after getting shot, he'd been distracted by shock and pain and hadn't paid much attention to it. Since then, he'd seen nothing more than Ada's room, the strange bathroom, and a bit of the hallway between them. Now, as he eased his way in the other direction down the hall, to the sitting room, one hand on the wall to keep his balance, Jonah paid attention. This was Ada's home.

The house was smaller than his own but brighter, and in the stark difference, Jonah saw how much of his home he'd let decay around him since he'd been alone with the children. All his attention had been on keeping them well—healthy and fed and loved—and he'd paid no mind to the house itself, except to keep it standing. Curtains put up maybe before he was born still hung in the windows. Paper peeled off the walls. Most anything of any value had been traded or sold off before he'd been in charge of the place, and he'd cast off nearly all the rest in the same way. He'd used castoff newspaper from Hez Cummings' place to fill in and cover up places in the walls that gapped or leaked, without ever thinking once what things looked like. His home was spare and grim and grey.

This little house was neatly kept. Humble and worn but cheerful, too. The paper on the walls was faded and stained in places, but not decaying. The furniture was sparse but comfortable and well-tended. There had been a rug on the floor of the front room; he could see the faint mark on the wood floor where that rug had lain a long time.

Turning the other direction, toward the chatter of the other people here, Jonah saw the kitchen. And what an odd thing it was.

A room all to itself, and small, but bright, more like the bathroom than the other rooms. White walls, white table, white chairs, white cupboards, but everything with a cheery red trim. A white sink, twice the size of the one in the bathroom, and another hot-cold tap.

There were strange white contraptions as well, big enough to make the small space feel cramped. He'd seen something like them up at the Cummings' place, back where Esther made her pies and pastries, but hers were black and wooden. An oven and an ice box. To keep food and cook it. 'Modern conveniences,' he'd heard them called.

He really was from another world entirely, just a few hours away. He was like one of those space monsters Elijah had told him about, from the stories he read.

Elijah, Bluebird, and Ada's mother were sitting at the table. Ada stood beside the ice box, making something at the worktop. Bluebird was chattering about something, and Bess, Ada's mother, was smiling and nodding.

Chancey stood near the door, his flat cap in his hand. Jonah hoped that meant the boy was on his way out.

"Pa!" Bluebird stopped her cheerful prattle—Jonah hadn't yet devoted enough attention to her words to know their topic—"Are you better?"

Ada spun around. "Jonah! You shouldn't be up!"

He felt a little wobbly and suddenly too exhausted to stand, it was true. Getting his overalls on had been harder than he'd expected. His left knee buckled as if to agree with Ada, and he stumbled into the ice box.

Chancey stood right where he was, holding his hat, but Jonah wouldn't have wanted his help, anyway. Ada was there, and Elijah, too, and they got him to the empty chair at the table. Getting to that seat burned like a house afire, but he managed it and gave out a relieved breath when he was down. Seated at the table with his children. With his family. It was what he wanted.

"You're supposed to stay in bed for a few days, Jonah. A few days. Until your blood replenishes."

He looked up at her and said the only thing his mind offered to his mouth: "Lonely."

That made her smile, and she leaned down and kissed his cheek. "Alright. The children and I were going to bring you supper later, but if you promise to let me know when you need to lie down again, you can stay while we make it."

"Maybe I should stay, too, Mizz Ada," Chancey said. "'Case you need me."

Jonah enjoyed the sharp look Ada sent to that boy. "Thank you, Chancey, but we're fine. Go on home to your momma."

The boy hesitated a bit longer before he nodded. "I'll be by tomorrow, then. Help you with the field."

Ada answered only with a short bob of her head.

"Thank you, Chancey," Bess said. "Don't know what we'd do without you."

"I'm here for you, Mizz Bess. Don't worry none 'bout that." And with that, the boy finally left.

Jonah watched until the boy was in his noisy, smelly truck and backing out.

"Can I get you a drink?" Ada asked. "Water, or tea? Milk?"

"Water's fine." He smiled at Bluebird. "What you chatterin' 'bout, baby girl?"

"I was tellin' Grammy Bess 'bout Lulubelle 'n how she likes to sleep under my legs."

Jonah sucked in a breath to hear his girl call Ada's mother by that name. The stretch of muscles in the gasp added fuel to the fire in his belly, and he grunted, earning a keen, examining look from Ada. He put a smile on his face, but she didn't seem especially reassured.

Lulubelle was one of the new goats born this spring. She was a tiny thing, and thick as a post, but she'd picked Bluebird as her special favorite person, and would likely be more pet than farm animal. Small as she was,

Jonah didn't see her breeding. But she made his girl happy, so she had her purpose, too.

"The children was tellin' all about your place, Jonah," Bess said. "I know your people, or did. I was raised up in Red Fern Holler."

"Yes'm, that's what Ada said. I remember your mother, Mizz Dee, a little. She was a real good lady. Sorry I can't say I remember you."

The old woman smiled and waved a hand to dismiss his apology. He noted that she kept her hands resting lightly on the table, ready for use as surrogates for her eyes. "I come down the mountain long 'fore you was born, I reckon, and only went up for visits after. No reason you'd 'member me, livin' up in Cable's Holler like you do." She heaved a soft sigh, and her smile faded out. "'Tis a good life, up in the mountain. Ain't easy, but it ain't easy nowhere. Up there, people is who they say they is. Things is like they should be."

Ada set a glass of water — it had little cubes of ice in it — on the table before him and gave his shoulder a squeeze before she went back to her work.

Jonah couldn't disagree. Down here, he understood hardly anything. Down here, he'd been threatened and insulted and finally shot. He didn't belong down here. In Cable's Holler, he'd been mainly unhappy and barely living until recently, and he didn't have much, lived on the edge of failing every day of his life, but he had his children, and his ways of being that made sense.

"Yes'm," he finally said.

Bess's sightless eyes narrowed, and she seemed to stare right at him. "You get them hobo men up in the hollers, Jonah Walker?"

He turned to Ada, who was frowning at her mother, and chewing on her bottom lip.

"No'm. Ain't no place to get to from up there."

Her right hand covered her left, and she traced a finger over the narrow gold band on her third finger. "I reckon not. If you go up there, you're goin' home. Things is like they should be."

Jonah didn't answer. A thought had sprouted in his mind, and drew his attention.

Ada turned the talk from the shadows it had wandered into. She spread out a piece of newspaper in the middle of the table and set a strainer full of green beans on it. "Children, Momma, will you split the beans for me?" She lifted her mother's hand and set it on the strainer.

While Bess and the children got to work, Jonah sipped his water and let his thought take root.

They buried Ada's father five days after Jonah had arrived in his noteworthy way. By then, he was healed enough to stand with her through the service at the church, and the few words the preacher said at the graveside in the churchyard. He wore borrowed clothes that didn't fit right and borrowed shoes that pinched, but he was, he thought, presentable enough.

Ada remade a pair of trousers and a plain white shirt from her father for Elijah to wear, and she made Bluebird a whole new dress. His baby girl dizzied herself spinning around and around in that new frock. Most all she'd ever worn before had been Grace's house dresses, cut down and re-hemmed as well as Jonah could. But his stitching skill was in mending, not making. Ada had a talent.

Elijah and Bluebird had never been to a funeral before, but since they didn't know Zeke McDaniel, he didn't think they were stressed by it. If they had questions, they hadn't yet asked. Zeke's coffin was closed, with a spray of lilies lying on its plain pine lid.

Jonah hadn't been to a funeral since his family had died, when Grace had been there to see to things. He'd buried Grace alone, near her favorite place in the world, in a humble grave marked with a cross he'd made. Her name wasn't on it because, though he recognized the shape of it, he hadn't been able to make the letters right, and he hadn't wanted to ugly up her marker with his unschooled attempt at writing.

He kept by Ada's side, and she stayed by her mother's. The children sat with them in the church and stood with them in the graveyard, quiet and curious, but not overly upset. They understood enough to know why Ada and Bess were crying, and to feel the weight of those tears, but not to be overswept by grief of their own. They were simply subdued and respectful, and Jonah was as proud of them as he'd ever been.

There was a gathering after in the church, a potluck not unlike those sometimes held in Red Fern Holler. There was music, a fiddle and a bagpipe, and even a little bit of dancing. It turned out that the people of Barker's Creek were mostly of Scottish blood and not so far removed from the memory of that homeland. They sent their dead off with good cheer.

Jonah thought there was Scot in his blood, too. Or Irish, maybe. Maybe a little of both. But he didn't know for sure, and didn't figure it mattered. The only heritage he cared for loomed above his head. He was of the mountain.

At the wake, Jonah's wound and weariness began to get the better of him. The children were playing with the other children. Bess was seated at the widow's place, with Ada at her side, and they were accepting condolences from their friends and neighbors. He didn't belong amongst them; he was a stranger to them all.

This world was so much bigger than his own. He'd thought Red Fern Holler to be a thriving village, but there were more people at this wake than that whole holler held. At least two dozen cars and trucks were parked outside the church. All these people lived in a world of motors and electricity, of flush toilets and ice-cold milk in August.

And they all looked at him and whispered. In his ill-fitting borrowed clothes, Jonah tried not to notice the gossip he stirred up, but it was hard to miss. Just standing in amongst them like some folklore forest creature was near as tiring as the bullet wound.

Finally, he found an empty chair at the edge of the room, near the door, and took the respite it offered. When he was seated, he realized there were people talking in the little nook where the door was. Men, three of them, at least. One of them was Chancey.

Jonah wasn't around people enough to have strong feelings about many of them. He loved his children. And Ada. He'd loved Grace, and still loved the memory of her. He'd loved his parents and sister. Ada said he had friends, but if that were true, then he was a bad friend, because he thought of no one in that way. Except for the people he loved, he'd never cared strongly for anyone in one way or the other, good or ill.

But he was starting to feel hate for that boy. No good reason, really. Nothing the boy had done had been aggressive or even hostile to him. Not outright, at least.

Even shooting him had been about protecting Ada, not attacking him.

But that was where Jonah's animosity lay: in Chancey's presence around Ada. All the time. Hovering. Putting himself in the way to take care of her.

Watching her.

Chancey had his sights set on Ada, and Jonah hated that. The boy was half his age, and Ada plainly did not share Chancey's feeling, but Jonah still wanted him away from her. The thought of going back to Cable's Holler and leaving Chancey alone down here to insinuate himself into Ada's life made a wholly different kind of fire in Jonah's belly.

The thought of going back to Cable's Holler without Ada was bad enough.

Just around the corner from where he sat, Chancey was talking with two other men Jonah didn't know. He listened.

"They found the man in Letcher County. Pack half-full of coins and jewelry, little figures from some ladies' shelves. Nothin' he had leads back to Zeke's place, but he come through these parts, so likely he already sold off anythin' he took down here."

Jonah didn't know who that was speaking.

Chancey spoke next. "You think he the one killed Zeke?"

"Likely so," the first man answered. "Though we ain't had no more reports of hobos killin' nobody 'round these parts. 'Twas prob'ly a mistake, though that don't put breath back in Zeke's chest. From what I took the scene to be, Zeke caught him goin' through the house, faced off with him. Hobo picked up that radio they had—maybe he's even tryin' to steal that, but it was heavy, one of them tabletop models, you know—he picked up that radio and hit Zeke with it. Prob'ly jus' wanted to knock him down and get runnin', but he stove in the old man's head."

"What he get away with?" a third man asked.

"Not much. Ada's weddin' ring, and Zeke's. A couple cheap trinkets of Ada's. A silver frame with Zeke and Bess's weddin' picture in it. A brass candlestick he mighta thought was gold." The man who was obviously a lawman, and a bit older, chortled darkly. "Fool's gold."

Chancey grumbled, "Killed Zeke over nothin'."

"Yeah, and he'd'a swung for it, but his cellmate got him first. Kicked him so hard, put a rib clear through his heart."

The third man asked, "He dead?"

"As a doornail."

"Well, that's somethin', then."

"Don't help Mizz Bess or Mizz Ada, though, do it?" Chancey countered.

The third man, who sounded Chancey's age, chortled. "I figured you had that in hand, Chance. Or can't you get it done with that stranger lurkin' around? What's that, anyway? Who's he, stayin' in that house with the ladies?" He laughed again. "Maybe Mizz Ada ain't so sweet aft'all. She got a taste of it back when she was married, so I bet she needs it bad now. Bet a real hot fire burns under all that red hair."

The men laughed.

Jonah was on his feet again so fast he didn't have time to protect his sore belly or bother with the cramp that went through him. He swung around the corner and stood tall, energized by a fiery blaze of anger.

All three men—one his age, in a suit with a string tie, and the other two just barely men, in their Sunday trousers and shirts—gaped at him.

"Get her name out your mouths," Jonah said.

The lawman in the string tie had the decency to look abashed before he took on an aspect of authority, and the other younger man, the one who'd been so nasty, flinched back, but Chancey came to him, his face shaping into a mask of territorial aggression.

He stood toe to toe, two or three inches shorter than Jonah, and said, "I knowed Ada all my life. I been takin' care of her since she come back home. I'll talk 'bout her if I want. Who're you to crawl down here like some varmint from under a rock and spout off?"

Jonah felt himself grow bigger as Chancey challenged him. Never before had he felt this way, this violent need to do harm. He was a quiet man. He wasn't like this. He didn't need to be like this. Ada loved him. She abided Chancey, and just barely that. It was him, Jonah, she loved. He knew it as sure as he knew his love for her.

But Chancey lived here, where she lived. Not hours of hard riding away, as Jonah did.

And he didn't know if he could change that.

At the moment he decided to back down, that his fight wasn't here and this boy wasn't worth it, that he needed to talk to Ada, Chancey decided to make it a fight. He lashed out.

And punched Jonah in the belly.

The blow took the wind out of him and doubled him over as hot agony seared through him, flowing outward like the rays of the sun.

What it didn't do is take him off his feet.

What it didn't do is calm his irrational anger.

Instead, the blazing pain met with the fire of his anger and became an inferno. He stood tall again, forgetting entirely his pain. He was blocking the way from this nook to the main room, and the lawman was in the way of the door itself. Chancey was trapped.

Jonah grabbed the boy by the collar of his Sunday shirt and shot his fist into his face.

Chapter Twenty

Doc Dollens stood up straight and pushed his spectacles up on his nose. "Well, you're damn—" he cut himself short with a glance around the church sanctuary and then corrected himself—"real lucky, Jonah. There's no pull to the stitches, and I don't even see much bruising. I'd say Chancey got the worst by a fair amount. And Zeke, havin' his wake tore up like that." He shook his head sadly. "Poor Bess. You can close up your shirt."

Jonah stood up from the wooden pew and began to fasten the buttons on this borrowed shirt. The sleeve was torn, pulled away at the shoulder, and two buttons had been popped near the collar. It wasn't even his shirt.

He turned and sought Ada's eyes. "I'm real sorry."

She stood just behind his pew, out of the way of the doctor's work, but close enough for support. Her hands gripped the curved edge of the pew so hard her knuckles had gone blue. "It's not your fault. Sheriff Guthrie said Chancey threw the first punch. In your stomach. Of course you had to defend yourself."

He was defending her most of all, but he didn't know how to say that, or if he should.

If it had been only that brief exchange, just a punch apiece, maybe he wouldn't have felt so guilty. But after Chancey had rebounded from the blow to his face and realized his nose was bleeding and broken, something had snapped in the boy, and he'd flown at Jonah, sending him out of that little nook by the door, into the main room. Jonah hadn't been in a fight since he was a boy. But he was bigger than Chancey, and apparently stronger as well. He'd acted out of pure instinct, trying to stop the boy from making a ruckus at Ada's father's wake, and just trying not to get hit.

They'd knocked over the table full of food and sent a gaggle of ladies rushing out of the way to safety. Jonah had avoided most of the boy's wild blows before he'd managed to get over on him and slam his head on the ground until he went limp.

He was fine, or would be. Had a knob on the back of his head and the pain to go with it. Pretty light cost for attacking a man he'd shot the week before.

But it was Jonah everybody looked sideways at. Jonah they'd yanked up by the arms and shoved out of the room, to sit virtually alone while all the people of Barker's Creek fussed over their own. Jonah the doctor had made wait until he'd seen to Chancey first.

Ada was with him, though. She'd even left her mother to be with him here.

"Where're the children?" he asked her.

"With my momma. Bluebird was frightened. I think Elijah was, a little, as well. But they're alright."

He'd heard Bluebird calling for him while he was fighting Chancey off. Heard the fear in her wail. Jonah finished closing what buttons he could and raked his hand through his hair. "I'm sorry," he said again.

Ada was there, curling her pretty, pale hand over his arm. "Jonah, it's not your fault. Chancey did this. The children aren't afraid *of* you, they're afraid you've been hurt. They'll be glad to see you're not."

Doc Dollens chuckled. "I don't think our Chancey knew what he was lettin' himself in for." He closed his medical bag and squinted up at Jonah. "He says he punched you 'cause you were talkin' outta turn 'bout Ada."

"Jonah wouldn't!" Ada exclaimed.

"No, sir." Jonah didn't want to elaborate. He didn't want Ada to know anybody was talking about her in any way but seemly, but now the thought was out there, among all Ada's people. And he was a man in her house. He'd been nursed by her when his injury was fresh. He might be from the backwoods, but he understood how gossip worked. His stomach burned at the thought of what people might be saying about her. About them.

The doctor's squint deepened. "You're a stony one, Jonah Walker. But somehow, I think there's more to it. If I had to put the pieces of all this together on my own, I'd add in what I know 'bout how Chancey feels for our Ada, and how he feels 'bout you bein' 'round her. And I'd think on the witnesses. Joe Guthrie looked mighty uncomfortable when that accusation came outta Chancey's mouth. And Paddy—well, Paddy's who he is. If Chancey said jump, Paddy'd jump. Into a snake pit, even. Without a second thought."

"I didn't say nothin' 'bout Ada," Jonah asserted, but stopped short, again, of saying what he'd heard. It wasn't Chancey who'd said it, anyway. And yet the implication landed on that boy. And he'd been the one to act out.

Ada's hand slipped down his arm and grasped his hand. "Of course you didn't. Doc, I don't want this known, but … Chancey's been … unseemly with me before."

"What?" Jonah snatched his hand from hers and changed the grip so he had hold of her. "When?"

She shook her head and stayed focused on the doctor. "The night we had that accident, when he gave me a ride to town and back. He was drunk. I was driving. He …" Again, she shook her head. "I didn't let him get anywhere, but it's why we crashed."

Jonah's grip must have tightened; Ada set her other hand over his and muttered, "Jonah, please." He loosened his hold.

"I tell you this not to shame Chancey," she went on, still talking to the doctor, "but I don't want what he's saying out there to become the truth as people believe it. Is there anything you can do? Sheriff Guthrie was there. Can't he get him to stop saying that? There's got to be some story that doesn't drag Jonah's — or my — name through the mud. Chancey owes me that."

"I'll talk to Joe, but it might be too late. Ada, you've got a man in your house who's no relation. I know it's chaste, and they prob'ly do, too, in their hearts, but they don't care. People talk. They were already talkin'. It's what they do. Tryin' to stop that'd be like tryin' to catch a cloud."

Dejected, Ada dropped to the pew. "Can't I just have this day? I just want to say goodbye to Daddy."

Jonah still had her hand. He squeezed it — gently, this time. "C'mon, darlin'. I'll walk back out to the churchyard with you. Leave all them to they whisperin'."

The grave had only just been covered. There was no headstone yet, or even a cross. Only a plain stake at the head of the grave, with black letters Jonah assumed made up Ada's father's name.

All the mourners were still in the church, or had headed home following Jonah's scandalous dust-up with the boy. Elijah and Bluebird were inside as well, in the surprisingly attentive care of their 'Grammy Bess.'

Grammy Bess. Jonah's children had been trying to make Ada their own from the moment she'd first crossed their threshold. For not nearly as long, but for quite a while, Jonah had been trying to work out how that might come to pass.

He stood here, beside Ada, holding her hand. She stared at the mound of dark earth, without words, without tears, as if she were waiting for something to happen.

"D'you want to be alone?" he asked, after they'd stood silent for some time.

Her hand tightened in his. "No."

There likely was no worse time to say the words clamoring on Jonah's tongue. Standing at her father's grave, after tearing up his wake and causing a scandal through her whole town. But he didn't know how to hold them back.

"Ada."

"Yes?"

"Would you marry me?"

She flinched, and her hand went stiff inside his grasp. "What?"

He turned his head. She was staring at him, her eyes round and her jaw slack. Before his natural tendency to silence took him over again, he rushed into his reasoning. "I was thinkin'—couldn't you ride from the top down instead? The way'd be easier most days, since you'd already be on the mountain. I know we ain't got the 'lectric or one of them fancy toilets, and the house ain't so nice, but mainly that's 'cuz I ain't got no talent for keepin' it, and Bluebird's too young yet. It's a big house, plenty of room. We'd bring your momma up, and she won't never be 'lone. Maybe they's some folk in Red Fern she'd like to visit, time to time. You don't gotta be 'lone like I been. Isolated, like you say. It don't gotta be that way. They's people up there, if you want 'em."

"Jonah …"

"I know this is your world down here, and I been tryin' to figure if I could stay in it, but I jus' can't. I don't understand nothin' 'bout things down here, and ever'body looks sidelong at me. You fit better on the mountain than I do down here. And if you was with us, you could give the children some schoolin'. They love you like you was they momma, Ada, and I guess that's what you is, in all the ways that count."

"Jonah!" Her tone was sharp, and he closed his mouth and set his gut like he expected a punch. This one would hurt a sight more than Chancey's sucker jab.

Ada turned to face him fully, and picked up his other hand. There were tears in her eyes. He didn't know if they were for her father or for him, but in either case, she looked sad, and he wasn't ready for what she'd say.

"I'm sorry, Ada. I should'a kept my mouth shut. I know—"

"Do you love me?" she cut in.

"Huh?"

"Do you love me, Jonah? More than once, you've told me the children love me. But you've never said how you feel. I love Elijah and Bluebird, too, but I don't want to marry them."

"Don't you know?" He was stunned. She had to know.

"You've never said the words."

He slid his hands from hers and cupped her face. "I love you, Ada. I loved you before I knew it."

"I love you, Jonah."

He'd known she did, but the words were still beautiful. "Would you marry me?"

The tears flooded her eyes and dropped to her cheeks. They wet his hands. "I love you," she whispered again, each word breaking. But that wasn't an answer.

"Ada?"

Her hands hooked over his wrists and held tight. "I don't know. I can't think. I'm standing here at Daddy's grave, and everybody's at the windows watching us, and I don't know what my life is now! I don't know if I still have my job, or if I can even do it anymore. I don't know how I'm gonna take care of Momma, or how to keep up the farm, or what to do about anythin' if I say yes to you. I don't know if Momma can live on the mountain anymore. She's past seventy and blind. Soon, she'll be frail. I don't know, Jonah. I know what I want, but I don't know what I can have, or what I should do."

As she'd spoken, her flow of tears had become sobs. Jonah looked over his shoulder and saw that, indeed, the windows of the church meeting room were full of gawking faces. Refusing to let those people into this moment, he turned back to Ada. "What do you want, darlin'?"

"You!" she cried. "I want you!"

It wasn't an answer to the real question, and he didn't have a better solution to her worries than the one he'd just babbled at her. But just then, he didn't care. He didn't care that there was a church full of people watching, feasting their gossip-mongering eyes. He didn't care that her murdered father lay at rest beneath their feet. He didn't even care just then what her answer would be. He bent down and kissed her.

With a gasp, she went calm, and opened her mouth. Ah, she was so sweet. Every sweep of her tongue with his, every waft of her breath over his cheek, every fragile sigh that trembled against his lips sent a new burst of life through Jonah's grief-hardened veins. He'd been existing in the shadows for years, barely holding enough form to be a father to his children, wanting nothing at all for himself. All those years that he'd seen Grace every day, he hadn't been much more alive than she.

This woman, Ada, was bringing him back to the world. Making him remember what it was to live. Making him want it.

Her hands let go of his wrists, and her arms came up, insinuating themselves between his so she could wrap around his neck. He dropped his hands and circled his arms around her waist, and she rose onto her toes.

She arched in his arms, pressed her body firmly against his, felt what she did to him, and twisted her hips against him.

They both froze then. For Jonah's part, he was nearly unmanned. With just that slight twist, accompanied by that soft pressure, he was close to losing control of himself. He pulled back just enough to put a breath's space between their lips, and opened his eyes. She was staring up at him, her eyes full of shock, and maybe shame.

He didn't want to see that kind of look in her, not ever, and his concern returned to him a measure of control.

With a soft kiss, he set her fully on the ground and stood back. "You are the best of women, Ada Donovan. I love you. I will take care of you and your momma, too. Will you come up the mountain and be my wife?"

She was pale, but her tears had been shed. She slid her hands from around his neck and let them rest over his heart. "I love you, Jonah Walker. I know what I want, but I need to think of what's best for my mother, too. May I have some time to think?"

That wasn't a no. It was exactly the answer Ada should give.

"'Course you can."

That night, Jonah lay alone in Ada's bed. He was well enough to give up the bed to her again, to sleep on the sitting-room floor with his children, but she wouldn't hear of it. In her mind, he was still convalescing, for at least the week Doc Dollens had set as a minimum. Truth be told, he still had stitches in, and he wasn't yet full strength. That fight today had taken a lot out of him and left him scattered and weary for the rest of the day. He reckoned she was more right than wrong, so he'd given up the argument. Ada slept, as she had been since he'd been here, with her mother, on her father's side of that bed.

The rest of the day had been quiet, with a strange air about it. One of the neighbors drove them all home in his truck, with Jonah and the children jostling in the bed, and then they were all left alone.

No one said it out loud, but Jonah thought that kiss in the churchyard, more than the fight with Chancey, had been the spark the scandal about them had needed. He'd kissed her like that, she'd kissed him like that, in full view of them all, beside her father's grave, and then he'd come back to be the only man in this house. After beating one of their neighbors unconscious. He'd made the rumors true.

He had to get back up the mountain. Back to his home and the world he knew. He hoped to go up with Ada and Bess, but if she stayed, that was all the more reason for him to go. Once he and his children were gone, these people could forget about him and remember the Ada they knew.

She hadn't given him her answer yet. He'd caught her staring at him several times, as if lost in thought, but they'd barely spoken a handful of words to each other the rest of the day, and none of them private. He'd made his case—she didn't have to quit her job, he and the children could look after her mother, he and the children loved her and needed her. Now, she would have to decide what was right, and he would abide her decision. She understood better than he ever could what it was to live fully and live right.

Except for the sounds of a night summer rolling through the open windows, the house was quiet. Except for the light of a waning moon, the house was dark. Jonah was exhausted and sore, in both body and spirit, but he couldn't coax his mind to rest. Thoughts of his love for Grace, and for Ada, and his shadowy life between them, filled his mind with love and longing and regret.

The light cotton curtains wafted in a scant breeze, frogs chirruped at a pond somewhere in the distance, crickets rubbed their legs together, and whippoorwills sang their chant. At night, this world was as close to his as it ever got.

A soft knock at the door pulled him from his half-dozed musings, and he lifted his head from Ada's pillow as the door creaked open. The hallway was dark, but the moonlight slanted enough through the window and its fluttering cotton curtains that he saw Ada standing on the threshold. Her hair was loose and flowing over her shoulders. She wore a pale nightdress, voluminous but with slender straps over her shoulders that showed her full arms. Her collarbones made soft shadows at the base of her throat.

"Ada?"

She stepped into the room and closed the door. Without that pathway, the breeze settled, and the curtains lay over the window again, dimming the light. Now she was a faint white form at the foot of her bed. For a moment, his weary mind slipped, and she was Grace. He blinked, and she was Ada again.

He sat up, reclaiming full consciousness with the twinge through his belly, to make her stay that way. Grace was his past, and he would love his memory of her until the day he died. But Ada was his present, and, he hoped, his future. She was here, warm and alive. He wanted Ada. Only Ada.

"Ada. What is it, darlin'?"

"How do you love me, Jonah?"

"What?"

She curled her hands around the top bar of the iron footboard. "How do you love me? As a mother for your children? As a keeper for your home? As a teacher? How?"

For once in his life, the words came easily. "All those things, and more. I love you as a woman. A sweet, kind, beautiful woman who is better than me in ever' way. A woman I think of ever' moment I'm awake, and most when I'm asleep. I love your smell, and your taste. I love the sound of your voice and your laugh. I love the sight of you comin' to me, and my heart breaks to see you goin' away." Jonah held out his hand, and Ada eased around to the side of the bed and set hers in it. "I love the weight of your hand in mine. I love the way you feel in my arms. I love you, Ada. In ever' way a man can love a woman." He kissed her fingers. "What's vexin' you, darlin'?"

She didn't answer. She stood beside the bed, her eyes on their joined hands. There was something new between them, something so intense the crackle and spark nearly had sound and light. Jonah felt himself harden, and shifted so it wouldn't be apparent, in case the shadows of night weren't enough camouflage. He'd been long without a woman, and nearly as long without the impulse to take himself in hand. Lately, around Ada, he was like a newly quickened boy, going hard at the slightest provocation.

But this moment was no slight provocation.

She took her hand from his. Before Jonah had time to feel disappointed to lose that touch, she'd gathered the soft folds of her nightdress and pulled it up over her head. She let it drop from her fingers, and her hair settled over her bare chest, brushing her small, pert breasts, their pearly pink nipples that he'd tried so hard not to see over the weeks of her recovery and that had tormented him in dreams. Between her legs, a small, soft nest of burnished gold that had tortured him as well.

Bare. She was naked, not even a pair of drawers. Her body was so beautiful, pale and thin, but strong. Strong enough to hold her powerful will. Need cramped Jonah's body with such force he moaned.

"Ada …"

"Are you strong enough? Healed enough?"

Never in his life had anything mattered less than the wound in his side. "Yes. But Ada, do you got an answer for me?"

"Does it matter?"

Those words stabbed at him. They sounded like a no. "I won't take you, 'less you're mine."

"You're not taking me at all, Jonah Walker. I'm giving myself to you."

"As wife?"

For a moment, she was quiet, regarding him in the filtered moonlight. Then she nodded, and Jonah's heart stopped. "As wife. I love you."

The bed was narrow, too narrow for two, unless those two kept very close. Jonah meant to keep her as close as he could, from this day forth. He scooted to the side and turned the summer quilt down. Ada slid into her own bed like a guest.

As he rolled to hover over her, he asked, "You don't want to wait? Until after the words are said?"

Her hand came up and brushed his cheek. He hadn't shaved since he'd come down the mountain, and his beard was nearly winter-full now. "We've said the important words, haven't we?"

Indeed they had. Jonah slid his hand over her satin cheek, threaded his fingers into her whisper-soft hair. Just then, a change in the breeze pulled the curtains through the open widow, and a bright wash of dappled moonlight slanted over the bed. Her eyes gleamed up at him, deep pools of fresh water. They fluttered closed as he came down and put his mouth on hers.

Weeks, months, he'd dreamt of her, and now, at last, her body, all of her, was in his arms, nothing between them but his drawers, and he kicked those off and away as quickly as he could. Her breasts brushed against his chest as he kept his weight from her small frame. When he gave up her mouth to taste the rest of her, he felt her belly meeting his chest with each intake of her great, whimpering gasps.

He moved down, trailing his lips and tongue from her mouth to her jaw, following that graceful sweep to her ear, nibbling lightly there before tucking his face against her throat and breathing deep of her scent. A soft kiss of sweet flowers brushed his nose.

All the years he'd wanted nothing like this, felt no urge even for his own hand, and now it was all he could do not to mount her like an animal. But he didn't want that. He wanted to adore her, print her body into his so he'd never forget it, so he'd remember always this feeling of being reborn, being brought back to life, given the world.

Ada had told him once that that was her job: to carry the world up the mountain. She'd done exactly so for him — not this world where her house was, this alien place he didn't understand, that didn't understand him, but a world of feeling, of emotion and sensation, of will and drive, of love and desire and need. Of want. How good it felt to *want* again. To desire. To care. To live.

His hands roamed over her body, and his mouth followed. So soft, so sweet, so warm, so alive. In his hands, she writhed and moaned, and her hands skimmed through his hair, over his shoulders, his arms, his back, pausing in their travels to dig into the muscle wherever they were each time she moaned most keenly. Her legs flexed and shifted, twining with his, folding up along his hips, then extending again like a caress over his thighs, his calves.

Too long, he'd gone without this. Too keen was his need. His body strained for her, ached and throbbed for her. "Ada," he finally groaned when he thought he'd lose himself on the sheet, "Ada, I need ..."

"Yes! Yes, please," she cried in a frenzied murmur. Her legs came up and caught around his waist, and Jonah settled himself fully over her, propped on his hands, looking down at her. The dim light was enough for him to see love and trust, perfect and unconditional, in her clear eyes.

He reached between them to take hold of himself, and pressed at her entrance. She was hot and slick with want, and Jonah felt seared to his soul. He thrust, slowly, steadily, until he'd filled her. She clutched him everywhere, fit him like a sheath designed for him.

And then they both went utterly still. Jonah thought he'd break apart if he moved even an inch. Ada was beneath him, eyes wide, not breathing.

"It hurts?" he asked, forcing the words past a throat grown rigid with his holding back.

She shook her head, but in a brisk way that belied its own act. "No. Just … it's been nearly three years." Her shy chuckle moved through her body and tested his control.

"I can stop." For Ada, he thought he could manage it.

"No! Don't." Her hands slipped down his back and clutched his backside. "Stay. But go slowly?"

It had been near three years for her, but more than seven for him. It might as well have been his first time. Could he go slowly, when every shift in sensation was like a jolt from one of her electric wires? For her, he would. Whether he could or not, he would.

He waited another few breaths, building up all his will, and then began to move, as slowly as he could, easing out an inch or two, waiting there while he bent to kiss her, taking his time, until he needed a breath, then easing back those same scant inches while he breathed through his own desperate need. He found a rhythm like that, slow and easy, getting to know all of her body while he filled it, and in that rhythm he found his control. Eventually, as her body grew familiar with his, he felt strong enough to shift them both so he could reach a breast and draw its pink point into his mouth, still doing everything slowly, extending his flexes and thrusts a little bit more each time, until Ada's moans were continuous, rolling in keening waves, yet quiet, barely more than whispers full of need.

Then she began to rock beneath him, taking part in the tempo of their bodies, and everything changed for both of them. Then there was no more time to take. Jonah folded her in his arms, tucked his head at her shoulder, and they rocked together, faster and faster, driving each other closer and closer. The curtains billowed as a noisy breeze moved over them, rustling the leaves and grasses outside, but their own breaths were just as loud, and perfectly in time with each other.

"Oh! Oh! *Oh!*" Ada whisper-cried at his ear and went stiff, her fingernails digging into his backside. Jonah thrust deep, again and again, and then held there as her clutching spasms pushed him over as well. The release tore him apart, filled him with the world, and sewed him back together again. He bit down on the pillow lest he roar like a bear.

They held like that until their breathing found the rhythm natural to each of them. Jonah lifted his head. For a moment, he felt a flicker of shame, but it guttered out and went cold almost before he noticed it.

He opened his eyes and found Ada looking at him. She was smiling—a big, open smile, bright enough to illuminate the room. Her first real smile since he'd come down the mountain.

"I love you for the man you are, Jonah Walker. The man you are is everything."

Part Five

Chapter Twenty-One

With a soft squeeze of Ada's thigh, Jonah eased his hips back and pulled out of her. The sensation of his body leaving hers made Ada's back arch and her core flutter. She unwound her legs from his waist and let them fall where they would. Her every limb was limp and hot.

Shifting to her side, he grunted sharply and set a hand on his belly.

She sent her hand to the same place, felt his stitches, and remembered reality. "You're hurt! You weren't healed enough!" She should have known better; he'd been shot less than a week earlier, and he'd been in a wild fight only hours ago.

"Hush, darlin'." He covered her hand with his and stopped her fluttering. "I'm alright. Just a twinge."

It was too dark in the room to see his expression clearly enough to know if he was telling the truth. "I'm sorry."

"I'm not. I don't want you to be." His hand cupped her cheek, and he gazed down at her. The moonlight made his dark eyes gleam. "You just made me happy, Ada.

Happier than I've been in a long time. Happier than I ever thought I'd be again. So please don't be sorry."

"I'm happy, too. I can't believe I can say it. I buried my daddy today, and life is all turned inside out, but right now, with you, I'm happy."

He kissed her, brushing his lips lightly over hers, and then, with another grunt he tried to restrain, Jonah turned to his back, pulling her with him and settling her under his arm.

She nestled into that snug hold and set her hand on his belly. There was a line of hair down the center, crossing his belly button and ending at the thicker growth around his softening shaft. She wanted to touch him, to feel that heft that had filled her so wonderfully, but now, in this quiet afterglow, she felt shy. Her earlier boldness had faded. Never before had she initiated lovemaking, and in hindsight, she was a bit shocked at herself.

Not regretful, or ashamed. How could she be, when he'd been so glad to have her and shown her such breathtaking pleasure.

It was her mother who'd prompted her to leave her parents' bed and come to him. Not directly, she might well be scandalized were she to learn why Ada had gotten up in the middle of the night. But her mother's words had rung in Ada's head while she lay in the dark, echoing over and over, until they'd driven her to Jonah.

Momma wanted to leave Barker's Creek. She didn't want this house she'd lived in for decades. She didn't want this world where she'd made her life. She was lonely and afraid, and she wanted her real home.

The mountain.

Ada hadn't yet mentioned Jonah's proposal. She'd intended to do so as they prepared for bed, after she read to her from *Sense and Sensibility*. But as her mother settled against her pillows, in her bed she'd had since her marriage and the bedroom she'd had near as long, she'd said, *I'm tired and lonely, Ada. I want to go home.*

At first, Ada had thought her mother was wishing for death, and she'd reacted strongly, her broken heart breaking more at the thought of her mother's sorrow, and all the things they'd both lost, were still losing.

But she'd meant the mountain. She wanted to live out her years where she'd been born. Away from the constant pressures of this world. Away from wandering strangers with their hands out, and the dangers she now knew so well they might harbor.

With those sad words, she'd cleared the way forward for them both. Ada told her of Jonah's proposal, and the content of her mother's tears had changed, from loss and sorrow, to gratitude and hope.

After she'd drifted off to a calm sleep, Ada had lain in her father's place on the bed and stared up at the shadowy ceiling. What she wanted for herself more than anything was Jonah and the children. But she didn't want to lose all that she'd worked for, all she'd accomplished. The idea that she could ride her route from Cable's Holler, working her way down and back up, rather than the other way around, had never occurred to her. But it made easy sense.

If, that was, she still had that job. She'd gone another two weeks without riding, and she'd sent word to Mrs. Pitts to let her know what had happened to her father, and her doubts about how she'd keep working. Mrs. Pitts had sent word back that she'd keep her post open as long as she could, so long as Ada kept her informed as often as she could.

But Ada had sent June Avery to talk to Mrs. Pitts about work not long before her father's death. With June waiting to work, how long could Mrs. Pitts really hold the post for Ada?

Then again, until Jonah's proposal, and his insight, Ada had been sure she'd need to give up the job entirely to take care of her mother.

Her thoughts had spun and spun, until she'd known, at least, her answer for Jonah.

Lying with him now, in the cozy warmth of his spent body, listening to his heart slow toward sleep, Ada's head still spun.

What to do about the farmstead? The bank note was so sizeable it was hardly worth trying to sell the place to pay it off; with so many people in equally dire straits, there couldn't be much of a market for their humble patch. Her father had taken that loan a few years back, after the second poor yield in a row, before he'd understood that poor yields were a trend, not an anomaly. He'd replaced the rotting porch and the sagging roof, and bought a new kind of seed, hoping a fresh crop would enliven the soil. The third year had been the worst yet.

They could walk away from the farm. If her mother didn't want to stay, they could just walk away and let the bank take it. Go up with Jonah and the children and build a life there. Where wandering men didn't come. And where people they loved lived.

But could they live like that? No electricity, no plumbed hot water? Cooking on an old iron woodstove? Ada hadn't felt deprived during her weeks of recovery, but that had been spring, into summer, with long days and comfortable nights.

She thought she could. She knew how to do it. It hadn't been that terribly long since this house had had an outhouse and a cold-water pump at the kitchen sink. The outhouse still stood, converted now to a little toolshed.

How ironic to think that moving up to the top of the mountain, a place so remote there was barely a trail to it, let alone a road, was her best chance for keeping her job.

How surprising that she might get to keep her job and take care of her mother, give her want she wanted, and have what she herself wanted, too, by moving away from the world.

This was a rainbow. After a devastation, God's promise that good would return.

"Jonah," she whispered, and rubbed her hand over his belly.

"Hmm?" He'd nearly been asleep.

"I have to go. I can't be here with you when Momma and the children wake up."

He turned to his side and faced her, sliding his hand into her hair. "I want to know this ain't no dream."

"Only a dream come true." She kissed him, opening her mouth and pushing her tongue between his lips. When they pulled back, he sighed.

"I love you, Ada."

"I love you." With another quick kiss to his chin, she slid from the bed, scrabbled around on the floor for her nightgown, and pulled it on. "Get some sleep. We have plans to make."

The first plan was to make sure she had a job.

The very next day, Ada dressed for town and hitched Henrietta to the wagon. Jonah was sore from the day, and the night, before, but he entrusted her with Elijah and Bluebird, both of whom were beside themselves at the prospect of seeing a real town. They wore their clothes from the day before, the best clothes they had, and Ada packed a lunch basket for all three of them, with some carrots for Henrietta as well.

Ada, in return, entrusted her mother to Jonah's care, and knew with brilliant, blessed certainty that she was in the best of hands.

As they rolled down the road, Ada noticed neighbors watch them ride by. To those who raised their hands, she offered a raised hand in return. Those who only gawked, she lifted her chin and ignored.

The children sat on either side of her, their heads swiveling to and fro, taking in the sights, the rolling hills, the grazing animals, the farms and homes growing nearer to each other the longer they rode.

They'd gotten a later start than she would have on her own—after a family breakfast, and once the children managed to mosey their easily-distracted selves toward the wagon—so Ada pulled over at a pretty spot she knew, on an open field, and set up a picnic under a tree. They didn't tarry long; Ada wanted to keep her clothes nice, and she needed to be in town early enough to get her business done, but they had a nice lunch, and she let the children run a bit before she called them close.

It was nearing two o'clock when they passed the Callwood welcome sign. As they rode into the town proper, with its cars and trucks, and people walking in every direction, Bluebird scooted right up to Ada's side and clutched her little fists in Ada's dress. She was afraid of all the commotion and bustle. Elijah, on the other hand, leaned forward, so far that Ada finally reached over and hooked her fingers into his waistband to pull him back to the bench. That boy was like to take flight.

Ada led Henrietta to Second Street and stopped before the Pack Horse Library. It was always quiet on this street. Most of the shops were vacant, and the library itself wasn't much of a draw.

"Alright, children, I want you to come inside with me, but I need you to please be your very best selves. This is my place of work."

"You mean where the books live?" Bluebird asked.

"Exactly."

Elijah hopped down to the sidewalk. Then, charming Ada utterly, he turned and offered his hand to her. He was only nine and not tall enough yet to be of real assistance, but Ada went out of her way to take his hand as she stepped down from the wagon. She turned and lifted Bluebird down next.

Taking both their hands, she led them into the Pack Horse Library.

Mrs. Pitts's desk was empty, and the library was quiet. Both children looked around, their jaws unhinged.

"I ain't never knowed there *was* so many books!" Elijah exclaimed in a reverential whisper.

"This is only a tiny portion of all the books in the world, Elijah. You could read a book a day for your whole life and never read the same book twice."

"Can we get some to bring home?" Bluebird asked.

This library was more of a collection facility, to hold the books for the pack horse librarians. Ada didn't actually know if there was any kind of circulation directly from here. "I'll ask Mrs. Pitts."

As if hailed by the mention of her name, Mrs. Pitts came forth from the stacks. "Ada! So good to see you. I was sorry to learn about your father."

She didn't seem to notice the children, and Ada wasn't sure if that meant she'd rather pretend they weren't there. For now, she let them stand at her sides, and hoped they remained quiet.

"Thank you, ma'am. And thank you for understanding. I know this summer I've not held up to my responsibilities —"

With a cluck of her tongue and a shake of her head, Mrs. Pitts cut off her apology. "Ada. This program is a public service. Not only to the people we bring the joy of reading and community to, but to the people we employ as well. Besides, the people you work with have built strong bonds with you. You could not so easily be replaced."

"But Miss Avery … did she come to see you?"

"Indeed she did. I offered her Mrs. Castle's post. But she wasn't yet in a hurry for a post. She's happy teaching, and not planning to get married until next spring. I've told her I'll keep her in mind."

"Mrs. Castle isn't with us?"

"Oh, of course you wouldn't have heard yet. No. The bank foreclosed on her family's property, and her son-in-law ran off and left her girl with two little ones. Her wages with us weren't enough to keep everyone going, sadly. They've all packed up to look for work out west."

Ada had been so wrapped up in her own troubles, she'd forgotten that people were suffering everywhere right now. Despite everything, Ada felt blessed. She had lost a lot, but not everything—and she'd gained a great deal.

"I'm so sorry to hear it. I wish I could have said goodbye."

Mrs. Pitts agreed with a sigh. "As for your friend Miss Avery, there is a position open, but she would prefer to wait a bit. I haven't had any other worthy applicants yet for Mrs. Castle's route, so I certainly am in no rush to lose you, Ada. As I said, you are not easily replaced, and I mean that in both personal and practical terms."

"Oh. Well, I'm happy to hear it. I'll be so glad to get back to work."

"But you had mentioned in your letter that you weren't sure you could continue. That's resolved?"

"Yes ma'am. Well and truly, as long as it's alright for me to switch my route around a little. I'll be getting married and moving up the mountain, taking my mother with me."

Enlightenment shone on Mrs. Pitts' round face. "Ah. I suppose that explains your guests."

"It does, yes. I'm marrying their father."

Finally, she focused on the children and gave them a surprisingly warm smile. "And who do I have the pleasure to meet today?"

Elijah held his hand out. "Elijah Moses Walker, ma'am. From Cable's Holler."

She took his hand and gave it a sturdy shake, as if he were a grown man. "It's very good to meet you, Mr. Walker. I am Mrs. Edna Eugenia Pitts. And who is this young beauty?"

Bluebird ducked behind Ada's skirt. She wasn't a naturally shy child, but the harried pace of Callwood had rattled her.

"Bluebird, sweetheart, Mrs. Pitts is a friend. It's alright."

Mrs. Pitts bent forward, bringing her short, hefty body close to the girl's. "Bluebird. What a lovely name." She held out her hand.

"Bluebird Hope Walker," Bluebird muttered, but didn't take the offered hand.

"Well, that's doubly beautiful. A perfect name for such a beautiful girl." She stood straight and exchanged her offer of a handshake with an understanding smile. She lifted the same smile to Ada. "I don't imagine why it would be a problem for you to start your mornings at the top of the mountain. I'm pleased for you, Ada. You are too young to have spent the rest of your life in mourning."

Jonah was anxious to return to Cable's Holler. He'd been away nearly two weeks, and had left the state of his homestead to the Cummings boys—a greater trust than he'd extended to anyone in years, possibly ever.

Bluebird was anxious to go home as well. She missed her little goat, Lulubelle, and her little bluebird toy, the one Ada had made for her not quite a year before. And she missed her quiet little realm where she was princess.

Ada had begun her route just a few weeks shy of one year ago. In that time, it seemed she'd lived at least one full lifetime.

She was anxious to move up the mountain, too, and begin her next lifetime. Her mother was anxious to return to her roots and leave the troubles of this world behind.

Only Elijah seemed torn. He wasn't reluctant to go home, exactly, but of the three Walkers, he was the only one who found the busier, more advanced life lived down here fascinating.

His father faced the differences warily, still jumping every time a car or truck rolled over the gravel road, still wincing when the electric lights went on, as if they were as bright as the sun itself. He said the faint hum of the power, which Ada heard only when he mentioned it, gave him a headache and made him tense.

Bluebird was frightened by nearly everything different. Bubbly and irrepressible at home, here in Barker's Creek, she hid behind Jonah's or Ada's legs upon every new encounter, or curled up in Grammy Bess's lap and buried her head.

Grammy Bess. Ada had loved these children as if they were her own since before Jonah had truly noticed her, or she him. Even so, and even after she had begun to dream of being their mother, being Jonah's woman, she hadn't realized what that would mean for her mother. To be a grandmother, finally. To have little ones to love. Having Elijah and Bluebird here had reclaimed Ada's mother from the jaws of grief and hopelessness. She had been willing herself to die, to follow her husband and end her troubles. Now she was planning a new life.

Jonah coming down the mountain when he did, on the day he had, when her mother had been grieving so hard she'd made herself ill with it, and when Ada had felt the farthest reaches of her own despair—for the rest of her life, every day she lived, Ada would thank God for him, for bringing him and his children down to save them. To give them hope in the depth of their loss. To fill up lives that had gone empty. To bring them love.

In her job, as Mrs. Pitts so loved to say, Ada carried the world up the mountain. Jonah had carried it back down to her. And they would keep it with them wherever they were.

Ada and Jonah were married in her home church, in a tiny ceremony with only Doc Dollens as a guest and their official witness. Otherwise, only their family and the preacher were present. They invited no one else in Barker's Creek. Whether it was fair or not, Ada was stung by the gossip, and the way they'd all sided with Chancey, and how they'd all decided Jonah had tainted her.

Jonah wore the suit the doctor had lent him for the funeral and then simply given him for the wedding, so Ada was able to tailor it to fit a bit better. The children wore the clothes they wore to the funeral as well. Ada wore her best dress, the one George had bought her in a wild splurge. She'd been able to clean away from its fabric all signs of the wreck with Chancey.

She thought—no, she knew—George would be happy for her. All he'd ever wanted was her happiness. In his life, he'd worked every day to give her some small moment of joy, and he'd never failed. She knew he was looking down now and feeling glad. She'd given her heart to a man who was almost nothing like him, except in that: their care of her.

The ceremony was over in scant minutes, hardly a ceremony at all. But the words had been said, and that was all that mattered. After the papers were signed, they invited Doc Dollens over for a nice supper.

And that was Ada's, and Jonah's, second wedding day. Quiet. Humble. And perfect.

They loaded the wagon with kitchen goods, clothes and linens, books. They crated the chickens and loaded them on, and they loaded all the feed and a few haybales as well. Jonah selected a few hand tools he could use. They meant to bring Polly, the younger of their cows.

Everything else, including the farm itself, they'd walk away from.

The wagon wouldn't go all the way to Cable's Holler. It was too wide to get even as far as Red Fern Holler, but they had hope to ask for help from their friends and neighbors to haul things by horse, cart, and hand the rest of the way. Jonah was reticent about asking for favors he didn't know how he'd repay, but Ada understood better about neighbors, and knew there would always be chances to return kindnesses done.

In that spirit, despite her newly conflicted feelings about the neighbors she'd lived with most of her life, Ada didn't protest when her mother wanted to invite them all over to take what they wanted of the things they hadn't packed up in the wagon. Early on the Monday morning they meant to head up the mountain, Ada and her family watched her neighbors come to them, nearly all at once, streaming toward the house on foot, on horseback, by wagon, by truck.

Some of those people had run Jonah off their property on the end of a rifle only two weeks before. All of them had sided with Chancey barely more than a week before.

Jonah kept his distance. He stayed close enough to be there should Ada or her mother need him, but far enough that he wasn't convenient for people to disrespect him — or, for that matter, to apologize, should they be so inclined.

But when Chancey's truck rolled through the gate, suddenly Jonah was at her side.

She patted his arm. "It's alright. His momma's with him. He'll behave."

Jonah only growled, a deep rumble in his chest, and Ada couldn't help but chuckle to herself.

Mrs. Maclaren was a nice woman, who'd been good to Ada all her life, and a good friend to her mother as well. She'd been at her father's funeral, but Chancey was her son, so Ada gave her more leeway to take up for him.

Ada took a step toward them, meaning to greet Mrs. Maclaren and take her to her mother, but Jonah caught her hand.

She turned. "It's alright, Jonah."

"I don't want him close to you."

"We're leaving soon, and then he never will be again. His mother has been good to us. Momma will want to talk with her."

His dark eyes flashing, he gave her a curt nod and let her go.

When Ada went toward the Maclarens, Chancey's eyes skidded off to the side. She didn't know whether that was shame or contempt, but she didn't rightly care. She went to his mother and held out her hand. "Mizz Birdie. How are you this mornin'?"

Mrs. Maclaren smiled and took Ada's hand warmly. "Well, Ada, I'm feelin' a mite blue. I can't hardly reckon you and your momma bein' away from us."

"Come talk to Momma. She'll want to say goodbye."

Chancey's mother turned to her boy. "Don't you git up to no trouble, Chancey Maclaren. B'have yourself today of all days." She turned back to Ada. "We ain't here to take nothin', Ada. Don't feel right. I jus' wanna see to your momma is all."

Ada turned her attention to Chancey, who still wasn't looking at her. Adding weight to her tone, she said, "Don't worry, Mizz Birdie. Chancey didn't drive us away. He couldn't. It's just time for us to start off new." She turned back to his mother. "Is there anything you might need? He can look around if there's something that could be a help to you."

"No, I don't think so. But you're a dear. Chancey, wait at the truck."

Ada felt an unseemly portion of bitter satisfaction as Chancey shambled back and climbed onto the hood of his truck.

She glanced in Jonah's direction and saw the same feeling quirking the side of his mouth.

When their neighbors were gone and they and their possessions were loaded and rolling through the gates of the place she'd been born, Ada didn't look back.

Home wasn't a place.

Home was people.

Home was all around her.

Chapter Twenty-Two

"'Of my own thoughts it is folly to speak,'" Ada read, and looked up to scan the rapt faces of her audience. "'Swooning, I staggered to the opposite wall. For one instance, the party upon the stairs remained motionless, through extremity of *terror* and of *awe*. In the next, a dozen stout arms were toiling at the wall. It fell bodily. The *corpse*'" — she struck key words with eerie emphasis, and each time, the children gasped — "'already greatly decayed and clotted with *gore*, stood erect before the eyes of the spectators. Upon its head, with red extended mouth and solitary eye of fire, sat the hideous *beast* whose craft had seduced me into murder, and whose informing voice had consigned me to the hangman. *I had walled the monster up within the tomb!*'"

Aside from a few more stunned gasps and cries, her audience was silent and still as Ada closed the book: *Tales of Mystery and Imagination* by Edgar Allan Poe. "The Black Cat" was her favorite story to read during the month of October, as a teacher and as a librarian. More than any other of Poe's stories, it captivated a wide range of audiences. She refrained from sharing such a chilling tale with very young children, but from about eight on, they seemed well capable of enjoying the story without being unduly frightened by it.

The children and young people of Red Fern Holler sat with their eyes wide, absorbing the shocking end of the tale. Behind them, an array of their parents were equally overcome. Her audience included Elijah and Bluebird, and Jonah and Momma, too. They almost always came when she went to Red Fern for their regular 'book meeting.' Jonah had built a small cart Momma could sit safely on and he could pull so she could get down the mountain this far.

Virtually all the people her mother had known here were dead and buried, but their families remained, and the memory of her family was yet keen. She had rediscovered her people among their descendants, and had found a community of neighbors and friends among them. Jonah and Ada came down to Red Fern Holler with Momma and the children almost every week now, but the book meeting happened as part of her route, on the schedule she'd established, and her family met her here on these days.

After allowing a moment for her story's desired effect to be felt, she set the closed book on her lap and folded her hands on its cover. "What is the lesson we can take from this story?"

"Before you wall up somebody, check for cats!" the newly gruff voice of one of the teen boys called out, and a ripple of laughter went through the older members of her audience.

She laughed. "That's one lesson, I reckon, Jeb Smith. What's a better one?"

"Stay away from liquor!" said KayLynn Dickerson.

"That's a better one, yes. Good, KayLynn! Any others?"

"Be nice to kitties!" Bluebird said from her seat up front. "He was mean!"

"Yes, Bluebird. He was mean."

"Not mean—he were crazy," said another voice, but Ada didn't see who it was.

"Crazy and mean ain't so different."

Suddenly, her audience was scattering. The children were miming scary cats, and the older folks were arguing about the theme of the story. Ada leaned back and watched, well pleased. This was what books could do, were *meant* to do: not only tell a story or impart information but build, grow, strengthen community. They were meant to be shared.

There had been some consternation among the older people in her audience when the story began to get dark. KayLynn's father had wondered aloud if it was a godly kind of story. Ada had asked for trust, and been given it. She could hear among the various conversations how those who wanted a godly story had found it in Poe's words. A cautionary tale about the wages of sin. Others had enjoyed a scary, suspenseful story. No one was wrong.

Jonah, still not one to engage in lively discussions except with his special people, and even then only occasionally, had stood back and watched. Now, he walked around the scattering group and came to her.

Standing at her side, he set his hand on her shoulder and squeezed. "Ever'day, you amaze me. You are an angel, Ada Walker. Nothin' less."

Ada rested her cheek on her man's hand and was content.

Ada rode Henrietta to the barn and dismounted. The last of the autumn sunlight washed across the top of the holler, but it was dusk here at the bottom. This was the latest she ever was with this new route, riding down the mountain and back up. She'd cleaved a total of near twenty miles of traveling a week simply by not riding all the way to and from Barker's Creek. This route took her to Red Fern Holler every day, because that was the trail head to reach home, and that was a convenience as well. Today, she'd stopped at the Cummings to warm up for a few minutes and had left with a basket of pumpkin muffins and sweet-potato tarts.

There was one new challenge to her work, now that she lived in Cable's Holler, and the reason she was home at dusk tonight: getting to Callwood for the monthly meeting couldn't be accomplished in a day. She had to stay overnight in town. Jonah didn't like that, but one of the other librarians, Mrs. Galway, had a sister who ran a ladies' rooming house, safe and bright and tidy, so she took a room there one night a month—a clean bed, a hot supper, and a cold breakfast for twenty-five cents.

Ada enjoyed this monthly trip. She got to see her colleagues, to work together with them and discuss their joys and challenges, and she was able to do a bit of shopping and pick up a little something for each of the people she loved.

The bank had claimed her parents' farm, but it didn't matter. That place had been nothing but a burden for years, and her father had been killed there. They were blessed to be free of it.

Now, living in Jonah's family home, a humble place but free of debt, and with her work as a librarian, they had ease none of them had known before. They didn't need her wages to live; Jonah had forged a whole life on nearly no money at all, and she had skills to add to that endeavor. The great bulk of her wages they saved, against the day when times might prove even harder and needs greater. But she could afford a few luxuries, like books and magazines for the children, and nice yarns for her mother, fabrics for a few pieces of new clothes, and good shoes for them all.

Circumstances would change again, hopefully fairly soon, but this time the changes would be their plan, and they would be prepared. When June Avery was married and forced to leave her teaching post, Ada meant to free up her librarian position for her.

Because she and Jonah wanted more children, and she couldn't ride her route long while she carried a child.

But she already had an idea how she'd help keep her family secure and keep herself fulfilled when that time came.

She lit the lantern, then unsaddled Henrietta and brushed her down. At her back, the house was quiet, but she knew it bustled in the front room. The scent of a good dinner wafted up the stovepipe.

Hen nickered as Ada combed her forelock.

"Yes, I agree. We have a lovely new life." She led her horse into the barn. Jonah had built onto it first thing after they'd arrived home. Now there were three fully enclosed stalls, for Henrietta, and Petal and Polly, the dairy cows. The goats had an improved pen as well, and the chicken coop had been expanded to house a doubling of their flock. Jonah's young rooster, Junior, was pretty proud of himself with such a big harem of ladies to call his own.

Before she doused the lantern, Ada stood at the barn door and watched the serene animals, nibbling quietly at their greens or slumping calmly off to sleep.

She blew out the flame and picked up her saddlebags and the basket from the Cummings.

Jonah met her at the side of the house. "Hey, darlin'," he murmured and took her load from her and set it on the ground. His arms wrapped her fully, and she looped her her arms around his neck. As he claimed her mouth and she claimed his, he lifted her feet off the ground, and Ada wrapped her legs around his waist. This had become their greeting, and Ada could hardly believe she'd ever thought this freedom to love and desire completely had been anything less than magnificent.

She was dizzy when he set her back down.

His panting breath skimmed her face as he kissed her forehead. "We missed you."

"I missed you. I'm glad to be home."

"Good trip?" He bent and picked up her packs.

"Very good. We got a large donation of brand-new books in. I've got some with me. And I bought the children each a new book of their own as well."

They walked onto the porch. The front windows blazed with light, and Ada stopped for a moment to enjoy the view. The new curtains she'd made hung open along the sides, and she watched her family busily laying the table for supper. Bluebird set a stack of plates—from their kitchen in Barker's Creek—on the table covered with a tablecloth Ada's mother had made years ago, and Ada's mother set the plates at each person's place, moving from the memory she'd made of her new home and its contents.

Elijah brought the iron pot over, holding it carefully with towels so he didn't burn himself.

Jonah chuckled softly. "He made that stew, or mostwise, anyway. I cut up the rabbit, but he used a recipe in that scrapbook. He told me what it's called, but I didn't catch it."

"Hasenpfeffer," Ada said. "Mrs. Pitts made that scrapbook. It's one of her family recipes that she altered for more common ingredients. Elijah cooked supper?"

Her husband's arm came around her and drew her close. "'Round here, ain't no man's work or woman's work. For 'long time, there was jus' me to work, and ever'thing was man's work. Now, my woman goes off ever'day on a job."

"Does that bother you?" If it did, he'd been doing a stellar job of hiding it.

But he shook his head. "There's jus' work, and we all do what needs doin'. Seems right to me." With a squeeze, he led her to the door. "C'mon. He's proud of his supper."

The first time Ada crossed this threshold, she'd entered a home that, except for the children standing in it, had seemed abandoned. Grey and gloomy. Dead. Decaying.

Now, holding her man's hand, she crossed into a cozy room full of lamplight, with a warm fire crackling and a good meal waiting. The walls were still covered with newspapers, but there were cheery new curtains, and a few more chairs. There were toys scattered and books turned upside down, holding their places. There were bright rugs on the floor and children's artwork over those yellowed newspapers on the wall.

The sampler Grace had made still had pride of place in the center of the mantel. This family was still, and would always be, The Walkers, and Ada meant to do Grace proud and take care of this love that had been passed on to her.

Jonah stood behind her. Bluebird cried "Ma!" and ran to hug her legs, and Elijah stood beside the table, grinning with pride.

Momma sat at the table beaming with happiness.

They were the Walkers, and they were well blessed.

That night, Ada came upstairs after reading with her mother. Jonah had given up the large bedroom on the first floor so Momma didn't have to climb stairs. He and Ada shared the second bedroom on the second floor, across from the children's room. If life went as they'd been planning, someday maybe this house, big as it was, would need an addition with another room or two.

This room had been full of furniture and other pieces from the previous lives the house had held over generations. With the children's help, they'd emptied it out, returning several good pieces to use and making a nice bedroom for themselves as well. The few pieces that remained without a purpose were stored in the nook under the eave, at the end of the hall.

Ada stood at the top of the stairs. The only light came from their bedroom, but it was enough. What had once seemed to her eerie and unwelcoming was now a cozy dwelling full of happiness and love. In the few weeks of their marriage and this new life, they had begun to restore the old house to a worthy dwelling for a family.

She peeked in on the children. They were sleeping, each bundled under an autumn's weight of blankets. Soon, when winter's cold set in, they'd all sleep in the front room, but it might be the last winter for it. They were talking about adding small woodstoves to the upstairs bedrooms to keep them habitable through the cold months. The rooms had had them long ago, and the downstairs stoves had been piped between the upstairs walls through the roof, so new stoves up here could be fitted easily. They'd already put one in the downstairs bedroom, so Momma would be comfortable regardless.

Pulling the children's door to, she crossed the hall. Jonah was in bed, his chest bare despite the chill. Both lamps were still lit, one on each side of the bed. He sat against the headboard, and in his hands was the book Ada was currently reading: *The Awakening*, by Kate Chopin.

Every now and again, Jonah would show some subtle interest in the books around the house. Ada had once offered to teach him to read, and he hadn't reacted well; since then, she'd noticed but had not remarked on his occasional displays of interest. She was waiting for him to decide when he wanted it. If he never did, that would be fine as well; the state of his literacy had no bearing on his worth.

He looked up and smiled. His face seemed to glow with love. No, it didn't matter at all if he never learned to read.

"Everyone's tucked in snugly," she said.

"That's good. I had to wrangle Bluebird for a wash. She says I shouldn't help her no more. She's a lady, she says, and it shouldn't be her pa helpin' her wash. She can do it herself, she says, but she never gets the back of her neck or under her arms."

Ada laughed. "I'll talk to her. A lady remembers to clean all her parts."

"Why's she think I can't help her? Girl's too young to be thinkin' like that. Ain't she?"

The true answer was probably that Bluebird had grown more than this one year in terms of her experience. She was reading and learning about other people and other lands. She was fascinated by fairy tales and stories about princes and princesses and true love, and she was spending more time among other girls her age or near it. She was beginning to understand that there were differences between girls and boys, and that some of those differences were meaningful.

"It's not a terrible thing if she feels a bit modest. Is it?"

Jonah shrugged. "I reckon not. It's hard to see my baby girl push me off, though."

"You will always be her hero. Trust me. I know the bond a girl has with her daddy."

As a sudden burst of melancholy ran through her, Ada went to the bureau and picked up her brush. On either side of the bureau mirror hung a sampler: the children's birthday samplers. The sampler commemorating Jonah and Grace's marriage was stored away—a keepsake, never to be forgotten, but no longer to be displayed.

Ada had not made a sampler for her and Jonah, and she didn't intend to. She wasn't replacing Grace. She'd merely come after her.

She brought the brush with her and sat on the bed, her back to Jonah, and ran the brush through her hair for her nightly routine: one hundred strokes. She could feel his gaze on her.

After sixty-one strokes, she felt his fingers, drawing through her hair, skimming down her back. Though she wore a nightdress and shawl, the touch raised gooseflesh over her skin.

"You are beautiful," he murmured.

Ada set the brush on the bedside table — sixty-seven strokes was enough tonight — and turned to her husband. "And you are magnificent." She nodded at her book, still in his hand. "I don't think you'd enjoy that story. It's about a woman who can't find a way to be happy in the world she must live in. Finally, she kills herself."

He made a face and set the book on the bed between them. "Do you like it?"

"I do. It's sad, and sometimes the main character is frustrating, but it's beautifully written. And, I suppose, I understand her in part."

"What part?"

"It is hard for a woman to make the life she wants."

"Ain't it hard for ever'body?"

"Sure, but … if I were a man, I'd still be a teacher. I wouldn't have been fired for getting married."

"You still are a teacher. You teach the children ever'day. You teach me ever'day. And all the people you bring books to." He picked up her hand and laced his fingers with hers. "You're a teacher in your soul, darlin'."

There was a bigger point he wasn't quite getting, but suddenly, Ada didn't really care. Up here in their tiny nook of the mountain, the pressures and injustices of the world below couldn't reach them. Life was hard here, but it was simple. It was like he'd said when she'd gotten home: there was no man's work or woman's work here. There was work, and people to do it. There was life, and people to live it. There was joy, and a family to share it. There was love.

She had the life she wanted.

She picked up her book, meaning to set it on the table and spend their remaining time before sleep doing something other than talking, but Jonah set his hand on hers.

"I'm too old," he said.

"Too old?" He was thirty-seven; hardly an old man. Then she realized his statement was really a question, one he was ashamed to ask. "No one is ever too old to learn anything, Jonah. And you are smart and perceptive. Do you want to learn to read?"

He stared at the book under their hands. "Sometimes … sometimes I think I'm … I dunno." His eyes came to hers. "I watch you with the children, sittin' by the fire, readin' to each other. I watch when you give 'em lessons, and see their little minds workin'. I listen when you and Bess talk about the books you read her. I'm so proud, Ada. Of you, of the children, of ever'thin' you brought to them. To us. But sometimes, I feel a little lonesome about it, too." He shook his head as if dismissing the weight of his doubts. "I don't know. Silly, I reckon."

"It's not silly. Whether you read or not makes no difference in what a good, worthy, wonderful man you are. It doesn't make you less smart, or less strong. But if you want to be part of this thing the rest of us share, there's only good in that. I would be honored to teach you to read."

"I don't want to stand off to the side no more."

Ada set *The Awakening* on the table and wrapped her arms around her man.

"We'll start tomorrow," she said and pulled him down on top of her.

Chapter Twenty-Three

It hadn't taken Momma long at all to know this new house. She didn't go up the stairs, but she moved nearly as well as a sighted person through the big front room, the narrow hallway, and the bedroom that had been made hers, and they'd made a space outside, with a rope guide circling the house, so she could be outside enjoying good weather, even as the others tended to their chores.

Elijah and Bluebird had learned to be careful about leaving things lying about on the floor, and to say out loud when they set something down in a place their Grammy might encounter it. It had become an easy habit for them to call out the placement of dishes on the table and food on the plates, and to describe in vivid details the things they wanted her to 'see.' Because she had not always been blind, she had a keen understanding of color and shape and, over the years she'd been without that sense, she'd tied her others tightly to her memories of sight.

Watching the children with her mother, Ada saw that they were gaining new understandings of the world around them through the ways they described things to her.

Ada thought the same was true for her, and for Jonah as well. Seeing the world for someone without sight, perhaps especially for someone who'd once had that sense, required that one truly *see* it, and take none of it for granted.

The children loved her mother like a gift they'd never even imagined they might have, and her mother loved them the same. Despite all her losses, despite her keen grief for Ada's father, Momma was happy.

The loss of plumbing and electricity, of the flush toilet, the gas oven and the ice box, bothered Momma not at all. She'd lived most of her life without them and had simply reverted back to that condition. Ada, on the other hand, did lament their lack, especially of the plumbed bathroom. There was a washroom in this house, but it was simply a small room, behind the stairs, where washing of bodies or clothes could take place indoors. The water still had to be heated on the fire and drained from the wood tub with buckets. And personal business was conducted behind the house, in the privy, or, in the cold nights, in pots they kept under each bed.

It was how things were as she'd grown up, but she'd lived long enough since in more modern circumstances to feel inconvenienced. Reading by sunlight or lamplight or candlelight was not a bother. Warming a home with a fire was cozy. Cooking with a woodstove was no trouble—and not, in the main, her chore. But she missed her soaking baths. She hadn't realized how luxurious—how *decadent*—they'd been.

It was a small thing, though, and no need at all, particularly in light of all their blessings. Still, Ada harbored a small hope that one day the little washroom would be plumbed.

She carried a basket of wet clothes from the washroom and went into the front room. November was full winter in Cable's Holler, and the temperature hadn't reached above freezing, despite the clear sky and bright sun. She'd strung the clothesline back and forth across the front room, before the fire. Once she got these things hung, they'd dry in a couple hours, hopefully before Jonah and Elijah were back from their hunt.

Normally, Jonah didn't hunt on days Ada didn't ride. He wanted to be home when she was. But that morning, as they were tending to the animals, a big flock of turkeys had wandered through the woods, and Thanksgiving was only a few days away. So, with Ada's blessing, her men had finished their chores and collected their bows and gear.

Bluebird was asleep near the hearth, curled up under Ada's bearskin, her cheek on the pages of her fairy tale book.

"Let me help," her mother said, setting aside her knitting and rising from the rocking chair near the table.

"Thank you. Watch the lines. Three of them, starting four steps directly ahead, about thee inches above your head at their lowest point right now." Ada set the cotton bag of pins down. "Pins are on the table by the hall door. Bluebird's sleeping on the floor, right in front of the hearth. She takes up about two steps of room. She's under the bearskin."

"Can't decide if I hate that skin or not," Momma said as she picked up a shirt and felt for its hem. "My only girl hurt by a bear."

Ada still had no memory of the bear, and could only take Jonah's word that one had made the scar on her side, or that the skin he'd tanned was of the same bear. But it was a beautiful thing, dark and soft and warm. Bluebird had more or less claimed it for her own, and Ada didn't mind.

"I'll be glad when you get to growin' this family and set that job aside," her mother added.

They weren't really trying yet to grow the family. Occasionally, she and Jonah would be caught in a moment and unwilling to separate in time to be sure of preventing it, but, for the most part, they had a plan, to wait until spring, because Ada didn't want to give up her route yet. Her work was a calling, and she wasn't yet ready to turn from it.

But yes, the pull to have a baby was powerful, to grow life inside her and nurture a child from its very beginning, a thing she'd always wanted but had once thought lost to her. Elijah and Bluebird were hers now, and when they'd begun to call her Ma her heart had nearly exploded with joy. But she wanted more children. She wanted to fill this revived house to its rafters with love.

As for her mother's consternation about Ada continuing to work, Ada let her grumble and didn't bother to argue. Momma had been proud of her when she'd been a teacher, but she didn't think a married woman should work away from home. It was the husband's job to take care of his family, she thought, as most people did. Ada thought Jonah was doing a brilliant job taking care of her by understanding that she loved her work, that it had value and made her happy.

So she let her mother's statement hang until it faded, and focused on the work before them. Together, they hung their family's wash. As Ada moved across the line, she glanced at her mother's momentarily discarded knitting, and thought of a way to change the subject. "Looks like you're almost done."

Momma nodded. "Another foot, and then I'll do a finishing edge. How's the pattern?"

Ada wiped her damp hands on her apron and cast a glance toward the hearth. Bluebird was snug asleep in her furry nest. She went to the bundle of knitting and spread it out. Dozens of tiny bluebirds and little pink bows on a pale yellow background. She kept it bundled in a basket so Bluebird wouldn't see what the project was becoming; the blanket was to be a Christmas gift.

It had come from a pattern Ada had found in Callwood. She'd read the pattern to her mother until she had it memorized, and she'd separated her colors as she always did. Her blind mother hadn't missed a stitch. "It's breathtaking, Momma. Just beautiful."

Momma grinned. "Good, good. Bundle it up again—don't let her see. Soon's it's done, I'm gonna start one for Elijah. When you go down to Callwood next, see if you can find a nice pattern. I think somethin' in red."

Ada laughed. "I'll do that." Her mother might not like her job, but she sure liked Ada's regular trips down to town because of it.

A sharp, bitter wind sliced straight down the mountain, blowing snow like tiny blades into Ada's face. Henrietta snorted and dropped her head, giving it so firm a shake Ada nearly lost the reins.

"I know, lady, I know." Ada turned off the trail and found a place to stop where the trees made a bit of a windscreen. She swung down from the saddle and grunted as her cold feet hit the ground.

This weather wasn't unknown to them; winter on the mountain meant snow, wind, and cold. But familiarity didn't make it easier. These were hard days; sometimes, like right now, they seemed too hard, and Ada felt ready to give up the job. There was plenty of work to keep her busy and fulfilled at home. She had two children to educate—more, when she and Jonah had more children. Or if she started a school in Red Fern Holler.

Or both.

She shuddered and glared at the snow flying sideways. She was dressed in layers—a pair of sturdy cotton stockings, two sets of long underwear, three pairs of woolen socks, sturdy boots, heavy dungarees, two shirts, one of them flannel, a wool sweater, and a heavy deerskin coat, a thick wool scarf, knitted fingerless gloves under lined leather gloves, and a thick knit cap under the coat's hood. She was as layered and bundled as she could be and still ride. But the cold got in anyway.

Henrietta had her thick, shaggy winter coat, and a winter-thick blanket under the saddle, and she was built for the weather, but she wasn't much happier today.

Tucked behind this natural screen, Ada pushed the hood back and slipped off the leather gloves. She dug into a pack for a treat for them both—a bit of biscuit with wild strawberry jam for her, and some dried apple bits for Hen.

"Not much longer, Hen. Just Bull Holler. You get a stable for a bit, and I get a fire, and then we can ride on home. And at *home*, there's a good brushing and a big blanket in your future."

Her girl snuffed in her palm for more apple. Ada gave her the last crumbles and shook out the cloth the apples had been wrapped in. "Okay. You ready?"

Henrietta gave her a sidelong look and a snort. Ada laughed and kissed her nose.

As always, the snow slowed Ada and Henrietta down. The holler was near full dark when they rode down its center, and they were both frozen to the bone. But Ada reined Henrietta in about a hundred feet from the house anyway. The horse stopped, and Ada rested her hands on the saddle fork and took in the sight before her.

The windows glowed bright yellow, lighting up the world around the house enough that Ada could see the swirls of smoke from the big stone chimney and the little stovepipes. Wood smoke and roasting venison wafted through the smells of winter forest. Through those big, golden windows, she could see the Christmas tree they'd put up a few days before, with its bows of white ribbon and its garland of dried berries. She and the children had baked bread-dough ornaments, too.

She'd thought it would be their first Christmas tree, until they'd reminded her their pa had helped them put one up the year before, and given them each a gift.

Ada remembered that day in every detail, when she'd hectored him about not giving his children Christmas. Later, alone, she'd been astounded at and ashamed of herself, for meddling in affairs not her own. But she'd made an impression. She'd reached Jonah, brought him a little bit back to the world of the living.

And now, here they were.

It was a humble house, showing the hard wear of its long years, and they lived a humble life inside it. But it was full and warm and happy, and Ada had never felt more alive and full than now.

She lifted the reins and squeezed her legs against her horse's side. "Come on, Hen. Let's go home."

The house was asleep for the night. Jonah and the children were nestled on the floor by the fire, arrayed around their simple Christmas tree like the best presents Ada could ever have dreamed of, and Momma was tucked in her bed, with her room's little pot-bellied stove stoked for the night.

Outside, the night was quiet and calm. The thick blanket of snow and the blade-sharp cold had muffled any kind of noise being made. A bright, waxing moon slanted down the center of the holler and bathed the white world in blue light.

Ada sat at the table with an oil lamp for light and a mug of warm milk and a butter cookie for comfort. One of her scrapbooks had begun to wear past its use, and she was rewriting some of the recipes and stories that had become illegible for various reasons—spatters of food, dirty hands, water smears, or the paper wearing out at the stress points of her simple lace binding.

A sudden wind went through the holler and rattled the windows in their frames. It died quickly out, but left behind the memory of her freezing ride that day. She shivered and snugged her thick woolen shawl more tightly around her shoulders.

Whether the knock of the wind woke him or something else, Jonah sat up. He looked her way, and she smiled.

"Ada," he said, and she knew he wanted her to come to bed. So often, with only the two syllables of her name, her husband managed to convey whole needs, feelings, ideas.

"Just a little longer," she answered, keeping her voice low.

She went back to her writing but heard him stir. The floor creaked and the shadows shifted as he came and stood behind her. When he bent low and wrapped his arms around her, she saw he had the bearskin around his shoulders.

When he tucked his face against her neck, she couldn't help but close her eyes and rest in his embrace.

"Come to bed," he murmured. His lips brushed her skin as he made the words.

"I just want—"

"Not to sleep. To bed. Upstairs."

There was no heat upstairs. They were saving her wages to buy stoves in the spring, when they were discounted.

"It's cold up there." Getting dressed in the mornings and undressed at night was lately an exercise in speed.

"I'll make you warm. Promise."

They hadn't been able to love each other like that for a few weeks, since the hard cold had set in. Sometimes, lying on the floor by the fire, they kissed and caressed each other until they were nearly mad with need, but with the children sleeping so near, they'd refrained.

"Ada," he murmured and said the world.

She capped her pen and closed the scrapbook. Jonah took her hand and pulled her to her feet. Wrapping the bearskin, warm from his body, around her, he led her upstairs to their bed.

The pillows and quilts were downstairs, and the mattress was chilly, but the bearskin was thick and heavy and warm. They lay under it, still dressed, and Jonah curled over her, easing the ends of her shawl to the sides. They hadn't brought up the lamp, but the bright moonlight still lit the holler and streamed through the windows to light the space between them.

She loved the way he looked at her. So full of love and delight. She saw in his eyes her own feelings for him.

As Jonah ducked his head, nosing the edge of her nightdress from her shoulder, so he could taste her there, Ada closed her eyes and eased her hands down the sides of his body. He wore a union suit, as always, and it was buttoned, as always, to the two buttons closest to his throat. Wanting more than to lie beneath him and be adored, she squirmed and pushed until he laughed and rolled to his back.

In the months of her marriage to Jonah, Ada had learned things about marital love she'd never known before. George had been a kind and compassionate lover, but he'd been a God-fearing man and, she now knew, a bit prim. He'd been nearly as innocent of some things as she had been.

Jonah had no fear of God, and he felt shame only for those things he thought were shortcomings. In bed, he didn't come up short. In any way. Once they'd been married, he'd shown her many ways to give and receive pleasure, and Ada had found some to be particularly powerful — and empowering.

Such as this: putting him on his back and looming over him. He grinned as, under the cover of their bearskin, Ada opened the buttons of his underwear, all the way down. When the buttons were open, he shrugged his shoulders and arms free, and she helped him escape from the thing entirely. Then he lay there, bathed in blue moonlight, naked under her hands, her gaze.

Such a handsome man he was. Such strength, such power. She brushed her hands over his shoulders, his arms, felt the rise of his biceps against her palms. Over his chest, his belly, his hips, his sides. Always, she paused at the scar the bullet had left behind. Always, she bent down and kissed it, letting her tongue feel the rough pattern of its healing.

Always, he moaned at that touch and tangled his hands in her hair.

She wrapped her hands around the part of him that was only hers, and on this night, she did something she'd wanted to for some weeks but hadn't yet found the courage. She put her mouth to him and kissed his tip.

Sometimes, he put his mouth on her. She'd never heard of such a thing before the first time he'd done it. But oh, how she liked it, and she wanted to give Jonah the same pleasure, if he wanted it.

He took in a sharp breath, so noisy it was nearly a cry. "Ada," he said when that breath was released.

It seemed that he wanted it.

She kissed him there again, and this time let her tongue out to taste him. His hips shook as she flicked her tongue over the silky-soft skin that topped the velvet rod that brought her so much bliss.

"Ada!" he groaned, and his hands clenched at her shoulders.

No longer interested in play, Ada did what she'd intended when she'd squirmed to turn him over. She straddled his hips, took hold of him, and mounted him.

He liked it when she 'rode' him. Ada liked it as well. There was a heady power to being in control of this act. She set the pace, and the depth. He could only lie beneath her and feel what she did to him.

Actually, there was more he could do. His hands roamed all over. They gripped and pulled and grasped and caressed, and sometimes he set his feet on the bed and joined in with her rhythm.

"Ada!" he groaned as she rested on him and he filled her full. Oh, how she loved the feel of them joined together like this. She was so full and alive she quivered.

He took hold of her nightdress. "Take it off, darlin', take it off."

She wriggled free of her nightdress, trying not to dislodge the cozy bearskin from her shoulders. Jonah took hold of the fur and kept it in place. When she was naked, he tugged on the fur, encouraging her to lay her body on his. The feel of his chest, his warm skin, his firm muscles, his soft hair, turned her nipples to knots, and she moaned.

Then he took her face in his hands and kissed her.

The way Jonah kissed—by now, they'd shared hundreds of kisses, but every time, whether it was an affectionate peck before she left for her day's ride, or a ravishing possession like this one, his kisses took her breath. From the first one, which had surprised her, to this one, which devoured her, each and every kiss filled her full of his love and his need. His desire. His life.

His love nourished her. And hers, him.

"Stay close, darlin'," he whispered when he pulled back for breath. "Stay here."

"Always," she answered.

He wrapped his arms around her, holding her as close as he could. Enclosed in his perfect embrace, Ada began to move, and sought his kiss again.

Santa didn't come to Cable's Holler. Jonah remained adamant that he wouldn't lie to his children with that story, or make them promises he had no certainty he could deliver on. Ada regretted sharing Christmas stories with the children, but they seemed content to believe they lived too remotely for Santa to reach. Soon, they would be too old for Santa, anyway.

But they had a wonderful Christmas nonetheless. In the afternoon, they'd have roast duck and mashed potatoes, fresh bread and pumpkin pie. But in the morning, there were presents.

Jonah and Ada and her mother had each been working for months now on gifts for the children, and Ada had helped the children make gifts for their father and grandmother. They'd also made festive wrapping paper out of old newspapers she'd brought up from the library, and a box of crayons she'd bought at the dry goods store.

On Christmas morning, the children, and the grownups, woke to a healthy scattering of presents under their little tree. Ada and her mother had knitted blankets and sweaters and socks for everyone. Ada had made a ragdoll for Bluebird, not unlike the smaller one she'd loved as a girl, and still kept safe in a drawer, but this one looked like Bluebird, with yellow yarn pigtails and bright blue button eyes, and a little striped flour-sack dress. Jonah had made Elijah a wooden train with rolling wheels, with an engine and a coal car, a box car, and a caboose. For Bluebird, he'd made a little copy of this house, with simple pieces of furniture for every room, and five little wooden people. Ada had helped that project by sewing tiny curtains for the windows, covers for the beds, and clothes for the people.

She'd also bought books for everyone, according to their tastes — used, but in good condition. Everyone. Jonah included. He'd been learning to read for less than two months, but he was picking it up quickly. He was a very smart man and keen to learn. She'd bought him a collection of essays by Emerson — too advanced for him just yet, but not for long. And she thought Emerson would really speak to Jonah, once he could understand.

They sat before the fire, with the mouthwatering aroma of fresh bread wafting around their noses and wads of Christmas paper drifting around their feet. The children's cheeks were rosy with joy. Ada's mother sat happily in her rocker, wrapped in a fluffy knitted shawl and wearing a big red paper rose in her white hair.

Bluebird had learned to make paper flowers at Auntie Esther's house and was festooning their world with them.

Ada had been managing the gift-doling, and still had a little stack of wrapped gifts beside her after the others had opened theirs. While everyone else played with their toys or oohed over their soft sweater, Jonah watched her open her gifts. A pretty purple scarf from her mother. She'd hoped when she'd bought the yarn that it would end up as something for her—purple, especially this reddish shade, was her favorite color, even if it clashed with her hair. Bluebird had made her a bouquet of paper flowers. She thanked her mother and daughter sincerely, and welcomed Bluebird's flying hug.

Then she opened Elijah's present. Something like a wooden tray, made of pine and sanded and buffed to satiny smoothness. A wood piece rose from the base at a slant. Ada studied it for a moment but couldn't make sense of it.

"Thank you, Elijah. It's beautiful work. But what is it?"

"A book rest! You can set your book on it so your hands don't get tired when you're readin' in bed!"

"He worked out the shape hisself," Jonah said, pride ringing in his voice.

"Oh, I'm so impressed. This is wonderful, Elijah! Thank you!"

Her boy beamed like the sun.

Her stack of packages was gone. She looked around at her happy family and met Jonah's adoring eyes. "Well, I don't know about anyone else, she said, "but this is the best Christmas I ever had!"

"Wait!" Bluebird cried. "Did I miss it?" She stood by the tree and squinted around the room. "Pa! Where's it at?"

"I didn't bring it yet." He unfolded from the floor. "Elijah, come help me. Bluebird, make sure your ma don't peek."

Bluebird ran over and jumped in Ada's lap to cover her eyes. "No peekin'!"

"Alright, alright, I'm no cheater. I won't peek."

"Better not."

There was a bit of of a shuffle-scuffle and a couple of thumps, and then Jonah said, "Alright. Merry Christmas, darlin'."

Bluebird freed her and jumped from her lap.

Sitting on the floor before Ada was a beautiful chest. It was pine, made of plain planks, but, like Elijah's book rest, sanded and buffed until it shone like satin. Thick leather bands wrapped it, one at each end, with simple brass buckles for closures.

Carved into the middle of the chest, centered on the top, were three letters in careful, even capitals: ALW.

Ada Lee Walker.

She slid from the chair to her knees and set her hands on the top of the chest. It was cool and smooth. The wood and leather were wonderfully fragrant.

Tears welling, she looked up at Jonah, whose smile was soft and enigmatic. "You made this?"

He nodded. "For your special things."

"It's so beautiful."

"Not half as beautiful as you, and this life you give us all." He crouched beside her. "Open it."

She unfastened the buckles and pushed the lid up. The scent of cedar rushed at her. He'd lined the chest so her things would stay safe.

And on the bottom, in a simple pine frame, was a sampler, done in threads of red, purple, and white.

JONAH & ADA

WALKER

September 3, 1937

Beneath their names and the date of their wedding was a large red heart wrapped with a thick white bow. Beneath that, a verse from the Bible: Psalm 147, verse 3:

He healeth the broken in heart, and bindeth up their wounds.

Ada took that treasure in her hands and lifted her stupefied gaze to her husband.

There were tears lurking in his eyes, too. He grinned and brushed his hand over her hair. "I made the frame, but I didn't take up stitchwork, don't worry. Esther helped me. I tol' her what I wanted and asked if she'd make it. Offered to trade some work, but she wouldn't hear of it."

"Did you pick the Bible verse?"

He laughed. "Naw, Esther took that on herself. I like it, though." His grin widened. "And I like I can read it."

Suddenly Ada couldn't hold back her tears anymore.

"Ma?" Bluebird said, worried. "You're s'poseda like it!"

"I do, sweetheart, I do! I love it! I love you all! These are happy tears!"

"Ada Lee, show me," her mother said. "Jonah tol' me what he's doin', but I wanna see for myself."

Ada pushed her tears away and scooted on her knees to her mother. She set the sampler on her lap. It was framed but not under glass, so she lifted her mother's hands and set her fingers on the cloth.

"Oh, this is nice work. Colors?"

"Red and purple and white. It says 'Jonah & Ada Walker, September 3, 1937.' There's a beautiful red heart in the center —"

"Yes, I feel it."

"It's wrapped with a white bow. Beneath it, it says, 'He healeth the broken in heart, and bindeth up their wounds.'"

Her mother's eyes filled with tears. "Indeed he does. Well, this is beautiful, Ada Lee. Just beautiful."

Ada smiled over her shoulder at her husband. "Yes, it is."

Chapter Twenty-Four

"Bluebird, come here. Come help."

Ada stood in the middle of the patch and arched back, pressing on her hips to ease the cramp between them. She'd been tired and sore all day—the past few days, in fact. Each evening she'd come home from her ride and felt dizzy with exhaustion.

Today, she was home, and there was too much to do to give in to weariness. They were using this good day, after real spring warmth had set in, to get things set up for the warm months and beyond. Jonah and Elijah had set out early that morning for Red Fern Holler, towing an empty wagon, in hopes that the pot-bellied stoves they'd ordered on discount from the Sears wish book might have arrived.

Here at home, the women were at work. While her mother sat in the sun and knitted, Ada and Bluebird were sowing their patch.

Well, Ada was sowing the patch. Bluebird was distracted by the new kids. Their little herd of goats was getting big enough that they'd need to trade off one or two—or butcher them, but since they all had names, it was unlikely they'd end up on their table.

"Blue, come now. I need your help."

Bluebird finally trotted over, her ponytail swinging. She wore a little pair of patchwork overalls Ada had made from scrap fabric. They'd turned out cute.

"Sorry, Ma."

"You can play with the babies when we're done. Follow behind me and cover up the seeds, like I showed you."

Bluebird nodded, and they got to work.

"I know their names now," Bluebird said as she patted earth over the lettuce seeds. "They told me." She insisted that she understood the animals, and that she didn't give them their names. They told her their names. Since Ada had had some of her most serious conversations with a horse, she wasn't one to dispute her daughter's truth.

"They did?"

"Uh-huh. The boy with the white face is Arthur, and the girl is Aurora."

Ada smiled. Names from legends and fairy tales. "Those are very good names."

"That's what I tol' 'em."

At the end of the row, a strong bout of vertigo struck Ada suddenly. The remains of her breakfast spun in her belly as she lurched to grab a fencepost and keep her feet under her.

"Ma? What's wrong?" Bluebird ask, coming up behind her.

Henrietta came over and brushed a worried nose on her arm. On her free days, the horse grazed contently among them, with the run of their yard. There wasn't a pasture for her to run in, just the small paddock where Petal and Polly lazed their days away, and the crowded goat pen. But Henrietta didn't need more exercise than she got every day, and she enjoyed moseying through the yard like a giant dog.

The world settled, and Ada took a breath. "I'm alright, sweetheart," she assured her daughter. She leaned her head on Henrietta's nose. "I'm alright, Hen. Just a little dizzy."

Her mother's preternatural hearing picked up every word. "Ada Lee? You dizzy? Come sit and rest. You should be off your feet."

"Momma …"

"Don't 'Momma' me. Come sit. Rest."

Maybe for a minute or two. She really was tired. "Okay, Blue. You can go back to the goats—but come when I call you back."

"Yes, Ma!" she chirped and ran back to the goat pen.

Henrietta followed behind Ada like she expected to be needed.

As Ada sat beside her mother, she said, "I really need to get the patch planted, Momma." But she leaned back in the chair and turned her face up to the spring sun. Already, she felt a bit better.

Momma's hand came up and reached for her. Ada took it. "The seeds will be sown, Ada Lee. Never you fret about that. 'Tis the time for sowin'. How long since you've had your time?"

"It's due, I think." Ada sat straight and thought. "Yes, it is." She put her free hand on her belly.

They'd decided to wait until spring to really try for a baby, and Jonah had completely stopped withdrawing about two weeks ago, when it was consistently warm enough for them to return to their own beds each night. They'd never been diligent about preventing it happening sooner, though. From their very first time, their commitment to waiting had only been slightly better than even, and she hadn't caught pregnant yet.

She and George had never been blessed. In those days, Ada had wondered whether it was something possible for her. She supposed it was too early yet to pick up that worry again.

Especially if her weariness now might mean hope.

"Do you think?"

Her mother turned and faced her, and looked so keenly at her that Ada nearly forgot she was blind. "You been run down all week, and you's dizzy today. I think it's worth bein' careful, yes I do."

Ada rested back again and closed her eyes to think. A baby. A child growing inside her. Oh, she hoped it was true. But it would mean giving up her work.

She'd known that, prepared for it. Made a choice— her own choice, not one forced upon her. But it would not be easy to give up the work she loved.

Her life would be full and happy here without the work. In fact, in many ways, she would be happier without it. Certainly, she'd be glad to be home with her family, and could devote her time to a full curriculum for the children. They didn't need her wages to live day to day, and they'd saved a tidy nest egg over these months, to cover them should trouble arise.

Moreover, the people of Red Fern Holler, neglected for years by the state board of education, had raised the idea of Ada teaching their children, coming down once or twice a week to give lectures and correct assignments they did on their own during the other days of the week. She wouldn't earn a wage that way, but she'd accumulate both goodwill and favors owed—and personal fulfillment as well.

It would be hard to leave her route, but there was ease in the choice. And joy to be growing their family.

But she wanted to be sure. "Don't say anything yet, Momma. I want to wait a little. I have my meeting in Callwood next week. If my time hasn't come by then, I'll see Doc Dollens while I'm down the mountain. I don't want to say a word about this until I see the doctor."

Her mother made a face. "You should be stoppin' that work right now, if you got a seed growin'."

Her mother knew better than that. Mountain women didn't have the luxury of putting their feet up while they carried a child. But she still didn't like Ada's job, and latched on to any opportunity to make it end. Still, it was true that her work had risks she wouldn't want to take for long in this condition. "If I am, a seed is exactly right. Tiny as that, and safe because of it. I will work until I show. And Jonah is already fretful about the thought that I'll someday carry a child. Remember how he lost Grace. When he knows, he'll start worrying that very moment and not stop until the baby's born and we're both well. I want a little time to live with the idea before he knows. Please."

Ada could see her mother didn't like it, but she nodded, and that was as good as a promise. "It's your news to tell, Ada Lee. Only yours."

"Thank you, Momma."

The following week, after her trip down the mountain, where she'd seen Doc Dollens and had her librarians' meeting in Callwood, and a fairly long private meeting with Mrs. Pitts as well, Ada rode Henrietta up to her perfect, beautiful, humble home.

Since she stayed in Callwood overnight, there was still a gleam of afternoon sun in the holler. The spring day had been summer warm, and her family was still outside. Elijah and Bluebird chased the new puppy they'd given Elijah for his birthday, from a litter one of the Dickersons' hounds had whelped. Jonah and Momma sat on the porch, chatting. Jonah had his book of Emerson essays upside down on his lap. He struggled with some of Emerson's vocabulary and turns of phrase, but he kept trying and learning and improving.

Jonah rose and came down the porch steps, walking to meet her. It was one of her favorite things in the world: to see that man, her man, so strong and quiet, so beautifully devoted to her and their family, walking toward her, a smile full of love spreading over his ruggedly handsome face.

She swung down from the saddle and snuggled close when his arm came around her.

Her mother stood, too, and stepped to the porch rail. She faced the direction Ada had come from, her sightless eyes not quite in line with Ada's position. Her mother knew what today might mean, and Ada wished her mother could see her. If she could have, Ada would have simply nodded.

She'd kept the news from Jonah until she was sure. Now it was time for him to know. But not quite yet. Tonight, when they were in bed. Alone, in their most private, personal, intimate togetherness. When she could assuage his worries and be sure he felt all the joy.

He wrapped her up tight, and lifted her from the ground. She coiled her legs around him, and they kissed each other until his knees buckled. Then he set her down and kissed her head.

"Hey, darlin'." He took Henrietta's reins from her. "Missed you."

"I missed you."

"Good trip?"

"A wonderful trip," she said and held him close.

Epilogue

Present Day

"That was Uncle Easy she was carryin'—Ezekiel, named for her daddy. Hold on—lemme see." Lizzie's mother rose from the sofa and knelt before the bookcase across the room. Lizzie was surprised to see how dim Nannie's front room had gotten, and she leaned over to switch on a lamp.

The hours of this long day had rolled by unnoticed. At some point, they'd decided the attic was too hot and dusty, and they were thirsty, so they'd carried the scrapbook and a few other pieces from the chest and come downstairs. They'd sat at the kitchen table and had a meal, and they'd eventually meandered to the front room to sit among Nannie's carefully tidy things, but now, the memory of all those actions and decisions seemed as faded and curled as the pages of Mamaw's scrapbook. They'd spent these hours in a haze of story, Momma telling all she knew, and remembering more as Lizzie asked questions. The 1930s seemed far more real to Lizzie just now than the year they were actually sitting in.

"Here, I think this—yeah, this is it." Momma brought an old photo album over and returned to her place at Lizzie's side. The album was the kind with little paper corners glued to the pages, and each of the grainy, faded photographs was trimmed with a scalloped white border. She flipped past a page or two without more than a glance, and then stopped. "Here. This is all of 'em, right out in front of that old house."

Lizzie leaned over and studied the photo. Three rows of people, men and women, girls and boys, seated and standing, were arrayed on the steps of a long wooden porch. Though the photo was old, and sepia-toned, Lizzie could see the age and wear of the wood. The porch, and its house, looked as if it had been standing long past its best days and was ready for its time to end.

She was a little shocked. Though her mother had said many times in her story that the family was so poor money hardly featured in their lives, that those lives were hard and humble, the image that had been painted in her mind had been different. She thought of bright windows and cozy fires, of good food and good cheer.

The house she'd hardly heard of before today and now felt as if she knew its every wall and corner was remade to her once more. This was the home of a poor Appalachian family, like those she'd studied in school, with little in the way of comforts or conveniences.

Yet all those faces were happy. Most were smiling broadly. They sat and stood arm in arm and hand in hand.

"That's Mamaw," her mother said and put an elegant fingertip on the figure of the oldest woman in the photo. Wearing a loose, simple dress, she was small and thin, and had a braid of pale hair wrapped around her head. Her smile was bright and pretty. She had an infant in her arms. "She's holdin' Micah, so this'd be about '48, I guess? He was her last, and the only one that was sickly. He died 'fore he was two. That makes Mamaw about thirty-eight here, and Papaw" — she tapped the tall, serious man beside Mamaw, wearing bib overalls and squinting at the camera — "forty-eight or forty-nine."

Her mother's accent had deepened through the day until she sounded just like Nannie, every word full to the brim with the mountain.

"Where's Elijah? And Bluebird?"

"The boy in the uniform, that's Uncle Eli. He's too young to join up durin' the war, but he wanted it somethin' fierce. Nannie al'ays said it broke Papaw's heart when he joined up soon's he made eighteen. Made a life of it. He was a combat pilot. Fought in Korea and did four tours in Vietnam. Came home in a box from the last one."

"Oh no!"

Her mother sighed and nodded. Lizzie felt her heart crack a little. Elijah had died long before she'd been born, and she'd never thought of him before this day, but now she loved him fiercely and mourned his death.

"And Bluebird? Is this her?" She pointed to a lovely young woman with long, straight hair, so pale it looked white in the photo. With that hair held back with a plain band, she looked like Alice in Wonderland.

"That's Aunt Blue, yep. She loved the mountain and never left it. Married a boy from Red Fern Holler, and they fixed up one of the old houses by Mamaw and Papaw and lived there her whole life. We went to her funeral, but you were jus' six or so."

Lizzie didn't remember.

"That there would be Uncle Easy," her mother continued. "The one she was carryin' when she quit the librarians."

"I understand why she quit, but it must've broken her heart. She loved the work so much." That much, Lizzie had known before, from the stories Nannie had told about her mother's life as a librarian. Mamaw had always spoken wistfully of those days, when she'd carried the world to forgotten people. When she'd met her great love and built a vibrant life.

"She did, yep. Even though she chose to stop and build a family, she missed the ride. But Mamaw wasn't one to sit and feel bad. She got to doin'. She had all those babies, one right after another—and two at once, even—so she had her hands full, but she taught 'em all every subject, and she even started a little school down Red Fern Holler, towing her babies along, sometimes with one swaddled on her chest. Didn't get no pay, but it didn't matter. She was a hero to those folks. They stopped the librarian program a few years later anyway, but she kept teachin', and doin' her book parties, until they finally got a road all the way up to Red Fern and the state remembered they was children up there. They brought in one of they own teachers, and Mamaw didn't teach down there no more, but she al'ays taught her own."

"I can't believe they didn't let her teach for the state, just because she was married. That's nuts."

Her mother shrugged, and suddenly she was a Chicago heart surgeon again. "Lizzie, you grew up in a very different world than Mamaw, or Nannie, or even I did. Every generation, things have gotten better for women, but it's still a fight. You know damn well it's still a fight."

Lizzie nodded. She'd experienced her own kinds of unfairness because she was a woman.

Her mother returned her attention to that humble photo full of riches. "And there's Uncle Luke and Uncle Luther—the twins—and that's your Nannie, right between 'em. Look how pretty she was. You look just like her, you know. She was a real beauty."

Lizzie considered that pretty little girl, just five years old or so, with dark pigtails and a serious look. Not

Nannie back then. Just Bekah Rae, with the whole world before her.

She'd seen plenty of photos of her grandmother, as a girl and a young woman, a newlywed, and a young mother. With her dark hair and eyes, she'd looked like Rita Hayworth. Lizzie had dark hair and eyes, just like her mother did, and her mother was beautiful, but she didn't think her own resemblance extended to that degree of beauty. Lizzie was cute, not breathtaking.

"And that little sprite makin' the face, that'll be Aunt Ella Beth."

"So many children."

"Mamaw wanted a big family, and she got it. When her kids started having kids of their own, the family got enormous. I remember that house. It was rundown as hell, but I never really noticed it when I was little. By then, it had plumbin' and electric and propane, but I still thought I was roughin' it. It was fun, and always busy and full. I'd go up in summers and spend weeks with Mamaw and Papaw, and those were the best times. It wasn't ever jus' me, a buncha cousins'd be there. Like our own little summer camp. Even chores was fun. And Papaw, he was quiet, but he loved to watch our play. The whole holler was full, too. Aunt Blue and Uncle Cade lived there with their kids, and Uncle Easy and Aunt Lottie with theirs. They built the old houses back up and moved in. For a while, it was bustlin' as much as it ever did, but the world below finally made it up that high, and after that, people started drainin' off again. Once it got easy to get down the mountain, people stopped goin' up. The kids grew up and went down to live and work, and when the old folks died or got brought down, the holler jus' died off. Papaw and Mamaw both lived into their nineties, and they stayed in that house till he died. Then Mamaw came down here to live with Nannie. Those last years without him, she was like a lady at a train station, sittin' quiet and prim, waitin' for her time to go. When she died, the family finally sold the holler off."

Lizzie sat back and swallowed down a lump of tears. "Well, that breaks my heart."

But her mother smiled and took her hand. "No, Lizzie. Cable's Holler was wonderful, but without Mamaw and Papaw, it was just a place. They made a home, and a family. They made a whole world, and every one of us carries it with us every place we are."

The End

ABOUT THE AUTHOR

Susan Fanetti is a Midwestern native transplanted to Northern California, where she lives with her husband, youngest son, and assorted cats.

She is a proud member of the Freak Circle Press.

Susan's website: www.susanfanetti.com

Susan's Facebook author page:
https://www.facebook.com/authorsusanfanetti
'Susan's FANetties' reader group:
https://www.facebook.com/groups/871235502925756/

Freak Circle Press Facebook page:
https://www.facebook.com/freakcirclepress

Instagram: https://www.instagram.com/susan_fanetti/

Twitter: @sfanetti

Carry the World Pinterest board:
https://www.pinterest.com/laughingwarrior/carry-the-world/

Printed in Great Britain
by Amazon